Talmid
The Book Of
JOHN

W. R. Sander

Talmid - The Book of John

Copyright © 2014 by W. R. SANDER

All rights reserved. No part of this publication may be reproduced, stored in a retrieval system, or transmitted by any means – electronic, mechanical, photographic (photocopying), recording, or otherwise – without prior permission in writing from the author.

Printed in the United States of America
ISBN: 9781494931469
ISBN 10: 149493146X

First Edition

For more information, go to:
www.TheBookofJohn.net

Scripture quotations are taken from the Complete Jewish Bible by David H. Stern. Copyright ©1998. All rights reserved. Used by permission of Messianic Jewish Publishers.
www.messianicjewish.net.

Cover design by W. R. Sander
Cover illustration copyright of Leah-Anne Thompson
Used with permission of Shutterstock.com
Published in the United States by CreateSpace, an Amazon Company.

From:

Date:

Dedication

This book is dedicated to my sons, Brad and Ben, so that you can come to not only know the gift God freely gave two thousand years ago, but to appreciate His love firsthand.

To Sharon & Ed,

Never Stop Believing

W. V. Sander

Table of Contents

Dedication 5
1 A Boy's Life 9
2 The Official's Visit 19
3 A Friend Revealed 29
4 A Warning 45
5 The Palace 55
6 A Stranger Arrives 73
7 A Task Completed 85
8 Secrets in the Night 99
9 The Visitor 111
10 A Revelation 123
11 A New Threat 131
12 An Invitation 141
13 The Plan 157
14 The Celebration 179
15 The Visitors 189
16 The Followers 199
17 A Faith Shaken 227
18 The Triumphal Entry 247
19 Chaos at the Market 255
20 The First Confrontation 263
21 The Pesach Meal 271
22 In the Garden 277

23 The Second Confrontation	281
24 The Trial	289
25 The Shepherd	295
26 The Final Confrontation	305
27 The Death of Yeshua	317
28 Redemption	329
29 A Life Saved	341
30 Wanderings	349
About the Author	357
Author's Notes	359
Scripture Verses	363
Glossary	365
Coming Soon	367

1

A Boy's Life

"Winnowing fork ... threshing floor ... unquenchable fire ... winnowing fork ... threshing floor ... unquenchable fire."

The stranger drew in a sharp breath between each disjointed phrase. His sudden appearance startled John as he sat on an enormous boulder on the edge of the path leading to the deep desert. The figure lurched along with surprising speed. Grateful the setting moon was to his back, and certain the stranger could not see him, he jumped silently off the large rock. His slender frame made hardly any noise as it hit the sandy ground. Bracing himself for a quick escape, John eased his head above the boulder for a second look.

The man swayed as he moved, his large frame faltering as he navigated the uneven path. Dried mud and twigs spotted his disheveled black hair, also liberally coating his beard. A leather wineskin hung from a thick brown belt about his waist. The dried mud caused his stiff robe to chase his movements. Robe was not quite the right word. It looked like he wore the skin of a camel. His bare feet and calves were thick with a combination of dust and mud.

As he passed, John let out a sigh of relief.

The stranger stopped suddenly and held his breath as an archer sighting quarry.

John prayed, *Adonai, protect me.*

The man hesitated only a moment, and then, returning to his chant, continued into the city.

The man looked familiar, but John could not place a name to the face. He knew he was not one of the townspeople, or a Roman, or any of the other foreigners living in his country.

So startled was he at the man's sudden appearance, it took him several minutes before deciding to head back into town. Only when the first rays of the morning sun had completely cleared Mount Korazim did he dislodge himself from the rock, certain the stranger would not return. As he followed the path into the city, the name came to him.

Yochanan had returned.

John's eyes darted as he tried to detect movement on the darkened streets. A shadowy figure stood alone by the town well. John adjusted his path to hide his approach, but soon realized his fear was unfounded. The person at the well was too small to be the stranger.

"Is he here?" John asked.

The young girl wore a faded blue full-length tunic, with the yellow sand pasted to its hem, and a white veil covering all but her eyes. She unlatched the veil, allowing it to drop alongside her head. If his appearance startled her, she did not show it. "Is who here?"

John strained to see in the dim sunlight as he continued to scan the still streets. He saw no movement and relaxed, believing they were alone.

"Myriam, I was up on the path out of the city, you know, the one we take to go down to the river. I saw a big man coming in from the desert. I don't know what he was doing out there at night, but I didn't want to find out."

"Somebody was out in the desert all night?"

John nodded.

"Who was it?"

John paused a moment, considering his next words. He knew how Myriam would respond to the news. "It was Yochanan."

Myriam stopped fidgeting with the bucket she had brought to fetch water, and her eyes grew wide in excitement. "He's back? Are you sure?"

"It was him. He looked far worse than the last time he was here." John thought back to their last encounter with the stranger. Yochanan had been preaching on the steps of the Temple. His manners were bizarre, to say the least. He gestured wildly as he spoke, and his comments made no sense. John never understood why Myriam and the others so readily sought to listen to him.

"Did you see which way he went?"

"No, I was so startled I just jumped out of his way. I

didn't want to talk to him, so I hid behind a rock."

"What were you doing out on the path, anyway?"

John was not sure how to explain it to her. *Because I like to get away by myself?* She would not understand that. "I woke up early this morning and couldn't get back to sleep. I thought a walk under the stars might tire me out."

Myriam picked up the empty bucket and prepared to leave.

"Where are you going?" John asked.

She gave him a disbelieving look. "To find Yochanan, of course."

John reached out and grabbed her upper arm, preventing her from leaving. "I really wish you wouldn't. You should have seen him. He was covered in dirt and filth. And he was talking strangely, as if possessed by a demon."

Myriam tore away from his grip. "Don't you say that. Yochanan is a good man, sent by Adonai, God."

John tried to think of something he could say to stop her. "He's a false teacher. You should go to Temple and follow the teachings of our rabbis."

Myriam snorted her disapproval. "All they talk about is old, dead legends. When will they help us with our real needs? All they care about is their own wealth and standings. I'm surprised you listen to them at all."

Now it was John's turn to become defensive. "You need to repent. You don't know what you're talking about."

Myriam lifted the empty bucket and replaced her veil. She reached out with a lithe hand and touched John's cheek. "You are so trusting of what they teach. I know it's your desire to become one of them, but I pray you will not become like them."

John furrowed his brow in confusion.

"Go to the Temple and learn Scripture. But don't use it to keep others in chains, as they do. Open your eyes and heart and see if you really think Adonai would want us to behave as they do."

She walked into the city, heading towards the Temple. Her comments confused John. The priests he knew were great men. His only prayer was that one day he could take his place among them.

With the morning sun already full upon the sky, John returned home to begin his work before Temple. He hooked up the family donkey to the cart that carried the daily load of fish from the docks to the marketplace, allowing his family to generate a meager living.

Things had been different five years ago when his father was still alive and one of the greatest fishermen their town had ever seen. But after his father's death and with the arrival of his brother, John's uncle and now stepfather, things had taken a hard turn for his family. His mother spent her days between the market, trying to make a profit on the fish his uncle purchased, and this home, which had lost all of its laughter.

He checked inside, but his mother had already left to set up their market stall. The only sound he heard was the gentle breathing of his little brother David, asleep.

John was glad to hear him asleep. It was only when he was asleep that his stepbrother had any peace from the torments that plagued him his entire life.

Pale light streamed past the mountains as the sun rose even higher into the early morning sky. Fine sand blew in from the west, from Korazim, littering the streets of his town, K'far-Nachum, and it coated John's feet and sandals. The cart left light marks in the road as he navigated through the streets to the shoreline of the sea.

The Sea! Well, that is what the townspeople called it. In truth, it was Lake Kinneret. The Yarden River, which began its journey seventy-five miles to the north on the slopes of Mount Hermon, flowed into and fed it from the north, and the Yarden continued its journey through Y'hudah from the southern end of the lake, eventually ending at the Sea of Salt. Lake Kinneret had been the lifeline of his town for centuries. The fish caught there fed thousands all across northern Y'hudah.

As he navigated the steep road to the waterfront, the morning sun illuminated about two dozen fishing boats making their way to the shore. They were of all sizes, some large, some small, some with oars and others with sails. Several had already docked and off-loaded their catch, and John had to maneuver his cart around several other merchants heading up the road to market.

John pulled up to one small boat as two men worked to

secure it.

A large man with dark hair, a dark complexion, and an even darker attitude stood on the docks by the bow.

"Where have you been?" the man bellowed. "They've already docked. You're lucky these fish are still alive, or it would be you I'd be bringing to market to sell."

Trying to ignore his uncle as the man cursed him, he looked into the hold of the boat. From the amount of fish, he could see the night's catch had been good.

John called out, "Papa, I will have the fish to market shortly." He hated calling the man by his father's name, but if his uncle's demands were not met, John knew it meant another beating.

Without waving, the man turned as he walked up the shoreline into town.

John loaded baskets of fish into the cart.

"How do you stand him?" a voice asked from across the water.

A man secured his boat at the dock. John recognized him and smiled. He was Shim'on, one of John's oldest memories. While John's father was still alive, he had taken Shim'on in as an apprentice, at twelve, like John was now. John's father taught him all of his tricks for catching fish, and after his death, Shim'on bought his father's boat. Now, Shim'on had become the finest fisherman their town knew. His arms were as thick as John's thighs, and his beard was full and black. Stripped to the waist, he coiled one of the fishing ropes. The morning sun glistened off the sweat clinging to his bare chest.

"The Torah says I must respect him."

The man snorted a laugh. "But it doesn't say you must like him, eh?"

John smiled but said nothing.

"I grieve for you. If you ever want to leave your father—"

"He is not my father," John barked in anger. "He is my uncle. He married my mother. That may make him my stepfather, but he will never be my father." John knew Shim'on was just speaking politely about his uncle, but the thought that anyone could mistake that man for his real father made him angrier than his uncle in a room full of crooked tax collectors.

Shim'on's smile diffused the situation. "I'm sorry. I meant no disrespect to your father's memory. I loved him too. I only meant that I am always looking for hard workers."

Now it was John's turn to laugh. "I may have to sell fish, but I'd never want to catch them," he admitted. "No, if I do leave, it will be for good. If I do go, it will be somewhere far away, somewhere special." John loaded the last of the catch into the cart.

The man reached out with one of his enormous hands and playfully tussled John's curly black hair. John pulled back from him, partially because of the strong odor of fish and partially because he really did not want the man touching his head. "You are a good boy," Shim'on said. "I have no doubt you will grow into a fine man." He reached into his bag and pulled out a *lepton*. "Here, take this and buy yourself something." He offered John the coin.

John accepted it, and placed his hand to his chest as if to protect his new wealth. "Thank you, sir. Thank you." A broad smile crossed his face.

"Boy, those fish will go rotten if you don't get them to your mother!"

His uncle's voice startled John, especially since he thought his uncle would be halfway into town by now.

"If I lose all my money because you don't have the common sense to get fresh fish out of the morning sun—"

"I'm going now," John said.

John led the donkey off the dock.

"Worthless fool. He hasn't a wit in his skull..." John heard his uncle mutter as he walked off into the distance.

Someday I'll show him.

John delivered the fish to market, and walked down the dusty streets towards the Temple. It was the largest building in their town, set almost in the center. He could see its clay roof and stone columns, even though several buildings impeded his path to its doors.

There were several children standing outside the door to the Temple schoolroom. John saw Andrew, Shim'on's brother, who was sixteen, and his friends Ya`akov and Yochanan, the sons of Shim'on's partner Zavdai. Like him, they were twelve years old and entering into the final months of their Temple studies. But unlike John, they were not very good students and the best they could hope for was to apprentice to a fisherman and join their father in the fishing trade. While they had been his tormentors for the last five years, he felt pity on them that they would grow up to know such a difficult life. Still, John tried to place some children between him and the boys, hoping they had not noticed him.

Then he recognized the faded blue tunic he had seen this morning.

"Myriam," said John, as he walked up to her. "Did you find him?"

Myriam shook her head. "He is not in the Temple, or on the streets. No one has seen him but you. Are you sure it wasn't a ghost?"

John nodded. "He's here, somewhere." He decided to change the subject. "Look what I have." He held out the coin in his palm.

Myriam held out her hand and he dropped the coin in. "Where did you get this?" she asked.

"From one of the fishermen my uncle does business with."

"Why you, why not to your uncle?"

"I don't know. I think because he is my uncle."

Myriam giggled. "If that's the reason, he should have given you double."

John smiled. He had always found it easy to talk to her.

"What are you going to do with it?"

He had not thought about it. "I don't know. What would you do?"

"If I had this much money, I would buy a donkey and travel far from this little town. I would move to a faraway city, maybe even as far as Yerushalayim, where I could be somebody, somebody different."

"Myriam, it's not a lot of money."

Myriam had a far off look in her eyes that meant she was not listening. "John, maybe this money is a sign from Adonai. Maybe we should do something with it. Let's do something right now."

"I don't think Adonai intends for us to skip Temple."

"How do you know what God intends?"

John feared she would begin one of her long rants on the meaning of Scripture, a conversation they had too often in the past. For years, after school, they would sit on opposite sides of the wall that separated their homes and discuss in depth the studies each had completed that day. Unlike the boys in his class who delighted in the end of lessons and the opportunity to play, she shared his desire to understand what Adonai had written down and what it meant. And John had always been amazed at her ability to argue Scripture and its meaning with him. She was actually far better at interpretation than many of his classmates. It was too bad that when her schooling was over, she would not be allowed to continue in her studies, as he hoped to do. Instead, she was expected to marry and raise a family.

"I don't feel like going to Temple today," she continued. "Let's do something fun."

"What do we have here?" Ya`akov sneered. "Fishface and his girlfriend?"

"Just leave us alone," said John.

"*Just leave us alone,*" Ya`akov repeated in a high-pitched squeal, trying to sound like a girl. "I don't think we can do that. We don't like having filthy fish carriers stinking up our Temple."

These boys had picked on John for five years. It all started when he was seven and didn't join his father on the boats like other boys his age. Neither did it help matters that they were also a foot taller and fifty pounds heavier.

Ya`akov grabbed John and pushed him into Andrew. Before John knew what was happening, they were pushing him faster and faster in their little circle.

"LEAVE HIM ALONE!" The voice boomed off the walls of the buildings. The pushing immediately stopped. John fell to the ground.

John turned to see where the voice had come from. He was relieved to see his best friend Philo approaching. Philo was well built, even bigger than Shim`on. His curly black hair was cut in the Roman style, and his arms were large and muscular. John had seen Philo only fight once, and he had so dominated his opponent that no one had ever thought to challenge him again. Even though Philo was six years older than him, they had been friends from the moment John had entered the Beth Sefer, as he helped Philo with his studies.

"Why, are you going to fight all three of us if we don't?" Ya`akov asked, although the tone of his voice showed he was scared.

Philo walked right up to Ya`akov's face until their chests almost touched then looked down at him. "I don't have to fight all three, just you."

The boy swallowed hard and took two steps back, never taking his eyes off Philo. His friends stayed safely behind him. "We don't want any trouble. We were just playing with him."

"The next time you 'play' with him, I won't give you any warning. Now get into class or maybe I'll start 'playing' with you."

The boys took three steps backwards, and then turned and started to walk away. Philo stomped on the ground as if he was coming after them, and they burst out running.

Philo laughed as he offered John his hand to help him to his feet. "Thank you for saving me, again," John said.

Philo shook his head. "For someone who lifts fish every morning, you need to build some muscle."

John smiled at his friend. *"He will guard the steps of his faithful, but the wicked will be silenced in darkness. For it is not by strength that a person prevails."*

Philo seemed confused. "Y'hoshua?" he asked, his voice betraying his lack of certainty.

John shook his head. "No, Sh'mu'el."

Philo just looked on in disbelief. "I don't know how you do that," he said. "My father and Gamli'el are the only rabbis I know capable of remembering Scripture the way you do."

"When I close my eyes, it's like I can see the scrolls before me, and I just read them."

Philo let out a low whistle. "That would be so helpful."

"Why aren't you in class?" Philo asked.

"I was headed there when those boys showed up."

"My father is sending me on an errand," said Philo.

John knew if his father sent him on an errand, it had to be important. Philo was the son of Kayafa, the religious leader of this entire area.

"Someone from Rome is arriving this morning. I need to bring him to see my father. Do you want to join me?"

"Who's coming to see your father?" asked Myriam.

Philo furrowed his brow, and gave a quick smirk as if dismissing her question. "Not that it's any of your concern, but it is a Roman on official business."

The mention of the garrison made John nervous. Their town had been under Roman occupation for years, from well before he was born. Still, no one was comfortable with it. He knew that many, though not all, of the Roman soldiers stationed there hated their assignments and took out their frustrations on the local townspeople. Philo himself had been beaten by a Roman soldier many years ago for the crime of walking on the same side of the street. Other townspeople who had tried to stand up to their tyranny were treated similarly; or worse, just disappeared. No one walked near the garrison without a reason.

"I don't want to go there," said Myriam.

"I didn't ask you," said Philo. "It would be best if you went inside."

Myriam crossed her arms in anger, and then spun around without saying a word. She walked away at a brisk pace, as if trying to put distance between herself and the boys.

"You really should be nicer to her," said John.

"Why? She's your friend, not mine."

"Still, I don't think you're setting a good example when you act like that."

"Like what?"

John could not believe Philo did not know his actions were hurtful.

As Myriam disappeared from view, John felt sad, even if it was for the best. He did not want to provoke the Roman soldiers in any way. He knew, being with Philo, he would be safe. Probably.

2

The Official's Visit

They turned a corner. At the end of a long street, John saw white walls about ten feet high. A black iron gate blocked the entrance into and out of the building. On either side stood several Roman soldiers loosely holding on to their long spears, unconcerned with any danger the townspeople might pose. Through those gates, in the darkness of the trees in the courtyard, stood the garrison. John paused at the sight, then quickly caught up to Philo, who had not broken stride.

Huddled against the walls, Roman soldiers wore their short military skirts, metal-studded sandals, and shin guards. Red cloaks hung from their shoulders, allowing them to fall from their frames as a loose-fitting garment. The emblems that signifyed their rank were attached to their outer garments. Short bronze swords hung from their belts.

The gates were crowded with Jews and Roman officials alike. As Philo approached, he motioned to a guard. "I am Philologus. I have been sent to lead the Roman visitors to the home of the High Priest Kayafa." One guard checked a manifest of names then signaled his colleague without making a sound. The gate was opened, and Philo and John moved through the crowds and entered the main courtyard. Where the morning sun beat down upon it, it was empty. Romans and Jews serving the Roman Empire sat in the shade of the sprawling olive trees along the edge of the wall. Each tax collector had a seat and a table. Upon the worn tabletops sat scales and papyrus, the tools used to determine the taxes required for their Roman occupiers. The Jewish merchants wore solemn expressions as they stood in silent lines to pay their tributes to the tax collectors. The mood was quiet, the opposite of the noisy marketplace.

John saw his uncle at a table, arguing with a tax collector. "Five shekels for tribute on six baskets of fish?" he complained. He placed his hands on the table and bent to eye level with the official. "Levi, Levi, my old friend, why are you doing this to your own people? This tax is tantamount to blackmail. I beg you, don't do this."

"I'm sorry, but the amount is correct." Levi offered the receipt slip. "*Teleō.*"

John recalled the first time he had heard a tax collector utter the phrase. He was with his father, who had included him on a visit just a week before he died. He remembered asking his father why the man said that. "It's a Greek word," his father told him. "In the common tongue, it means, 'It is finished.' The tax collectors have to say that at the end of a contract to say the debt was settled, that the bill had been paid in full." It was funny how he remembered that now.

Uncle seemed not ready to give up his case. He continued to talk, drawing the attention of the Roman soldiers. Two walked over to see what the disagreement was. "Is everything all right?"

Startled at the sudden appearance of the soldiers, Uncle stared at them, and then withdrew his argument and placed the appropriate coins on the table. He reached out and yanked the receipt from the tax collector's hand.

As he turned to leave, the guards relaxed and returned to their conversations.

Philo moved to one corner of the courtyard, and passed through the doors into the submagistri's office, John following right behind.

The room was dim compared to the bright sunlight of the courtyard. John opened his eyes wide trying to get a better sense of his surroundings.

Though large, the room had very little furniture. A wooden desk took up one wall nearest the window. A woven rug covered most of the dirt floor. The only chair in the room was for the use of the submagistri seated at the table. Other than an unlit lamp stand, there were no other furnishings. A door on the far wall opened into an adjacent room, but it was too dark in there for John to make out anything.

The submagistri looked up from his table. "Yes, what is it?"

Philo stepped forward to deliver his well-practiced line. If he was nervous before such an important man, he did not show it. "Long live Caesar! My name is Philologus. I have been sent by my master to lead our esteemed guests to the home of the High Priest Kayafa." Philo bowed his head in reverence to the official.

John knew better than to interrupt the official greetings. He was not an official member of the party, just an invited guest.

Several men emerged from the adjacent room, one dressed in the simple toga marking him as a Roman citizen. He stepped forward. "Long live Caesar. I am Sergius Paulus, praetor of Judea from the Roman garrison in Yerushalayim."

John stifled a giggle at how the man pronounced the city's name. Although his Roman accent was thick, he tried to intone as a Jew would. John did not expect that from a Roman official.

"I have been sent with an important message from Valerius Gratus, curator in Judea for the Roman Empire and Tiberius Caesar, to Kayafa, High Priest of the Jewish peoples in settlement about Lake Kinneret." Sergius spoke the formal greeting in a low voice, with much rising and falling in tone, as if reciting some grand speech. He did not return the bow of Philo.

"This is my friend, John."

"Who?" demanded the Roman.

Philo bowed his head in apology. "I mean, Yochanan, son of Elioenai of Yerushalayim."

The Roman took no notice of John.

It had been a long time since John had heard his name pronounced so formally. Ever since he could remember, his mother and friends had called him John.

"Come, follow me, and I will lead you to my father's house."

The party walked in silence as they navigated the narrow streets. It was mid-morning, and a crowd of perhaps two hundred people stood at the steps to the synagogue.

A man stood on the upper step, speaking in a loud voice, waving his arms to emphasize each point. He did not speak in Greek, the common tongue used by the townspeople, but in traditional Aramaic. He ignored the questions and calls of the crowd. It was almost as if he was talking to himself with two hundred eavesdroppers listening in.

Paulus stopped. "Who is that individual and what is he saying?"

Philo seemed reluctant to answer. "His name is Yochanan."

"*That* is Yochanan?" the Roman said. "I've heard of him, but he is not what I expected. He doesn't look important. Where does he live?"

Philo stood with a blank look on his face. "I... I don't know that he lives anywhere."

"He has no home, no place he retires to at night?" His eyebrows arched up in amazement.

"I saw him this morning coming in from the desert on the outskirts of the city," offered John.

Paulus ignored the comment and went back to staring at Yochanan. "What is he saying?"

Philo listened. He hesitated to translate Yochanan's words. "He is speaking of the Hebrew prophecy of a redeemer."

"What is he saying?" Sergius asked again, emphasizing the first word with authority.

Philo swallowed and bowed his head in shame. "Forgive me, praetor, he is saying, *'After me is coming someone who is more powerful than I—I'm not worthy even to bend down and untie his sandals.'* It is an ancient Hebrew prophecy." Philo let his voice trail off without further explanation.

Paulus looked at Philo, and then at John. "Do the people believe this? Do they believe this one will free their land from the Roman Empire?"

Philo did not offer a response.

"That is the prophecy," said John.

Paulus snorted. "Prophecy..." he said, under his breath, and resumed his walk.

John opened the gate to the courtyard and saw Philo's father, Yosef Kayafa, Cohen Hagadol of the Pharisees in Galil, stood at the door to his home waiting for his expected visitor. Apparently, this visitor was most important, for he was dressed in his finest priestly garments. He wore a blue robe with no sleeves, but only slits in the sides for the arms to come through. A trim of blue, red, and crimson pomegranates decorated the bottom, with a bell of gold between each one. He wore a turban of dark blue with a thin gold plate on the front engraved, "Holy to the Lord," fastened with a dark blue cord. He stroked his recently groomed black beard. Other members of the Council stood with him.

Philo stepped aside to allow Sergius to enter the gardens past the front gate.

"Long live Caesar. I am Sergius Paulus, praetor of Y'hudah from the Roman garrison in Yerushalayim."

"Long live Caesar. I am Yosef Kayafa. These are my colleagues." Kayafa introduced many members of the Council, but the only ones John recognized were his teacher, Ya'ir, and one other, Nakdimon.

All the men greeted the praetor with "Long live Caesar," then Kayafa invited Sergius into his home. All removed their sandals and stood before the door. Philo rushed forward and poured cool water on the men's feet, cleansing them. Only upon completion of the ritual did the men enter.

Afterward, John stood with Philo alone in the courtyard.

"I wonder what this is all about," said Philo.

John shrugged.

"This Roman has come a long way, and he doesn't seem too happy to be here." Philo moved quickly but cautiously through the house towards the back. "Come on, follow me." He disappeared around the corner.

As John crept along, he saw Philo climbing a tall olive tree in the backyard. He crawled onto a thick branch hanging above a window, and then waved to John, who crawled up after. Philo motioned to him to keep silent. "If we are caught, my father will have both of us crucified," he said.

While they could not see anyone, they could hear voices.

"We have put up with your kind and your religion for decades," Sergius was saying. "We do not object to your temples, but when we hear one of you is plotting to overthrow Rome, we must not stand idle."

"Proconsul, no one is plotting to overthrow Rome,"

argued a voice that sounded like Kayafa's.

"Then why do your people look for a king to rule? I have been from one end of these lands to the other, and in every settlement I visit, your people stand idly by as usurpers and crazed men tell them of a coming king. Who is this king?"

"My lord, our people may have no nation of their own, but our ways are handed down to us by our fathers and their fathers of old. What you speak of is but one part of our life. Our Tanakh says,

> *Adonai will raise up for you a prophet like me from among yourselves, from your own kinsmen. You are to pay attention to him.*

"It is a redeemer, a mashiach, who will release us from our bondage."

"So, you freely admit this, then?" asked Sergius.

As John leaned closer to hear their conversation, he slipped on the branch. Philo grabbed him and pushed him firmly back against the tree. "Be more careful," he said under his voice.

"Thank you," was all that John could whisper back.

Kayafa's voice was quiet and soothing. "Proconsul, this person is spoken of in our writings. He could come today, he could come tomorrow, or he could not come for a thousand years. No true worshipper wastes time on such searches. To spend time searching for a mashiach would neither add nor detract from my daily religious life."

Sergius sounded puzzled. "Then why? Why do your people spend so much time wasted on such a search? As I was led here, I saw hundreds listening to yet another lunatic. I have seen him before. He has stood in the streets of Yerushalayim, he has been seen around Y'hudah, and draws people to the Yarden River. Large crowds follow him. What power does he have over your citizens?"

"Because people need him. Forgive me, Proconsul, but our people have been under the rule of others for so long. Their desire is to live again as free men some day. To believe in a leader, even a leader they may never see, gives them hope."

Sergius stuck his head out of the window, taking in the courtyard view. John held his breath. If Sergius happened to look up, he would catch two very large birds sitting in an olive tree.

Sergius' head disappeared back into the house, and John heard Philo release his breath, too.

"Rome will never permit a ruler of Jews to come to power," said Sergius. "If these people believe in one, even one who does not exist, they become a threat. We do not care for your wants and desires. We care only that peace stays in this area and those whom we rule fulfill our needs."

"Peace is in our lands. These people pose no threat to the armies of Rome," pleaded Kayafa.

Sergius laughed. "No threat to Rome? I would hope not. Yet, with the right words, one lunatic can raise an army. It would be suicidal to attack Rome. We would spill much blood. We do not desire this."

"Neither do we, praetor," agreed Kayafa.

"Allow me explain why I am here. There is a man in these parts, a man named Yochanan. He has traveled up and down the Yarden River, speaking to anyone who will listen to him that this mashiach, this ruler of the Jews is coming. Are you aware of this?"

"We have heard of him, but not of his wanderings. He came through here a few months ago."

"And you did not arrest him?"

"For what, Proconsul?"

Sergius sighed. "For inciting your people! For telling them that they can look to someone besides Rome to meet their needs. As I was brought here, I saw him spreading his teachings. Many people have taken his word as truth. There have been several skirmishes between our soldiers and townspeople. He is preparing your people for war. This is why Gratus dispatched me. The governor of Y'hudah has grown tired of his rants. The time has come for us to silence him. You must dissuade the people from listening to this man. You must disperse these crowds and get them to return to their homes. You must keep them from gathering together in the first place."

"I must?" asked Kayafa incredulously. "My lord, if I may ask, why me?"

"Because," replied Sergius, "if you don't, we will. You are their religious leader, are you not? They will listen to you."

"I do not want to see the armies of Rome attack this or any other town." Kayafa sounded very uncomfortable. "However, we have had many of these types before. Some time ago, there was a rebellion under Todah. He claimed to be somebody special, and maybe four hundred men rallied behind him. Upon his death, his whole following broke up and it all came to nothing. Another one, Y'hudah HaG'lili, led an uprising back at the time of the enrollment for the Roman tax. He got some people to turn form their teachings and follow him. But he too was killed, and all his followers were scattered.

"In this present case, Proconsul, my advice to you is not to interfere. Leave these people alone. If this idea or this movement has a human origin, it will collapse."

"Nonetheless," replied Sergius, "we want him stopped, now." Sergius' tone said the discussion was over and it was time to finish this task. "If you do this, if you succeed, my superior is prepared to offer you the presidency of the Sanhedrin in Yerushalayim."

Philo gasped. "Presidency of the Sanhedrin!" he whispered to John. "He would preside over the Temple in Yerushalayim, and distribute the money. He would have supreme religious and civil authority. He would be the head of all Y'hudah!"

"My father-in-law, Anan, already sits at the head of the Sanhedrin," said Kayafa. "The high priest has been chosen for life. How can this happen?"

"With Rome, all things are possible. We will allow Anan to remain as high priest *jure divino*, and he will have authority in spiritual matters, while you, Kayafa, will be the official pontiff recognized by Rome. Anan will be the high priest while you will hold the office. Do you accept?"

"You come in the name of Gratus, curator in Y'hudah for the Roman Empire, yet isn't the governor of Y'hudah someone named Pilate, responsible for the makeup of the Sanhedrin?"

"I'm impressed," said Sergius. "I was not aware you were so knowledgeable of our leader's comings and goings."

"I make it a point to know what happens in Yerushalayim. Will the governor honor Gratus' offer?"

"He will," said Sergius.

Kayafa remained silent for several moments. "I cannot be bought with appointments," he began, pausing as if carefully choosing every word. "However, I am well aware of the dangers this man poses to the children of Y'hudah. I will take measures against this man and anyone else who teaches this prophecy."

"On behalf of Rome, we welcome any assistance you offer."

John and Philo scurried down to the lowest branch and jumped out of the tree, making it to the courtyard moments before Paulus exited the house. The Council members bid him farewell from the doorway.

"May I escort you back to the garrison, praetor?" offered Philo.

The Roman officer grunted as he shook his head. "I can find my way." He left through the gate and disappeared from sight.

"Do you think Rome will invade?" John asked.

"I don't know. I wouldn't put it past them."

John tried to imagine what it would be like to have Rome send armies against them. True, they did have soldiers at the garrison, but they were a small group. If the citizens of K'far-Nachum organized and really chose to rise up against them, the soldiers would not be able to hold them off for long.

A Roman army, though, was a different thing. John had heard tales of their armies laying waste to whole towns in their wars, leaving not one stone atop another. He shuddered to think what such an army might do to his town. As much as he desired to leave it, he did not want to see it destroyed.

"You heard what Yochanan said on the steps. Do you think he's trying to raise an army?"

"I doubt it. But it doesn't matter. If Rome says he's a problem, then he's a problem. My father will have to silence him now."

John shook his head. "It's not right, Rome telling us what to do to our own citizens."

Philo scoffed at him. "Don't tell me you're going to defend that heretic."

"Of course not. He doesn't speak as our teachers do. I just don't think he should be 'silenced'—whatever that means."

"What that means," said Philo, puffing out his chest as he assumed an air of authority, "is my father will give him one choice: stop preaching or face arrest. If he doesn't choose wisely, he'll be imprisoned."

John nodded, although deep down he did not understand why everyone was so upset. This Yochanan was only one man, and not very likely a military genius. John suspected everyone was making a big deal about nothing.

3

A Friend Revealed

"John, is that you?" asked the soft voice.

John wiped sweat from his forehead. The afternoon sun burned hot upon his bare head as he repaired the nets for the third time that week. He squinted and raised a hand to block the sunlight as he strained to see who had called him. He focused on the silhouette of a young girl. "Myriam?"

When she nodded, it lifted his spirits.

"How is everything going?" he asked, returning to the repairs.

Myriam became very still, and took a few moments to answer. "It's my mother. She saw another physician yesterday."

"I take it things didn't go well?"

Myriam shook her head. "It's not fair. My mother's a good person. She's never cheated or lied to anyone, yet she's been so sick for all these years."

She paused before continuing, wiping tears from her eyes. "Do you know what the worst part is? Everyone who sees her thinks she's the cause of this, that Adonai is punishing her for some hidden sin."

"That's so unfair."

"I know. She is the most wonderful, sweet person, but because she can't control this..." She struggled for the right words. "...this bleeding, everyone avoids her and speaks about her behind her back." Myriam stepped forward so only John could hear. "They think they're getting away with it, but I know. I hear them."

"I wish I could do more to help," he offered. "I know this is difficult for you and your parents." He let his thoughts trail off. He knew his sympathy was an empty gesture.

"I don't know why God would do this to her. You want to become a rabbi. Maybe you can pray to God, ask Him to reveal why He is punishing her?"

"Do you think..." He swallowed hard, fearful to ask the question. "Do you think maybe Adonai wants your mother to be this way?" For as long as he could remember, Myriam had asked everyone for prayers to heal her mother— John, his mother, rabbis and teachers, strangers. All had prayed for a healing, but no healing had ever come. The illness consumed her father so that he spent his days looking for miracle healers and his nights obtaining foods and scraps to feed his family. John always feared she would go from asking God to blaming God for her mother's illness. Now that fear seemed to be coming true. John could not bear the thought of anything coming between her and God. "Maybe He has a purpose for her illness."

Myriam's mouth dropped open. "What? How can you say... how can you even ask such a thing?" she stammered.

The tears in her eyes made him realize how wrong his statement sounded. "Myriam, please understand, I only mean that everything God does, He does for a purpose."

Myriam closed her eyes tightly, and then wiped her tears with the palms of her hands. She sniffed in her despair. "Maybe so, but I still want Him to heal her. She's suffered long enough."

Then I will pray for both of you."

The two of them sat in silence for several moments.

"I want you to come with me," she said, changing the subject.

"Where are you going?"

"I saw Yochanan preaching at the synagogue yesterday. His words were ..." she struggled for the right word. "Different from the last time he was here. He's not just saying the mashiach will come some day, he seems to know something."

His mind raced back to yesterday, when he and Philo sat on the tree limb outside Kayafa's home, and he remembered the decision the Council made. "No, I don't think it would be a good idea."

Myriam frowned with her eyebrows. "Why not? I saw him speak. His words are very different from what your rabbis preach in the synagogue. You should see him. He's at the Yarden River right now. It's only a few miles away. Will you come with me?"

Her eyes pleaded with him to join her, and for a

moment, he considered it.

She leaned closer and lowered her voice. "He says he is Adonai's prophet. I think he's a true prophet."

John sighed. "Myriam, how many of these 'true prophets' have you and your parents followed? A dozen? Two dozen? A new one comes through every few months and it's always the same thing. You listen to him for a few weeks, and then he leaves, often with all of your money."

"But he is different. You have to see him and hear him. He is not doing it for money. Won't you come?"

John feared that if he told her about the arrest the Council planned, she might run off and warn Yochanan, or worse, blame John. "I can't, not today." He saw the disappointment in her eyes. "Maybe another day," he offered, hoping it would be enough for her.

"He'll be there until the Sabbath. If you change your mind, we'll be at Beit-Anyah, on the east bank of the Yarden River. You know the spot. It's the one we played in a few summers ago."

John knew the exact spot. While the main river flowed so fast they would have to dodge logs and other things in the water, they discovered a small pocket off to one side where the water lapped in soft circles. When they played here, they never had to worry about the current dragging them into the lake, and afterwards, they sunned themselves on the grassy hill off to one side. "Maybe I will see you there," he said.

John watched her disappear up the road. Part of him wanted to walk beside her and the other wanted to drag her back.

So engrossed was John in the repairs at the dock that he didn't notice the approach of his friend until he was almost beside him.

"My father needs to see you immediately," Philo barked.

"What for?" asked John, somewhat apprehensive. "Kayafa has never asked to speak to me. What could he want?"

Philo maintained a stern look. "I don't know, he didn't tell me. You'll just have to find out when you get there. Come along."

Philo took off with such speed John had to quicken his pace to keep up. They rounded a street and entered Kayafa's courtyard. Philo's father stood impassively, his black beard and hair making him look even more demanding than usual. Several men stood within the courtyard, but John, noticing Kayafa's cold stare, bowed in respect.

"So," he growled, "you have brought him."

Philo nodded.

"Ya'ir tells me you know our Tanakh. Is this true?"

John could not imagine what Ya'ir had told him. "If you mean, can I memorize Scripture, then it is true," he answered without raising his head out of respect for the man's authority and fear of his stare.

"Are you familiar with the writings of Yesha'yahu, the great Jewish prophet of our fathers?"

"Yes, sir."

"Complete this section:

The Spirit of Adonai Elohim is upon me, because..."

John closed his eyes. He searched his memory for the proper scroll, opening it within his mind's eye. When he came to the point, he answered in a loud, strong voice.

The Spirit of Adonai Elohim is upon me, because Adonai has anointed me to announce good news to the poor. He has sent me to heal the brokenhearted; to proclaim freedom to the captives, to let out into light those bound in the dark; to proclaim the year of the favor of Adonai and the day of vengeance of our God; to comfort all who mourn, yes, provide for those on the Temple Mount who mourn, giving them garlands instead of ashes, the oil of gladness instead of mourning, a cloak of praise instead of a heavy spirit, so that they will be called oaks of righteousness planted by Adonai, in which he takes pride.

John opened his eyes. Kayafa still stared at him, but the look had softened, his eyes opened wide in wonderment. Within seconds, Kayafa regained his composure and returned to his threatening appearance. John swallowed hard under the man's glare.

"What does it mean?" asked Kayafa in a loud voice. "Of whom is the prophet speaking?"

John spoke in a loud voice. "He speaks of the mashiach."

"What do you mean?"

"This is only one of the scrolls depicting the coming of the mashiach. The prophet describes Him and His kingly office. When He arrives, He will free His people from the dominion of sin, and also from the fear of Sheol."

Kayafa's scowl disappeared, his face softening in admiration. "Can you offer an understanding of the next line?"

This cannot be happening to me. John's mind spun futilely in search of an answer, but none came. *Just go back to the Scripture.*

John closed his eyes and took a deep breath to calm down, then continued.

"When the mashiach comes, he will take vengeance on our enemies. The prophet speaks of ashes and oil to say his people no longer are slaves, as a mourner wearing ashes, but instead our lives will be filled with joy, as one who is anointed with oil."

"And does the text tell you in what form the mashiach will appear?"

John shook his head. "It does not."

"Do you believe the mashiach will come dressed in rags, as a vagabond or a vagrant?"

John flashed back to Yochanan's appearance that morning. "When the mashiach comes, He will come as our new king. He will free us from those who keep us captive."

"And if you should see a man preaching on the street, wearing rags or making crazed statements, should you listen?"

"No, he is a false prophet. When Adonai sends our Savior, He will come as a conqueror, not as a beggar."

Kayafa addressed the assembly about the courtyard. "Do you want your king mistaken for a beggar?"

The men shook their heads, some crying, "Adonai, no."

It took John a moment to remember there were others in the courtyard, so focused was he on Kayafa. He looked about and recognized several members of the Council, and several men he did not. He saw his teacher, Ya'ir, smiling broadly.

He expected more questioning from the older man, but Kayafa's stance softened, and he even managed a smile. "Your answers impress me. I did not expect you would possess such knowledge of the passage's true meaning."

Ya'ir stepped forward and spoke before John could answer. "That shouldn't have surprised you. It is as I told you. He does the same thing in his studies."

The older man nodded. "Yes, but speaking up in a class of peers is one thing. When surrounded by elders is another. Not many his age could."

Kayafa's smile dropped, and again he was all business. "Have you given thought to what you would like to do with your life?"

John paused so as not to appear too anxious. His knees almost buckled as he tried to calm himself before the rabbi. "I have."

"Your teacher and I have spoken at length. You have a tremendous gift from Adonai. Your understanding of our ancient Scriptures in many ways surpasses some in our own Council."

For his entire life, John could not remember anyone giving him such praise. "Thank you."

"Under normal conditions, I would have you demonstrate your knowledge of the Torah, but I have no need to test you. I know from your teacher and from the way you have answered, you have memorized not only the Torah, but also much of our Scriptures. I am not altogether convinced continuing on in school will accomplish anything."

As Kayafa's words registered, John felt his dreams and aspirations fading from him.

Ya'ir walked forward. "With the High Priest's permission, I would like you to consider becoming my apprentice."

"What... what do you mean?" John asked. He had never heard of a twelve-year-old apprentice to a rabbi.

"Most boys your age either continue in Beth Midrash, or leave schooling all together to apprentice in a trade, such as carpentry or fishing. I do not expect you to become a fisherman, but a rabbi," Ya'ir replied. "You have a gift, one that needs to be nurtured and watered. You are far too young to become my talmid. However, I do not see how having you sit for seven years until you reach the proper age to become one of my talmidim will be a benefit to you.

"Therefore, I would like you, as other boys your age do, and accept an apprenticeship. Though this apprenticeship will not be to learn a trade, but to learn how to become a rabbi."

The words he had longed to hear! An opportunity to get away from his uncle, to get away from fish, to become his own man. John was overwhelmed.

Ya'ir did not give him time to respond. "I ask you because I truly believe Adonai Himself has gifted you for this position."

"Yes sir," said John, "I would be honored."

"What of your parents?" asked Kayafa. "Will they approve this arrangement?"

John tried to imagine how his uncle would respond. *Would he be happy to be rid of me, or upset to lose his free labor?* " I do not know," he answered.

"You must speak to them," said Ya'ir. "I am certain that once you explain what is being asked of you, they will approve."

John opened his mouth, but no words came out.

"I will speak to them on your behalf, if you wish," offered Ya'ir.

John shook his head. "No, let me speak to them first. If this is what Adonai wants, He will make it happen."

Kayafa addressed the men in the courtyard. "Then I so ordain, from this moment forward, Yochanan Ben-Elioenai will be apprenticed to the house of Ya'ir. He will enter into this position effective immediately."

A few of the men offered a smattering of applause at the announcement.

John glanced at Philo. His mouth was open, his eyes unblinking. John got the distinct impression that Philo neither knew about nor accepted this decision.

Kayafa did not give them time to talk. "Now to the

matter at hand. The Council has decided. Nakdimon and Ya'ir."

The two priests stood before Kayafa. "By order of the Council, you are assigned to arrest the heretic, Yochanan the Immerser."

As if listening, a dozen soldiers entered the courtyard. They carried spears and short swords; they were not the Roman soldiers from the garrison, but local men under the employment of Rome to keep the peace. Still, they were formidable fighters, and well armed.

Nakdimon stepped forward and spoke to the captain of the guard. "Follow me. We last saw this man at the synagogue."

The captain barked an order, and the soldiers shouldered their weapons and fell into line.

John remembered what Myriam told him about the river, and he struggled with his decision. Betray the trust Myriam had in telling him, against the duty he felt to his new teacher. He knew what he must do. "Masters," he cried, running after them. "The man you seek is not there. He is at a pool called Beit-Anyah, on the east bank of the Yarden River, with his followers."

"How do you know this?" demanded the captain of the guard.

"A friend of mine has seen him speak there."

Philo shot him an odd glance.

"She said he will be there preaching all week."

"If what this boy says is true, then it will make his capture much easier," said Nakdimon. He spoke to John. "Do you know where along the Yarden? Can you lead us there?"

"Yes."

"Then come with us," Nakdimon beckoned.

John's heart ached at the thought of what the arrest might do to Myriam. Then he and Philo fell in line behind the priests, with the soldiers following them.

Yochanan stood waist deep in the Yarden, lines of people in the water with him. One by one, people walked up to stand next to him. The followers would cross their hands in front of their chests. Yochanan would then place one hand on their crossed arms, and the other in the small of their backs. He whispered something into their ears, but John could not make out what he said. The follower would become limp, and without a sound, be lowered into the waters until completely submerged. After a moment, he brought them back up, where they drew in air, a huge smile on their faces. The waiting crowds said nothing as they watched the ritual repeat.

"Is he purifying Jews?" John asked Philo softly.

"It certainly looks that way."

John tried to understand what the man was doing. It was true that when Jews felt unclean, they performed a ritual immersion to restore themselves to ritual purity.

"Why would he do that to Jews?" John asked, to no one in particular.

After a time, Yochanan strode towards shore.

Some four hundred men and women crowded the hillside. He stood and addressed the mass.

"Turn from your sins to God, for the Kingdom of Heaven is near!"

As he spoke, his voice carried along the surface of the water and up the shore. Even from their distance, John could clearly hear every word.

With an uneasy excitement, the crowd moved forward.

"When is the time, Prophet?" yelled a man in the crowd. "Are you our deliverer?"

"After me is coming someone who is more powerful than I—I'm not worthy even to bend down and untie his sandals. I have immersed you in water, but he will immerse you in the Ruach HaKodesh."

"Ruach HaKodesh?" asked Philo.

John was dumbfounded. "The Holy Spirit. How can anyone wash with a Spirit?"

Philo shook his head, equally confused. "This is not how a rabbi teaches. All rabbis teach from Scripture, of things already past. How can he speak of what is to come?"

John leaned over and whispered into Philo's ear. "Do you think maybe he's a prophet, like Mal'akhi?"

Philo turned to John, an incredulous look on his face. "What made you say that? It has been four hundred years since prophets spoke the words of Adonai." Philo shook his head. "Ya'ir makes you his apprentice and suddenly you think you have all the answers? You've got a lot to learn. It might be best if you keep your mouth shut until you have something intelligent to say."

John cowered, surprised at his friend's sudden burst of anger.

Nakdimon and the soldiers were finally in place. He signaled the guards to move forward to make the arrest.

Nakdimon stood at the edge of the lake. "You there, Yochanan Ben-Z'kharyah," he called out, addressing the crowd more than the man. "By what priestly authority do you make these claims?"

"You snakes! Who warned you to escape the coming punishment?"

"We have committed no sins. We are not under threat of punishment."

"If you have really turned from your sins to God, produce fruit that will prove it!"

"You have no authority to speak." Nakdimon gestured at the other priests for the crowd's benefit. "We have the authority. We are sons of Avraham, not some lowly peasant who immerses our townspeople in a filthy river."

Yochanan would not back down. "Don't start saying to yourselves, 'Avraham is our father'! For I tell you that God can raise up for Avraham sons from these stones!"

"I have never seen anyone question Nakdimon this way," said Philo.

John sensed the crowd's tension. Many people appeared moved by these words. None of them had ever heard their own rabbis speak with such authority, or of such matters.

"You are treading on dangerous ground," Nakdimon said. "I knew your father, Z'kharyah. Your father sleeps with his ancestors, and your continued insolence only brings you closer to him."

Yochanan's eyes glazed over, as if fixated on an object in the distance. He did not even seem to notice or hear Nakdimon. "The axe is at the root of the trees, ready to strike; every tree that doesn't produce good fruit will be chopped down and thrown in the fire!"

"Does he mean us?" John asked.

Philo nodded.

Yochanan was attacking the priests. They were the trees to be burned. Yochanan could only be implying that the fate of the priests, of all who follow their traditions, would be the fiery pit of Sheol.

From the back of the crowd, a man cried out, "Are we to be burned? Or will you immerse us in these waters to save us?"

"I am immersing you in water so that you might turn from sin to God. But the one coming after me is more powerful than I—I'm not worthy even to carry his sandals—and he will immerse you in the Ruach HaKodesh and in fire."

Nakdimon sought to regain control of the discussion. "I said, who gives you this authority? Answer me!"

Yochanan appeared as if in a trance. "He has with him his winnowing fork, and he will clear out his threshing floor, gathering his wheat into the barn but burning up the straw with unquenchable fire!"

John recognized the words from the encounter at the edge of the desert. His appearance was so very different from the rabbis and leaders John had grown up with, so much different from Kayafa, Nakdimon, or Ya'ir. While most of his kind was trying to earn a living, Yochanan could not be doing this for money. Other "true prophets" demanded payment for their revelations. If there was one thing of which he could be certain, this particular individual had no desire for material riches. Instead, his clothing, his manners, all of it, reminded John of another prophet of old—Eliyahu.

Kayafa's appearance filled him with pride. He was a priest of Adonai. He often seemed to hold himself so far above others it was hard for John to relate to his teachings.

Yet this man, this prophet, held himself below others.

Ya'ir tried to assist. "Who are you?"

The question seemed to bring Yochanan back into this world. "I am not the Messiah."

"Then who are you?" Ya'ir asked again.

"Are you Eliyahu, returned to us?" yelled someone from the crowd.

"No, I am not."

"Are you 'the prophet,' the one we're expecting?" asked another.

"No."

Ya'ir pressed on. "Who are you? So that we can give an

answer to the people who sent us. What do you have to say about yourself?"

The only sound was the slow roll of the waters of the Yarden River lapping against the shore. Everyone there stood mesmerized by the man in the water.

Yochanan broke the silence with a shout. "I am the voice of someone crying out in the desert. Make the way of Adonai straight!"

John remembered his Scripture. It was from the scroll of Yesha'yahu.

> *A voice cries out: "Clear a road through the desert for Adonai! Level a highway in the desert plain for our God!"*

Ya'ir was so upset he almost walked into the lake, stopping just short of the shore. "Are you claiming that you are the one spoken of in the prophecies?"

Yochanan said nothing.

Nakdimon pulled Ya'ir from the edge. "If you are neither the Messiah nor Eliyahu nor 'the prophet,' then why are you immersing people?"

Yochanan replied, "I am immersing people in water, but among you is standing someone whom you don't know. He is the one coming after me—I'm not good enough even to untie His sandal!"

Nakdimon looked nervously about at the crowd then turned to Yochanan and tried again. "Why are you immersing people?"

Yochanan became silent.

The exchange fascinated John. He had never seen such disagreement over the Lord's teachings.

One of the townspeople on the edge of the shore walked over to stand by Yochanan in the Yarden. "So then, what should we do? Do you need money to answer?"

Yochanan addressed the crowd in a loud voice. "I do not want money. If you have freely to give, then give. Whoever has two coats should share with somebody who has none, and whoever has food should do the same."

A man stepped forward into the waters and walked right up to Yochanan. John recognized Levi, the tax collector his uncle dealt with. "Rabbi, what should we do, for I do have monies in abundance?"

Yochanan placed his arm on the man's shoulder and smiled. "Collect no more than the government assesses," he told him.

Nakdimon signaled the captain of the guard. "I have had enough of this. Go down there and arrest him."

The captain looked about nervously. "Do you think," he asked, "that is wise, considering the size of the crowd?"

Nakdimon glared at him. "Do as I instruct."

The captain signaled two of his men into the river. They walked up to Yochanan and stood on either side of him.

"What about us? What should we do?" they asked.

Yochanan smiled to them, and placed his hands on each one's shoulder. "Don't intimidate anyone, don't accuse people falsely, and be satisfied with your pay."

"What are they doing?" Nakdimon cried to the captain.

The captain had no answer.

Yochanan again turned to the crowd. "It is true, each of you breaks the laws of Adonai, and you need to repent. Your tetrarch, Herod, has done many more evil things. He murdered his brother and took his wife as his own."

Nakdimon approached the soldiers. "You there, go down and arrest that man and those two idiots."

The man looked at his captain, who slowly shook his head.

"You deny my orders?" asked Nakdimon

The captain spoke in a low tone. "I will not arrest my own men. They have done nothing wrong."

John stood there fascinated at the interaction of the priests and the soldiers. All was silent except for the gurgle of the river as it lapped against the shore.

Ya'ir walked over and placed himself between the two men, preventing Nakdimon from getting any closer to the soldiers. "Come, there is nothing more we can do here."

They turned from the river and headed back into town.

The sounds of the river faded as the crowd's whispers rose in response to what they had just witnessed. This man, this unkempt, wild-looking man, had single-handedly defeated the religious leaders of their city. The whispers turned to jeers as the priests left.

Several of the soldiers surrounded Nakdimon and Ya'ir,

protecting them as they exited. Philo joined them for the walk back into town.

Many others waded into the waters.

John just stood there as they walked off. He felt a tap on his shoulder.

Myriam's eyes sparkled with pride.

"What did you think?"

"Th-th-that...that was amazing," was all John could stammer.

"Did you see how he talked to that priest? I've seen nothing like it."

John's smile faded.

"What about his message?" she asked, "Didn't you hear his message?"

"What message? What did you hear?"

"John, don't you want to go into the river?"

John thought about it. He was a Jew, and did not need to go into the waters as the Gentiles did. "No," he answered softly, "he did not speak to me. Do you think I am one of the ones he was speaking about?"

Myriam nodded.

John did not know what else to say. He turned and began the long walk back to town.

Myriam joined him. They walked in silence until the crowds were well behind them.

"He is wrong, you know," he began. "The laws of Moshe are quite precise."

"He does not speak for Moshe. The priests do."

John fought to keep his anger in check. It would do no good to explode at her. He had to think as a rabbi would.

"Do you believe he is the prophet?"

"Yes. You heard him speak. His words come from Adonai."

"I did hear him speak. I did not hear any of Adonai's words, other than his claim to a mantle that is not his. He does not speak from Scripture."

Myriam walked in silence.

"He is a vagrant. He dresses as a mad man. If he walked on our streets and you had not heard of him, you would cross to the other side to be away from him." He paused, trying to think of the right words. *Adonai, use me, insert your thoughts into my speech.*

"But what if he is right?" she asked. "What if he has seen the future, and knows who the mashiach is? What if the mashiach is here on earth right now? Wouldn't that be glorious?"

John prayed daily for their redeemer to come, but it was without any expectation that it would happen today. It was ludicrous and quite terrifying to think that he lived in the time, dreamt about since the time of Avraham two thousand years ago.

"I know Scripture, I have read the prophecies. This man does not know what he is saying. It would not surprise me if a demon has possessed him."

"You should not think like that about Adonai's servant."

"If he was Adonai's servant, I couldn't think that about him."

They continued in silence.

4

A Warning

"Where have you been?" Philo asked gruffly.

"I was delayed. I'm here now."

Philo turned his back on John and began walking away at a quick pace.

"Wait. What's wrong?"

Philo continued walking, ignoring John's question.

John ran up and grabbed Philo's arm, spinning him around. "What's wrong? Are you still upset about what happened at the Yarden River?"

Philo raised his fist as if to strike John, and then backed down. There was a look of anger in his eyes. "I cannot believe my father made you Ya'ir's apprentice."

"What are you talking about?" John asked.

Philo stared at the ground, refusing to look John in the eyes. "All my life, I have been a good son. I have followed my father's commands, done everything he has asked."

John nodded in agreement. "What does that have to do with my apprenticeship?"

Philo raised his head and glared at his friend. "I have been in Beth Midrash for six years. I have one more year to go and then a decision has to be made, do I continue as a talmid of a rabbi, or do I quit my desire to join the priesthood and learn a trade."

"I know all of this," said John meekly. "I still don't understand why you are mad at me?"

Philo's anger exploded. "You don't understand?" he shouted. "I want to be like my father, the cohen hagadol of K'far-nachum. To do that, I have to become a talmid. There aren't that many openings available."

Suddenly, John realized what his friend meant. "You're afraid my apprenticeship means that Ya'ir won't be able to take you in next year as his talmid?" he asked timidly.

Philo's breathing became labored. "It is all I have ever wanted. I had everything planned out. But I had never expected a twelve-year-old apprentice. Such a thing has never happened before."

Tentatively, John reached out and placed his hand tenderly on his friend's shoulder. "You're afraid no one else will accept you as a talmid? That's ridiculous. You're Kayafa's son. Of course someone will take you."

Philo pulled away from his touch.

John understood. Philo had often come to him confused by the lessons he had been learning at Beth Midrash. Many times John had to help him understand what the lesson meant and what he was trying to interpret. Philo was unsure he would be accepted by anyone other than Ya'ir. And now John had taken one of the few available spots.

"I am not a talmid," John said. "I am an apprentice, whatever that means. I do not know what is going to happen in the next year, and neither do you.

"I did not ask for this. I was only hoping they would let me continue my studies in the Beth Midrash."

Philo grunted. "That's where you should be."

It hurt John to think that his friend could not see that he deserved this position. "We shouldn't argue about this. Neither of us can change your father's edicts. We must accept what has happened and move on."

Philo grunted. "That's easy for you to say. You got what you always wanted."

"What I wanted," John said in a soothing voice, "was to get away from my uncle, to get away from the fish and the poverty and, most of all, to become something more than what was expected of me. I praise Adonai that I have this opportunity. I do not know what it means to be a rabbi's apprentice. I just hope one day that I have the same opportunities you have already—the opportunity to be a talmid, and someday, a rabbi."

"You really don't understand how this works, do you?"

"Please, explain it to me."

They had reached Philo's home. They sat down in silence to remove their sandals, but neither moved.

"Here in Galil, boys and girls go to Beth Sefer. Boys study the Torah, and the girls study the scrolls of the Tehillim, Mishlei and D'varim. At age twelve, if a boy knows the Torah by memory, he'll continue on in Beth Midrash, studying and memorizing the rest of the Tanakh. At age nineteen, if they find a rabbi who will take them, they become his talmid.

"I have been attending Beth Midrash under Ya'ir for six years. I have worked hard to memorize the Tanakh. You have not put in your time. You have not put in the effort I have. I don't think you deserve to be a talmid, at least not before me."

"I'm not a talmid, I'm an apprentice."

"Who has heard of a twelve-year-old apprentice?"

"You're jealous?"

"Of course I am. Ya'ir can only have so many boys under his wing. If you fill a role as an apprentice, he may not choose another to be his talmid. If you take a position away, I might not get to be one."

"That's ridiculous. Can't your father make you his talmid?"

"My father has already told me Ya'ir will not accept me."

"Why?"

Philo shrugged. "I have not memorized the Tanakh. There are many scrolls I am struggling with. He doesn't think I have what it takes to be a rabbi."

"Well, he's wrong. I mean, he's a great man, but he doesn't know what he's talking about. You'll make a fine rabbi someday."

"Not if I don't become a talmid."

"I can help you with your studies. If you want, I can work with you day and night to help you memorize."

Philo shook his head. "No you can't. Because now you must stay with Ya'ir day and night."

Suddenly, Philo let out a long sigh and allowed his shoulders to droop. He began unlacing a sandal, and John followed.

"Stop, you're doing it wrong," said Philo.

"What do you mean? How can I take off a sandal wrong?"

"If you are going to become a rabbi, you need to know things. The law says you must remove your right sandal first, never the left one."

"Why?"

Philo looked puzzled. "You know, I'm really not sure why. But that is the law."

And like that, they were again friends. John did not

understand why Philo had been so angry, or why he suddenly wasn't angry anymore, he was just thankful his friend was his friend again.

John removed his right sandal, and then his left. He poured cool water over his feet to cleanse them, and then they entered the home quietly. Philo guided him to a small room off to one side of the main hall, a room that offered them some privacy to talk.

"What did you think of Yochanan?" asked Philo.

John swallowed and considered what to say. He thought about what Myriam had said on the road. He knew his questions would anger his friend, but he also had to know that his answers to her were true. "Do you think...is it possible he is who he claims he is?"

"No, he is just another false prophet, trying to make his living off the hopes of the lost."

"But, the way he spoke, the message. No other prophet has ever done that. Did you see how he was dressed? He wasn't after money, he was after souls."

"Don't anger me. My father will not allow this to continue."

"I'm not trying to make you angry. All I'm saying is you should consider what he said. He talked in ways I have never heard before, not from your father, not from Nakdimon, not from Ya'ir."

"I cannot listen to this anymore. This is blasphemous, to think a man could—"

Philo never finished his sentence, as there came a loud pounding at the door. Philo and John retreated into the shadows of the room as a servant ran to see who it was. The man argued with the hidden newcomer, then the door flung open and Sergius walked into the front room, followed by several Roman soldiers from the garrison. The servant ran off into another room, and then Kayafa came out a moment later, with Nakdimon and Ya'ir.

"What," Kayafa asked, "is the meaning of this intrusion?"

Sergius was unfazed. "I have just received a report you spoke to that man, that prophet." He practically spat the last word. "And he humiliated you in front of the entire city. Is this how you plan to deal with the situation?"

"My dear Sergius," Kayafa began softly, "your

information is not accurate. I have not begun to deal with the situation personally, although these colleagues did see the man today."

"Several of the garrison soldiers happened to be in the crowd when your 'colleagues' confronted the man."

"Spies?" asked Kayafa.

"Let's call them 'observers,' shall we? They reported that this man humiliated your men."

John and Philo listened in silence.

"Excellency, you came to me only last month with your concerns. We were not aware of Rome's anger regarding this situation. We dispatched two men to meet with this individual. We do not normally deal with such trivial matters."

"Rome does not consider insurrection trivial."

"And we do not consider one lunatic yelling in the river an insurrection." Kayafa paused, regaining his composure. When he spoke again, his voice was much softer. "My men met with this man and asked him several questions. By his responses, he believes himself to be one of our old prophets. A dead man returned to life. He is insane."

"And you?"

"Governor, I have learned we should not invest our time or energy worrying about the ravings of a lunatic."

"Yet your people do. My men reported there were hundreds there."

"He really doesn't matter. Our people have seen his likes before. He comes in, he riles people up for a few weeks, but the people tire of his rants and soon forget him."

"I've got to get closer," said Philo, as he moved to a better view. John stayed near his friend, aware that if caught, Kayafa would have much more to deal with.

Kayafa stepped towards to Sergius. "I understand Rome's concerns. We will hunt this man. I doubt he will make an impact on our town."

Sergius spoke softly to the soldiers, who turned and left. He strode after them, pausing at the door. "I hope for your sake, and the sake of this town, you are right. You have thirty days. If you do not silence him in thirty days, we will."

The Roman and his soldiers left the house. Kayafa turned to the two priests in the room. "My friends, the stakes we are playing with have grown much higher. Where is my son?"

John followed Philo into the room. "Here I am, Father," said Philo.

"Good," said Kayafa. "I want you to find the other members of the Council. Tell them to join us here immediately. Take John with you."

"Yes, Father." The two boys quickly left on their mission.

"What just happened?" John asked as they tied their sandals.

"Not here," Philo whispered. "My father has spies everywhere."

They left the house and gathered their belongings. They walked out of the gate in silence. It was not until Philo felt they were far enough away from the house before he spoke.

"I have never heard of Rome taking such an interest in one of our own. I was surprised when he first showed up at my father's, but today's little tirade..." Philo let his words trail off.

John thought for a few moments. "What did 'we will' mean?"

Philo shook his head. "That is a very bad omen. I fear if Rome thinks he is a threat, they will send armies to come in and arrest him."

"Would that be so bad? Our own soldiers were ineffective. Maybe we should go to the garrison and ask the submagistri to help. Do you think your father would do that?"

"My father has spent a considerable amount of his time trying to mediate between that outpost and our townspeople. For the last several years, there have been numerous violations of our citizens by those foreigners. I doubt my father would trust them with the job."

John did not press him for details. He had heard rumors of atrocities conducted by the Roman soldiers, mostly attacks on women, but did not personally know anyone who was involved.

"He gave my father thirty days to deal with this, which really limited his options."

"Thirty days is a long time."

Philo laughed, and slapped John on the back. "That's what I love about you. Always joking."

John considered arguing, but backed down.

"Thirty days will pass in a flash. We don't even know where Yochanan will be tomorrow. What we need is a spy in his network, someone who can tell us where he is at a moment's notice."

John's mind immediately thought of Myriam. Her distrust of the priests would prevent her from helping them, especially if she found out what they were planning.

Philo knocked on the door of the first Council member's house. "My father has been given an ultimatum, which means he is now on Rome's time and not his own," he said as he waited for the door to open. "He does not have the luxury to wait for an opportune moment. He must act swiftly and decisively, or we might have Roman soldiers arresting not just Yochanan, but his followers too."

Roman soldiers with orders to arrest anyone they thought was associated with Yochanan. John knew that such a mass arrest would pit the inhabitants of his town against the brutal Roman army. The thought horrified him.

When the Council had convened, Kayafa spent several minutes telling them of the recent exchange between Nakdimon and Yochanan. Several were openly fearful of what it all meant.

"What can we do?" asked Nakdimon. "Our own people turned on us and our own soldiers failed us."

"We cannot arrest him ourselves," said one member.

"We certainly cannot let Rome do it," said another.

"Perhaps if we interview each soldier before we go, make sure they are on our side," said a third.

"No, that would take too long," added the first again.

The Council went around and around about various options, but none seemed acceptable. The men were at an impasse.

While the Council members argued and spoke amongst

themselves, Philo leaned in and placed a hand to his father's ear. "It is not my place, but perhaps other soldiers, ones who do not readily believe such blasphemy, are needed."

"What do you mean?" asked Kayafa softly.

"Herod is still king over this territory. Perhaps he would be interested to hear what has been going on? Doesn't he need Rome on his side to rule?"

Kayafa raised his hands. All of the other Council members became silent.

"Perhaps," he said, "it is time to bring in new soldiers, if ours do not follow our commands."

"Not Rome, they will kill him."

Kayafa shook his head. "I knew his father, Z'kharyah. Death is too extreme. Yochanan may be a lunatic, but he does not deserve to die.

"No, I propose we travel to the tetrarch of Galil and Perea, Herod-Antipas, and enlist his aid in arresting Yochanan the Immerser. You heard what he said about Herod and Herodias. Surely this is more than enough to gain his arrest?"

Everyone applauded Kayafa's solution.

"Yes, if Herod imprisons Yochanan, everything else will take care of itself," said Ya'ir.

Kayafa walked over to a young man seated by the door. It was the first time John had noticed him. He was not a member of the Council, or with any of the other officials John had seen.

The man was slim, with the beginning hints of a beard. He was dressed not in the purple priestly robes of the others, but wore a simple white robe, fastened with a belt made of rope. A blue and white prayer shawl hung about his neck.

"Sha'ul," Kayafa said "What is your opinion?"

"Who is that?" John whispered to Philo.

"That is Sha'ul of Tarsus. He is a talmid of Gamli'el."

John's eyes grew wide. While he had not heard the name Sha'ul before, everyone knew the name Gamli'el. He was a legend in their town. Gamli'el was a s'mikhah rabbi. There were only a handful of these rabbis throughout Y'hudah. They knew more about the Law and the things of Scripture than even Kayafa. They were so knowledgeable and well respected they could do what few rabbis dared: provide new insight and teachings on the Scriptures. All other rabbis, including Kayafa, limited themselves to only what their own teachers taught them. To be a talmid of such a great man was an honor John could not imagine.

Sha'ul remained gjpqy seated. "This situation is intolerable. By what authority does Yochanan offer these new interpretations?"

"Several times we asked him that same thing," said Nakdimon.

"Sha'ul," Kayafa said, "neither you nor your master serve on this Council, but, as he is the wisest of our order, and as the only s'mihkah rabbi in these parts, I humbly ask that he make the formal request. I fear that Herod may decline if he believes the request comes from the Council. Will he accept?"

Sha'ul pondered the request. "Of course, I cannot speak for my master, but I believe that he will share my concern over this situation. I will make the request, and I assure you, he will agree."

Kayafa smiled. "Wonderful. Take Ya'ir and travel to Tiberias. Have your master meet you there."

"Yochanan speaks the truth when he says Herod is a murderer and an adulterer. However, Herod is the devil we already know. My master knew Yochanan's father, Z'kharyah. He would not stand for his son's accusations."

Sha'ul sighed, and a look of sadness crept into his eyes. "My master often told me a story. Before Yochanan's birth, Z'kharyah suffered a breakdown. Perhaps some of that insanity transferred to his son."

"Are you ready to travel?" Philo whispered to John.

"What do you mean?"

"Now that you're an apprentice of Ya'ir, you'll be traveling with him to Tiberias."

John let statement sink in. Traveling? To another city? He had never done that before. What would it be like? What would his mother say?

Sha'ul continued questioning the Council. "Do you believe Herod is our only hope?"

"I do," said Kayafa.

The man sighed, and then, leaning on his staff, arose.

"Then I will do as you ask."

A broad smile broke over Kayafa's face. "I will dispatch a courier with a request for an audience. Be ready to travel at a moment's notice."

The Council members turned to leave, the meeting finished.

"My brothers," Kayafa said in a deep voice, stopping all in their places. "I cannot impress upon you how important this has become. We must not fail."

5

The Palace

"John, where have you been? Your father and I have been worried about you."

John entered their small room and immediately moved to embrace his mother. He held her longer than he had before.

"What is wrong, little one?" she asked. "Is everything all right?"

John broke his grip and smiled into her eyes. "Everything is wonderful. I have had the most amazing day. I don't even know how to begin to tell you."

His mother returned his smile, clearly delighted in her son's happiness. "Then you must tell me. Tell me everything that has happened."

John looked around at the empty room. "Where are Papa and David?" he asked.

Her smile left her. "Your brother had another episode. I was with him most of the afternoon. Only this evening, when his father returned, did he calm down. The two of them left to give me some time to recover."

John sighed at the news. Ever since his birth, David had been difficult to handle. Some days, he would say nothing and barely move, while others, he would have a tantrum and spin uncontrollably, lashing out at anyone who tried to stop or help him. Today must have been one of those days.

John took his mother's hand and led her to the only table in their room. They sat on the floor together as John began.

"Mama, I have some news. You know that I enjoy Beth Sefer, that I do well with my studies and my master appreciates the effort I put in."

His mother beamed. "Oh, John. Have they asked you to continue in Beth Midrash?"

John shook his head and her smile disappeared. "Even better. Ya'ir has asked me to become his apprentice!"

His mother's face did not change. "I don't understand.

Aren't you supposed to go to Beth Midrash for another seven years?"

John nodded, smiling, and she couldn't help but smile too. "That's just it. Ya'ir thinks I don't need to go to school. He wants me to start apprenticing with him now."

John's mother still did not understand. "As his talmid?"

John shook his head. "No, not officially. I cannot be a talmid until I am nineteen. But I am to begin learning how to be a rabbi starting tomorrow."

"I'm confused. You are not going to school to be a rabbi, but you are apprenticing to be a rabbi, but you are not a talmidim?"

John paused to consider what she said. "Yes... yes I think that is right."

His mother bent over and threw both arms around him. "A rabbi! I cannot believe this. I am so proud."

She released him and pushed him back, concerned. "Does this mean you will be living with Ya'ir?" she asked.

John nodded. "I will be spending some nights with him, but because I am not a talmid, I can spend nights here also."

She embraced him again. "That is wonderful news. Your father will be so proud when he hears."

Uncle! John suddenly worried what his uncle would say about this.

"Do you think he'll be mad?"

His mother shook her head. "No, no. He will be very proud. Just as I am."

John wasn't so sure. "It means I will be spending all day, from sun up until past sun down with Ya'ir. Not just for schooling, but other times as well."

"You needn't fear. I can take care of your father."

John wasn't so sure. "I have more news, Mama."

"I am not sure my heart can take more news like the last."

"Ya'ir has been chosen by the Council to visit our king, Herod, in Tiberias. He will be leaving as soon as the preparations are ready."

John's mother didn't seem to understand.

"That means that when he leaves for Tiberias, I will accompany him. As his apprentice, of course."

"You will have an audience with the king?"

John nodded. "I won't be speaking, of course. But I will accompany Ya'ir there and will be with him in the royal chambers."

Again she threw her arms around him and squeezed tightly. "That is wonderful. I am so proud of you."

"What's wonderful," said a dark voice as the door closed. John turned to see his uncle and stepbrother.

"John has been telling me about his day. Go ahead, tell your father."

The man walked over and stood by the table, glaring down at John.

Where to start?

"I met with our cohen hagadol today."

"Kayafa, that corrupt politician," his uncle spat.

"Please don't talk about our priests like that," John's mother implored. "You don't want Adonai to hear you."

Uncle addressed his wife. "Adonai knows his heart." Then he turned to John. "But why would he speak to you?" Uncle's mood seemed particularly unpleasant.

"My teacher recommended me to him. Kayafa made me an apprentice of Ya'ir today." John closed his eyes, afraid to see Uncle's reaction.

There was no response but silence. Then, "What did you say?"

John opened his eyes. Uncle was staring at him with a burning anger. "I accepted. What else could I do?"

Uncle made a move as if to strike John, causing John to flinch in fear. But instead of hitting him, he walked to the other side of the room. "You could have said no. You could have told him you have responsibilities at home."

"He had to say yes," John's mother said, speaking in his defense. "One does not tell the cohen hagadol he is wrong."

A bitter laugh escaped Uncle's lips. "Ha, I will gladly tell that viper he is wrong. He has no right to decide what is to be done in my house."

John felt his future slipping away. "What if this is Adonai's decision, not Kayafa's? Do you want to step between God and His will?"

His uncle turned his anger on John. "I decide what happens to my family. Not God!" he shouted.

John's mother bowed her head in respect. "Adonai, do

not say such things!"

Uncle's head jerked violently to view his wife's. "I am master of my house."

"No," John said timidly. "Adonai is master of your house."

Uncle walked back and stood beside John, who flinched, certain a beating was coming for being so direct. "Do you believe Adonai wants you to become a rabbi?" he asked.

John nodded vigorously.

Turning to his wife, he asked, "Do you want your son to be a rabbi?"

John's mother stood and gently took his hand. "I want my son to be happy. If serving Adonai as a rabbi is his calling, then, yes, I do."

Uncle pulled away from his wife. "What of his chores? Will he be able to still bring fish to market?"

"I will, Papa, whenever Ya'ir does not need me at sunrise."

Uncle considered what this meant. "When will you begin?"

John stood up, convinced that his uncle would accept this decision. "I am to accompany my master to Tiberias, as soon as he receives word. Until then, I will stay here with you and Mama, attending classes as before. Nothing will be different, I swear."

Uncle grunted. "It better not be."

"Then he has your blessing?" his mother asked.

Uncle headed out the door. He said nothing, but a wave of his hand seemed to indicate that he accepted the situation.

In the silence, John asked, "Does this mean I can be Ya'ir's apprentice?"

His mother looked at him with a big smile. "Of course you can. He was just trying to act like he was in charge. He will be fine with it, I promise you. Go, go to Ya'ir's. Become his greatest student."

John wasn't sure how to respond. "What of my chores?"

"Leave that to me. You need to concern yourself only to learning. I will take care of everything else."

John gave his mother a tremendous hug. "Thank you, Mama. I love you."

"I love you too, son. Now go, quickly, before I change my mind."

John sprinted out the back door so as not to see his uncle.

Exactly one week later, John arrived at the shore of Lake Kinneret. At the dock sat a great ship built of cypress wood, over one hundred feet in length, a row of thirty oars stacked neatly along its side. These would be their wind, as the slaves assigned to them would quickly take them across the sea.

His master's luggage had already arrived. John looked at the half dozen wagons on the dock, and began removing Ya'ir's.

He felt a slap on the back, and a hand from behind him pointed. "Those three over there," said a familiar voice.

"Philo," John exclaimed. "I didn't know you were coming on this adventure."

Philo brushed past him and grabbed several bags off the nearest cart. "My father assigned me to Sha'ul."

"As his talmid?"

"No, as labor. I have to carry his bags and do his bidding."

John sensed anger in his friend's voice.

"Like a talmid?"

Philo scowled. "More like a servant. I couldn't believe my father would treat me like this."

"Maybe he just wants Sha'ul to see what you were like. Maybe you can become Shau'l's talmid."

Philo lifted that last of the luggage from the wagon and began carrying it to the ship. John followed, struggling with just one of Ya'ir's bags.

"I cannot become a talmid of a talmid," Philo continued. "Sha'ul is still Gamli'el's talmid."

"But surely he is close to thirty. Won't he become a rabbi soon?"

John was falling behind his friend as he struggled with the heavy bag. Philo waited for him, then continued on at a slower pace. "I do not know. I do not know what the future holds. I only know"—he paused at the gangplank leading into the ship—"that I don't want to be here, doing this." Philo carried the bags onto the ship.

John heaved Ya'ir's bag upon his shoulders, and began to walk unsteadily across the gangplank.

Philo quickly reappeared. "Here, let me take this, before you fall and your master's things get all wet." He lifted the bag with ease from John's shoulders. "Go back and get the next bag. "I'll wait here until you get back."

John thanked his friend and ran back to where the other bags were waiting. Philo may not want to be here, but John was glad anyway.

K'far-Nachum grew steadily smaller in the brightening sky as the oarsman whisked them away from the docks and into the open seas. The weather was calm, and the ship sliced through the waters quickly.

The initial excitement John felt in the morning with the departure quickly faded as he found himself with little to do. Philo had followed Sha'ul below decks and neither had emerged since they left the docks.

Ya'ir had given him several small scrolls to memorize, so he decided to sit down and pursue his studies. But the rocking of the boat, the lapping of the waves and the steady drone of the oars made his mind quickly wander, no matter how hard he tried to concentrate. After several fruitless hours, he stood up and walked the deck.

John knew very little about Herod Antipas, the man they were going to meet. While he knew Herod was tetrarch, or king, of Palestine, and he was a cruel king at that, he knew very little else. He sought out his new master.

"What troubles you?" Ya'ir asked.

"I am having difficulty concentrating on my studies," he answered. "I thought a small walk would help clear my head."

Ya'ir looked about the cramped quarters of the upper deck. "This is indeed a small walk, but I sense there is more on your mind than your studies."

"It's this visit to the palace."

"You're not sure what is to be expected of you?"

John nodded in agreement.

"Little one," the older man said in a kind voice, "nothing is expected of you. You are merely here to accompany me."

"I know, but what will happen? I know so little about King Herod or his palace."

Ya'ir motioned for him to sit on the deck near the rail of the boat, and then took up a similar position across from the young boy.

"So you wish to know more about Herod-Antipas."

John nodded.

The older man sighed. "First, understand that we use the term 'king' only as a courtesy. He is not a king in the same vein as David or his son Shlomo. Herod's true title is tetrarch of Galil and Peraea. He is not even Jewish."

John gasped. "He's not?"

"No, he is the son of Herod the Great and Malthace, a Samaritan woman. He is half Idumean, half Samaritan, and has not a drop of Jewish blood in his veins."

"Then how did he become our king—I mean—our tetrarch?"

"When his father died, his older brother Archelaus inherited the throne and much of his father's lands. Herod Antipas traveled to Rome to contest the will of his father."

"So Rome assigned him to be our king?"

"Rome upheld the will of Herod the Great, and assigned to him the tetrarchy of Galil and Peraea, as his father had set apart for him.

"Herod is the ruler of Galil and Perea, but he is under the rule of Rome. Now, he may pretend otherwise, but the truth is he is under the authority of Valerius Gratus and, of course, Tiberius Caesar."

Ya'ir paused to allow John to absorb this information.

"I hear he can be very cruel."

Ya'ir's countenance fell. "Actually, Herod has not always been so cruel. When I was young like you, I visited his father. He was a cruel man. Just before he died, he ordered the slaughter of all males under the age of two in the town of Beit-Lechem, all because soothsayers from the east came looking for a small child they believed was the mashiach."

John's eyes widened at the thought. "The mashiach?" he asked.

Ya'ir shook his head. "No evidence was found to support these claims. Still, they murdered almost a dozen infants to satisfy the tetrarch's demands. The entire village wept over the loss."

John felt a great sadness.

"After Herod the Great joined his fathers," Ya'ir continued, "and Herod-Antipas took the throne, he began his reign by repairing much of the ill will his father had created. The Roman occupation and rule he despised actually influenced him until he became just as cruel and corrupt as the Romans.

"Herod the Great had a gift for flattering Rome, which Herod-Antipas inherited. This makes him very dangerous."

John remained silent, fascinated by the account.

"With his power, he decided to build a new city on the southern shore, and named it Tiberias. This is his capital, the city to which we are now sailing."

Ya'ir looked about to see if anyone else was watching, but no one took any interest in their conversation.

"While you are there, you may meet the queen, Herodias," Ya'ir continued. "When they met, Herod's entire life changed."

John spoke softly. "Is this what Yochanan meant when he said Herod had stolen his brother's wife?"

The older man shushed him. "Never say that in the palace. If Herod should hear, we cannot protect you."

John grew silent.

Ya'ir lowered his voice until it was barely a whisper. "When they first met, Herodias was married to Herod's half brother, Phillip. Herod himself was married. Caesar summoned Herod to Rome, while at the same time Herodias was in route to visit a friend. They met on the road to Rome. To Herod, she was the most beautiful woman he had ever seen.

"The two parties decided to travel together, and Herod and Herodias spent much time together. Herod soon became obsessed with her, and quickly decided she would become his wife. He proposed before they reached Rome, and she, being equally ambitious, left her husband to become Herod's wife, taking her daughter Salome with her."

When John heard this, he knew what an evil man Herod was. Their temple laws forbade a man from marrying his brother's wife while he was still alive. The fact that Phillip had a daughter was doubly sinful.

Ya'ir continued in his low tone. "This situation directly led to our great war with the Nabataeans. The father of Herod's first wife was Aretas, king of the Nabataeans. Herod had married her only to negotiate a peace with the Nabataeans. When he divorced her to marry Herodias, Aretas sent troops to war against Herod. Even today, Jews are dying for the sake of Herod's lust."

Ya'ir again cautioned John not to speak of any of this while in the palace. The council had condemned Herod for the act, but he was still tetrarch, and a powerful ally with Rome.

John promised he would say nothing.

John stood at the side of the boat as they swept into the bay and approached the city docks. The tall basalt cliffs he had been watching for hours came into sharp focus. What had been only black lines earlier in the day revealed themselves to be jagged cliffs rising some two hundred feet into the air, providing an impenetrable wall, safe from an attack by sea.

"Is that the palace, on top of that cliff?" asked John.

"That's it," said Philo.

Even from this distance, John could make out many richly carved arches and wooden terraces. Generously sprinkled amongst the arches were watchtowers, both for protection and aesthetic design.

Sea birds squawked above as the boat drifted up against the city docks. Several locals caught lines thrown from the boat by the sailors and began to secure the vessel. As John and Philo began the work of unloading their masters' luggage, John took his first notice of the city. He was surprised at how similar it was to his own home, only slightly larger. The docks seemed almost familiar.

Even though they were only expecting to be there a day or two, the priests had brought several different sets of clothes, prepared for whatever they might encounter.

"Not much different than when you worked for your uncle," noted Philo, as he tossed the last of the packs from the ship.

"At least these smell better," kidded John.

Both boys laughed at the joke.

Servants from the local synagogue met the party with pack animals and wagons. John and Philo loaded the packs on the wagon.

"I'm glad to see this," said Philo. "The route to Herod's palace is difficult."

"Have you been here before?" asked John.

Philo nodded. "Two years ago, my father was invited to one of the celebrations, and brought me. We had to move through and around people's homes to arrive at the palace walls."

"I thought this city was built by Herod recently."

"It was," said Philo. "How did you know that?"

"I talked to Ya'ir a little on the way over."

Philo shrugged. "Herod designed the city himself. This makes it impossible for an army invading from the west to protect itself. While they are trying to negotiate the narrow, winding streets, Herod's own forces rained arrows and projectiles down on them from the palace above."

"But wouldn't he be firing on his own citizens?"

"Yes. He was using the townspeople as a buffer. But remember, these people are Jews. Herod rules them, but has no blood ties to them."

John looked up and saw a wide, wooden balcony attached to the side of the palace that faced the city. Thick poles thrust high into the sky. Attached to the poles, a canopy of bright reds, yellows, and blues protected anyone beneath from the noonday sun.

It must be huge to be visible from this distance.

Hundreds of flat-roofed white homes lay scattered along the gently sloping hill. An occasional white dome appeared to provide some variance. Behind the homes were high green mountains, a few scattered white dwellings upon their slopes.

As they moved through the city, dozens of smaller lanes branched from the main road. Men and women, children and livestock, filled the streets, pressing against each other as they forced their way along.

"This is worse than the market at home," said John.

After some time, they reached the end of the homes. Ahead was a great crevice in the rock itself. John looked up the rock walls, fully conscious of how narrow it was.

They were at the mercy of whoever lived above. Herod's palace was already intimidating, and they had not even arrived.

At the palace, servants showed the parties to their rooms. They were given time to recover from their journey before Herod summoned the delegation to the Great Hall.

The room John was assigned was unlike anything he had ever imagined. Daylight streamed in through the grated window, illuminating rich purple silks that covered the walls. Their color was so dark they appeared to soak up the sunlight. Unlike his own bed, just thrown to the floor, this bed was suspended on a frame of dark wood with much ornamental carvings. Gold bands decorated the posts, and a fine lace hung overhead to keep him cool during the night. Thick cushions of down made up the mattress. John had never seen such opulent furnishings. He could only imagine Ya'ir's room, if this was how the servants were treated. He lay on the bed, sinking into its rich luxuriousness.

I could get use to this.

A knock on the door woke John from his light sleep. Herod's servant was there to escort John and Philo through the palace to the throne room. He dressed quickly and met Philo at the door.

"Where are Sha'ul and Ya'ir?"

Philo pointed ahead. "They are in a different wing of the palace. We will meet them in the throne room."

The servant began walking, and the two friends fell into line behind him.

Compared to the splendor of his room, the gray walls of the palace felt cold and uninviting. The steady glow of dozens of lanterns illuminated richly embroidered tapestries. Their footsteps echoed in the hallway as they walked to the hall.

"John, do you notice anything unusual?"

John looked around, but to him, everything was unusual. "What do you mean?"

Philo motioned at the halls as they passed. "There are no guards."

It was true. While there were servants around every corner, John had not seen a single soldier.

"Is that bad?"

Philo looked puzzled. "I don't know. I would expect Herod would have someone to keep him safe."

"From whom?" asked the man leading them. "No one here would dare attack the king."

Just then, they rounded a corner, and there stood Ya'ir and an older man John didn't recognize. He was shorter than Ya'ir, with a pronounced belly and a long, white beard. Behind the man stood Sha'ul.

"Who is that?" he whispered to Philo.

"That is Gamali'el."

With the entire party present, the doors, which looked as tall as their synagogue back home, opened and they walked into the Great Hall.

Herod-Antipas, Tetrarch of Galil and Perea, sat at the opposite end of the hall on one of two identical gold thrones. He wore a richly embroidered robe that appeared to change colors as he moved. Golden bracelets set with precious stones adorned his wrists, gold rings glittered on each finger, and a fine gold filigree crown sat on his head. Bands of fine gold held his long black hair and beard in place. Two slaves stood on either side, gently fanning him with palms.

Ya'ir, Sha'ul, and Gamali'el wore identical clothing, the dress of the P'rushim. Their outer robes were purple, draped from their foreheads, which held phylacteries of gold. Underneath, their white inner robes were punctuated by dark blue stripes. Gamli'el had the most stripes, befitting his station as the elder of the group, while Sha'ul had only a few. Each one stepped forward, bowed to Herod, and then knelt upon the cushion that sat in front of him. John and Philo stepped behind their masters and knelt on smaller cushions.

"What news do you bring me from the north?" asked Herod.

"Greetings, Herod the Great. All is well with your lands," began Ya'ir. "Your people bid you greetings."

Ya'ir cleared his throat. "May I first introduce my colleagues. On my right is one of our greatest rabbis, Gamli'el, and on my left one of his most promising students, Sha'ul. We have news for you of a small—no a tiny—difficulty we must report to you."

Herod leaned forward on his throne. "Gamli'el. You I have heard of."

Sha'ul had no reaction to the apparent slight.

Ya'ir began his mission and told Herod about Yochanan the Immerser, and the demands of Sergius Paulus.

Herod listened without interrupting, stroking his beard as he took stock of the report. "I do not like this, not at all. I need Rome as an ally, not an adversary. What have you done to fulfill Sergius' request?"

"Excellency, with all due respect, we immediately sought to bring this man into custody. However, crowds constantly surround him, and it is difficult to get near him. Roman troops would only enflame the situation."

"Perhaps," added Gamli'el, "if his Excellency were to decree it? Hmmm…?"

Even John could see through Gamli'el's transparent attempt to get Herod to issue the order to arrest Yochanan.

"You want me to commit my troops to capture a man you can't control? Perhaps I should replace you bumbling fools. Wouldn't that make more sense?"

Gamli'el and Ya'ir cast nervous glances at each other.

"It is not a question of leadership," began Ya'ir, "but a question of crowd control. We have neither the strength nor the authority to take on this man."

"Perhaps you should have dealt with him when he first arrived, rather than waiting for the situation to escalate. You have placed me in a difficult situation. Are you aware that I know of your position regarding my marriage, and have said so to your congregations?

"To have my own people condemn me for my legal decision weighs heavily on my rule."

"What would you like us to do, Tetrarch?" Ya'ir asked. "The laws of Moshe cannot be rewritten, even for a king."

"Nor should they," Herod replied. "Yet I cannot help but wonder how much easier such decisions could be made without having to worry about how my own people perceive me."

A great crash interrupted the tense situation as the doors to the Great Hall flew open.

A woman strode into the chamber. She had to be the most beautiful woman John had ever seen. Tall and thin, her ink black hair was a stark contrast to her alabaster skin. A bright gold necklace drew attention to her graceful neck, offsetting her eyes which shone like emeralds.

She walked past the priests and took a seat on the throne next to Herod.

"Forgive the interruption. My queen, Herodias," Herod said.

Herodias did not give the priests an opportunity to greet her. "Who are these men, dear, and what is their business with the great king of the Galil?"

The king cleared his throat. "Tell her, Ya'ir. Tell her the news from the north."

Ya'ir stood and bowed to Herodias, introduced their party, then, again kneeling on the cushion, repeated the news of the north.

"Yochanan!" she exclaimed. "I know this man of whom you speak. We have met."

Everyone seemed surprised.

"Have you, dear?" Herod replied. "Where have you met this man? Tell me all the details."

"It was on the road to Gilead. I was traveling to purchase the perfumes you find so intoxicating when he walked with a dozen of his followers in the opposite direction."

A slave brought her a golden chalice filled with wine. "He was a strange man, dressed in animal hides," she continued, as she gestured with the cup. "His hair was unclean and his beard untrimmed. I thought he was a bandit.

"When he saw me, he stopped and pointed at me. I could not look away. 'Jezebel, harlot,' he cried out in a loud voice. 'Go back to your husband. Your daughter cries for her father. Leave the fox and be right again with Adonai.'"

The crowd gasped at the insolence that was shown their queen.

"He just kept repeating this. I was horrified and embarrassed, and could hardly leave the road quickly enough."

Herod seemed quite thrown by the story. It appeared he was hearing it for the first time. "Is this true? Does he make comments against me and my marriage?" he asked.

Ya'ir lowered his head in humility. "Yes, my lord, I fear it is true. He tells the crowds, 'Turn from your sins to God, for the Kingdom of Heaven is near!' And I am afraid you and your queen are one of the examples he uses."

"My lord," Herodias said, "if this man is raising followers, you must put a stop to it. His words could lead to war amongst our people."

Herod sat silent for many moments. After some time, he stood and announced, "I do not believe it is in the best interests of my kingdom for Jew to fight Jew. However, what you have said greatly concerns me. I will have the captain of the guard and a platoon of my best troops accompany you to see this man. If he finds you have spoken well, he will escort the man back to Tiberias, so that I may meet with him and learn from him."

Ya'ir and Gamli'el smiled at each other.

"They will depart in the morning. You may accompany them. In the meantime, you may return to your chambers and rest for the night."

He clapped once, and servants appeared and escorted them back to their rooms.

The three priests left with the captain of the guard to discuss what to expect when they met Yochanan and his followers.

Left alone, Philo and John decided to explore the palace. While many areas were off limits, many others were not. John was most amazed at the size; it seemed to go on forever.

They came around one corner and saw half a dozen children their own age. Most were dressed in plain robes, and appeared to be the children of servants. One stood out among them. She was taller and wore a bright blue robe fringed with gold. A golden necklace and golden bracelets adorned her wrists. An emerald stud graced her nose, highlighting her green eyes. Her dark, curly hair fell to the small of her back. She ordered the other children to do what she wanted.

"Who are you?" she demanded when she saw them. "And what business have you in the palace?"

Philo stopped, but no words came from his mouth. He had a look of utter astonishment. Whether it was her beauty or her attitude, John could not tell.

John spoke up. "I am John, and this is my friend Philo. We are apprentices of the P'rushim from K'far-Nachum. We have accompanied our masters to meet with the Great King Herod."

The girl's eyes danced when she heard the answer. "K'far-Nachum! That is a city I have always wanted to visit." She dismissed the other children with a wave of her hand.

John could not imagine someone who lived in such a grand place wanting to visit his dirty old city. It was almost amusing to hear her speak as though it rivaled this great palace. "I can tell you about it if you want—" John stopped, unsure of her name.

"I am Salome, daughter of Herodias, the Queen of the Galil."

During Ya'ir's story on the ship, John had pictured her as an infant.

"Tell me of your city."

He spoke to her of many things. The things he thought most boring she seemed most interested in: the market, the garrison, and the desert to the west. As they talked, he became very conscious of her presence near him. She wore perfume, unlike the girls from his town. Her dress flowed and billowed as she walked, unlike every other girl he knew, who seemed to have dust caking and stiffening their robes. How different she was from Myriam, although they seemed to be the same age.

Abruptly, she changed the subject. "Your friend is very cute," she said. "Is he deaf or mute?"

John laughed then quickly clasped his hand over his mouth to stifle it, so as not to embarrass her.

"I speak," said Philo.

"Then why do you let this little one do all the talking. Are you uneducated?" John did not believe she was trying to insult Philo, just genuinely confused.

Philo stood proud and tall, "My name is Philologus. I have been sent by the High Priest Kayafa to speak with King Herod on a matter of great importance."

Salome looked at John, almost as if to ask if he was kidding. "Yes, yes, I believe you."

John went into detail about why they were here, and

Philo added to it. Back and forth they went, almost as if in competition for her attention. Salome seemed to enjoy it.

Again, she abruptly changed the subject, as if to prove she was in charge. "Well, Philologus, sent by the High Priest of the province of Galil, and little John, son of the great city of K'far-Nachum, I have enjoyed meeting with both of you. Now, I must leave. I hope we can meet again and talk some more."

She turned and walked down the hallway without glancing back. John and Philo watched, unblinking, until she had disappeared from sight.

Morning came too quickly. It had taken John a long time to fall asleep, his mind filled with images of the sea, Herod, and Salome.

The return trip to the docks seemed much easier. Before long, they were boarded and underway. John noticed a second ship keeping station in the harbor, ready to accompany their own for the return trip.

"That is Herod's ship. It is filled with soldiers," said Ya'ir, who had joined him on deck.

Once out to sea, John looked back at the palace as it slowly shrank from sight, overwhelmed by everything that had happened.

Philo stood near. "Isn't Adonai amazing? Last week you carried dead fish to market. Now look at you."

John only smiled. He glanced about and saw Sha'ul and Gamli'el were also on the deck. As he stood next to Ya'ir, he finally felt that he was where God wanted him to be.

6

A Stranger Arrives

"I can't do this." John slammed his writing reed onto the worn surface of the writing desk. It rolled several inches, leaving a small trail of black ink dots.

Ya'ir looked up briefly from the scroll he was studying, arose and walked over to John's desk. He picked up the pen and placed it in its inkwell. "What is it this time?"

John took a deep breath, trying to calm his frustration. "It's this writing. I can't understand how you make these letter strokes come out the same. Every time I try to copy yours, they come out all fuzzy."

Ya'ir looked down at the practice parchment. Rows of large letters dominated the top half of the page, each getting progressively larger and more difficult to read. "Have you sharpened the reed at all?"

John looked down sheepishly at the paper. "Of course I did," he muttered under his breath.

Ya'ir picked up the pen and inspected the nib. "When, the first time you used it? We've been at this for weeks. You know that you have to sharpen your nib at least after each row, to keep it fresh. Look here ..." He motioned towards the page, "You have three rows of letters and I'll bet you haven't touched the nib since you started."

The older man took the knife and carefully cut the end of the reed pen, making certain it was sharp and at the right angle. "Now let's look at those letters, shall we?"

John offered Ya'ir the sheet. After studying it for a few moments, he put it down and handed John the original parchment. With a practiced eye, Ya'ir pointed out first the good letters before harping on the poor ones. "You are too hard on yourself. Even the original has good and bad examples."

"I can't tell the difference," John said with disgust. "I don't even know why I have to learn to write. I thought a rabbi recited the Tanakh, not copied it. That's a job for Scribes."

"Ah, but how can you speak the Word if you cannot

write the Word? How can you be certain of the truth if you have not written it on your heart?"

"Of course, Master," John replied in response to the man's instruction.

The first weeks of his apprenticeship had been difficult. He had tried to be at the docks at sunrise to help his uncle as he promised, but that often made him late to his lessons. Ya'ir finally interceded with his uncle and John was allowed to live at Ya'ir's fulltime.

In the afternoons, Ya'ir and he scoured the reeds on the edge of the Yarden River looking for the right kind to make into the pens they would use. To John, each looked exactly like the last, but Ya'ir kept pointing out subtle differences in color and texture that made one reed a better candidate then another.

Then he had to learn to cut them to the right length, carve the edges to the right thickness, and then load them with the correct ink. Twice he had cut himself trying to carve too much off the reed at one time.

That was the easy part compared to the writing. In Beth Sefer, they had never had to write, learning only how the letters made words. With a pen in his hand, he was discovering how difficult it was to control the instrument while making the shapes that now seemed so foreign to him. It was not just the shapes of the letters. Before he could copy Scripture, he must learn to write in a certain way, in a certain number of columns, with everything aligned. The more he practiced, the worse he seemed to get.

"John," said Ya'ir, putting down the scroll.

"Yes, Master."

"This reed is too worn to continue. You will need to start with a fresh one."

John looked at the pen. It seemed fine to him.

"I want you to return to the Yarden and choose some fresh reeds. This writing can wait until tomorrow."

"But Master, I have several other reeds in my room. Would you like me to use one of them?"

"No, I think you need fresh reeds. I have some errands to run in town. Use the next several hours and come back with some quality reeds. Then, we will begin anew."

"What if Yochanan returns?" Secretly, John hoped he

would. He was fascinated by how Yochanan stood up to authority. It would be interesting to see how he responded to Herod's men.

It had been a month since they had been to the palace. When they returned, they discovered Yochanan missing, possibly going into the desert. For the past several weeks, Herod's soldiers remained on their ship anchored off shore, awaiting his return.

"If you should see him, come and let us know. Otherwise, we will continue with our lessons."

"Father?" asked a small voice from the doorway.

John turned and saw a young girl, maybe a little younger than Myriam. She was dreesed in a clean blue robe, and her long black hair was held back with a blue ribbon.

Ya'ir motioned for her to come in. "John, this is my daughter, Rivkah."

Rivkah bowed to John, which he thought was a strange thing to do.

"It's nice to meet one of my father's students," she said.

"And I to meet someone from his family," John said. Although he had been an apprentice for several months, this was the first time John had met anyone from Ya'ir's family.

"John is one of my new students," Ya'ir said. "He joined before I went to visit King Herod."

"Oh," said Rivkah. "That was a long time ago."

Ya'ir smiled. "Not that long ago. John was just leaving to run an errand."

"It was nice to meet you, sir," Rivkah said.

"And you."

"Now, off on your errand," Ya'ir said.

John folded out a crease in his new, white linen robe. Since he had received it his first day, he was amazed at how people treat him differently. As he walked along the streets, people stepped aside and seated people rose out of respect for his position. Two months ago, he carried dead fish to market; now the burden seemed almost overwhelming.

As John walked up the last hill, he heard voices in the distance. At the top several hundred villagers stood by the edge of the lake, watching Yochanan, who again immersed people in the Yarden.

He stopped, unsure what to do. He knew that he should inform his master that Yochanan had returned, but he also felt drawn to the river. He just stood there under the cloudy skies.

"Don't you look special in your white robes. Are you here because you want to be baptized, or are you here to spy for your new friends?"

Myriam, arms crossed, stood next to him. She refused to glance in his direction, instead maintaining an icy stare at the people in the river.

"Neither. Actually, I'm just here to get some new reeds."

Myriam gave him a look of disbelief.

"It's true. I had no idea Yochanan was here. I only came because Ya'ir told me to."

Myriam snorted and walked slowly towards the river. John had no choice but to follow. "Yochanan hasn't been here but a few minutes, and you want me to believe it's purely a coincidence that Ya'ir's lapdog is here? You are either Ya'ir's fool or his liar."

John breathed rhythmically to try to calm the anger welling inside him. He reminded himself that all of K'far-Nachum had seen the ship arrive. Word spread through the small town very quickly. John was more amazed that Yochanan would reappear before the soldiers gave up and returned to Herod.

"I'm sorry," she said, "that was uncalled for. Philo told me what the Council plans to do with him. It makes me so angry."

"Do you still believe he is a prophet sent by Adonai?"

"Yes."

"Then Adonai will protect him, right? I mean, if he really is a prophet, there is no way Adonai would allow us to arrest him."

Myriam's eyes lit up at the idea. "I never thought of it that way. You could be right."

"Of course I'm right. If Yochanan is here to do Adonai's bidding, then he will be just fine, and you have nothing to worry about." Even as he spoke the words, John was unsure if it was a lie or the truth.

"How about you, have you decided?"

"What?"

"About immersion? About following Yochanan and what he teaches?"

It was John's turn to form an icy stare at the river.

"I am apprenticed to Ya'ir. My duty is to follow the teachings of Ya'ir, and what Ya'ir teaches is the Scriptures, not this." He paused and waved his arms at Yochanan in the river. "Not this messy, water-based feelings that he professes. I cannot begin to consider anything Yochanan says until he proves himself to be a true prophet."

"But how can you see if you refuse to listen?"

John remained silent.

Myriam turned to him, her eyes pleading. "John, your eternal security is at issue. Just listen to what he says. Now, not when he is arguing with the Council." She pronounced the last word such that there was no secret of her opinion of the P'rushim.

John opened his mouth to argue, but without warning, a murmur went through the crowd. John looked back up the path to see a man walking towards them. John did not recognize him as one of the townspeople. Perhaps he was a visitor from a neighboring town. His robe was a dark brown that matched his hair. He held in one hand a long staff of cypress, and wore old, beaten sandals on his feet. On his chin was stubble, with the beginnings of a beard.

John noticed his eyes most. They were dark brown, like the robe, but appeared to be almost bottomless, as if John could see deep into his soul. His nose was just slightly crooked. John wondered if it might have been broken sometime in the past.

The crowd murmured quietly, aware of the stranger's approach. "I think he is from Natzeret," said someone in the crowd.

"Natzeret," snorted another. "Can anything good come from Natzeret?"

The man passed John and Myriam and walked to the shore of the river. He removed his outer, brown garment and carefully folded it before placing it on a rock upon the shoreline. Underneath, he was dressed in a plain white robe, not unlike the one John wore. He appeared to be in his late twenties or early thirties.

"Who is that?" he asked Myriam.

"I do not know. I have never seen him."

"Yochanan Ben-Z'kharyah," said the stranger.

So busy was Yochanan with immersions, he did not see the man approach. As soon as he recognized him, his eyes grew wide in horror. "You are coming to me? I ought to be immersed by you!"

The stranger answered him, "Let it be this way now, because we should do everything righteousness requires."

Before Yochanan could respond, the stranger walked into the Yarden. Everyone awaiting their time with Yochanan stepped aside, allowing him to walk to the front of the line.

Yochanan and the stranger exchanged a few words, which John could not hear. The stranger bowed his head. Yochanan closed his eyes and looked to the sky. "*Yoreh Yoreh. Yaddin Yaddin*," he said. Then Yochanan cupped his hands in the waters of the river. The stranger raised his left hand and Yochanan allowed the water to dribble over it as he again spoke the phrase. He then purified the right hand. This was repeated two more times.

A ray of sunlight broke through the thick clouds, touching Yochanan and the man on the head.

Yochanan turned to the crowd and shouted, "Look!" So forceful was his cry that the last people in the crowd who were not paying attention stopped what they were doing and turned to him.

John noticed dozens of people suddenly falling to their knees, then prostrate, on the ground, including Myriam.

Yochanan pointed at the stranger, the man from Natzeret. "God's lamb! The one who is taking away the sin of the world!"

At that announcement, the rest of the crowd knelt in worship.

John's eyes slowly moved from Yochanan to the man, who stood there, unashamed of the praise Yochanan placed upon him. He said nothing, making no effort to dispel or contradict Yochanan's claims. But he also did not seem joyous about Yochanan's comments. He stood there, dripping, as if he was just waiting for the next line or phrase in a play.

As more people began to kneel, John tried to understand why. This man seemed no different than the others. Why would they submit themselves so willingly before a total stranger? John refused to bow in reverence to this man.

The stranger slowly walked out of the Yarden.

John was one of only a half-dozen individuals still standing when the man from Natzeret stepped upon the shore.

John watched as the man, without a sound, picked up his dirty brown robe and old sandals and walked up the hill. Many of those lying on the ground glanced up, confused to why the man was leaving.

"Immerser," cried one voice, "is he the mashiach? Why does he leave?"

But Yochanan also began walking from the water, and said not a word.

"Could he be the real thing?" asked Myriam, after getting to her feet. Together they watched the stranger disappear over the ridge of the hill.

"When the redeemer king comes, he will be a noble descendant of David, not some commoner bathing in a river. This man is no king," John declared.

Before Myriam could answer, Yochanan called from the shore. "This is the man I was talking about when I said, 'After me is coming someone who has come to rank above me, because He existed before me.' I myself did not know who He was, but the reason I came immersing with water was so that He might be made known to Isra'el."

Almost everyone rose. Several began to head up the hill after the man from Natzeret, but most turned to Yochanan and demanded an explanation.

Yochanan motioned to all of them, and after everyone was seated, he said, "As He walked down the hill towards us, I saw the Spirit coming down from heaven like a dove, and remaining on Him. I myself did not know who He was, but the one who sent me to immerse in water said to me, 'The one on whom you see the Spirit descending and remaining, this is the one who immerses in the Ruach HaKodesh.'"

The crowd's voices rose at the statement. Cries of, "I didn't see that," or "I didn't hear that," rose from the ranks. Yochanan quieted them down.

"I have seen and borne witness that this is the Son of God."

Everyone leapt to his or her feet. Some came close to Yochanan, angry at his assertions. Others sought to protect him. Many ran off, perhaps to find the stranger.

"Now do you believe?" asked Myriam, shouting above the noise of the crowd.

John took her to the water's edge, away from the people.

"Did you see the same things I saw?" asked John.

Myriam nodded, but did not speak.

John rubbed his eyes, trying to get the words right. "I saw a man walk down the hill, get immersed in the water, and walk back up the hill. That is all I saw. Is that what you saw?"

Again, Myriam only nodded.

"Did you see this dove Yochanan spoke of?"

"No."

"Did you hear the words Yochanan heard?"

"No."

"All I heard the stranger say was, 'Let it be this way now, because we should do everything righteousness requires.' He spoke no other words."

Myriam nodded in agreement.

"Then how," John said, his voice filled with disbelief, "can you say that he was anything other than another man being immersed in the river?"

"Because Yochanan declared it."

John shook his head. "No, no, you cannot have faith on his words alone. You must think for yourself. Other than his statement, which could be a lie, do you have any other evidence that what Yochanan said is true?"

Myriam considered his statement. "No," she finally admitted.

"Then why believe Yochanan?"

"Why do you not?" she asked. "Are you so blind by your studies that you are willing to dismiss what is plain in front of you?"

"My studies are with good men who have been given the authority to teach from Scripture. Who gave Yochanan his authority?"

Myriam remained silent.

"You are listening to the cries of one man in the wilderness," he said, deliberately echoing what Yochanan had stated last month. "Who is to say if those cries are from a prophet or a lunatic?"

Myriam considered a moment. "Faith alone is what is needed. Faith alone can differentiate between the truth and lies."

John scoffed. "Faith? In what? Two men who, for all you know, could have been planning this for months? Where are you going to go now, to follow that stranger? You have no reason to accept anything you have seen as truth."

Myriam sighed, and placed one hand on John's shoulder. "I know how difficult this must be for you. It is difficult to accept faith, especially when it contradicts your own beliefs. But I have listened to Yochanan, and I have faith that what he said was truth. So yes, I will follow the man my prophet anointed as the Son of God." She began to walk up the hill.

John stood there alone. "This is all a lie," he shouted. He looked around and saw that, while many people were walking up the hill, two dozen remained with Yochanan. All eyes turned to John, and he quickly felt very vulnerable.

He sighed, and followed her up the hill.

Upon his return, Ya'ir immediately took him to Kayafa's house, where the entire Council was called to be told about the latest event.

"So, you saw this man, this Yochanan, of whom we have been searching for months, and you did not choose to return to the Council with this news?" demanded Kayafa.

"I meant to, Master," John said, his head bowed in deference, "but it all happened so quickly."

"But look at the good that has happened," interrupted Ya'ir. "Had John not been there, we would have no news of this new threat from Natzaret. It is one thing to have a man say he is a prophet talking about a mashiach, it is quite another to have one declared to be the mashiach."

"I don't understand," Nakdimon said. "We've had dozens of these false mashiachs come through over the years. Are we really so worried about this one?"

"Yes, we have seen others," Ya'ir said, "but they have all been self-claimed. No one has ever stood up and proclaimed another as the one, true mashiach. Well, except for their deluded followers."

"This is most unusual. I have never heard of a situation where one of these rebels confers his flock onto another. What would he gain?" Kayafa asked, to no one in particular. He turned to John. "You said he called him God's lamb for everyone's sin?"

"And Son of God."

"Anyone trying to get money from the people would never give up that kind of power. It doesn't make sense."

"Our teachings have given us the signs to look for in the coming mashiach," Sha'ul said. "For thousands of years, our ancestors prophesied that a mighty ruler would rise up and free our peoples from the slavery we have endured. We look for and welcome our king.

"We are in the fourth millennium since the creation of Adam. We look forward to this as our time, as we seek out and await our king."

All of the members of the Council nodded in agreement.

"My brothers," he continued, his tone growing darker and more sinister, "do either of these men fit your understanding of who our king will be?"

They all shook their heads.

"We know our God," Ya'ir declared. "It is spoken of in our most important commandment.

> *You are not to use lightly the name of Adonai your God, because Adonai will not leave unpunished someone who uses his name lightly.*

"No man could come forward as a god; to do so would be blasphemy against Adonai himself.

"For Yochanan to say, 'This is the Son of God,' that should be enough for this Council to send them both to prison.

"Our own prophet Yesha'yahu tells us who this mighty mashiach will be," said Ya'ir.

See how my servant will succeed! He will be raised up, exalted, highly honored!

"Does a man who mocks our laws by wearing the skins of dead animals, or someone from Natzeret wandering through the wilderness, fit this prophecy?"

Again there was silence from the assembled men who could only shake their heads in agreement.

"Our ancestors tell us our mashiach will be a great deliverer and king; he will drive out our oppressors. Does Rome still rule? He will sit as king over all Y'hudah. Did we not recently speak to Herod?" shouted Kayafa.

Now the Council shouted their agreement in unison.

"My friends, if I thought either of these men fulfilled Scripture, I would be amongst the first to support them," said Kayafa. "You know how much I hate Rome and its oppression. Yochanan mocks our laws and our teachings. How can either of these men be our mashiach?"

John found himself joining the masses as they yelled their support.

"What shall we do, Master?" Ya'ir asked him.

Kayafa spoke in low, measured tones. "I say to you, this is the most dangerous threat to our way of life I have ever witnessed. This Yochanan has our citizens in a frenzied state. He must be stopped at all costs. We must move swiftly to use the support Herod has given us. Nakdimon, move in at sundown tonight. Find Yochanan and arrest him. There must be no mistakes this time."

"And what are we to do with the stranger from Natzeret?"

"I know nothing of this man. If he is there, take him into custody and bring him here to me so I may question him. Take a few of our own guards too, in case Herod's men refuse to do this. Ya'ir, you will accompany Nakdimon and be in charge of our troops, so there is no question we acted on this."

The men nodded that they understood their tasks. "And I, Master?" asked Sha'ul.

"You, my friend, will depart immediately for Yerushalayim. You will seek out Anan and let the high priests know of this situation. If Sergius is a man of his word, I will meet you there soon.

"I need not remind you of how precarious our situation is. We must handle this swiftly and finally. If this is allowed to go beyond our borders, I fear we will suffer grave consequences."

7

A Task Completed

John led Nakdimon to the edge of the river where he had seen Yochanan and the man from Natzaret earlier that day. But the area was empty; only depressed grass and footprints in the sand showed that anyone had been there.

"Where have they gone?" asked Ya'ir.

John shrugged.

The captain of the guards spoke up. "Fan out in an orderly manner. Search every blade of grass and every footprint. Find out where they have gone." Herod's soldiers began to spread out from the water's edge.

"Did you see them leave?" Nakdimon asked.

John nodded. "They went up this way, over the hill."

One of the soldiers cried out an alarm, and several came running to assist him. "He has found the tracks of one of them. Yochanan, he believes," said the captain to Nakdimon. "This way."

The captain and his soldiers began a fast march up the hill. Nakdimon and Ya'ir followed at a quickened, though statelier, pace.

They followed the tracks to the edge of the town. They did not enter the town, but instead followed along its eastern edge heading north. A few times, the soldiers lost the trail only to pick it up again. They continued following the tracks until they came to the northern edge of the city.

John recognized where the tracks were heading. "He is returning to the desert," John told Ya'ir. "We are about to pass the rock that I hid behind months ago when I first saw Yochanan emerging from the wilderness."

Up ahead was the very rock. A man stood next to it. With his back to them, he was unrecognizable.

"You there," called out the captain, "have you seen a man run through here?"

The stranger turned. There, resting against the rock, was Yochanan himself.

"It's him," cried Ya'ir, "and he's all alone. Arrest him!"

Herod's soldiers rushed up, swords drawn, spears at the ready, but Yochanan made no movement to defend himself or flee. He just stood there, resting.

Two soldiers grabbed his arms so he could not get away, but Yochanan did not struggle. Another brought some chains and clasped them around his wrists. Yochanan said nothing.

"Yochanan Ben-Z'kharyah, I have been sent by the Council to arrest you for blasphemy against God and for inciting riots," said Nakdimon. "These soldiers are sent by King Herod himself for the purpose of returning you to Tiberias for formal questioning and trial. Do you have anything to say?"

Yochanan stood tall and proud, actually taller than most of the soldiers there. "I only wish to thank Adonai that I was able to be a part of His plan for redemption. My time is through. I look forward to the rest and reward He has prepared for me."

"Herod's palace will give you no reward, and Herod's dungeons no rest. Take him away!" said Nakdimon.

The soldiers surrounded Yochanan and led him into the city. As they disappeared from view, Ya'ir said, "That was too easy. I would have expected him to try and run or hide or fight."

Nakdimon stroked his beard. "Yes, I don't understand why he gave himself up so easily. Perhaps he knew he had no hope."

"We may never know."

Both men began to follow the soldiers into town, with John on their heels.

Several weeks past Yochanan's arrest things settled down for John. There was no sign of the man from Natzaret, and the followers of Yochanan, as the Council had predicted, had dispersed. Things were returning to normal.

Ya'ir raised the parchment to the lamp stand to illuminate the writing. He squinted at the text, scrutinizing the writing from top to bottom. He remained silent, only punctuating his review with a few "hmms."

John stood by as his master made his inspection,

bouncing lightly on the balls of his feet. He glanced around the Temple, but the few men there were deep in prayers and paid no attention the two of them.

After a few moments, Ya'ir brought up a second parchment, and glanced between the two. It took several moments, but he finally placed both on the desk.

"I must say I am impressed. Your writing has improved dramatically over the last month."

John beamed at the older man's compliments.

"If it were not for the quality of the parchments, I would truly be unable to distinguish between your hand and the original."

"Thank you, sir," said John. Even if he personally found it loathsome, John had become determined to succeed at this assignment. Now that it was finished, he found it hard to believe that it had been so difficult.

"I believe you are ready for your next test."

"What is that, Master?"

Ya'ir removed a scroll from and brought it to John. "This is a copy of the scroll of Mal'akhi. One of my students created it at the beginning of his apprenticeship. I would like you to begin work on duplicating his effort."

The master's offer surprised John. He knew that someday he would be required to copy a scroll of the Tanakh, but he had no idea it would come so soon.

"I am flattered. When should I begin?"

Ya'ir chuckled. "You have plenty of time. Before you can undertake such a task, you need to learn the proper way. This is not just looking at one scroll and writing on another. No, in good time, you will be taught all of the techniques and ceremonies that go into creating a scroll."

John felt relieved. While the master's task of completing a copy of the scroll was flattering, he dreaded the upcoming hours of meticulous detail such a task would require.

A servant came to the door. "My apologies, Master, but there is a young man here to see you. He says it is urgent."

Ya'ir looked upset by the interruption. "Who is it and what does he want?"

From behind the servant, Philo leaned out. "Forgive me, rabbi, but my father has need of your presence immediately."

Ya'ir waved off the offense. "Your apology is unnecessary. Of course I will come at once."

Philo bowed and dismissed himself.

"Sha'ul must have returned from his meeting with Anan in Yerushalayim. Come, we will go there together."

"Me? I am to accompany you to the Council meeting?"

"You are my apprentice, are you not? Then you must accompany me, if for no other reason than to observe and learn. Besides, you want to know what he has to say, don't you?" Ya'ir gave him a sly grin.

The two of them quickly exited the Temple.

By the time they arrived, most of the members of the Council were crowded into Kayafa's home. While John was pleased to see he was not the only boy here as, several of the other members had brought their apprentices and talmid with them, he didn't see Philo anywhere. Would Kayafa exclude his own son?

It took almost another hour to get everyone into the house and quieted down. Finally, when everything was in place, Sha'ul began the meeting.

"My brothers, I have returned from Yerushalayim, and we have much to discuss."

There were many shouts welcoming him back, and Kayafa raised a hand to quiet the group.

"With Yochanan safely imprisoned in Herod's dungeon, Rome no longer looks upon our region with concern."

Men shouted, "Praise Adonai," at the news. Again, Kayafa had to quiet them.

"While I was in Yerushalayim, I met with the new Roman governor, a Pontius Pilate."

Many began to murmur at the man's name. Most Jews knew of Pilate's great hatred of them.

"Pilate complimented the Council for the quick work in apprehending the Immerser. He praised our handling of Herod, and being able to convince our tetrarch to imprison Yochanan in Tiberias, away from most Jews, and not involving Roman troops."

Several members of the Council were about to exclaim their joy at the news, but a glare from Kayafa silenced them.

"Pilate has named Yosef Kayafa, cohen hagadol here in K'far-Nachum, as the new president of the Sanhedrin in Yerushalayim. He is to tie up all of his affairs here, and then leave immediately."

A great cheer went up from the Council members. Pride showed through at the thought that one of their own would assume the mantle of leadership of all Y'hudah. Kayafa made no attempt to quite them.

Finally, Kayafa walked next to Sha'ul and the room quieted down. "Thank you, my brothers. I am overwhelmed and humbled by this news. I had not expected anything like this. Before I name my successor here, I have one final duty to perform. Gamli'el."

The old s'mikhah rabbi came forward.

"Gamli'el has served as master over his talmid, Sha'ul, for now eleven years. As Sha'ul turns thirty today, Gamli'el has an announcement."

The crowd became absolutely still as the revered rabbi spoke. "It is with great pride that I announce before you today that Sha'ul born in Tarsus of Cilicia, trained at my feet in Yerushalayim, has shown himself worthy to become a rabbi. Sha'ul?"

Sha'ul moved and knelt before his master.

"I have trained you since the age of nineteen. You have shown yourself worthy and diligent in your studies. You have learned our Tanakh and can read it from memory. You have been a good student, with sound advice and a willingness to follow and lead."

A man stepped forward and handed Gamli'el a silver chalice. "I hereby pass to you my s'mikhah." Gamli'el closed his eyes and looked heavenward.

Yoreh Yoreh. Yaddin Yaddin.

"What is that?" whispered John to Philo.

"Ancient Aramaic. It means, 'May he decide? He may decide! May he judge? He may judge!'"

Kayafa's stern glance silenced Philo and John's questions.

Sha'ul held out his left hand, and Gamli'el poured water onto it while repeating the chant. Then the right hand, then each hand two more times.

John thought back to Yochanan and the stranger in the Yarden.

Sha'ul stood and Gamli'el threw his arms around him. The Council broke into cheers. Kayafa also hugged Sha'ul, as did several others visiting from Yerushalayim.

Kayafa raised his hand to quiet the room. "Now that he is a rabbi, Sha'ul must begin to train another and is in need of a talmid. I have discussed with him several of the boys here at K'far-Nachum as we tried to choose one worthy of this great honor."

John could not believe what he heard. A talmid for a rabbi!

"There is one boy here who stands out among all of the others. His study of the Tanakh is impeccable. He has repeatedly demonstrated knowledge well beyond his young years, and his assistance in the apprehension of Yochanan was extraordinary."

John held his breath at the thought that he could soon find himself studying with Sha'ul.

"Philologus," called Kayafa.

John's heart sank as he saw Philo step forward from the back of the room. He had changed out of the dirty clothing he wore while inviting the Council members. He now wore a white robe, similar to John's, with a red rope tied about the waist as a belt.

Sha'ul walked forward. "Now that you are turning nineteen, with the High Priest's permission, I would like you to consider becoming my talmid."

"Yes sir," said Philo, "I would be honored."

Kayafa addressed the room. "I so ordain, that from this moment forward, Philologus Ben-Yosef Kayafa will be assigned to the house of Sha'ul of Tarsus as talmid. He will enter into this position effective today."

John heard the men around him praising Philo's selection. Philo himself had a wide grin on his face. John felt numb from the announcement. He had been so sure that Kayafa was going to name him.

"As President of the Sanhedrin, as my first act of authority, I name Nakdimon ben Gorion as my successor here in the Galil region."

A large round of applause rose from all the men in the room. Unlike Philo, Nakdimon had a look of surprise as he slowly began to smile.

His duties complete, Kayafa turned and quickly left the room.

"Thank you, my friends. It is with greatest humility that I accept this appointment. My first declaration as your new leader is to announce that our esteemed colleague Ya'ir is named as a full member of our Council."

Applause and murmurs of appreciation echoed through the room.

"My first announcement is to let you know that Sha'ul of Tarsus has agreed to stay on here as our new synagogue leader, replacing Ya'ir."

Additional congratulations echoed throughout the room.

It took a moment before Nakdimon realized it was now his responsibility to end the meeting.

"My brothers," he called out, "today has been one of many announcements and decisions. I wish to thank all of you for your support, and I ask your assistance over the coming months and years as I try to prove myself worthy of this great honor bestowed on me. And now, as we have no further business, I dismiss you to your daily routines."

Several men came forward to congratulate Nakdimon; others, Ya'ir and Sha'ul; and still others congratulated Philo. Some left the room. John, unsure what to do, just stood there.

"Aren't you going to offer your congratulations to your friend?" asked Ya'ir, inbetween congratulations.

Not sure what to say, John said nothing.

"What is wrong, young John?"

"I thought," John paused, carefully considering his words. "It's just, when Kayafa began describing boys fit to serve as talmid, I thought he was speaking about me."

Ya'ir began to laugh, and then quickly caught himself. "You are my apprentice. I would not abandon you like that."

John knew Ya'ir was right, but it did not make his pain and disappointment go away.

"Are you still my master, or do I have to go to Sha'ul now?" John was torn, he would have liked to be learning with Philo but he knew nothing about Sha'ul.

"No, you will remain my apprentice, since Sha'ul will

have his hands full with your friend, I'm sure. Come, we'll congratulate both of them on their appointments."

There was a large crowd around Sha'ul, so they stood by Philo.

"Congratulations," John offered, although his tone did not sound very happy in his own ears.

"Thank you, thank you. I really was not expecting this."

John was not sure he believed him. "Does your father's appointment mean you'll be moving to Yerushalayim with him?"

"No, as Sha'ul's talmid, I will stay with him. However, my father has always held Sha'ul in high esteem, so I expect we will travel to visit often."

John did not have much more to say. The silence became awkward, so Ya'ir steered them over to congratulate Nakdimon.

"It is time for your lesson, young one. Let us leave now for the Temple," Ya'ir said.

His feelings unresolved, John followed his master out of the home.

Ya'ir appeared to be in no hurry as the two of them walked slowly to the Temple.

"The position of talmid to someone like Sha'ul is made neither lightly nor without much consideration."

"Did you know of this, Master?"

Ya'ir paused before saying, "I discussed Sha'ul's needs with Kayafa."

Suddenly, John felt betrayed by his master.

"Your studies go well, you show much promise," Ya'ir said. "Your knowledge of our ancient texts is unequalled to anyone your age, except perhaps for Sha'ul himself. Your willingness to leave your family and apprentice with me is also admirable for one so young. But your path and Philo's are not equal. He has to travel along his own path. Did you really expect to be named Sha'ul's talmid?"

"I don't know what I expected. As Kayafa spoke, I became convinced he was talking about me."

"He did describe several attributes you possess. But do you really believe you could apprentice with me for such a short time and then be named talmid for another?"

John knew in his mind that idea was impossible, but it

did not dispel the sadness he felt at losing the opportunity.

"I am sorry, Master. I know I should be focused only on your lessons."

"Your disappointment will leave you soon, as you realize that you do not possess the talent and experience necessary to take on such a position."

Ya'ir's words wounded John almost as much as Philo's appointment. "I thought you said I was making great strides in my writing. I already have more of the Tanakh memorized than Philo does. I think I could be a good talmid."

"Someday, perhaps, but not now. Your time has not yet come. You still have so much to learn."

John did not appreciate Ya'ir's honesty. Maybe it was true that he was not fully ready to be a talmid. He still hoped that he had made enough of an impression that Ya'ir could at least think of him that way. They arrived at the Temple.

"I think we shall cancel our studies for this afternoon, in light of the announcements and your reaction to them."

John could not remember another time Ya'ir canceled lessons. Ya'ir came faithfully every day, even if he was sick.

"What shall I do, Master?"

Ya'ir opened his leather moneybag. "I am in need of some fresh fish for the evening meal. Purchase me two carp." He reached out and dropped a silver shekel into John's outstretched hand.

His master's request hurt John the most out of everything else today. Getting fish was a job for a servant, not an apprentice, though John knew better than to question his master's demands.

"Give yourself time outside to consider today's events and what they mean. Place yourself in the now, not the future or the past."

"Yes, Master," John said as he placed the coin in his own moneybag.

"And make sure they are fresh. Most fish have been sitting in the hot sun all day. I do not want any sour fish spoiling my meal."

John kicked a stone along the dusty road that lead to the docks. It was a road he walked a thousand times, yet today it seemed so strange and foreign.

"What are you doing here?" a voice asked.

John looked up to see Philo approaching in his new white robe. "Why are you alone? Where is Ya'ir?"

Philo's appearance was unexpected. "I could say the same about you. Where is Sha'ul?"

"He is still with my father and Gamli'el. I had some business to attend to before my father left. And you?"

"I'm... I'm going to the docks."

Philo's eyebrows shot up in surprise. "Why would you go there?"

Ya'ir's errand embarrassed John. "Ya'ir asked me to bring him some fish."

Philo laughed. "Some things never change. Are you still carrying fish for a living?" he teased.

John scowled. His anger at Philo's appointment still burned, and he did not appreciate any sarcastic comments his old friend might make.

"I do whatever my master asks," John said. "I don't question why."

"Do you mind if I join you?"

John shrugged and Philo walked next to him.

They walked in silence for several minutes until John became uncomfortable. "Congratulations again on being named Sha'ul's apprentice."

"Talmid," Philo quickly corrected. "You know that is much more than just learning the trade."

John shrugged his indifference.

"What's wrong with you? I thought at least you could be happy for me."

John stopped and both boys stared at each other. "I am happy for you. I just..."

"What?"

John did not say a word, but the resignation in his face spoke volumes.

John turned and continued walking. "I just thought, the way your father introduced you, and then I remembered all the problems you had with me being named Ya'ir's apprentice, it just..." Again, he could not finish the sentence.

"You think you're better than me?"

John had to think quickly. "No, well, yes, in some things, like memorization, I am, but in other things you're better than I am."

"You're right, I am. I deserve this position more than you."

The discussion was not going as John hoped. He did not want Philo against him.

"I'm happy for you, truly I am. I'm just disappointed. I don't know why, but I just feel sad. I'll get over it soon, I promise. I'm sorry for acting like this."

Philo said nothing, but walked along in silence.

"I'll forgive you," he finally said.

The two friends walked along for a few moments.

"Why is Ya'ir sending you on this kind of errand? This is something a servant should do."

John agreed with Philo. "I don't know. I think I'm being punished."

"What for?"

"My anger at your announcement."

Philo laughed. "You didn't actually talk to Ya'ir about it, did you?"

John nodded.

"That was probably not a wise idea, but you can't change what has been done. I'd suggest that you apologize to Ya'ir when you get back."

They arrived at the docks. "I will."

Crews secured some of the boats, while others sat silently, moored to their docks, their crews resting from their work. A few of the docks were empty.

John saw Shim'on and his crew coming in late. "Shim'on," John yelled, "do you have fish for me to buy? It is for Ya'ir."

Shim'on strained to see who called him from the shore. "John, is that you?" he asked.

"Yes, Ya'ir has sent me to buy carp for the evening meal. Do you have a few you can spare?"

Shim'on threw John a rope. Recalling his days working with his uncle, John pulled the boat to the docks, and then securely lashed it.

"I was out all night, and even stayed late this morning. There were no fish to be caught."

John was surprised. Shim'on was K'far-Nachum's best fishermen.

Shim'on's brother, Andrew, spoke up. "It is true. I have never seen such bad luck in all of my days."

The sound of an approaching group caught John's attention. Three dozen men wearing different robes and all talking at the same time walked along the banks of the sea. Leading them was a man dressed in a white robe with a brown belt. Around his shoulders hung a prayer shawl, similar to Sha'ul's. John recognized him. It was the Natzeret from the Yarden River last month.

He spoke to his followers as a rabbi spoke to his talmidim. "The time has come, God's Kingdom is near! Turn to God from your sins and believe the Good News!"

Shim'on stepped off his boat. Without hesitation, the stranger walked along the dock until he stood before Shim'on. His followers awaited on the shore.

The two men exchanged glances. Even though Shim'on was larger and more muscular, he some how seemed slight next to the man. Without a word, the stranger pressed past Shim'on and stepped onto his boat.

Shim'on moved to protest, but his brother grabbed his arm and restrained him. "It is all right. I have seen this man before."

Shim'on gave him a puzzled look.

"Last month, on the banks of the Yarden. This is the man I told you about, the one who was baptized by Yochanan."

The stranger neither verified nor denied Andrew's claim, but said, "Put out into deep water, and let down your nets for a catch."

Shim'on laughed. "We've worked hard all night long, Rabbi..." Shim'on waited for the man to introduce himself.

"I am Yeshua."

"We've worked hard all night, Yeshua, and haven't caught a thing."

Yeshua repeated his request.

Shim'on sighed, tired from his long and fruitless work. "If you say so, I'll let down the nets." He motioned to John to untie the boat.

When they were a good distance from shore, they cast

out their nets. It took only a moment. As they began pulling the nets back in, the water erupted with the splashing of fish. Shim'on and Andrew pulled as hard as they could, but the amount of fish in the nets was too great and the net began to rip.

Another boat came next to them, and together, they tried to haul in the catch. The only way they had a chance to land all of the fish was to split the load between the two boats.

After some time, they finally succeeded in securing the catch. Another problem arose, as the weight of the fish was so great the boats' decks came perilously close to the waterline. One wrong move or tall wave, and both boats would begin taking on water.

The two crews relentlessly worked to get both boats and their cargo safely back to the docks. It was almost comical watching these two big boats bobbing, their owners fighting to save them, and the stranger just sitting there calmly, as if this was an everyday event.

When they finally reached the shore and docked, Shim'on, his brother Andrew, and two of the boys on the other boat, Ya`akov Ben-Zavdai and Yochanan, his brother, jumped from their boats.

Shim'on fell at the man's feet. "Get away from me, sir, because I'm a sinner!"

The entire scene, from the fish to the boats to Shim'on's confession seemed surreal to John.

Yeshua did not move. "Don't be frightened, from now on you will be catching men—alive!"

Yeshua's statement puzzled John. How does one fish for men? Would they be using the same nets?

Shim'on, his brother, and their friends followed the man from Natzeret into the crowd.

As they slowly disappeared from view, Philo and John stood there dumbfounded. Fish flopped around on the decks of both boats; the lucky ones fell back into the lake.

The amount of fish John saw was staggering. All of them appeared to be twice their normal size; there was not a single runt in the catch.

For a few moments, John did not know what to do.

"What just happened?" he asked Philo.

His friend said nothing.

"Have you ever seen anything like that? How do you think Yeshua knew there would be fish there?"

Philo shook his head. "There is no way he could have known."

"Then how do you explain it?"

"I can't."

"What should we do?" John asked.

Philo said nothing.

When he came to his senses, John grabbed several of the large carp.

"I'm going to get these fish back before they spoil."

8

Secrets in the Night

John completed his errand and headed to Temple. The afternoon services would begin soon, and Ya'ir expected his assistance. He arrived at the Temple, and entered the dimly lit room. Dozens of men were already there, some broken into small groups quietly praying, while a large group stood listening to a man speaking at the front of the room.

John walked forward, confused. It was too early for Ya'ir to have begun the service. He should still be in Beth Sefer for at least another half hour. One of the worshippers had the right to read the text and offer interpretations, but in the weeks that John had been with Ya'ir, he had never once seen one of the townspeople step forward in that role.

John approached the from behind. He tried to see who the speaker was, but the men were too tall and blocked his line of sight. The man's voice, though, was a clear, authoritative tone. John recognized the words from the scroll of Yesha`yahu the prophet.

> *The people living in darkness have seen a great light; upon those living in the land that lies in the shadow of death, light has dawned.*

This verse in particular John remembered well. It spoke about how his lands, the lands beyond the Yarden, the lands of Galil, would be among the first to see the light of the mashiach. He took great comfort in the words.

The speaker closed the scroll and returned it to the shammash. There was not a sound in the Temple as everyone awaited his interpretation.

"The Scripture speaks of the great ignorance of people to the coming of the mashiach. In darkness, you cannot see, you do not know where you go. If you are ignorant of Adonai and your duty, you are in the darkness. And what removes darkness?"

"Light," called out a voice from the crowd.

"You live in the ignorance and darkness of death. A great light has come to this region and shadow of death. Death stands between you and Adonai, casting a long, dark shadow on the nations.

"But be encouraged, for the prophet says that to your lands comes the light of the mashiach to illuminate the shadows and bring you to the Kingdom of God. The time has come, God's Kingdom is near! Turn to God from your sins and believe the Good News!"

As the man spoke, John walked around the crowd, trying to catch a glimpse of the speaker. No one he knew, not Ya'ir, not Nakdimon, not even Kayafa himself, spoke with such authority. The man's pronunciation of key words from the Scriptures was impeccable.

As John stood, a few of the men parted, and gave him clear view of the speaker. It was Yeshua. John gasped.

Yeshua, hearing John, stopped his comments and turned. Before he could speak, an evil cry rang through the building. All voices stopped at the sound. Again it rang out, even louder. Some of the men in the back whispered then the crowd parted and revealed the source of the noise.

A man came forward, if "man" was the appropriate word for him. His name was Hadad and for the last twenty years had terrorized the city. John met him on a street three years ago and barely escaped uninjury. Goose bumps spread across John's arms at the memory.

Attempts to capture Hadad had failed. So dangerous was he that he maimed several of the men sent to arrest him. At his sight, townspeople secured their doors and windows, or just fled entirely.

Dust and dirt caked his outer garments and he wore no sandals. His hair and beard were wild and unkempt. He walked forward with a pronounced limp, perhaps the result of one of the many attempts to capture him.

His most frightening feature were his eyes. They were blank, emotionless, almost lifeless.

About halfway through the synagogue, he dropped to his knees as if in great pain. With a voice that sounded like wind driven through a crack in a wall, he cried,

"What do you want with us, Yeshua from Natzeret? Have you come to destroy us? I know who you are—the Holy One of God!" He gasped, and dropped to the floor screaming and moaning in agony.

Yeshua did not move. In a calm, but authoritative voice, he said, "Be quiet and come out of him!" Hadad screamed in agony, as if every part of his body was aflame. He writhed on the floor, his screams growing louder until grown men covered their ears to mask the sounds. Without warning, all became silent.

Hadad lay on the floor, drenched in sweat, breathing heavily. There was no other sound in the building except his labored attempts to draw in air. Slowly his breath returned to a normal pace, then seemed still. A few brave men moved closer to see if he was alive.

Without warning, Hadad rolled into a seated position on the floor. Gone was the trembling that had gripped the man.

Some men crept closer, unsure what to make of this transformation. The closest one reached Hadad and tentatively offered a hand to help him to his feet. Hadad grabbed it and rose to a standing position. He embraced the man. A huge smile shown on his face and tears of joy rolled down his cheeks. One by one, every man came up to see Hadad for himself.

"What is this?" asked one.

Someone spoke up boldly. "A new teaching, one with authority behind it!"

"He gives orders even to the unclean spirits," said Philo, "and they obey him!"

Philo's sudden appearance startled John. "How long have you been here? How much did you see?"

"Enough," said Philo.

John looked back through the crowd, but Yeshua was gone.

"Where is he?" asked Philo.

So intent was he on Hadad that John had not seen him leave. Philo searched the area for a few moments, to no avail. "We must go tell Nakdimon of this, this Yeshua of Natzeret," he said, and he headed out of the synagogue.

John followed his friend.

As they neared Nakdimon's house, John and Philo realized word of the events in the synagogue was spreading faster than they could walk. A group of people busily discussed what happened. At the edge of the group, a small girl listened intently. Myriam. John approached his old friend, who now seemed so much different.

When Myriam recognized them, she smiled with joy. "Where have you been?"

"I have been with my Master."

She turned to Philo. "And you?"

Philo puffed out his chest with pride. "I am talmid for Sha'ul."

"Apprentice with Ya'ir, talmid for Sha'ul. What did you two do to earn such high honors?"

John stammered momentarily, and then said nothing.

"Did it have anything to do with Herod's arrest of Yochanan?"

John stared at the ground, unable to look his friend in the eye.

Myriam's joy at seeing her old friends suddenly dropped. "So, you're the reason Yochanan was arrested." Tears welled in her eyes. "I wondered. I wondered if the great Philo and his best friend John had anything to do with it. But no, I thought, not them. They are too decent to allow a man to get murdered for their own pleasure."

"No one is getting murdered," offered Philo.

Myriam gave him an icy stare. "Surely you don't think Herod is going to let him live, do you?"

She turned her back to John. "How could you? What gives you the right to play with a man's life like that?" Tears rolled down her cheeks.

Now it was Philo's turn to be angry. "What gives the P'rushim the right?" he yelled at her. "They are the ones who interpret Scripture, not some lunatic who screams at people in the desert."

Myriam looked shocked. "Well, now I know what kind of a person you are." She looked at John. "What kind of 'men' you both are."

"Myriam, it wasn't like that," John started to explain, but she would not listen.

"I don't want to hear it," she said as she walked away.

John turned to Philo. "What did you do that for?"

"Forget her. She'll get over it. She's the reason why these lunatics get started in the first place," said Philo.

That evening, John was summoned to Nakdimon's home to explain what had happened at the synagogue. When he arrived, he found Philo already there. Together, they both told Nakdimon what they had observed.

"This news is unexpected," said Nakdimon. "We remove one lunatic, only to have another replace him."

"This situation needs to be dealt with immediately," said Sha'ul. "If we allow it to continue, things will be difficult for us."

"Sha'ul," said Nakdimon, "we can do nothing this evening. You may return to your lodgings. Meet here at sunrise tomorrow.

"Philo, please go to each Council member and tell them what you saw. I want them here at the rise of the sun so that we may make our plans."

When Sha'ul and Philo had left the courtyard, Nakdimon turned to John. "Boy, do you know where I might find this Yeshua?" he asked.

John shook his head. "No, sir."

Nakdimon paused. "I need to speak to him, to see how he responds. But, it would be wrong for the chief priest of K'far-Nachum to wander about, asking to speak to Yeshua."

He dropped to one knee.

"John, I need a favor. Go and find out where he is, and then come back here. Don't tell anyone why you are looking for him."

Two favors in one day, John thought. The last favor had not gone as he expected. He headed out into the darkness of the streets.

After wandering about town for several hours, and asking different people, he finally located where Yeshua and his followers were staying. John led Nakdimon to a small house on the eastern edge of town.

"Stay behind me," Nakdimon told John. "I don't know what to expect, and I don't want you involved unnecessarily."

Shim'on, Andrew, and Ya`akov stood outside the door

to the small home. So animated were they in discussion of what had happened, Nakdimon's presence seemed to startle them.

"I am here to speak with Yeshua of Natzeret," said Nakdimon.

Shim'on walked up to Nakdimon.

"What is it you want, priest?" Shim'on's jaw tightened as he spoke. Clearly, he had as much trust for the P'rushim as John's uncle.

"I have come by myself, alone, to talk to your master," said Nakdimon calmly. "I have questions only he can answer."

Shim'on relaxed his jaw a bit. "What kind of questions are these? The kind you use to send innocent men to Herod's dungeons?"

Nakdimon shook his head. "No, you misjudge me. I have come not with the P'rushim, but by myself. I need to see your master and see if everything I have heard about him is real."

Shim'on almost smiled. "It is, you will see."

"And if you do, are you prepared to accept the truth?" asked Andrew.

Nakdimon kept his composure. "It depends on how he answers. May I see him?"

Ya'akov and Andrew gave John a menacing look. John felt a cold sweat roll down his back as he remembered how these boys tormented him at Beth-Sefer.

Shim'on turned to his brother. "Run inside and see if the Rabbi will speak to this..." He paused, looking Nakdimon up and down. "...This man."

Andrew ran into the house. A few moments later, he returned. "I have spoken to our master. He says you may enter, alone, if you wish."

"I have only this small boy with me. Surely your teacher is not afraid of him?"

Shim'on's eyes widened as he recognized John. "You certainly look different than the last time we met."

Nakdimon gave John a queer glance.

"I am."

Shim'on considered their request, and then moved aside to let both of them pass.

The inside of the home was dim. Only a few small oil lamps were lit. The home was a modest one, not unlike the home his family shared. It was nothing like the homes of Ya'ir or Kayafa that John had become accustomed to lately.

Yeshua sat at the far wall, deep in conversation with several followers John did not recognize. Before they even reached him, Yeshua seemed to sense their presence and invited Nakdimon to sit. John stood behind the priest.

After Nakdimon was comfortable, he said, "Rabbi, we know it is from God that you have come as a teacher, for no one can do these miracles you perform unless God is with him."

Nakdimon's words took John by surprise. Yeshua's followers seemed surprised the leader of the local priests would make such an admission.

"Yes, indeed," Yeshua answered him. "I tell you that unless a person is born again from above, he cannot see the Kingdom of God."

Nakdimon's eyes became wide in wonder. "How can a grown man be 'born'? Can he go back into his mother's womb and be born a second time?"

Yeshua replied, "Yes, indeed, I tell you that unless a person is born from water and the Spirit, he cannot enter the Kingdom of God. What is born from the flesh is flesh, and what is born from the Spirit is spirit."

Nakdimon still did not seem to understand. "What does it mean to be 'born again'?"

"Stop being amazed at my telling you that you must be born again from above!" Yeshua said. "The wind blows where it wants to, and you hear its sound, but you don't know where it comes from or where it's going. That's how it is with everyone who has been born from the Spirit."

Nakdimon furrowed his brow in puzzlement. John, too, had to admit he did not understand what Yeshua was getting at.

"How can this happen?" Nakdimon asked.

Yeshua looked about the room. Every voice was silent, every eye turned to see and hear their discussion.

"You hold the office of teacher in Isra'el, and you don't know this?" Yeshua asked.

John felt shame for Nakdimon when he heard Yeshua's

tone.

"Yes, indeed! I tell you that what we speak about, we know, and what we give evidence of, we have seen, but you people don't accept our evidence!"

Yeshua stood and offered a hand to help Nakdimon up. John strained to hear what the Natzerene said, for he spoke in a soft tone.

"If you people don't believe me when I tell you about the things of the world, how will you believe me when I tell you about the things of heaven?"

Yeshua tenderly placed his arm around Nakdimon, as one would when talking to his own brother. "No one has gone up into heaven, there is only the one who has come down from heaven, the Son of Man. Just as Moshe lifted up the serpent in the desert, so must the Son of Man be lifted up, so that everyone who trusts in him may have eternal life."

Nakdimon did not answer Yeshua directly.

John recognized the scriptural reference. Yeshua spoke about the time Moshe, the great Hebrew leader, led the Great Exodus from captivity in Egypt. During their time in the wilderness, the people complained against Adonai, and He sent fiery serpents to bite the people, causing them to die. When the people repented, Moshe created a bronze serpent at God's command. Anyone bitten by snakes needed only to follow God's command and look upon it, and God healed them.

Yeshua continued. "For God so loved the world that He gave his only and unique Son, so that everyone who trusts in Him may have eternal life, instead of being utterly destroyed."

Nakdimon asked Yeshua a question, but it was so soft and quiet only Yeshua seemed to hear.

He smiled. "God did not send the Son into the world to judge the world, but rather so that through Him, the world might be saved. Those who trust in Him are not judged; those who do not trust have been judged already, in that they have not trusted in the one who is God's only and unique Son."

"God has already given His judgment on those who do not follow the Laws of Moshe. What judgment will the Son bring?" asked Nakdimon.

Yeshua extinguished all of the oil lamps but one, which he held in front of him. "This is the judgment." He began to walk around the room as the meager light from the lamp flickered on the faces of his followers. "The light has come into the world, but people loved the darkness rather than the light. Why?"

"Because their actions are wicked," said John.

Yeshua smiled. "Because their actions were wicked. For everyone who does evil things hates the light and avoids it, so that his actions won't be exposed. But everyone who does what is true comes to the light, so that all may see that his actions are accomplished through God."

Yeshua walked out of the room, leaving it illuminated only by the light of the rising moon. After a moment, Nakdimon walked out of the house, with John behind him. They passed silently into the street, and began to head back to Nakdimon's home.

When they were outside and able to speak without Yeshua and his followers hearing, John asked, "What did he mean?"

"He is saying that he believes he has been sent here to teach God's truth."

"That is a good thing, is it not?"

"But that truth does not mean following the Laws of Moshe."

"Adonai, no," exclaimed John, "How can anyone claim to be teaching Adonai's truths and dismiss the Laws of our fathers? Surely a rabbi would teach God's Laws."

Nakdimon walked many steps in silence, and then answered. "I think he believes himself to be the mashiach. I fear this man does not follow our laws and customs. Do you recall him speaking of Moshe?"

John nodded. "It was from the scroll of B'midbar, was it not?"

Despite the seriousness of the situation, Nakdimon could not help but smile. "Ya'ir is right to speak so highly of you. Yes, you are correct. Do you remember of what it was telling?"

John had to think hard. It had been a long time since he had read that scroll.

"It was after the Sh'mot," began John, "when our

people fled Egypt. They were alone in the wilderness, and questioned God and Moshe."

Nakdimon nodded. "And how did God respond to their unbelief?"

John thought about the scrolls he had read. "He sent fiery serpents to bite them," he said, pleased to remember his studies.

"That's right, he sent serpents that bit the non-believers. And many of them died."

"And Adonai told Moshe to make the bronze serpent to heal them," John quickly.

"Quite right," said Nakdimon.

John was still puzzled. "But, Master, what does that have to do with the mashiach?" he asked.

"Did you recognize the reference to 'Son of Man'?" Nakdimon asked.

John shook his head. "No, is that in the Tanakh?"

Nakdimon nodded. "In the scroll of Dani'el, the prophet speaks of the mashiach. He calls the mashiach 'the Son of Man.'

> *I kept watching the night visions, when I saw, coming with the clouds of heaven, someone like a son of man. He approached the Ancient One and was led into his presence. To him was given rulership, glory and a kingdom, so that all peoples, nations and languages should serve him. His rulership is an eternal rulership that will not pass away; and his kingdom is one that will never be destroyed.*

"Do you not see? When he refers to himself as the 'Son of Man,' he is saying plainly that he believes he is the mashiach. The Son of Man stands in the presence of God."

John gasped. "Adonai, no!"

"When he said, 'the Son of Man be lifted up,' I was almost overcome with fear. This man speaks with authority, as if he believes he has been empowered by Adonai Himself."

Nakdimon walked for several moments in silence.

"I think this man believes he will die. I think he is

willing to die for his beliefs."

"Is that so bad?" John asked. "Won't he be silenced?"

"My boy," Nakdimon said, "Ya'ir tells me you show such promise as a rabbi, but you're a bit naive at world affairs. His death will only benefit us if we control the circumstances. If he controls the events surrounding his death, he could throw our entire world into war."

John was not sure what his teacher was saying. "War against whom?"

Nakdimon leaned down and spoke softly as if worried someone else could hear. "War against Rome, I fear."

"That would be suicide."

Nakdimon nodded. "I think that is exactly what he is planning."

9

The Visitor

At sunrise, all the members of the local Council assembled. Sha'ul and Gamli'el were also present, as was Ya'ir. John saw a stranger amongst the priests. He was a tall, impeccably dressed man with dark black hair and beard. He wore gold rings on his fingers and a golden amulet about his arm. His clothing and jewelry were of a finer quality than even Nakdimon's. John thought he must be a very important man.

"My brothers, I present to you a member of the Sanhedrin who journeyed several days to be with us," said Nakdimon. "His arrival is most fortuitous. Adonai has answered our prayers and brought him before us in this dark hour. May I introduce to you, Yosef of Ramatayim."

Yosef stepped forward and took his place before the Council. Nakdimon explained briefly what had happened yesterday at the docks, and then sat back to allow Yosef to speak.

"I bring greetings from the Sanhedrin." He did not speak with the same accent as other from Yerushalayim; instead, his tone was rich and deep. "This man you have seen, this Yeshua, he is known to us. We have made inquiries of the residents of both K'far-Nachum and Natzeret. To date, this is the information we have acquired.

"He is Yeshua Ben-Yosef. His father is a carpenter in Natzeret. The reports indicate he grew up as a first-born son in a home with his parents, with at least four brothers and some sisters. He is a scholar of the Scriptures. One person reported of a time before the boy's thirteenth year when he stood in the Temple in Yerushalayim and questioned the rabbis of the Law."

"When did this happen?" asked Nakdimon.

"According to our information, about eighteen, nineteen years ago. Apparently, the boy and his parents came to Yerushalayim to celebrate our Passover Feast. During their visit, he spent several days sitting in the midst of the teachers both listening to them and asking them questions. All who heard him were amazed at his understanding and his answers."

"This sounds like what we witnessed at the Temple with Hadad," said John. "He had everyone there mesmerized with his speaking."

Nakdimon glared at John for interrupting. "Please continue," he said to Yosef.

"After finding him, his parents took him home to Natzeret, where he learned the carpenter's trade. There have been no accounts of him since then. From all of our reports, he has been a model citizen."

Nakdimon stood and offered Yosef a seat. "Thank you for your report, and please thank the Sanhedrin on our behalf. The information you have furnished is most interesting.

"My brothers," Nakdimon continued, "we have before us a crisis. This Natzeret, whom both Yoesf and Hadad have identified as Yeshua of Natzeret, teaches an interpretation of Scripture that is drastically different than our own. This is a threat to our very way of life. He moves freely through our city and the surrounding towns. I have asked Sha'ul and Ya'ir to watch his activities. What have you found out?"

Ya'ir nodded to John, who stood. "With your permission, my master assigned me to watch this man and report back on his movements." As he began speaking, the sight of all of the P'rushim staring at him made his mouth run dry. He swallowed hard, and pushed on, growing stronger with each sentence.

"I have observed him on three separate occasions," he continued. "After the incident with Hadad, he returned to the home of one of his followers, a fisherman from here named Shim'on. Shim'on's mother-in-law was bedridden with a high fever. It was reported that Yeshua visited her in her chambers, and a few moments later she recovered and prepared a meal for him and about a dozen of his followers."

An audible gasp arose from several of the P'rushim members. "He heals, too?" several asked amongst themselves.

"After hearing of this, I went to Shim'on's home that

evening. A large crowd from all over K'far-Nachum gathered outside the door to watch. Yeshua spoke to them. The message he preached was the same as Yochanan the Immerser's at the Yarden River, with these words: 'The time has come, God's Kingdom is near! Turn to God from your sins and believe the Good News!' This message is..." John paused for the right word, "...different than what most of us hear when we go to Temple. He makes no mention of the Law or following the Commandments brought to us by Moshe."

John had a question, but feared to ask it. He took a deep breath before forging ahead. "Forgive me, my masters, but when the crowd saw me, they confronted me. I was asked why we fear what he speaks of. I did not know how to answer. He speaks of loving each other. Surely that is a good lesson to teach?"

There were murmurs and shouts from the P'rushim. While a few openly supported the question, most condemned it.

Nakdimon settled everyone down. "Now, now, the boy asks a perfectly good question. We must answer it, for it speaks to the questions our own people will be asking."

He faced John. "You are right to say this. He does talk of things that are good and right, if he speaks of loving each other. There is nothing wrong with that."

Nakdimon addressed the other priests. "The Torah clearly shows us that the mashiach will lead the Jewish people to a full observance of the Torah." He turned back to John. "Do you know the scroll of D'varim?"

John tried to remember his teachings.

Before he could answer, Nakdimon continued. "I will tell you what it says:

> *If a prophet or someone who gets messages while dreaming arises among you and he gives you a sign or wonder, and the sign or wonder comes about as he predicted when he said, 'Let's follow other gods, which you have not known; and let us serve them,' you are not to listen to what that prophet or dreamer says. For Adonai your God is testing you, in order to find out whether you really do love*

Adonai your God with all your heart and being. You are to follow Adonai your God, fear him, obey his commandments, listen to what he says, serve him and cling to him; and that prophet or dreamer is to be put to death; because he urged rebellion against Adonai your God, who brought you out of the land of Egypt and redeemed you from a life of slavery; in order to seduce you away from the path Adonai your God ordered you to follow. This is how you are to rid your community of this wickedness."

The other priests nodded in agreement. "The Torah says all of Adonai's laws shall remain binding, forever," said Nakdimon. "If anyone says he is coming to change the Torah, rest assured, he is a false prophet."

Nakdimon began walking amongst the Council, holding their attention at his every word.

"Remember what the Immerser said about Yeshua before the crowds. 'I have seen and borne witness that this is the Son of God.' There is only one God, and He reigns in heaven. Our teachings tell us conclusively He will give us a redeemer from the great line of David as a herald to the dawning of a new age of peace, compassion, and love. This man can be nothing more than an impostor, or at worst, a deranged man." Nakdimon sat, his point made.

The Council agreed with Nakdimon's statement. John bowed, and continued with his report. "I went to Shim'on's home that evening, as soon as I heard Yeshua was there. That evening at sunset, I saw him heal a great number people sick from many different kinds of diseases, and he ordered many of the demons to come out of their victims, as he did with Hadad."

Again, murmurs rose from the P'rushim. Nakdimon tried to quiet them down. "Let him speak." He turned to John. "You actually saw this?"

John nodded. "I saw him heal at least three dozen people, and cast demons out of at least another dozen more."

"Where did this take place?" someone asked.

"Outside Shim'on's home. The street to the Temple passes by it."

Nakdimon shook his head. "Surely, this is the worst news you could bring. Do you know where he is now?"

"No, I do not," John replied. "He has been to other towns within the Galil."

"I have reports from travelers he has traveled to many communities, preaching in their synagogues," added Yosef.

"Just preaching?" Nakdimon asked.

"Preaching and expelling demons, just as the boy spoke," Yosef said. "I have heard a report in Korazim of a man with leprosy who knelt in front of Yeshua, begging to be healed. After Yeshua healed him, he—"

"Of leprosy?" someone cried.

"Of leprosy," Yosef confirmed. "After Yeshua healed him, he told him to go to the priest and present himself to him. Yeshua told the man to take with him the offering required in the law for being healed of leprosy."

"Did the man go? Can the priest confirm the story?" Philo asked.

Ya'ir stepped forward. "The priest happened to be in K'far-Nachum on business last week," he said. "I met with him. The man did as Yeshua told him to and paid the offering. The priest also confirmed the man had been stricken with leprosy for twenty-six years, but now appeared completely healed."

"How is this possible?" cried Sha'ul. "Surely anyone with such amazing powers must be sent from Adonai?"

Nakdimon shook his head. "He does not speak of our teachings as one from Adonai would. He has declared himself equal with God, which by our law is punishable by death."

"Death," John whispered to Philo. "Can't we just arrest him, like we did Yochanan?"

Philo leaned in to keep his voice low. "Nakdimon speaks the truth. If this Yeshua seeks death, we should be the ones who administer it to him."

John shook his head. "No, no. I can't accept that. I can't kill a man, no matter what he does."

"Then it's a good thing you're apprenticing to be a rabbi and not an executioner."

Nakdimon glanced over at the two of them, and they immediately stopped talking.

"My brothers, don't you see what is happening?" Nakdimon said excitedly. "This is no prophet from Adonai we are dealing with. He has Ba'al-Zibbul in him. It is by the ruler of the demons that he expels the demons." He paused to allow the thoughts to sink in. "This man himself is demon possessed! He is sent not from Adonai, but from our great Adversary!"

Nakdimon sat as all of the P'rushim stood to argue. John could not believe what Nakdimon said. The man he had been sent to follow was Satan? This could not be.

Nakdimon waited for the discussions to calm down. "My friends, I know this is a radical statement. But we must look at the facts. This man is healing in his own name, not Adonai's. He has control over demons. He is forgiving sins. This is blasphemy! Who but Adonai can forgive sins? This man is setting himself up to be what Satan has always wanted, to be equal with God."

The P'rushim discussed Nakdimon's proposal, but quickly came to accept it. John was not so sure he was right. Yeshua certainly did not act like he was demon-possessed. He remembered how Hadad had appeared in the Temple. This was the image he expected of a demon-possessed man. Even his own brother David, when the fits came upon him, appeared more demon-possessed than Yeshua.

"We must move with extreme caution," said Nakdimon. "Unlike Yochanan, this one travels from town to town, amassing a large following. Our own townspeople vilify us for the role we played in Yochanan's capture. We cannot risk further damage in dealing with this Yeshua."

"What must we do?" Ya'ir asked.

"This man teaches in our own synagogues. We are the teachers of the Law. We must confront him, not with arms, but with truth. Expose him for the fraud that he is. Even Satan cannot stand up to God's Word. We must publicly challenge him every chance we get.

"Once the people see his true nature, it should be an easy matter to have him arrested. Sha'ul, Ya'ir," Nakdimon called. "I want you to keep constant surveillance at the Temple. One of you should be there at all times. When he returns, engage him in debate. Prove he is an impostor before the crowds."

Both men agreed.

It was several weeks later when John found himself sitting with Ya'ir in the Temple, waiting. Other than ten men quietly murmuring prayers, the building was empty. The torches on the walls illuminated their faces in a warm light of orange and yellow.

"Master," asked John, "what if he is wrong? What if Nakdimon hasn't really understood? We would be condemning an innocent man."

Ya'ir sighed and lowered his voice. "Are we to have this discussion yet again?" he asked. "I worry about that too. I don't doubt that Nakdimon believes what he says. However, I am not so quick to assume Satan walks amongst us. If this man is truly from Satan, we should be able to tell from his answers to our questions. And if he is from God, well, that too should be obvious."

Knowing that Ya'ir did not necessarily believe Nakdimon's arguments as the others did comforted John. At least Ya'ir wouldn't be quick to judge.

The doors to the Temple opened, and a man ran in. He went deliberately up to the seats where Ya'ir and John sat. "Forgive me, Rabbi," he said lowering his eyes, "but the man you seek has just crossed through the north gate."

"Yeshua?" asked Ya'ir. The man nodded. Ya'ir stood and adjusted his tunic. "Where is he?"

"He is at a small house, several blocks from here. Come, I can show you the way."

Ya'ir and John followed close at the man's heels.

When they arrived at the home, a crowd surrounded it. Ya'ir and John stepped past several men seated outside. The crowd at the door was thick, and allowed Ya'ir and John to make their way through the front door almost undetected.

It didn't seem possible, but there were more people inside than outside. John could not move without feeling someone pressing against him from all sides, making it difficult to see and hear what was happening. With so many men around him, John had no choice but to cling to Ya'ir, afraid that if they were to get separated, he would never again find his master. It reminded him of a family wedding he had attended several years ago in Gibeah. He and his mother and uncle had traveled for many days. They had met many relatives at this home, which was too small for the number of people inside. Even though they had stayed there for many days, they had never felt cramped because everyone there was family.

John had the same feeling in this house. He often could not see over the shoulders of the men pushed up against him. There were coughs and moans from the sick, men with crutches who could not move, yet no one complained. Each man treated the one next to him as a brother. John never expected this many people to be this friendly with strangers. It was as if they were celebrating the return of a long lost relative.

Ya'ir spotted Sha'ul, and made his way through the mass of people to stand next to him. Sitting was quite out of the question. John followed Ya'ir.

In the front, facing them, were five men. Yeshua stood in the middle. To his left stood Shim'on and his brother Andrew, and to his right were their partners, Ya`akov and Yochanan, the sons of Zavdai.

Yeshua had been speaking in soothing tones since their arrival. His message reminded John of Yochanan the Immerser's: "Repent, for the kingdom of God is at hand." John listened intently to the message, trying to hear miscues the priests might use in an attack.

He felt an itch on his ear, then his cheek. Dust floated down in front of him. He looked up. The roof was coming apart! Flakes from the plaster ceiling fell into the room, and already a large section was missing. Sunlight streamed in. A head popped into view, upside down, looked at the room below and then disappeared.

By this time, the room had grown silent. All eyes looked up at the opening, which quickly grew larger. John thought he saw four sets of hands, making it quite evident more than one man was at work.

After a short time, the work above stopped. Everyone was silent. Then the head they had seen before popped in and addressed Yeshua.

"Forgive our intrusion, Teacher," he said, "but the home is so crowded with followers we could not get in to see you otherwise."

Again the head disappeared, and then the sunlight streaming in was blocked. A rectangular form made of wood and straw appeared, holding a reclining man. His friends lowered him lightly into the room. As the stretcher descended, people pushed back until a patch of floor appeared between Yeshua and the crowd. The man's friends aimed the stretcher towards that. A man's head reappeared above while they struggled to lower the man evenly.

"This is our friend. He begged us to bring him to you when he heard you were here. He believes you can heal him of the paralysis that has gripped his lower body for fifteen years."

The man lay on the floor. To get him through the small opening, his friends had hideously curled his legs up under his body. From his appearance, John thought that if he had not already been paralyzed, he soon would be. He said not a word, refusing even to look up at Yeshua.

Yeshua knelt and placed his hand on the man's head. "Son, your sins are forgiven."

Sha'ul seized the opening. He addressed the crowd in a loud voice. "How can this fellow say such a thing? He is blaspheming! Who can forgive sins except God?"

Immediately the crowd began to talk excitedly. "He is right," said some.

Sha'ul and Ya'ir waited for the answer. Sha'ul's trap amazed John in its simplicity. If Yeshua admitted to the crowd he was God, the crowd would turn against him, believing him to be insane. If he admitted that he wasn't from God, then the crowd would leave, believing him to be a false teacher. It was a brilliant strategy.

If Yeshua was trapped, he didn't look like he knew it. He stood and faced Sha'ul. "Why are you thinking these things? Which is easier to say to the paralyzed man? 'Your sins are forgiven'? or 'Get up, pick up your stretcher and walk'?"

"Who gives you the power to heal here on Earth?" asked Ya'ir. He turned to the crowd. "People, consider this. What kind of power must this man have to control demons and sickness. Where does he get such authority?"

Yeshua looked at Ya'ir and shook his head sadly. "I will prove to you that the Son of Man has authority on earth to forgive sins." He then turned to the paralyzed man and said, "I say to you: get up, pick up your stretcher and go home!"

The man did not move for a moment, but then kicked out his legs as if in great pain. The man said not one word, but quickly jumped to his feet and grabbed his mat. He pushed his way through the crowd of stunned onlookers.

Unmoving, mouth open, John could not believe this sudden turn of events. Only moments ago, he watched his masters trap Yeshua. Now, the Natzerene had not only addressed the priest's charges, he had humiliated John's masters and given the crowd more reason to worship him than before.

Someone shouted, "He is from Adonai, God!" Others said, "We've never seen anything like this." Several accused Ya'ir and Sha'ul of lying. "We have seen extraordinary things today," they said.

Yeshua said no more. John's eyes locked with the man from Natzeret. John saw a look of love and compassion but sensed that even though Yeshua had won, he received no personal satisfaction from the victory.

The cries of the crowd tore John away from the Natzerene. They must sense the trap that the priests had laid before Yeshua. They began to turn on the priests, and John. For their own safety, Ya'ir and Sha'ul withdrew to the safety of the streets, to the jeers of the crowd.

John grabbed a cloth and began drying Ya'ir's feet. Philo did the same with Sha'ul's, both boys silent as they prepared their masters to enter Nakdimon's house.

"This will not go well for us," said Ya'ir.

Sha'ul only nodded in agreement.

The men stood and entered the house. John removed his own sandals and began cleaning the dust from his feet, as Philo did the same.

"I cannot believe that Ya'ir is in this situation," John said, as he began drying his feet.

"And I can say the same about Sha'ul," said Philo.

"How did Yeshua turn things around so quickly?"

Philo only shrugged as both boys followed their masters inside.

The two priests stood at the entryway to the main living space, waiting to be announced. When all was ready, they entered, John and Philo behind them.

Inside stood Nakdimon and the visitor from Yerushalayim, Yosef.

"What do you have to report? Did you see the Natzerene?"

Ya'ir nodded, and then proceeded to tell Nakdimon what had transpired. As the story concluded, Nakdimon's face twisted in rage.

"Fools!" screamed Nakdimon. "Imbeciles. You were supposed to prove him incompetent to the crowds, not have him prove you unfit to teach."

John had never seen Nakdimon so angry. Ya'ir just stood there, saying nothing.

Nakdimon turned to Yosef. "Forgive the inadequacy of my servants. We must inform Yerushalayim what has been done."

Yosef remained silent. Nakdimon sat down to compose a letter. Everyone in the house remained silent until he finished.

Nakdimon turned to Sha'ul. "I trust that only your talmid will be able to get this letter safely to his father. May I ask that you release him from your service temporarily so he may preform this important task?"

Sha'ul nodded.

Nakdimon called Philo forward. "Please deliver this to your father, Kayafa," he said as he handed the letter to Philo. "And let him know that the next time we confront this man, I will make sure it is done correctly."

10

A Revelation

Dear Philo,

It's hard to believe it has been a month since you left for Yerushalayim. So much has happened since we last saw each other. I'm not sure where to begin.

My assignment this week is to practice my penmanship by writing a letter to someone. I could think of no one else I would want to write to than you. You'll have to let me know if it is legible.

Since our last confrontation with the Natzerene, Nakdimon has refused any attempts to confront Yeshua publicly. I, along with Nakdimon's, Ya'ir's, and Sha'ul's other apprentices, have shadowed Yeshua and his followers whenever they are in town. I have followed him many times over the last few weeks, but Nakdimon has given us strict instructions not to engage them in any public debate. Instead, Nakdimon wants us to wait until he is alone, then come and get the P'rushim. Nakdimon wants to confront him with authority.

I must tell you, old friend, I don't agree with this position. Even if we do succeed in trapping this man in a lie, he will have time to think up a better answer before we can bring him before the people.

But Nakdimon's decision is to limit potential damage should Yeshua twist our words, before the confrontation spreads among the populace. So, I continue in my studies, and occasionally shadow this stranger when required.

It finally happened yesterday. Yeshua had spent the morning teaching near the shores of the lake. I took over the surveillance at noon. Rather than going into town to someone's home for a meal, Yeshua walked straight to the Roman garrison.

I watched as his talmidim refused to follow him into the complex. It was one thing to talk in rebellious tones to your followers in the wilderness. It was quite another thing to speak it directly to your oppressors. His talmidim knew Rome was not lenient of rebels seeking the freedom of Y'hudah, and had already put to death many thousands of Jews with more power than Yeshua.

When Yeshua entered the complex alone, I sent the apprentice with me to fetch Nakdimon while I followed Yeshua.

Old friend, I could not believe what happened next. Yeshua showed no fear as he walked the outer courtyard. He spoke not a word, but walked amongst the tables where the officials sat with their scales and their papyrus lists.

Do you remember Levi Ben-Halfai? He worked at his tax-collection booth and did not notice Yeshua as he approached.

"Follow me," Yeshua said to him. Levi thought about the offer for only a moment, and then put away his reeds and his papyrus lists. He took the monies he collected and placed them into a leather satchel, which he handed to a startled Roman officer.

"Levi," his co-workers called, "Where are you going? Why do you follow him and leave your job empty? You won't get it back if you leave now."

I must confess, old friend, I do not understand what causes these types of reactions. First Sh'imon, now Levi. What is it about this man that makes seemingly sane people leave their jobs and drop everything when he comes?

Getting back to my story, as he was leaving, Levi addressed his friends. "I know who this man is, and some day, you will too. You need to hear what he has to say. I invite all of you to my house for a meal. I want you to meet my new teacher and learn what he has to say. I know the message he brings. It is a message all of you need to hear."

After Levi left, the entire courtyard began talking about what had just happened. I followed Yeshua and Levi until I met with Nakdimon, who was approaching. I told him everything that had happened.

So tonight, I will accompany the P'rushim as they confront the Natzerene at the home of Levi. Nakdimon is certain that none of Yeshua's talmidim will be there and doubts any followers would dare enter the home of a tax *collector, especially if Roman officials and the others Levi invited are there.*

We have waited weeks for such an opportunity to trap this man, and this may be the best chance we get. I will write to you again tomorrow to tell you what happened.

I hope your father will send you back to us soon.

John

Nakdimon, Sha'ul, Ya'ir, and several of their apprentices met at Nakdimon's house and began the short walk to Levi's.

"Master," John asked Ya'ir, "Do you think this will work?"

Ya'ir glanced at Nakdimon, who did not appear to hear John's question. "What is, is," he said rather cryptically. "I'm sure Nakdimon knows what he is doing."

"Well I'm not," John muttered under his breath. He spoke loudly enough for only Ya'ir to hear. "We have been shadowing this man for weeks, trying to engage him alone. Now, suddenly, Nakdimon wants to confront him in front of a house filled with tax collectors and sinners?"

Ya'ir shushed John to keep his voice down. "Don't let Nakdimon hear you talk like this. We highly doubt any of Yeshua's followers will be here. In fact, I believe that having these tax collectors and sinners, as you call them, will benefit us. They will question Yeshua just as vehemently as we will. Try not to doubt, little one."

When they reached Levi's house, John was amazed at its size. It had to be the largest home he had ever seen, not counting Herod's palace. Like many of the tax collectors, Levi had a habit of taking extra money for his efforts and he had amassed a considerable fortune. The courtyard in front contained a garden, where many of his guests drank wine and acted wild. John saw several men passed out from the wine, along with several women of questionable character with the men.

Inside, it was no different. Men and women ran around, many of them drunk. The priests moved through the house carefully, trying not to interact with the other guests, as if they could become drunk from mere touch.

"So, now we see the kind of man this Natzerene really

is," said Sha'ul. "Appearing all holy and righteous around our people, but acting like a madman, getting drunk and," Sha'ul pointed a shaking finger at two men in a corner, "Acting like that when they are alone."

John felt he had to speak up. "Master, I do not see any of his followers. Many of these people are the tax collectors and Roman officials from the courtyard. I don't see even one of Yeshua's men here."

"Are you sure?" asked Ya'ir, looking around. "There are a lot of people here, and it is dark. Could you be mistaken?"

"No, I remember faces. None of these people have I ever seen at one of his teachings."

"Let's keep moving. Maybe he's at the rear of the house."

A large man with food and drink liberally sprinkled on his beard and shirt came forward. John recognized him as another tax collector who worked with Levi, another Jew working for the Roman occupiers. "Aren't you the priest from the Temple?" he said to Ya'ir. His slurred words made it apparent he had been drinking heavily. "What are you doing here? Are you a friend of Levi's?"

The man placed his arm around Ya'ir's shoulder. He made it look like an act of friendship, but John thought it was more to help him keep his balance.

Ya'ir removed it with disgust. "I am a friend to all, but I am here on official Temple business. Where is Levi? Is he the one pouring all this wine for his friends?"

The man tried to laugh, but it made him weave back and forth. "Levi, giving us wine? That's rich. No, since he met that fellow, he has no use for it. He dumped all of his wine before dinner. Darn rude of him, if you ask me. Invite us to a meal and deliver no wine. We had to bring our own. He's back there with his new friends, if you want to ask him yourself." The man belched and pointed into a room in the back. He then scratched himself before staggering past them and out into the crowds.

The three priests pushed through the mingled guests and entered a large dining room. Along the windows hung curtains made from a material John had never seen before. They seemed to shine in the lamplight. Although four dozen men could easily stand in here, only about two dozen sat quietly on the floor, listening intently to Yeshua.

Strewn upon the table were the remnants of a great feast. Two spits of roast, one lamb and one goat, occupied each end, cut down to the bones. Earthenware pots surrounded them, their covers removed, a variety of vegetables, beans, lentils, cucumbers, leeks and onions plastered to their sides. Servants passed the dessert of nuts, melons, figs, grapes, and sweet fried cakes. Woven reed baskets of goat cheese and wild honey were available for anyone who wanted it.

Yeshua sat under one window, with Shim'on on his left and Levi on his right.

"Master," John whispered to Ya'ir, "I recognize only Shim'on as one of his followers. All the others are tax collectors and Roman officials."

Yeshua saw the men enter and smiled. In the silence, all eyes turned to the priests in the doorway. Ya'ir's eyes filled with rage at the scene before him. He turned to Shim'on and asked, "Why does he eat with tax collectors and sinners?"

Nakdimon tried to quiet Ya'ir, but he was too late. Shim'on and Levi stood, ready to defend their teacher from attack, but Yeshua calmed them and addressed the priests. "The ones who need a doctor aren't the healthy, but the sick. I didn't come to call the 'righteous' but sinners!"

Nakdimon quieted Ya'ir, telling him not to speak. Then he addressed Yeshua. "Our Scriptures give many definitions of sinners, Teacher," he said. "Our laws require us to fast annually at the Day of Atonement, but my colleagues and I, we fast twice a week, on Mondays and Thursdays, as an act of piety. We observe fixed daily hours of prayers and take part in a weekly communal meal. We, not you, are the models of piety for this community. Do you not even know the very Scriptures you say you are here to teach?"

Yeshua said nothing.

"I am the one ordained by Adonai to preach His Word, not you. I am the High Priest of K'far-Nachum, who offers the lamb sacrifice to the Lord. Do you not understand the words of God?"

Shim'on pushed past Yeshua and stood within an arm's distance of Nakdimon. "He understands all; it is you who are blind. You hide behind your robes and traditions. Hear what He teaches, and maybe you, too, can learn."

Nakdimon took a deep breath, as if controlling the swelling anger within him. He looked around at all of the plates and cups, the waste left after the great meal. "Why is it that Yochanan's talmidim and the talmidim of the P'rushim fast, but your talmidim don't fast?"

Yeshua considered Nakdimon's question only a moment, and then asked, "Can wedding guests fast while the bridegroom is still with them? As long as they have the bridegroom with them, fasting is out of the question. But the time will come when the bridegroom is taken away from them; and when that day comes, they will fast."

John gasped at the implication. His teacher fasted with the other priests as part of their ordinary life. This is what the Tanakh required. Yeshua and his followers ate as part of their ordinary life. Was Yeshua saying that fasting was proper, but it is out of place in ordinary life, especially as a regular practice to advertise one's holiness?

Nakdimon had no response. This man had just declared their entire order in error.

As John had seen him do in the past, Yeshua gave Nakdimon a story, a lesson to understand. "No one sews a piece of unshrunk cloth on an old coat; if he does, the new patch tears away from the old cloth and leaves a worse hole." Yeshua held on to his own dusty clothing, as if to emphasize his point that new and old do not mix. "And no one puts new wine in old wineskins, if he does, the wine will burst the skins, and both the wine and the skins will be ruined. Rather, new wine is for freshly prepared wineskins."

Nakdimon closed his eyes and sighed deeply.

John saw what Yeshua was doing. He claimed their old, trusted traditions were about to be thrown away for his new ways. John looked about. This sinners and tax collectors, the ones Nakdimon seemed sure would not support Yeshua, now listened intently to the man's story. It was apparent they began to see and follow what Yeshua said.

John feared the worst. Yeshua again was turning Nakdimon's attack around on to the priests. If this conversation continued, John imagined the tax collectors supporting Yeshua. If that happened, he wondered how the citizens, Yeshua's regular followers, would react.

Could Nakdimon turn this to their advantage? Or would the support of these people further erode their position?

Nakdimon turned and left quickly, followed by the rest of the P'rushim. John hesitated only a moment, and then followed his masters.

Outside, Nakdimon's anger almost got the better of him. "How dare he accuse us in front of all of those people. Who does he think he is?"

Ya'ir responded, "That's easy. He thinks he is God. To him, those miraculous signs are all the proof he needs for him to believe God is with him."

"This is the same thing that happened to us when we confronted him," said Sha'ul. "He certainly has no respect for our way and our traditions."

"Or us," added Ya'ir.

Nakdimon calmed down. He turned to the other two men. "There is nothing more for us to do here now. Go to your homes and get some rest. Pray Adonai will show us how to deal with this man. We will meet again soon."

11

A New Threat

"My father sends you urgent news," Philo said in a most authoritative voice. Each trip to and from Yerushalayim took three days, and Philo had made four such trips since the incident at Levi's home. As he delivered one important message after another, he became more and more arrogant. Ya'ir recognized this, and spoke about it to John on more than one occasion, but there was little that could be done. With these matters, Kayafa trusted no one. That meant his son, whom he had only recently named a talmid, was in a position to instruct Nakdimon.

"My father is very upset with your lack of progress in resolving this matter," Philo stated. "Stronger measures need to be addressed. This man must be stopped before Rome finds out."

"What would your father ask us to do?" asked Sha'ul. "We have taken this man on and so far he has eluded our efforts to entrap him."

Philo was beginning to act less and less like a messenger. "You are the senior leaders here. It is you who should be telling me what you will do, not your talmid for direction."

Philo took a deep breath. "My father and I have talked at length about this. I have explained to him your difficulties in trapping this man. This Yeshua is cunning and deceitful. It's almost like he has a spy in our P'rushim, telling him everything we are planning."

Philo looked at John as he said this, implying he was running to Yeshua after every meeting and telling him what had been decided. John did not like the implication, and was about to say something when Philo cut him off.

"My father knows it will be difficult to get him to speak blasphemy in front of his followers. You are the leaders of your people. You are the only ones who can point out his lies and falsehoods to the masses. Use your knowledge. If you can't get him to speak his lies, than get him to break the Laws, the very Laws you guard."

Philo leaned in closer so everyone could hear. "Our Laws command us to rest on Shabbat, but he continues to preach and heal. Confront him. Get him to admit he has no regard for the Sabbath. Then we can arrest him and put an end to this."

What a brilliant idea, John thought. Use his own teachings against him.

Nakdimon pondered Philo's statement. "This is a good strategy, though risky. Confronting this man in our Temple in front of his followers has many dangers."

"Yes, not in the Temple," added Sha'ul. "Perhaps outside, as he headed in to speak."

Everyone in the Council agreed to Philo's suggestion. Now they needed only to wait two days until Shabbat.

If Yeshua saw the delegation of priests arrive and stand before him, he was not intimidated or concerned.

Standing to Ya'ir's left, John recognized a local beggar named Titus. John had spent many days at his mother's booth in the marketplace while Titus came and begged for even the rotten fish to eat. Titus could not work because his entire left hand was turned in so his fingers were touching his wrist. The man did not say a word, but Yeshua watched him very closely. "Come up where we can see you!" Yeshua said to the man. Titus looked around as if there might be someone else Yeshua was talking to, but, when he knew it was him, he slowly walked up to Yeshua.

Yeshua turned and looked at Ya'ir. "What is permitted on the Sabbath? Doing good or doing evil? Saving life or killing?"

Ya'ir looked to Nakdimon for help, but Nakdimon shook his head slightly, as if to remind him of the pact they had made. No one from the P'rushim said a word.

Yeshua's fists balled in annoyance at their unwillingness to answer. The priests remained silent, stoic, unmoving, and unwilling to get into a verbal argument in the synagogue.

Yeshua apparently decided not to try to engage the men in a debate. Instead, he did something that surprised John. He turned to the local man who stood in front of them.

"Hold out your hand," said Yeshua.

The man looked confused, and a bit embarrassed. Reluctantly, and a little slowly, he brought his hand up from his side, where he had tried to hide it from the crowd. As he straightened his arm, his fingers pulled away from his wrist. He spread his fingers, as if reaching for fruit. He held the hand, the now normal hand, up high for the whole crowd to see. There was much murmuring and gasps as the newly cured man stood before them.

Murmurs ran through the crowd like rippled waves on the lake. There was no silencing them. Nakdimon had lost the opportunity. With the gathred people in wonderment, he could not point out this act, however generous to the men, was in direct violation of their own long held traditions. They left the Temple quickly.

Outside, Nakdimon's anger blazed. "He attacks everything we stand for. He mocks everything we hold sacred."

The other priests were equally upset. John saw the anger in their faces. "If we allow this man to continue," said Ya'ir, "we will lose everything, our positions of respect in this community, our livelihood, our very way of life."

The priests spoke for several minutes, alone, outside the Temple doors. "Like Yochanan before him," said Ya'ir, "we have to consider we cannot stand against this man on our own. His fame amongst our people is too great. We must look again to Herod to have him arrested."

"Not Herod," said Philo. "My father has received reports Yochanan is still imprisoned in Herod's palace but Herod spends much time talking to him."

The other men seemed surprised. "What would Herod have to say to that wild man?"

Philo looked pleased to see he had information the others did not. "Herod respects Yochanan. He considers him to be a good and holy man."

"No!" said the men, collectively.

"That's not all," added Philo. "Yochanan is under Herod's protection. No one can see him or speak to him without Herod's permission."

John gasped. "Has Yochanan corrupted the tetrarch's

mind?" he asked.

Philo shook his head. "Herod is disturbed whenever he speaks with Yochanan, but even so, he likes to listen to him."

"We need to keep Yeshua from Herod," said Ya'ir.

"No," said Nakdimon. "We need to move quickly before Herod's help is lost to us."

"But we can't risk Herod hearing this man talk," said Ya'ir. "He will easily complete whatever Yochanan has started."

"He must be put to death," said Philo.

The priests looked at Philo horrified. "Jew killing Jew?" Nakdimon asked. "This is not our way."

John slid away from the conversation. He had understood the need for Yochanan's arrest, but this talk of killing made his stomach ill. He could not stand to be near Philo for another second. He sank backwards between the arguing men until he was outside the circle, then swung around and headed down the street. He had no destination in mind other than to be away from the discussion. He found himself wandering the streets, not sure where to go or who to talk to about everything that troubled him. His mind thought of different possibilities, and then suddenly he knew who he needed to see. He walked up to the door he knew well and slowly opened it.

"John!" The smile on his mother's face as she saw him brought a tear to his eye. He quickly wiped it away before she noticed.

John placed his arms around his mother and squeezed tightly. "Hello, Mama," John said, with a smile. It really felt right to be back in his home again.

"Let me look at you, let me look at you. My, you look all grown up and handsome."

John was blushing. "Mama, I'm still the same boy I was when I left here five months ago."

His mother shook her head. "You may feel like the same boy, but I can see you are different, more grown up, more sure of yourself. I can see it in your walk and in your eyes."

John spent many hours alone with his mother, telling her about his studies. He told her about Herod's palace, though not the reason for the visit. She listened as only a mother can.

Finally, he got to the reason for his visit. "Mother, have you seen Myriam?"

His mother was startled at the question. "Myriam? Why do you want to see her?"

John did not answer.

"John," she said in a soothing tone, "can you not tell your mother what is going on?"

John knew his mother would disagree with what he been doing. That knowledge made him question whether he should continue.

"But I can't really say," he said.

"All right, if you can't tell your mother, then you can't tell your mother. I don't like secrets. She has come to visit several times, along with her mother."

John's mother was one of the few people who talked to Myriam's mother, because of her condition.

"Wait here," she said.

John was alone in the only home he had ever known, a home that now felt very alien to him. It had all happened so quickly. For years, he had dreamed of having good clothes and good things to eat. He looked around the meager house. It was nothing to be ashamed of, yet he was. He hated to admit it, but he had begun to love his new lifestyle. He knew he should not feel this way, but he suddenly felt superior to his mother and all the others who lived like this.

"John," said a soft voice. "You wanted to see me?" Myriam poked her head through the doorway.

"I must go meet your Papa and David," said his mother. "You two stay and talk." She quickly disappeared out through the front, communal courtyard.

John offered her a seat next to him. "A lot has happened to you in the past five months," said Myriam. "I heard about your visit to Mattityahu's."

John seemed puzzled. "Who?"

Myriam smiled. "I guess you haven't heard. Yeshua has renamed Levi the tax collector Mattityahu."

John said nothing.

"Why did you want to see me then?" she asked.

John could not look her in the face. "Nakdimon and the others have vowed to stop him, you know," he said. "They will not stop until Yeshua is either discredited or imprisoned."

"I know," she said. "Why are you telling me this?"

John took a deep breath then looked her straight in the eye. "I don't want you to be hurt by it."

She smiled and took his hand. "John," she said, "I was hurt and upset when they arrested Yochanan. Those things you and Philo said, they hurt me. I have seen Yeshua up close. I understand Him now, and I have faith He will do all the things He promises."

John shook his head. "No, he won't. The P'rushim met this morning." John took a deep breath. "By this time next week, he will be in prison."

Myriam laughed. "Is your P'rushim really so arrogant? God allowed you to arrest Yochanan, because Yochanan's mission had ended. But this man, His mission is just beginning."

John got angry. "Why do you defend him? What is so great about this man? How has he so clouded your judgment?"

John's anger did not stop Myriam. "It is you who has had his judgment clouded. You've seen this man, you've seen His miracles. How can you not believe what He says?"

"This man is not a rabbi. He is not a teacher or a priest. He has no formal training in the Law. He is the son of a carpenter. Where does he get his knowledge?"

It was Myriam's turn to be angry. "Why are you the only ones who can interpret the Laws? Just because you are a follower of Ya'ir doesn't give you his wisdom. All that does is make you knowledgeable in the Laws." She took a deep breath to calm herself down. "If you would just come and listen," she said.

"I have listened," argued John.

"But only as a student, with Ya'ir and Nakdimon and all the others. Come listen as you. Please?" Her eyes pleaded with him to follow her.

John considered her request. What harm would it do? Nakdimon himself had met this man without the P'rushim. "I will not speak to him," he said. "I have no desire to get into an argument with him."

Myriam's eyes grew excited. "Yes. No talking, just

listening. I promise it will change the way you think." She grabbed his hand and headed for the door.

He quickly took his hand back. "What, now?"

She smiled. "Can you think of any better time to start?"

Myriam and John ended up by the lakeshore. Behind them, the sun was starting to set. The last rays of its light struck the edge of the lakeshore, turning the waters blood red as it reflected the light. A large crowd stood by the shoreline. One of the boats had cast loose from the docks and moored several cubits off the beach. John recognized several of the men in the boat. The central figure he recognized as the Natzerene.

John had difficulty hearing him from the back, so he and Myriam worked their way through the crowd until they stood only a few feet from the water's edge.

Yeshua stood in the boat as he spoke to the crowd. The last lights of the setting sun shown on his face in sharp contrast to the darkening skies over the lake. The light settled on his robes, which glowed as if illuminated from inside. The whole effect made him appear as if he was a spirit, which greatly troubled John.

John looked around at the people in the crowd. Many of them he recognized. Many of them had been people he had seen at the marketplace, either merchants trying to eke out a living or customers trying to stretch their meager incomes to feed their families. Some of the men here were soldiers, though not from Rome. They were local men with local families, here to listen, not to arrest. Some were wealthy businessmen; the most important merchants in their city. Some were mothers and children, unaccustomed to standing out in the streets with the men, but grateful to be able to hear the message. John was impressed with the incredible diversity in the crowd. This man certainly appealed to a large cross section of the city's populace.

John listened to his message. He looked around at the people in the crowd as they listened. There was no pretense in their expressions, no hidden agendas in the way they took in the words. He compared their way of worshipping to Nakdimon's. He made a great show of how he spoke the prayers, where he spoke the prayers, and when he spoke the prayers. He made it a point to dress as lavishly as possible when he worshipped. It was more important to set an example than to pray, John began to suspect.

These people were not like that. They did not care how they dressed or where they were. In fact, they were standing on the shore of a lake, wearing the same clothes they had on that morning. The lake emitted a foul odor this evening, like rotting fish, but no one seemed to care. This was worship, pure worship, simple and true.

Yeshua was not teaching them the Laws, as Ya'ir did. He did not tell them how they should follow what Moshe put down, or what penalties they should pay if they broke a rule. John did not even hear once anything he recognized from the scrolls he had memorized. Instead, Yeshua was telling a story.

"Listen! A farmer went out to sow his seed. As he sowed, some seed fell alongside the path, and the birds came and ate it up."

John watched the reactions of the followers. Several he recognized as farmers, who could easily visualize themselves walking along with a bag of seed across their shoulders. Others had at one time or another either planted seeds or seen farmers planting seeds. Taking large fistfuls of seed, the farmer would liberally spread the seed on his grounds. Often, flocks of large, black birds would follow the farmer for a quick meal. John listened to the rest of the story.

Yeshua continued. "Other seed fell on rocky patches where there was not much soil. It sprouted quickly because the soil was shallow; but when the sun rose, the young plants were scorched; and since their roots were not deep, they dried up," he said.

This John could understand. He had seen many plants like that, here one day and gone the next.

"Other seed fell among thorns," Yeshua said, "which grew up and choked it so that it yielded no grain." John had seen many farmers throw their seed in patches of weeds. Seed was cheap and the farmer's time was short. It made no sense for them to save a few handfuls from the thorny patches.

"But other seed fell into rich soil and produced grain; it

sprouted, and grew, and yielded a crop—thirty, sixty, even a hundred times what was sown."

This was how a farmer raised the crops not only for his family but also for the rest of the town. Good soil brought good crops.

Then Yeshua said, "Whoever has ears to hear with, let him hear!" He finished, and those on the boat with him brought it back to shore. He disembarked and headed into town. Most of the crowd followed him, although many went to their own homes.

Soon, he sat by himself with Myriam.

"What did you think?" she asked.

What could he think? The man did not say anything. He talked about some farmer making a living, but nothing else. Where was the discussion of God? Where was the discussion of the Laws?

"I don't know what to think," he admitted.

Myriam seemed disappointed. "Didn't you understand?" she asked.

"All I heard him talk about was farming. If I was a farmer, it might have made sense to me. Where was the talk of the Law?"

"Is that all you think about?" she asked. "Can you not see beyond your own thoughts? He's not here to teach the Laws. We have enough of you doing that already.

"He was speaking about the Kingdom of God. How we can spread the news throughout the land. How, as He walks around preaching, different people hear different things."

John shook his head. "I didn't hear anything."

"That's because you haven't opened up your mind to listen. You're still trying to force His words into your own ways of thinking. Expand your mind, and then you'll understand."

"I don't have any idea what you mean. I only know the way I worship, the way my father did, and his fathers before him. There is no other way."

Myriam closed her eyes and clasped both hands across her face. She sighed then continued. "I know. This is why you struggle so much. I hope God can open your eyes and your heart so you can understand."

She left him there alone with his thoughts.

12

An Invitation

A month had passed since John had last seen Yeshua or Myriam. He continued to excel at his studies with Ya'ir, and, without the Natzerene around to follow or argue with, John began to feel almost normal.

Just after morning prayers, his sense of normalcy ended as he heard a familiar voice outside the door in Ya'ir's courtyard.

"Hey, Fishface," said Philo. "Are you still stuck here? I thought you'd have been running this place by now."

John jumped up, put down his study papers and rushed out to see his old friend.

"Philo, when did you get back? How is Yerushalayim? What word do you have on the Natzerene?" John yelled as he raced to hug his friend.

"Slow down, slow down. One at a time. I have a lot to tell the P'rushim, but we can talk before they assemble. I'm here to get your master. Can you let him know that Nakdimon needs him to come now?"

John went back into the house and found Ya'ir, who agreed to come immediately. John returned to the courtyard to visit with his friend.

As John tied his sandals, Philo remarked, "You haven't changed a bit."

John looked up to see his friend silhouetted by the morning sun. He squinted to block out some of the rays. "Really? Everyone says I'm different."

"Well, I'm sure they don't know you as well as I do."

John smirked at the comment and rose.

"Come, walk with me," said Philo.

"What about my master?"

"I'm sure that he knows the way."

John hesitated and Philo read the concern in his eyes. "Don't worry, you won't get in trouble. If Ya'ir says anything, I will tell him it was all my fault."

Reluctantly, John started to follow his friend, glancing back to the door to see if Ya'ir was coming until they were no longer in the courtyard.

"The reports my father's been getting have been highly complimentary of you. You have been a huge asset in keeping track of the Natzerene."

John was amazed that any report to Kayafa would even mention him, much less praise him. John was embarrassed, and tried to change the subject. "What is Yerushalayim like?"

Philo took a deep breath, and a smile crossed his face. "Yerushalayim is the most beautiful place I have ever seen. The Temple that Herod built is the most amazing building in the world. It is truly a work of art by itself. And huge." Philo's face alit as he described it. "I have never seen such a building anywhere in the world. It rivals anything any Gentile country could build. You need to come and see it."

John longed to go to Yerushalayim. He had heard so many amazing things about it, and now that Philo had been there, he felt a twinge of jealousy that his friend had seen it before he did.

Things became quiet as they walked. John took a deep breath, and then asked the question that was most on his mind.

"Have you heard anything about Yeshua?"

Philo's smile left his face at Yeshua's name. "That is why my father sent me back. That is what I am here to talk to the P'rushim about. Things are beginning to unravel."

John shuddered at the thought. Because Yeshua had not been around for several weeks, he assumed that things had begun to calm down.

"What has happened?"

Philo hesitated. "You'll hear most of this in a few minutes, but I can tell you what I know. The Natzerene," Philo could not come to call the man by name, "has been wandering about Galil with his followers. Great numbers follow him from all around through Y'hudah, Yerushalayim, Idumea, the territory beyond the Yarden, and the Tzor-Tzidon area."

John gasped at the thought. He had always assumed, apparently incorrectly, that Yeshua was only a local problem, as Yochanan had been. This man must be moving a lot to have been to all these towns since they last saw him.

"But that is not the worst. His talmidim travel the Galil as emissaries. They preach his filth even when the Natzerene is not there."

"How many are there?"

Philo stopped at the steps to Nakdimon's home and sat down to remove his sandals. "He has twelve who are close to him, that he calls his talmidim. The first and closest to him is—"

"Shim'on?" John interrupted.

"Yes, the fisherman from our town. But he no longer goes by that name. The Natzerene has given him another name, Kefa."

"Why Kefa?"

"Because it means 'rock' in our ancient Aramaic."

John didn't understand why Yeshua kept renaming his followers. Philo continued.

"There is also Ya'akov Ben-Zavdai, and Yochanan, Ya'akov's brother—to them he gave the name "B'nei-Regesh.""

"The Thunderers?" asked John.

"Apparently, your old nemeses have shown some fiery zeal for this man."

John thought about how the boys had tormented him in the past. He couldn't imagine them using their "skills" to help Yeshua. "That's three. Who else does he have? I know about Levi."

"You mean Mattityahu. Yes, he is now part of the Natzerene's inner circle, as is Andrew, Philip, Bar-Talmai, T'oma, Ya'akov Ben-Halfai, Taddai, Shim'on the Zealot and Y'hudah from K'riot."

John had not heard of or met any of those others. "I don't know anything about them."

"Nor would I expect you to." Philo stood, barefoot and ready to enter Nakdimon's house. "We know little about them also. That is why I am here, to see if we can learn about these men. Bar Talmai, we believe, is the son of an Egyptian ruler. Shim'on the Zealot is, of course, a member of the Zealots."

John knew this group. They were a dangerous fringe of men set on revolt against their Roman conquerors. "Is he recruiting for war against Rome?"

"That is what we have to determine." Philo turned and disappeared into the dark hallway. With nothing else to do, John followed him.

It had been two weeks since Philo's return with the news that Yeshua's band had grown and become a much greater threat. Nakdimon had immediately pledged to gather intelligence on Yeshua and his followers and bring it to Kayafa. As before, he placed Ya'ir, and by default John, in charge of this task.

But Yeshua remained outside the borders of their town. Part of John's daily tasks now included trying to gather information about Yeshua's whereabouts. He turned to Myriam first, but when she realized what his intentions were, she refused to give him any information. Other townsfolk were less skeptical, almost daring the P'rushim to take on this man, so sure were they that the Natzerene would win.

It was during one of these excursions that John noticed a large crowd gathering around one of the homes on the eastern side of town, away from the docks and merchant stalls. As John approached, he heard whispers and excitement announcing that Yeshua was in the house teaching again.

"Is it Yeshua?" John asked one of the men on the fringe of the crowd.

When the man saw John and his robe, he turned without speaking.

John grabbed at another man and asked the same question, and got the same response.

He saw a woman and two boys standing just a few feet off from the edge of the crowd. John approached them.

"Do you know Yeshua of Natzeret?" he asked.

The woman turned to see who was asking the question. John did not recognize her, but he immediately felt a connection with her, though he did not know why. Her robes were caked with dust and dirt, as if she had traveled a great distance. The two boys with her were similarly dirty. Her hair was long and dark under a formerly white scarf. He guessed she was older than his own mother, but her eyes were young and alive.

She smiled at his question. "I should hope so. He is my son."

Her answer caught John off guard. He had considered many things about Yeshua, but until this moment, he had never given a thought to his having a family.

"Do you know my son?" she asked.

John wasn't sure how to answer. "I have met him," he finally responded.

"And what do you think of what He is doing?" she asked.

John sought to avoid the question. "What do you think about what he is doing?"

"We think he's out of his mind!" one of the boys said.

John smirked at the boy's impetuousness.

The woman shushed him quiet. "Do not mind what my sons say."

John wanted to speak to the woman longer, but knew he must let his master know that Yeshua had returned. He hastily bid her farewell and ran to Ya'ir's house.

"His own brother said that?" asked Nakdimon, as they walked briskly to the house.

"Yes, Master," said John. "'We think he's out of his mind,' were his exact words."

"I wonder if this sentiment is shared by his mother?" asked Yosef.

"It would make things easier for us if we could get her to take him back to Natzeret," added Ya'ir.

Nakdimon forced his way into the house, with Ya'ir and Yosef close behind. Philo and John followed the three men in.

Yeshua stood in the middle of the room, his twelve talmidim sitting in a circle surrounding him. John recognized the man standing next to Yeshua. He was another of the poor souls who lived in their town, by the name of Cabul. He often sat along the streets to the Temple begging, unable to see, hear, or speak.

All eyes turned to see the priests entering. Whatever Yeshua had been speaking about disappeared as the room grew silent. Yeshua reached over and, without a word, placed his hands on the mute man's ears, and then over his eyes. John swore he could actually see color returning to the man's irises, so sudden was the transformation.

The man glanced around, taking in the setting and the people. "I can see," he said, that single sentence extolling the fact that not only was his sight restored, but also his speech.

Nakdimon and Ya'ir exchanged nervous glances. Yosef exhibited no change in his appearance, but Philo looked shocked.

Someone in the back of the room shouted, "This couldn't be the Son of David, could it?"

The phrase terrified John because of the implications. David had been their strongest and mightiest king. "Son of David" could only mean the crowd expected this Yeshua to take up that mantle. John knew if that happened, the people would seek to break from the control of Rome, and war would ensue, a war they would most certainly lose.

Nakdimon moved quickly to quiet the crowd. "He has Ba'al-Zibbul in him," he said.

Yosef took up the call. "It is by the ruler of the demons that he expels the demons."

Yeshua smiled, not at all the reaction John was expecting. Again the man did not seem afraid of these religious rulers. He approached Nakdimon.

"How can Satan expel Satan?" Yeshua asked.

Nakdimon did not answer.

John immediately understood what he was saying. If this man was truly from Satan, then he would not undermine the work of his demons. That wouldn't make sense. If anything, he would be trying to bring more under the control of demons.

"If a kingdom is divided against itself, that kingdom can't survive, and if a household is divided against itself, that household can't survive. So if Satan has rebelled against himself and is divided, he can't survive either; and that's the end of him," Yeshua said.

Dozens in the crowd nodded their approval. To John, the logic was impeccable. He thought back to the meeting with Yeshua's family. Is this how an insane man thinks? Surely no one who is losing his mind can make such leaps of pure logic in such a short amount of time.

With the Torah-teachers silent, Yeshua took the opportunity to expound on his point. "Furthermore, no one can break into a strong man's house and make off with his possessions unless he first ties up the strong man. After that, he can ransack his house."

Yosef finally pulled out of his silence. "He has an unclean spirit in him. This is how he can say, 'I forgive sins.' Only Adonai forgives sins."

Yeshua pounced on the opening. "Yes! I tell you that people will be forgiven all sins and whatever blasphemies they utter. However, someone who blasphemes against the Ruach HaKodesh never has forgiveness but is guilty of an eternal sin."

Upon hearing this, Yosef turned and left, with Nakdimon and Ya'ir close behind. Philo lingered momentarily then followed the other men, leaving John there alone. John felt all eyes on him, and he suddenly felt unworthy to be in that room.

John remembered his meeting earlier, and sought to change the direction of the discussion. "Your mother and brothers are outside asking for you," John said.

If Yeshua was surprised by this comment, he didn't show it. "Who are my mother and my brothers?" He walked around the outer ring of his followers, touching each of his twelve on the head. "See! Here are my mother and my brothers! Whoever does what God wants is my brother, sister, and mother!"

John didn't know how to respond. Without any support and alone, he felt extremely vulnerable. He turned and the crowd parted without saying a word to let him through.

Outside, he found his master and friends. "What happened?" asked Nakdimon. "Why did you stay so long?"

John told them about what he and Yeshua said to each other.

Nakdimon looked disappointed. "It would have been good to have his mother on our side, trying to shut him down."

Yosef nodded in agreement. "I can make inquiries with my colleagues as to the status of his family. This is not an idea we had before."

Ya'ir shook his head. "No, if he has disowned his family, as it seems he has, then we cannot use anything they say against him."

John piped up. "Couldn't we ask his mother to take him back to Natzeret? Surely if he was in her presence, she might be able to talk some sense into him."

The others laughed at the thought. "I'm afraid if his mother believes what she believes and had the ability to do what you suggest, she would already have done it," said Ya'ir.

"I agree," said Nakdimon. "I don't think this is an area we can exploit."

With no clear idea what steps next to take, the priests turned and began the walk back to Nakdimon's. John and philo followed a few steps behind.

Months passed and John continued with his studies, memorization one day, writing another, and just observing Ya'ir and his ways almost continuously. While copying one of the ancient scrolls, John was so deep in concentration that the knock on the door startled him.

"John, go and see who is here," said Ya'ir.

Sighing, he carefully replaced his pen in the inkwell and stood up. His legs were stiff from having sat for so long. He moved slowly as the visitor knocked for a third time.

He opened the door, blocking out the morning sun with his right hand. There was a figure there, though the head was bowed and he could not make out who it was.

"Yes, can I help you?" he asked.

"Forgive me, sir. I know it is not my place, but might I be allowed to speak to one of your apprentices, Yochanan Ben-Elioenai?"

John recognized the voice. "Myriam?"

The figure lifted her head and removed her veil.

John hurriedly left the house and closed the door quietly behind him. "What are you doing here?"

Myriam looked into his eyes then dropped her gaze in deference. "I know it is not my place. I know..." her voice trailed off.

"What do you know?" John demanded, a little more angrily than he meant to.

She did not respond to his question.

John grabbed her arm and forced her to look up at him.

"What is it Myriam? What has happened?" Myriam had a look of sadness and longing that made his heart melt.

"Yeshua," she said.

"Yes, what about him?"

She took a deep breath. "He is here, in town."

John was puzzled. He knew that Myriam did not approve of the plans the Council was making to have this man arrested. For the past few months, Yeshua had been far from K'far-Nachum, and they had not been able to move forward with their plans. This news would change that.

"Why are you telling me this? You know what I must do."

This time Myriam reached out to grab his arm, preventing him from returning into the house. "Don't do it. I beg you."

John sighed. "Myriam, why are you here?"

She bit her lower lip to keep it from trembling. "I need you to come with me. Not with Philo, not with Ya'ir. Just you, alone."

"Why me? What is going on?"

"I need you to hear Him speak. I need you to understand."

"I do not believe as you do," John said forcefully, making Myriam wince. "You know that. I've listened to him enough to know he is not who you think he is."

"And I've listened to Him enough to know that he is."

John turned away from her. "I can't do this."

Myriam continued to plead. "You must. Your life depends on it."

John turned back to her.

"He is here, down by the sea. He is talking about the Kingdom of Adonai."

John snorted. "He is always talking about the Kingdom of Adonai."

Myriam shook her head. "No, this is different. It is not about what you should do or how you should act. It is about what that kingdom will be like. John, He knows."

John's eyebrows furrowed as he tried to understand. "Knows what?"

Myriam's eyes alighted. "He knows what the Kingdom of Adonai is like."

John became intrigued. It was true, they all knew the rules and laws to follow to enter Adonai's Kingdom, but they did not know what it was like to be there.

"Come with me and see for yourself." Myriam took hold of his hand, and tugged him gently off the step.

"I can't," John protested. "I am in the middle of my studies."

"Think how much more important your studies will be if you know the truth about Adonai's Kingdom."

John hesitated, torn between his desire to be with her and his desire to be a good student. "I must let Ya'ir know where I am going."

"No," said Myriam. "Don't have the Council come and try to arrest this man. Just come and listen."

"Then what shall I tell him?"

"Tell him your mother is sick and needs you."

Lie to my master? John could not conceive of such a thing.

He opened the door and stuck his head in. "Master, I need to run an errand," he called out.

A voice floated in from the house. "Is it important?"

John looked at Myriam then turned to answer. "Yes, it is very important."

"You have one hour."

John bent down and grabbed his sandals, and quickly followed Myriam out of the courtyard.

When they arrived at the shoreline, there was already a large crowd gathered. Many stood listening intently to the Natzerene speak, while others lounged nearby, content only on being in the presence of Yeshua.

John pushed his way through the crowd with Myriam following. He heard some grumblings as he passed, and he suddenly felt very isolated and alone.

They arrived near the edge of the shore, and John saw the twelve talmidim lined against the edge of the sea. Yeshua, as seemed to be his custom, was preaching from a boat launched about a dozen feet from the shoreline.

"A lamp isn't brought in to be put under a bowl or under the bed, is it? Wouldn't you put it on a lamp stand?" said Yeshua.

John, like everyone around him, murmured in

agreement.

Yeshua continued. "Indeed, nothing is hidden, except to be disclosed; and nothing is covered up, except to come out into the open. Those who have ears to hear with, let them hear!"

When Yeshua mentioned ears to hear, John swore that he was looking straight at him.

"What does he mean?" he whispered to Myriam.

Myriam merely shushed him so they could continue to listen.

"Pay attention to what you are hearing!" Yeshua continued. "The measure with which you measure out will be used to measure to you—and more besides! For anyone who has something will be given more; but from anyone who has nothing, even what he does have will be taken away."

John gasped. "Is he saying that the rich will get richer while the poor will get poorer?"

Yeshua sat down, and Myriam seized the opportunity to explain to John. "You have to see it from His point of view. It is not about material things. It is about the Kingdom of Adonai. The lamp is what Yeshua is doing, spreading the good news about Adonai's Kingdom. Think about it, John, if you had some really good news, news that could change my life forever, would you tell me or would you keep it to yourself?"

John didn't have to think about his answer. "Of course I would tell you."

Myriam smiled. "I know you would. You're a good person. You want the best for the people you love."

So intent was John on what she was saying that he missed that last part. "So what you're saying is—"

"What I'm saying is, I know the truth. It is a truth that will set you free from the bondage of this life. John, I need you to hear and understand the truth."

John shook his head. "I don't accept this as truth."

"John, think about what measure you are using to measure yourself and others. It is the Laws of Moshe."

"Laws that have served us well for millennia."

"And all you can do is measure me by those same Laws, measure Yeshua by those Laws."

John was puzzled. "What are you saying?"

"Do you believe Adonai cares one jot or tittle if you wash your hands before a meal, or whether you pick grain on the Sabbath?"

"They are His Laws. He wrote them."

Myriam sighed. "What does washing your hands have to do with eternal salvation?"

John became indignant. "Only those who prove themselves worthy of Adonai because they have followed His Laws will receive eternal life."

Myriam shook her head. "You are wrong. And that is what Yeshua is saying. Live by the Laws. Follow the Laws, Judge others by the Laws, and that is all you will get. A bunch of empty Laws. Follow Yeshua, and learn what means to live free! I understand Yeshua, and because of that, my knowledge and understanding of the Kingdom of Adonai will only grow, while what little you understand will be taken from you."

Before John could reply, Yeshua stood again and began to speak, and those around him demanded he be quiet.

"The Kingdom of God is like a man who scatters seed on the ground. Nights he sleeps, days he's awake; and meanwhile the seeds sprout and grow—how, he doesn't know."

Myriam turned to John, almost as if to say, *I told you so.*

"By itself the soil produces a crop—first the stalk, then the head, and finally the full grain in the head. But as soon as the crop is ready, the man comes with his sickle, because it's harvest time."

John whispered to Myriam, "Again, he talks about farming. When will he talk about the Kingdom of God?"

Everyone around him shushed him to be quiet. John had no choice but to continue to listen to the man in the boat.

"With what can we compare the Kingdom of God?" continued Yeshua. "What illustration should we use to describe it? It is like a mustard seed, which, when planted, is the smallest of all the seeds in the field; but after it has been planted, it grows and becomes the largest of all the plants, with such big branches that the birds flying about can build nests in its shade."

John threw up his hands, turned, and started to walk

out of the crowd.

"Where are you going?" Myriam yelled, as the people around her pleaded for quiet.

John said not a word until they were on the outskirts of the crowd once again.

"He is not a rabbi. He is not a Torah-teacher. His stories, they don't mean a thing. Why can't he just come out and say what he means?"

Myriam sat down on the cool grass and motioned for John to do the same. He paced for a moment or two then decided it would be less conspicuous if he sat next to her.

"Do you want to understand?" she asked quietly.

John considered the question before answering. What if she could make sense of what Yeshua was saying? Would that change anything?

"Yes," he finally replied.

"Then I will tell you what Yeshua was saying to me, what I heard."

John moved to an empty patch of grass and lay down, his right elbow on the ground supporting his head. "Tell me."

Myriam took a deep breath and began.

"When we got here, Yeshua was talking about a lamp, and whether it should be placed on a lamp stand or hidden under a bowl."

John thought of a snide comment, but wisely kept it to himself.

"The light Yeshua was referring to was the Good News He was preaching, about the Kingdom of God. That is why I came to get you. You see, like that lamp, I too know the Good News, the light that will disperse the darkness of this world. Now, what should I do with that knowledge?"

It was a rhetorical question, so John didn't answer.

"If I was to keep it to myself, to not share it with anyone, to not tell it to you, then it would not be like a lamp on a stand, but like a lamp under a bowl."

"A lamp under a bowl is ridiculous," said John.

"Exactly! And hearing the Good News about Adonai's Kingdom and not saying a word about it is just as ridiculous. I have to tell you. I have to tell everyone."

John had to agree that interpretation made sense.

"But what about the measure?"

"As I said before, whatever you believe will be what you are measured against. Now John, you believe in the Laws and Commandments of Moshe."

John nodded. "They are the truth of our existence."

"And what if you break one, even the smallest of them? Like when you told Ya'ir you had an 'errand'?"

John knew what she was getting at. Failing to keep even the smallest of the Laws meant they were not keeping all of the Law. That is why Ya'ir and the others impressed upon them the need to be exact in their following of the Laws. "What is your point?"

"My point," said Myriam, pressing on, "is that eventually all the weight of trying to maintain all of those laws perfectly will fall on you and suffocate you. You have nothing. When you are dead and gone, all of those Laws will not mean anything."

"But I will be with Adonai, where the Laws have no meaning."

"Are you saying that in God's Kingdom, you won't have to wash your hands before you eat?"

John had never considered that. Would he have to continue to follow the Laws even in the presence of Adonai?

"Won't every day be a Sabbath?" said Myriam. "Won't you have to feel love towards each other?"

"I don't know."

"These Laws you hold to are not meant to be a way to God's Kingdom, they are meant to be a way to identify God's Kingdom. That's what Yeshua meant when He said that the Kingdom of God is like a seed growing in the ground."

John sat up. "See, there again, you've lost me. How can the Kingdom of God be like a seed?"

Myriam smiled. "How does a seed grow?"

"Water? Sunlight? I don't know."

"Is there anything the farmer can do to make the seed grow?"

John thought of all he knew about farming. It was true, the farmer scattered the seed and maybe tried to clear a few weeds to let it grow, but it was Adonai who actually made the seed sprout.

"Your Laws make it look like you are doing something

to earn the favor of God. There is nothing you can do to earn God's favor. We are talking about Adonai, the Creator of the World! Do you really think He cares if you follow any silly law?"

John stood, angry at the way she characterized their Commandments. "These are His Commandments, not mine! He gave them to Moshe on Mount Sinai. He demanded that we follow them. He even gave us a solution if we should fail to follow them. Who is Yeshua that he can decide that these Laws are no longer valid?"

"Sit down, please," Myriam pleaded.

John gathered his composure and sat back down in the grass.

"Let me ask you a question. How do you grow in knowledge and understanding of Adonai?"

"By reading the Tanakh, by following His Laws," replied John.

"But when you first started, when you were young, how did you grow?"

John thought back to his first teacher of the Law. "I was taught the Law from my mother."

Myriam shook her head in disagreement. "You were taught the Law from rabbis. You mother taught you about God's love for you."

John could not disagree with her.

"Yeshua teaches the same thing. That God loves you. If you can understand this simplest of truths, then you will be like that tiny mustard seed. Your knowledge and understanding of Adonai will grow until it consumes you.

"Today, you are consumed with learning Laws and memorizing words. Tomorrow, you will be doing the same thing. Your life will be only about following rules. This is not how God intends us to live. Not to be concerned with following rules, but with following Him."

Again John stood. "I cannot listen to this. Yeshua has poisoned your mind against the Laws of our forefathers. I must leave."

Myriam stood and grabbed his hand. "No, please stay. Listen to what we have to say."

John yanked his hand from hers. He saw the pain in her face, the hurt that he would not accept what she said, but he had no choice. "I must leave." He turned and ran from the spot.

Myriam pleaded with him to return, but John pretended not to hear. As he ran, tears bluirred his vision, and he slowed to a quick walk. He wiped the tears from his eyes, and turned to see if Myriam was following him. But she had also turned and walked away.

John feared he may have forever lost his friend.

13

The Plan

It was later that evening when John finally returned to Ya'ir's home.

"Where have you been?" Ya'ir demanded. "You disappear during your studies, no word as to why, then just decide to come back?"

John had never seen Ya'ir so upset.

"Forgive me, Master," he said, head bowed in deference to the older man. "I was told that Yeshua had returned, and I sought to find out where he was preaching."

"And did you?" Ya'ir replied, not easily calmed.

John nodded.

"Then why did you not return and tell me?"

John refused to lift his head to return his master's gaze. "I... I was with a friend..."

"A friend of Yeshua's?"

Again, John nodded.

"Is this how you know his comings and goings, through this friend you both share?"

"Yes, Master."

"And why did you not return when you discovered his location?" asked Ya'ir in a calmer tone.

John dared glance at his master. "I didn't want to lose my friend."

Ya'ir for the first time began to see the terrible burden John was carrying in their quest to contain Yeshua. "Come," he said, "I understand. I forgive you for running off this time." He gently grabbed John's shoulder and helped him to his feet. "You are probably hungry. Dinner is prepared. Go and join the others."

John rose and began heading to the dining room.

"And, John," Ya'ir added, "you are never to do this again, are we clear?"

John nodded, then turned and continued walking.

"Quiet, quiet," said Nakdimon, as all of the P'rushim seemed to want to talk at once.

"I've never seen them so worked up," John whispered to Philo.

Once the murmuring had ceased, Nakdimon continued.

"We all know what this Yeshua of Natzeret is capable of. I myself have seen him on a number of different occasions. I have even spoken to him in private, away from the P'rushim, in the hope that I might be able to dissuade him from continuing his dangerous path."

"And what was the result?" came a question from the back.

"My worst fears have been realized. This man not only claims to be sent by Adonai, he claims to be Adonai in the flesh."

Gasps rose from the assembled members, followed quickly by numerous discussions. Again, Nakdimon tried to gain control.

"I know, I know, my brothers. It is such a blasphemy that even I cannot fathom why he would make such a claim."

Sha'ul stepped forward. "We can no longer wait. The time has come to deal with this matter more forcefully."

The murmurs drew silent as the great rabbi spoke.

"I have just returned from Tiberias. I went there seeking to meet with Herod and ask for his assistance in this matter."

"Will he help?" asked Philo.

Sha'ul shook his head. "Alas, Herod was not there. I did get to speak to one of his subordinates. He has arranged for us to meet with Herod in six weeks. I have sent dispatches to Kayafa. A delegation from the Sanhedrin will join us. Together, we will convince Herod that he needs to arrest this man just as he did Yochanan."

"What if he takes him to the palace, like Yochanan? What if Herod listens to his blasphemy?" Nakdimon asked.

"We will ask Herod first to arrest him. This will limit this man's influence on our region, and will calm Rome," Sha'ul answered.

The room erupted into cheering at the news. Nakdimon quickly sought silence.

"This is good news, yes. However, being granted an audience with Herod is easier than convincing him to act.

I will travel there personally. Sha'ul and Ya'ir will accompany me."

John turned to Philo with anticipation. "Do you think we'll be able to go?"

Philo shushed him.

"The delegation from Yerushalayim will be here within the month," finished Sha'ul. "Until then, we are to keep Yeshua under observation only. Do not attempt to speak with or interfere with him."

Nakdimon turned and left the room, signaling that the meeting had ended.

"I wonder if we will go?" John asked again.

"I wonder if we will see Salome?" responded Philo.

After everyone was asleep, John awoke and grew restless. He rose and quickly dressed, then headed into town, trying to process everything he had seen that day. He walked alone for a long time, and found himself down by the docks where he had first seen Yeshua.

There was a large crowd of people there. They stretched up from the docks where Shim'on had kept his boat to the road that lead to the marketplace. Many were sleeping, while a few stayed awake and stoked several small fires. John could not see their faces or hear exactly what they were saying. It all mixed together, some talking about the day's events, some dealing with unruly children, others telling stories and laughter and still others debating the meaning of some small phrase or story Yeshua had told. They all blended in unison, like the smells of the meals and fire pits wafting together. He was sure they were followers of Yeshua, so he kept his distance.

"Beautiful night, isn't it?" said a soft voice.

John turned to see Myriam. He was glad to see her, after everything that had happened earlier.

"Yes, the stars are quite gorgeous tonight."

"Do you mind if I sit with you?" she asked.

John patted the ground next to him invitingly. She sat down, and neither of them said a word for several minutes. He couldn't even look at her. Finally, she broke the awkward silence between them.

"John, I want to apologize if I offended you today," she

began. "My intention was not to argue with you, only show you the truth."

John bristled as she mentioned truth. "We have a difference of opinion on what truth is," he finally responded.

She smiled in the moonlight. "Yes, I'll agree that we do."

John felt calmer with her response. She was again acting like the old friend he knew.

"Can I tell you something?" she asked.

"Is it about Yeshua?" he replied. The last thing he wanted to do was get into another fight about Yeshua.

"Only indirectly," she said.

John considered her request then acquiesced.

"We have known each other for a while now," she started. "I have seen you when you were happy and when you were sad, and you the same with me."

John nodded his agreement.

"And you have thought of me as a dreamer, haven't you? I was always looking off into the future, hoping for something better."

"I did too," John admitted.

"And now look at where we are. You are away from your stepfather, studying hard for that life you always wanted. Maybe you didn't think about becoming a rabbi last year, but the lifestyle and people are the same as what you did desire."

"Do you have a point to make?" John asked.

"Your life is finally becoming everything you could have dreamed of."

"Adonai has been good to me," he said.

"Yes, He has. But I have one question. Are you happy?"

John didn't even hesitate. "Of course I am. Why do you ask such a thing?"

Myriam turned and looked at him for the first time. "Because all I see with you is anger and hatred."

John was taken aback at her comment. Anger? Hatred? Had he really been acting that way?

"You have become an angry, bitter person. The more you see of Yeshua, the worse it gets."

In the distance, he heard a rumble of thunder.

"That isn't what being a rabbi for Adonai should be

about," she continued. "Adonai is a loving, caring God. Yet you and your friends use Him as a weapon against others. Why?"

John took a deep breath and exhaled before answering. "Adonai is a loving God, yes, but He is also a vengeful God. He will take vengeance on those who do not follow His Laws."

Myriam turned to him. "I am not here to argue. Do you believe that, if you become a rabbi, your job will be to help people to more deeply love Adonai, or to force people to accept Adonai?"

John didn't understand the question. "My job will be to teach them about God and His ways. His ways are the only thing that matters."

Myriam turned away and stared back at the fires. Another rumble of thunder rolled in, a little louder this time.

"There is more to Adonai than His Laws," she said.

"But to our people, they are the most important thing."

"Why?" she asked, turning again to face him. "Why are they so important?"

John couldn't believe what he was hearing. "I'll tell you why. Because the Laws are the only thing that separates us from the Gentiles. It is what sets us apart as special in Adonai's eyes. It is the Law that brings us closer to Adonai."

Myriam shook her head. "I have to disagree with you."

"You can disagree all you want, but it is the truth."

Another rumble of thunder interrupted their discussion, this one too loud to ignore. They both turned to the sea, where the sound came from.

Off in the distance, under the moonlit night, John saw a large storm cloud by itself. Above the cloud and to its sides the stars were out, but the cloud itself was dark and terrifying. He saw flashes of lightning inside of it, followed almost immediately by the rumble of thunder.

John felt the winds stirring, as the breezes shifted from the coolness of the lake to warm, dry heat from the center of town. The breezes picked up, and the leaves in the trees began to rustle in the winds.

John looked up. The stars were still strong; there was not another cloud in the sky. He looked back at the sea and storm cloud seemed to be gathering strength moment by moment. But it stayed far out to sea, no immediate threat to them.

"Have you ever thought about why Adonai loves you?" Myriam asked.

"I don't understand."

Myriam turned and took hold of his hands. "Do you believe Adonai loves you?"

"Yes, I guess I do."

"You shouldn't guess, not about something so important. Do you know deep in your heart that God loves you?"

John did not answer.

"Not loves what you do, not loves what you've become, but loves you, Yochanan Ben-Elioenai?"

John nodded his head in agreement, but no words came to him.

"You see, this is where we differ. Since I have met Yeshua, since I have heard Him speak, I have come to realize that Adonai His Father loves me, Myriam, not because of what I am doing, not because I follow any silly law or try to convince others to believe in Him, but because of who I am."

"I still don't know what you are talking about. Adonai loves all Jews. He has set us apart for His purposes. You didn't know this before?"

Myriam shook her head. "No, this has nothing to do with that. Think about it. Why would God make you? Why would God make me? Because He needed someone to do His work here on Earth? That doesn't make any sense. God doesn't need anyone to do His work."

John had to admit that was true.

"God made you, God made me to love and be loved. To love Him and be loved by Him."

John didn't know how to respond. He wished Ya'ir was here to show him what to do.

"And this is Yeshua's message. That God loves us. That God wants us to love Him. This is His Law to us. Not some silly rituals. Not following a particular rabbi. To follow Adonai only. In love."

Another clap of thunder interrupted their conversation. They both looked back at the sea.

The storm cloud had grown exponentially. It now covered the entire center portion of the horizon. John saw in the flashes of lightning that the waves had risen. And judging by the distance, if he could see waves, he assumed they were gigantic. The wind from the center of town had risen steadily. It was now strong enough to bring dust, sand, and bits of debris as it raced seaward to join the cloud. John thought to their upcoming journey to see Herod and hoped they would not see a storm this intense.

He snapped back into the present. "I do follow Adonai. I demonstrate my love for Him by following His Laws. That is how we demonstrate our love to Him. It is in His first and greatest commandment to us.

> *I am Adonai your God, who brought you out of the land of Egypt, where you lived as slaves. You are to have no other gods before me. You are not to make for yourselves a carved image or any kind of representation of anything in heaven above, on the earth beneath or in the water below the shoreline; you are not to bow down to them or serve them; for I, Adonai your God, am a jealous God, punishing the children for the sins of the parents, also the third and fourth generation of those who hate me, but...*

"And here's the important part," John said,

> *but displaying grace to the thousandth generation of those love me and obey my commandments."*

Myriam giggled. "Do you believe Adonai can't tell if you love Him unless you're following some silly law?"

John was becoming angry. "They are not silly laws. They are Adonai's Laws."

Myriam backed down. "I'm sorry. That was rude of me to call them silly laws. But the question remains, do you believe Adonai can't see that you love Him unless you're following His Laws?"

John considered her question. She was right. It didn't

make sense. "No, I believe that He knows everything."

"Let me ask you another question. Do you think someone could obey the Laws and not love Adonai?"

John snorted. "That's ridiculous. Why would somebody follow His Laws and not love Him?"

Myriam shook her head. "I'm not saying they do, just try to imagine it. Could someone who doesn't love or believe in Adonai still keep His Laws?"

"I guess they could. I don't know why they would, but I guess they could."

Myriam smiled. "Exactly. They are just rules to follow. If you knew all the rules and strove to follow them daily, yet did it not out of respect for Adonai but out of fear for yourself, would that be showing Adonai love?"

John had to admit the truth. "No."

Myriam leaped at the opening. "This is what I have been trying to explain to you. God loves you, Yochanan Ben-Elioenai. Not because you are becoming a rabbi, not because you've memorized His Word, but because you are His special creation."

John admitted to himself that that sounded good. "I can accept that," he said, "but it doesn't negate the need to follow Adonai's Law, His Word and everything He has ordered us to do. Let me ask you a question. Can you love God and not follow any of His Laws?" John smirked, sure that he had trapped her in her own little game.

"Why would you do that?"

"I'm not saying they do, just try to imagine it," John replied, repeating her earlier argument.

"But no one would," she replied. "Your mother loves you, would you disagree with everything she said or did? Of course not. Love is not about following rules because you have to, love is about following rules because you want to.

"It's a silly question, because you could no more love Adonai and not want to do for Him than you can chew and not swallow, inhale, but not breathe. You follow Adonai's Laws not because they bring you closer to Him, but because He is closer to you."

This made no sense to John. "I must disagree. God's Laws are the very tools He created for us to love Him."

Myriam took his hand. "I know you believe that now. It

is what you are being trained to believe. We have had discussions like this throughout our time in Beth Midrash. But there is another truth out there, God's truth, and that is He loves you, not because you do these things, but because of Him."

John pulled his hand from hers, looked past her shoulder, and gasped.

Myriam turned to look at the sea. It was flat and calm, with not a cloud to be seen.

"What happened to the storm?" she asked.

Sleep had not come easily for John that evening, and morning came too quickly. He replayed over and over the events with Yeshua and the P'rushim the day before. He had to admit that he was confused over what to believe. Was the man a true prophet or a complete lunatic?

As he dressed, he became fearful of the impending trip back to Tiberias, back to Herod. John felt nothing good would come of it.

"Please, Lord," he said quietly during his morning prayers, "let this trip be postponed until I know for sure what to do."

Ya'ir arranged for a ship to meet them at ten o'clock that morning. John completed his morning chores quickly, and packed for the trip. At nine o'clock, he still had not seen Ya'ir. Hoping the P'rushim had changed their minds, John headed over to the main house.

A dozen people were there, speaking in quiet, subdued tones. John entered the home and saw many members of the synagogue. Ya'ir and his wife were in one corner of the home, five women around them speaking quietly.

Myriam huddled in a corner. The edges of her eyes were red. "What's going on?" he asked.

"Haven't you heard?" she answered. "Ya'ir's daughter has fallen ill."

"Rivkah?" John asked.

"Yes," Myriam said quietly. "Her skin is hot, like it's on fire, and they have been unable to wake her." She began crying again, and John put his arm around her to comfort her.

"The physician is here," someone cried, and the crowd in the home parted to let him through. He was an older man with a long white beard. He carried a satchel made of leather. Ya'ir and his wife followed him into Rivkah's room.

They were in her room for about ten minutes when Rivkah's mother cried out a pained moan.

Ya'ir appeared at his daughter's door, his ashen face bathed in sorrow. "The doctor has said nothing can be done. She has only a short time left," he announced to no one in particular.

Several women let out gasps, and the men shook their heads. Several men recited prayers.

Myriam began crying and held on to John.

The whole thing happened so quickly, John did not know what to do or what to say. Myriam broke from his arm and ran into the street. John hesitated a moment, then followed her.

Outside, Myriam turned angry. "This does not make any sense. You two sit there and you attack a man who has the power to heal her, yet your pride stops you from admitting it."

John moved closer to her, but she backed off.

"Don't come near me." She spat the words at him. "He can save her. Let me go get Him. Please."

"No," John said, "we can't." John swallowed hard. "He is nothing."

She fell on her knees and took his hand, tears flowing freely. "Please, I'm begging you, let me talk to Ya'ir. I can convince him, I'm sure of it."

He dropped her hand and turned away. How could he even approach Ya'ir, let alone ask him to do this one thing. It went against all of their plans.

He looked back at the house and saw Ya'ir standing in the door. He had no look on his face, not sadness anger or pains, just a blank, unblinking stare.

He staggered out and walked up to John. His face was emotionless. "She's dying, John, and no amount of prayer will stop that." He stood there.

"You're wrong, sir," said Myriam. "Your lack of faith is what will kill your daughter."

John could not believe Myriam would say that.

"Who are you?" Ya'ir demanded.

Myriam bowed her head in deference, but held her

ground. "I am Myriam, a follower of Yeshua."

Ya'ir looked down at her. He took a few deep breaths, as if to calm himself, but the anger in his eyes and the furrowing of his brow showed that Myriam's charge had wounded him.

"You dare accuse me of having a lack of faith?" he repeated back to her. "I have been on my knees since before the sunrise. I have pleaded my case before God for the past five hours, but she just gets weaker. I am a leader in this community, a keeper of the Laws." His voice had been building until his words echoed off the surrounding buildings. Myriam cowered at the fury of his anger, but it suddenly dissipated, like a puddle of water in the afternoon sun.

Myriam regained her courage and stood up to him.

"I, I, I," Myriam repeated back to him. "Teacher, you were there in the synagogue when He healed the man with the deformed hand. You saw that miracle. You know His reputation throughout the lands. Go to him. Ask His forgiveness. Ask Him to heal Rivkah."

Ya'ir looked with anger at Myriam, but she did not flinch in the heat of his gaze. Ya'ir softened his stance then considered what she said. He lowered his head and spoke, his words barely audible. "I cannot. I am called on to uphold the Law. I cannot approach this man who blatantly disregards our ways."

"Why?" Myriam asked defiantly.

Ya'ir looked away.

John touched his teacher's back and spoke in soft tones. "Master, I have a thought. Perhaps we can use this against him."

Ya'ir shot him a strange glance.

"I am not convinced Yeshua is in fact the Son of God as some claim, but I cannot deny he has a healing nature. We have always wondered if his healings were staged. We know that this illness is real. If we ask Yeshua to come and he fails to heal her, then at the very least, her death will have meaning."

Ya'ir shook his head. "No, it goes against my beliefs. I cannot do it."

John felt great sorrow for what Ya'ir must be going through. "I know this must be destroying you inside. You love your daughter, and you love your God." John knew what he had to do. "It comes down to one decision," he said, "your only daughter or the only faith you have ever known."

Ya'ir looked at John. Gone was all of the pain and anger. "My son, some day you are going to make a fine teacher." He turned to Myriam. "Can you take me to this Yeshua?"

John went back into the house. Several people asked for Ya'ir, but all John would say was that he had an errand.

The doctor stepped out of the girl's room. "I am sorry," he announced, "but Rivkah, daughter of Ya'ir, is no more."

Great cries of anguish filled the room. Someone grabbed John's shoulder.

"You, you're Ya'ir's apprentice, aren't you?"

"Yes."

"Then go out there and find him. Tell him his wife has need of him."

John left and headed down the road.

John had no idea where to find Yeshua. It was even more difficult because he was becoming known as Ya'ir's apprentice and it would not do for him to be seen asking for Yeshua. After awhile, he ran across a large crowd gathered along the shore near the docks. He headed there.

John tried to make his way into the crowd, but it was too large and he could not get through. He saw Myriam and Ya'ir. They had made their way to the shore and where right in front of Yeshua.

Ya'ir had fallen down onto his knees in front of Yeshua, burying his face in the wet sand. Small waves lapped against him, but he did not move.

"My little daughter is at the point of death," he cried in a loud voice. "Please! Come and lay your hands on her, so that she will get well and live!" He buried his face again in the sand.

Several of Yeshua's followers were there. They recognized Ya'ir from the dinner. "You seek to have him come now and heal your daughter? Be gone, and stop wasting our time."

Ya'ir did not move. "She is about to die," he said in

desperation. "Please come and place your hands on her. Heal her so she can live."

His talmidim were about to say something else, when Yeshua raised his hand and said, "I will come."

Ya'ir remained prone for just a moment, and then slowly rose to his knees. "Bless you," he said.

Yeshua stepped onto the shore and walked into town. Ya'ir rose and walked beside him. Most of the crowd parted to let them pass, but there was still much pushing and jostling. John no longer saw Myriam in the crowd.

Suddenly, without warning, Yeshua stopped and said in a loud voice, "Who touched my clothes?"

Andrew responded. "You see the people pressing in on you, and still you ask, 'Who touched me?'"

Yeshua refused to move, and continued to look around, as if to find who had touched him.

A woman stepped forward. She lowered her eyes as she came forward, making it difficult to see her, but John recognized her. It was Myriam's mother. She fell down at Yeshua's feet.

"Forgive me, Lord," she said. "I have suffered from bleeding for twelve years, since the birth of my daughter. Doctors have been unable to cure me, and I have spent everything I have had to pay them, but I was no better."

Myriam's mother lowered her eyes. "I thought to myself, 'If I touch even his clothes, I will be healed,' and when I did, immediately the bleeding stopped, and I could feel that I had been healed!"

Yeshua smiled down at her and placed his hand upon her head. "Daughter," he said to her, "your trust has healed you. Go in peace, and be healed of your disease."

Myriam ran to her mother's side, and they embraced, tears streaming down their cheeks. Everything that John was wanted to go to them and congratulate them, but he knew he had to reach Ya'ir before he spoke to Yeshua again. John pushed through the crowd until he stood next to Ya'ir. "Your daughter has died. Why bother the rabbi any longer?" he spoke softly into Ya'ir's ear.

Yeshua heard, and turned to Ya'ir. "Don't be afraid, and just keep trusting."

John looked up at the Natzerene. Even though John knew the truth, the words of this man soothed him.

Yeshua turned to the crowd. "I will go with this man. What I must do is between a father and a child. Wait and I will return to you when I am finished."

Yeshua walked through the city. John walked beside Ya'ir and Shim'on, Ya`akov and Yochanan, Ya`akov's brother, walked beside Yeshua.

Yeshua and his talmidim said nothing during the walk to Ya'ir's house. They moved along at an easy pace, as if in no hurry at all, as if they were merely walking to visit a friend. When they finally reached Ya'ir's house, it had filled with mourners. Some of the crowds flowed out into the streets. Most of the women were crying. Loud wails could be heard from the inside of the home, and many of the people were moving back and forth, jostling each other. Yeshua ignored the people in the front of the house and went inside. The rest of them followed him.

Yeshua searched the faces of the people. Some were relatives or friends of Ya'ir. To these, he offered comfort and hope. But the professional mourners, those sent in to provide a proper atmosphere for the death of a family member, Yeshua ignored. Perhaps Yeshua knew the professional mourners were the ones wailing, tearing their clothes and their hair, putting on the public show that allowed the family to mourn privately.

Yeshua moved to the center of the room. "Why all this commotion and weeping? The child isn't dead, she's just asleep!"

"Asleep," one of the men said. He laughed at the thought. "What gives you the right to come in here and say such a cruel thing?" Several of the men broke from their conversations and walked threateningly towards Yeshua.

Ya'ir stepped in front of Yeshua. "I give him the right. I have asked him into my home."

When the men saw Ya'ir, they immediately stopped and stood where they were, never once taking their eyes off Yeshua.

"Everyone, go outside," Yeshua said. Slowly, the room emptied until only Yeshua, his three disciples, Ya'ir and his wife, and John remained. "Come with me," said Yeshua, and everyone but John went into Rivkah's room.

John watched the scene unfold through the open doorway. The small party surrounded the girl's bed. The air was absolutely still, and John heard no noises. With her mother and father at the head, and his three disciples at the foot of the bed, Yeshua gently went down onto one knee. As someone might unseal a letter from a loved one, he lifted the sheet off Rivkah's face.

Rivkah certainly appeared gone to him. Her eyes were closed and there was no movement to her form. She looked to be more than asleep. There was no sign of pain on her face, only peace.

Yeshua reached down and stroked the girl's brow. John was amazed to see this. This man knew all of their Laws and customs, yet he seemed to have no regard for one of their most important ones, the purity law that forbade someone of his stature from touching a dead body lest they would have to perform the purifying ritual afterwords.

Yeshua looked at her parents as if to comfort them, and then gingerly held the girl's hand as if it were spun gold and would break. He said to her in a gentle tone, "Talita, kumi! Little girl, I say to you, get up!"

Rivkah's eyes instantly opened and her lungs drew breath. She sat up in the bed. Ya'ir grabbed his wife to support her, an expression of wonder on their faces.

Rivkah swung her feet of off the bed, and Yeshua helped her to stand. She walked around the bed, past the stunned disciples, and stood by her parents, embracing each of them.

Ya'ir looked down at his daughter, returned to him by this man he had planned to imprison, and then looked up at Yeshua. Tears streamed down his cheeks, but his lips were silent. Ya'ir's wife also was equally still. Only Ya'ir's strong hold on her kept her upright as her knees buckled, completely overwhelmed.

Yeshua stood and faced them. "Your faith has returned your daughter to you," he said. "Tell no one of what you have seen today." He smiled at Rivkah, who returned his smile.

"She is hungry. Give her something to eat."

Yeshua turned and exited the room. After a moment, his three talmidim followed him. They exited the home and walked through the crowds milling outside the front door.

John accompanied Ya'ir as he went into the kitchen.

"Master?" John began, but Ya'ir waved his arm, demanding silence. John watched his master grab a serving plate, place bread on it and then pour honey into a bowl. He filled two wine cups, handing them to John, and brought the food and drink to his wife and daughter. The girl dipped the bread into the honey, eating as one who was famished. Ya'ir took the wine cups, gave one to his daughter and the other to his wife, who slowly sipped the wine, not once releasing her hold on her precious daughter. No one spoke a word.

Several of the mourners who had been waiting outside made their way back in. Ya'ir intercepted them, telling them their services no longer needed. Many did not understand and insisted on entering. It took almost an hour to get everyone to leave. When they asked Ya'ir what had happened, He only replied, "The Lord has answered our prayers." By midday, only two close family friends remained, along with John. Ya'ir had allowed him to stay because of what he had said to get Ya'ir to go to Yeshua.

Several times, they asked Rivkah what had happened, but she had no memory of the events. To her, she had been but asleep for a few moments.

When he was finally sure she was alive, and would stay that way, Ya'ir invited John outside for a walk. They walked through the quiet streets, with no particular destination in mind.

"I cannot explain to you what happened today," said Ya'ir. "My wife, myself, our friends, even the physician, we all knew she had died."

"But not Yeshua," replied John. "He told the crowds, 'She is only asleep.' Could it be that everyone else was wrong and he was right?"

Ya'ir laughed. "My boy, you have had an excellent beginning in your studies. Yeshua did not mean she was sleeping. I have been listening to what everyone has said about this man without listening to the man himself.

"Asleep? No, she was not asleep, anymore than you or I will be when we breathe our last. I do not believe our Lord was deceived. On the contrary, He knew she would rise again."

John was puzzled. "Our Lord? Does this mean you now believe what the people say about him?"

"I do."

John was in turmoil. The man who had been his mentor, who had given him such hope for his future, had gone over to the other side.

"What of all of your statements, your plans? Just last night, you were to go to Herod demanding his imprisonment."

"I was. And I am glad I did not."

John could see no turmoil on the man's face. It held a peace and calmness that denied the events of the last few months.

"My own pride has blinded me to this man's teachings. I can no longer deny the truth."

"The truth? And what truth is that?" John asked. "I saw her too. She looked dead to me. Now she lives. She had to be asleep. It is the only logical answer. A man cannot raise someone from the dead."

Ya'ir reached out and placed his hand on John's shoulder. "I know how difficult this must be for you," he began, but John broke away.

"You taught me the truth," cried John. "I have learned our Laws. They are the only truth that matters." Tears welled in John's eyes as he struggled to understand everything that had happened today.

Ya'ir turned from John. "Laws are not truth. Truth is truth. I can see now that my blind belief in the Laws has kept the truth from me."

He placed his hands over his eyes, then grabbed his robes and tore them from his body.

"My God," he cried up to the sky. "My God, for too long I have hidden myself from you!" He stood there in his underclothes. "I stand now before you ashamed at what I was." Large tears fell from his eyes. He sank to his knees. "Forgive me, Adonai. I didn't understand what I was doing." He sank to the ground and began sobbing.

John waited until the man regained his composure.

Ya'ir rolled over and sat down.

"I cannot accept this," John said quietly. "I cannot

believe that this Yeshua is anything other than a simple man. I admit, this is an exceptional man, but he is just a man. I do not know if he is a prophet or a lunatic, but I will find out."

Ya'ir stood and gathered his clothing. "I understand. And I will pray that God helps you to see."

Holding the shreds of cloth in his hand, Ya'ir turned to John. "I release you from my service. If you wish to continue your training, I will recommend you to Nakdimon. You are a smart boy, a credit to your family.

"But for me, I cannot continue. I have met my Lord, and I must follow Him." Ya'ir rolled his belongings into a ball and walked back to his home.

John saw his master disappear around a corner. He thought about what the man had said. Yesterday, he was a rabbi's apprentice, everything seemed so right. Now, it was upside down.

John wandered around until sunset. With no place else to turn, John ended up at the gates to Nakdimon's home. He sought out Philo who was studying alone in the garden.

Philo stood up and embraced him. "I heard what happened to Ya'ir's daughter," he said.

"Where is Sha'ul?" John asked.

"He is in a meeting with the Council. He specifically asked me not to go with him."

"Why?"

"I do not know. I trust he has very good reasons. Were you there when Ya'ir brought Yeshua?"

John nodded.

"Was she..." Philo's question trailed off.

John finished it for him. "Dead? No, she couldn't have been. The doctor must have misdiagnosed her condition."

"And Ya'ir ran off to the heretic," Philo said. "He has made things more complicated. Now, the Council will have to put a stop to this."

John watched anger welling up inside his friend. "Unfortunately, I won't be here to see it," said Philo. He looked at his friend. "I received a letter from my father today. His house is set up, and I am to leave for Yerushalayim in the morning."

"How can he do that? You are Sha'ul's talmid."

"My father is cohen hagdol in Yerushalayim. He can do anything he wants, spiritually. He has a rabbi in Yerushalayim who will continue my training."

John was used to Philo's coming and going, but this seemed different.

"I won't be coming back," said Philo, kicking at a stone in the courtyard. "My father wants me to complete my training near him."

After Ya'ir's betrayal, Philo's statement hit John like a punch to the stomach stronger than any tormentor. His whole life, which had seemed so wonderful over the last few days, was gone.

"I've got an idea." Philo said. "Why don't you come with me? I'm sure my father will have plenty of rooms in his house. You could stay with us and learn from my father."

The offer was very tempting to John. To leave K'far-Nachum and had always been his goal. Is this how Adonai would fulfill his wish, by ripping his world apart?

"I'll think about it," he said. He thanked his friend, wished him well, and headed into the night streets.

John walked for a long time only to find himself again in front of Nakdimon's house. He was confused and tired, angry and sad, all at the same time. He did not understand everything that had happened, but he knew God had a plan. There was a reason why this man was walking around, doing what he was doing. There was a reason why Philo was leaving and Ya'ir too. He did not know what these reasons were.

He stood in front of the door. Nine months ago, Ya'ir offered him a new life. Now, that life was in tatters.

John knew deep down he was a good person. He had lived a good and righteous life. He did not deserve these attacks on his beliefs. If Myriam could not see that, then he would have to help her.

He made his choice. He walked up to the door to offer his services to Nakdimon.

Before he could knock, he heard men engaged in an intense argument. He cautiously opened the door and slipped quietly into the front entrance of the home. Inside were several members of the P'rushim, with Nakdimon standing at the front.

"I have just spoken to Ya'ir. He has left our service."

Sha'ul spoke up. "We heard what happened to his daughter. Surely, he is just in a period of uncertainty. Perhaps tomorrow he will—"

Nakdimon cut him off before he could finish the sentence. "This has nothing to do with his daughter. Her illness was unfortunate, and could not have come at a worse time for us. No, this is about Yeshua."

"We heard he brought her back from the dead," said another.

Nakdimon clenched his fists in fury. "She did not die. This man, this carpenter, this thorn in our flesh, merely took advantage of the doctor's misdiagnosis. Things have become much more complicated."

The other men murmured at Nakdimon's assessment of the situation, but no one chose to challenge him.

"What has happened shook Ya'ir's faith, and he has chosen to leave our course of action. This is not going to help us in our quest to rid ourselves of this man.

"Philo is set to return to his father in Yerushalayim. I have given him a letter explaining to the High Priest, in detail, all that has transpired over the last few days. I have asked for Kayafa's guidance in our next steps."

Sha'ul spoke up tentatively. "Then we will not ask Herod to arrest this man?"

Nakdimon looked troubled for the first time. "I fear that Philo, for all of his arrogance and pride, may have been right. The more we let this man walk amongst our people, the more we let him infect the masses, the greater our troubles will be."

A few men gasped. "Teacher, surely you're not suggesting we ask for this man's death?" There were several low murmurs as the others sought to reconcile this new and dangerous course.

Nakdimon stood silently, carefully choosing his words. "We must put aside our own discomfort on this matter. This man has controlled us and thwarted our every move. We must take action, quickly and decisively. We must silence this man, or give up our own way of life."

Nakdimon circled the men. "Death? I do not know if death is appropriate at this time. Without a doubt, if we do not regain control, then all other options quickly end.

We must convince Herod, for the good of our people, to arrest this man and imprison him.

"I do not make this decision lightly," Nakdimon said. "This is a terrible thing we are talking about. After all I have seen and heard, I now know, in my heart, this man must not be permitted to further infect the masses. His followers will be angry at first, but you saw how Yochanan's followers scattered when Herod arrested him. The same will happen here, I assure you."

John stood silently in the darkened corner. His thoughts were in turmoil, knowing what he knew, and hearing these words. He made his decision. "I saw what happened in my teacher's house," he said, stepping into the lamplight. "I have seen Yeshua and heard his words. Nakdimon speaks the truth."

The sound of John's voice made the men jump.

"What are you doing here, and how long have you been listening?" demanded Nakdimon.

John bowed his head. "Forgive me, Master, but my own teacher sent me here to offer my services to you. I have only heard very little, the very last parts." John raised his head and looked Nakdimon in the eye. "But I assure you, what you say is true."

The other men began to move towards John, but Nakdimon held them back. "Let's hear what the boy has to say."

John swallowed hard and began. "Yeshua is a good man, and the words he teaches are fine words, but he openly denies the Law and all we have learned and attempt to teach." John paused to gather his courage. "Ya'ir was my mentor, and, in some ways, was like a father to me, but he has betrayed us. I for one will offer my service to Nakdimon, and ask if I may help him in any way I can. If that means returning to Herod and asking for his assistance, then I will do this."

The men stood silently. "Such wisdom from one so young," said Nakdimon. "Can you not see that even this child knows the right thing to do?"

Nakdimon placed his arm around John, bringing him into the light. "Ya'ir spoke very highly of you, even when he came to tell me he was leaving the P'rushim. I now see why. I will take this boy on as my apprentice."

All of the fear, all of the despair he had felt since he had spoken to Ya'ir vanished at the man's words.

"It is decided," said Nakdimon. "Tomorrow, we travel to Herod."

14

The Celebration

John woke before sunrise. He arose from the bed he had been given in Herod's palace. It all made him feel a bit unsettled. Here I go again, beginning yet another new life.

The delegation met just inside the gates. Several members of the High P'rushim of Yerushalayim were there also. They were dressed in regal robes, befitting men of their stature and grace.

Nakdimon introduced all of the men, but the only name John recognized was Anan. Kayafa referred to him as his father-in-law months ago when he first met Sergius.

"We have heard of all of the difficulties you have had," said Anan. He was an older man; his beard was black with a streak of silver running from his mouth to its tip. He wore the same robes that the other delegates wore, the same as the Council, although the material was much finer. His most outstanding feature was his size. He was the shortest man there, almost the same size as John himself, yet he probably weighed the most of all the men at the same time.

"It is difficult to believe men of your high training and knowledge have so quickly come to this decision. Can you not handle even one small, insignificant man?" Anan continued.

Nakdimon dipped his head as if to hide his shame. "Forgive us. This man is like no other we have seen. Our decision comes neither lightly nor without great debate. We truly believe Herod's help is needed in this decision."

Anan stroked his long beard. "I am not unhappy with this course of action. In fact, it was I who had Philo suggest it in the first place. And after what I have heard of Ya'ir and his daughter, I am even more convinced we need to move forward quickly to defeat this man, before the situation becomes worse."

Sha'ul stepped forward boldly. "Teacher, what news of Yochanan? I hear he is here in this citadel with Herod. I hear he now has Herod's ear. Will Herod be with us or against us?"

"Adonai is on our side," replied Anan, "and I believe He will guide us in our talks with Herod. We will not fail."

Slaves led the men deep into the fortress. There were far more people in these corridors than the last time John visited. There were times he was bumped and jostled and feared he might get separated from the others. It seemed as if half the population of Yerushalayim made the journey. Yet every time, he managed to catch up to the tail end of the visitors.

Today was Herod's birthday, and at noon, a great celebration was to take place. Men lined the halls and filled the rooms, drinking and generally making merry.

Servants led the combined delegations into the Great Hall. John looked about in amazement. He had thought the throne room had been impressive, but this one was beyond comprehension. It was at least twice the size of the throne room, with white marble columns topped with gold leaf ringing the outside walls. They held up the ceiling, upon which was a great fresco painting depicting Herod's many battles. The floor was a tan marble with streaks of red in its grain, as if stained by blood. There was an elaborate pattern on the floor, but because of all the guests, John could not fathom what it might be.

Anan and Nakdimon stepped into the room.

Revelers stood around the outside edge of the Great Hall, food and drink in hand, oblivious to the comings and goings of the party. At the far end sat Herod Antipas, tetrarch ruler of all Y'hudah, and his queen, Herodias.

The P'rushim members approached until they were almost to the foot of the thrones. Neither Herod nor his wife noticed them, so intent were they on enjoying the festivities of the day.

Herodias was the first to see the priests. The moment her eyes met Anan's, her smile dropped and her body became rigid in anticipation of a confrontation.

"So, our illustrious High P'rushim bids pay us another visit," she said, getting Herod's attention. "And what brings you on such an occasion as this, to offer congratulations to your king, perhaps?" Her very words spat at them as if they were the lowest slave.

Anan chose to ignore the blatant disregard with the way the queen treated him. "My lord," he started, in his most soothing, calming voice, "my delegation and I come to you on this grand day of celebration bearing gifts." Anan turned to one of the servants accompanying him, who immediately handed him a wooden box. "In here, we have forty-three silver didrachon, in honor of our lord's forty-third birthday, a gift in honor of all you have done on our behalf this past year." Anan laid the wooden box at Herod's feet and knelt deeply, never raising his eyes above Herod's knees. All the rest of the visitors knelt in unison, and John soon found himself following suit.

John was astonished. Never had he heard of the Council giving such a generous gift, nor had he seen Nakdimon kneel in such abject humility.

Herod shifted uneasily on his throne, but did not utter a sound.

Herodias spoke first. "What he has done on your behalf?" she said, in a mocking tone. "Certainly you don't refer to that evil sorcerer you had him bring into our home, do you?"

"I fear I do not know of whom you speak. What sorcerer resides in the palace?" Nakdimon replied, his voice filled with sarcasm.

The Great Hall grew silent, reinforcing the seriousness of the conversation, as if every partygoer was listening.

Herod chose to rescue his wife. "She refers, of course, to the wild man you had me arrest. Yochanan."

Nakdimon slowly turned his attention to the tetrarch. "And do you, sire, refer to him also as an 'evil sorcerer'?" asked Anan.

"It is true," Herod said, "since Yochanan has arrived here, I find myself talking with him whenever time permits. I find his ramblings more entertaining than evil.

"My wife, however, is not amused. Often, this Yochanan has said to me, 'It violates the Torah for you to marry your brother's wife,' as if he had the rights or privileges to tell me what to do."

John remembered the conversations he had with Ya'ir during their first trip to see Herod.

"My sire has firsthand knowledge of how treacherous this man can be," Nakdimon said to Anan, "and how important it was to get him away from his subjects. If he is willing to be that blatant before his own king, you can only imagine the issues we had to deal with."

Herod nodded.

"Indeed, sire, if one man can so upset the harmony of your household, you can imagine how easy it was for him to upset the harmony of your subjects."

Herod again shifted uneasily. "While it is true I often do not enjoy hearing what Yochanan has to say, I must admit I respect him, knowing he is a good and holy man. I have kept him locked up here under my protection." Herod appeared, if only for a brief moment, remorseful over the entire situation. "Even so," he continued, "whenever I do speak with him, I leave..." Herod paused, searching for the right word. "Disturbed." Then the old Herod returned, the wily sneak everyone knew. "Yes, he is a strange man, one who deserves the dungeons. But even so, I like to listen to him."

Herodias saw an opportunity and stepped in before the priest could answer. "My lord, this is not the day to talk of prisoners or dungeons, but to celebrate. May I present my gift to you?"

Herod's eyes lit at the suggestion. Ya'ir had mentioned that Herod Antipas was in many ways like a small child, especially when it came to gifts and presents.

Herodias stepped off her throne, and Nakdimon took two steps back to stand with the other members of the council. If he was angry with the queen for stealing the conversation away, he did not show it.

Herodias' brilliantly white dress shone in the noonday sun streaming through the windows as she strolled out until she stood in the middle of the great hall. All of the guests in attendance melted back to the walls of the room not sure what the queen had planned and not wanting to be unwitting participants.

Herodias turned and addressed her king. "Oh great and kind ruler of all Galil and Perea, we stand here this day in celebration of your birth two score and three years hence."

Herod seemed especially pleased with the regal way his wife was addressing him.

"Such a great and kind ruler is not in need of more gold

and jewels, as such trinkets do not enhance is stature amongst his people."

Herod's smile fell.

"No, for a ruler so fine and great," continued Herodias, "only an ethereal gift will do, a gift of such grace and beauty that, in the years to come, it will forever be remembered as the only gift given such a king. For your gift tonight," she stopped and loudly clapped her hands twice, a cue to the court musicians to begin playing, "I give the gift of the art of dance."

Herodias bowed low to her king then quickly walked back towards the main entrance doors, never releasing her bow. For years, people spoke of her respect.

The people spoke about what happened next for far longer. From behind the main doors stepped a girl, a girl who hid her face behind an exquisitely beautiful mask. A murmur rose from the men in the room, as this girl became only the second female in the room.

She wore a dress of the finest silks, bright reds, yellows, and blues that moved gracefully as she danced. She appeared as a living, breathing flame. The music contained no lyrics, no song, yet through the movements of her dance, the entire room knew the story of which she spoke.

First, she is a young girl traveling along the road. She meets a man, an important man. They enchant each other. He wants to know her better, but she cannot. Another awaits her. He is saddened, but her beauty intrigues him. He tries again. She admits she too is attracted to him. Alas, it cannot be. His heart is broken, but, in his moments of sadness, she realizes she loves him, and agrees to marry him.

John had never seen dancing like this before; the beauty and grace of the girl's movements caused his eyes to swell. He wiped away a tear. Her arms and hands were so graceful; they almost spoke the story aloud. The movements of her feet were so precise they punctuated every image. Through her dance, she expressed feelings, passions, and acts with surprising effect.

When the girl finished, she lay at Herod's feet, her chest heaving mightily as she tried to catch her breath.

The crowd gasped. Who was this girl, so brazen as to sit

at the king's feet?

The guards moved in to protect Herod, but Herodias stopped them.

The king looked down at the girl in bewilderment. Who could be so bold as to publicly showcase his marriage, and to sit on his own dais. "Who are you to dance such a dance on my birthday? Reveal yourself," he demanded.

The girl looked down at the floor, then removed her mask and looked up at her king.

There was a great cry from the guests as they recognized the dancer. Even John had met her before.

"Salome," cried Herod as he recognized his stepdaughter.

John realized immediately what had happened. It was obvious Herodias planned the entire dance as a public profession of her love for him.

A broad smile broke over Herod's face, and then he laughed a deep resounding laugh.

"Oh, my beautiful girl. Today, you have given me a gift no one else could give, not king or lord or even the emperor of Rome."

Herod was obviously feeling pleased, as his guests were nosily discussing the dance and how well it had been performed. "And so I would like to return the favor. Ask me for whatever you want," the king said to the girl. "I will give it to you." Then he promised, "Whatever you ask me, I will give you, up to half my kingdom."

Herod and his guests laughed at this pronouncement, at the idea of giving a thirteen-year-old girl half his kingdom for a dance. There was much talk and speculation as to what her gift might be.

"I'll bet she asks for jewelry," said one voice.

Another said, "If it was me, I'd ask for one of his palaces."

Salome said nothing, but ran to her mother, who stood only a few feet from John. Her breathing was labored from her performance of a few moments ago.

"Mother," she whispered, "what should I ask for?"

John saw Herodias' brow furrow in deep thought. It was apparent this was an unexpected opportunity, and the queen needed to plan something befitting it.

The queen glanced at Anan, and a look of hatred and

loathing came over her. She stared right into Anan's eyes. "The head of Yochanan the Immerser," she said, without breaking her stare.

Salome gasped at the thought. "Yes, Mother," she said, and hurried back to the king.

Herod had been discussing the finer points of his offer with two wealthy guests when he noticed his daughter return.

Herod raised his hands, and the entire room grew very quiet. "My friends," he said in a loud voice, "my daughter has returned with her decision." He smiled broadly, and placed both hands on his daughter's shoulders. "Tell me, girl, what is it you desire? Whatever it is, I promise I will give it to you."

Salome could not look him in his eyes, but she said in a strong voice, "I want the head of Yochanan the Immerser."

"What?" said Herod, dropping his hands and stepping back, horrified.

Salome looked her father straight in the eyes and said in a loud voice so all of the hall could hear, "I want you to give me right now on a platter the head of Yochanan the Immerser."

Herod stumbled back and fell onto his throne in a great heap. He looked at his wife, who smiled broadly.

The king sat unmoving for a few breaths then his face scowled in anger. He looked around at the guests at his party. Every eye in the room was on him, wondering what he would do. John saw now that Herod was trapped. If he said no, he would be a liar to his daughter, and if he said yes, a man would die. John looked at Herodias, who still wore her regal smile. What a brilliant woman, he thought.

Herod sat up and barked his orders. "Call forth my executioner!" he said in a loud voice.

It took several minutes for the man to appear before Herod. He bowed on one knee before his king.

"My daughter has asked for Yochanan's head. Go to the royal kitchen, get my finest silver serving tray, then go to the prison and remove Yochanan's head from his body and bring it to me."

The crowd gasped at the command.

Herod rose and stood next to the man, then leaned

down and spoke into the man's ear, only loud enough for those closest by to hear. "Be kind, for he deserves our kindness. And use your finest blade, so the end is as quick and painless as possible."

The man ran off, and Herod returned to his throne, a mixture of despair and anger on his face. He never once looked at his wife.

Before the ringing of the new hour, the soldier returned reverently carrying the silver tray. On it was the man's head.

What struck John as odd was the look of peace and contentment upon it, as if Yochanan not only expected his death but actually looked forward to it.

The soldier bowed deeply and offered the grisly gift to his king, who accepted it and called forth his daughter.

"I would have been happier if you had taken half of my kingdom," he said, and he handed her the plate.

Salome took it and looked at the head. She looked as if she might get sick, but she rose and regally walked over and handed the tray to her mother.

Herodias took the tray, took a long look at Anan and Nakdimon, and handed it to a slave who quickly removed it from the room.

Herod stood and addressed the room. "As a result of this," he said, "I am no longer in a mood to celebrate. As my guests, you may stay and enjoy the food and wine, but as for me, I will now retire." With that, he quickly exited the room.

Nakdimon moved to intercept the king, but he was too late. Herod moved quickly before anyone could stop him to talk to him.

The guests were speaking loudly, and the members of the Council discussed the situation, regardless of who might overhear.

"What do we do now?" asked Sha'ul. "Should we stay until tonight, or tomorrow, to try and get an audience?"

Everyone looked to Anan for an answer. He thought long before replying. "No, after today, Herod will not consider taking action against another so quickly."

Nakdimon stepped forward. "We must thank God for our good fortune. While we still have Yeshua to deal with, the Immerser is silent. We can watch and see how his followers react." Nakdimon turned to Anan. "Perhaps this turn of events will open the eyes of some of this Yeshua's followers, and his strength will dissipate.

"I will return to K'far-Nachum at once, spread the news of event so he and his followers will know the path they have chosen is a dangerous one, and one that may lead to an untimely death."

"And I shall return to Yerushalayim," said Anan, "and consult with Kayafa as to our next steps."

With that, they turned and left the group standing there, dumbstruck.

15

The Visitors

John awoke, remembering today marked the six-month anniversary of Rivkah falling ill and John becoming Nakdimon's apprentice. Since his master was out of town on an errand this morning, John arose and quickly and dressed, looking forward to spending some time by himself, away from his studies.

John walked along the empty streets of K'far Nachum. Despite the warm morning, there were few townspeople walking about. That suited John fine, as his errand this morning was personal, and he did not look for conversation.

His studies had progressed well. He was proud of the scholar he was becoming. He had memorized almost the entire Scriptures, and his handwriting had improved to the point that he was routinely called on to make copies for the Beth Sefer. John had never felt so alive and so needed in all of his life. He never missed an opportunity to bring a korban as an offering for Adonai in thanks for the transformation he had received.

In fact, that was where he was headed, to the local temple to give his offering. Being an apprentice of Nakdimon had proven very lucrative, and he often found himself with extra money available to make these offerings.

John walked down the street, barely acknowledging the comings and goings of the other townsfolk. If someone approached him from the opposite direction, they often steered clear of him, giving him plenty of space so that he did not have to break his stride. John enjoyed the stature and position he had attained, both with Nakdimon and with the townspeople.

Along the side of the street, resting against a building, sat several beggars. Dirty, unkempt and with a strong odor that almost made John nauseous, they were there every day. Whenever anyone passed, they would call out, begging for money or food. The sight of them sickened

John, and he thought about crossing the street to the opposite side so that he wouldn't have to deal with them.

"Can you spare something for an old man?" cried one of the beggars.

"I have not eaten in three days. Can you spare a morsel?" said another.

"I have nothing for you," John said loudly. "Leave me alone."

He picked up his pace to pass them as quickly as possible.

"Is that you, John?" said the last beggar.

John stopped in his tracks and turned to see who had addressed him.

The last beggar rolled over onto his hands and feet, and then slowly raised himself off the ground. Once he was erect, he turned and faced John.

"Is that you, Uncle?" John asked.

The man said not a word, only nodding a response.

John was shocked at his uncle's appearance. He was slim and gaunt, and all of his muscles had wasted away. His eyes were sunken into his face, and his usually chubby cheeks had disappeared. Had the man not spoken, John would never have recognized his stepfather.

"You look well. Ya'ir has been good to you," said the old man.

"I am no longer apprenticing with Ya'ir," replied John. "I am now studying with Nakdimon ben Gorion." Pride filled John that he could make such an announcement to this man.

"I'm impressed," said his uncle.

It was the two words John had never thought he would hear from the man.

"It appears that becoming an apprentice under Ya'ir has worked out well for you."

John beamed at the encounter. This moment made up for the years of hardship he had suffered.

"What happened to you?" he asked. "Why are you begging for money?"

His uncle's shoulders drooped in resignation. "After you left, everything fell apart. Did you hear about Shim'on?"

"What do you mean?" John asked.

"He left with some prophet from Natzerene," his uncle

said, practically spitting the words from his mouth. "Both he and his brother just quit their jobs in a moment. There went my source of income."

"But there are other fishermen. Didn't they sell fish to you?"

"No one would trade with me. I tried, John. I tried for months. But they all accused me of gross lies."

John smiled as he thought of how his uncle's unsavory business ethics finally caught up with him. "What did you do?"

The old man lowered his head. "There was nothing I could do. Your mother helped as much as she could, but I've lost everything."

John became alarmed at the thought of his mother still with this man.

"Where is she now? What is she doing?"

"She is home, taking care of David. The bills from the doctors have been mounting. He has been getting worse and worse. I can't find any way to earn money other than to beg here in the street."

"Is it enough?" John asked.

His uncle nodded. "Barely. You have no idea how humiliating it is to spend the entire day here begging for handouts." John's uncle for the first time seemed to notice John's fine cloak. "But you, you seem to be doing well."

John took a step back as his uncle's eyes suddenly began to clear and focus on him.

"Yes, you look as if being an apprentice to a rabbi has its benefits."

The man took a step towards John, and John in turn took another step backwards.

"I'm sure you have access to some money, what with these fine clothes he gives you." His uncle reached out with his right hand and grabbed John's sleeve. John tore away, noticing a dark stain where his uncle's hand had been.

"I have nothing for the likes of you!" John shouted, his anger and hatred for this man returning.

His uncle took another step towards him, and John swung his hand as hard as he could in defense. He struck his uncle square in the nose. The man was not at all prepared for an assault, and the blow knocked him back to the wall, where he slowly sank to the ground. John saw a small stream of red leak from under one nostril.

"Stay where you belong, in the gutter," cursed John. "Whatever I have no longer belongs to you, but is for Adonai!"

John turned and ran before his uncle could regain his feet.

By the time John completed his errand at the temple, his fear and anger had left him. He felt pity, not to the man his uncle had become, but for his mother and brother. He had not been to visit them in such a long time. Maybe now would be a good time fix that? But he also knew he had to be back for afternoon lessons. Maybe he could find some time later this week.

John returned to Nakdimon's by a different path so he wouldn't risk an opportunity to see his uncle again. John sat down and began studying a portion of a scroll he had been handed. Nakdimon left him alone to his studies.

John tried to concentrate on the scroll, but his mind kept wandering, to his mother, to his brother, to his friends Philo and Myriam, whom he had not seen in many months. Each time he wandered, he forced himself to return to the scroll, only to find himself wandering again by the next line.

Most days, his studies strengthened him. While Yeshua no longer bothered with K'far Nachum, they did receive reports almost daily of his travels. The man sure seemed to get around. There were reports of him from far north, where he had caused much mayhem in some small towns ill equipped to deal with his brand of heresy, all the way down to the outskirts of Yerushalayim. John was thankful that, at least for the time being, Yeshua was someone else's problem.

The afternoon was quiet as John sat under the shade of the olive tree in Nakdimon's courtyard. The sun was warm against his robes, and he felt a sense of calm and peace.

Several men dressed in purple walked through the front gates, stern looks upon their faces. As John rolled up his scrolls, he recognized one of the men from months earlier. He was Yosef, a member of the Sanhedrin who had accompanied Philo on one of his first trips.

John crossed the courtyard when the doors to the house burst open and one of Nakdimon's servants ran to him.

"You there, apprentice. Nakdimon has need of the Council. Go and tell them to come here immediately."

John stood dumbfounded. No servant of Nakdimon's had ever spoken to him like this. He was about to say something, but the man motioned him to go. "This is an emergency. The Council must meet immediately. Go, run, you're the fastest student the master has."

John ran off to the other Council members' homes, relaying the news. It took about fifteen minutes for the entire Council to assemble in Nakdimon's home. John, too, stood outside the large room, listening intently.

Nakdimon raised a hand, and the murmurs became silent. He spoke. "We are honored to have such distinguished visitors. This is Yosef, a member of the Sanhedrin, and his associates. What news do you bring us from Yerushalayim?"

Yosef said, "I have spoken with Kayafa of Herod's decision not to interfere. This Yeshua has become a bigger problem than just for K'far-Nachum."

"How so?" asked Nakdimon.

"You rightly dealt with Yochanan ben-Z'kharyah, but this son of Yosef of Natzeret is far more dangerous. He has more followers than Yochanan. Crowds may have loved Yochanan, but the masses that follow this Yeshua come from all across northern Y'hudah."

Yosef bent down and retrieved a scroll from his pouch. "I have here a letter from Kayafa. May I read it to you?"

Nakdimon's eyes shifted repeatedly between the Council members and the visitor. "Please."

Yosef cleared his throat and read. "To Nakdimon and the leading priests at K'far-Nachum, greetings from Kayafa, High Priest of Yerushalayim.

"I have received word that Yeshua of Natzeret continues to preach his heresy in Y'hudah and that your attempt to enlist the assistance of Herod has failed. This is most troubling. Worse yet, Sergius Paulus is aware of your failure."

There was a murmur through the assembly at the mention of the Roman official's name. A glare from

Nakdimon quickly silenced any discussion.

"The path is clear. You must remove this man and his influence. If you should fail, the governor here, Pontius Pilate, may take a military interest in suppressing this man. This is a path neither Rome nor Y'hudah wish to walk."

John could not believe that Rome would send an army into K'far-Nachum because of one man.

"I have sent Yosef along with several colleagues to assist your attempts to silence this man. If you cannot discredit him before his followers, then you must see to it he is arrested by the local Roman command."

Yosef stopped reading and put the letter down. "The rest of this letter is Kayafa's decree that I am to take charge of the arrest and detainment of this man."

The Council members all talked at once. Nakdimon raised his hand, and there was instant silence.

He turned to Yosef. "My friend, this man is well versed in the words of Scripture. He is also quite good at manipulating words to his own advantage." He paused for a moment, and then continued. "Yochanan the Immerser was difficult to arrest, but he was small compared to this man. This man has large crowds that follow him and look to him as a true prophet of God. After word got out of the death of the Immerser, I fear the crowds may prevent us from even getting near him."

Yosef scoffed. "Surely he is just one man. He can be silenced on his actions alone, no?"

Nakdimon smiled, "We have said before, we welcome any help Yerushalayim can give us in this matter."

"That is why I am here," said Yosef. "We have been following his movements. He is on his way, and will be here before sunset."

"Adonai, no!" came a shout from the back. All of the Council began talking loudly, and it took several tries for Nakdimon to get them quiet.

"Where will he go once he arrives in town?" asked Yosef.

"It is difficult to say," said Nakdimon. "He owns no land, no property here, so he is at the mercy of his followers for a place to rest. But in the past, he spent his time at the town square."

"Good. I will deal with him when he arrives. Lead me to your square."

The men stood and headed out of the house into the courtyard. John followed right behind them.

The priest arrived at the square, Yeshua and his men were already there teaching, surrounded by about a hundred townspeople. When his talmidim saw the approaching delegation from Yerushalayim, they instantly became alert. John felt every eye was upon him and the Council, preparing for the worst.

Yeshua paid no attention to the priests, and continued teaching. After a few moments, food arrived for him and his disciples, and they ate.

Yosef saw this and scoffed, "See, right here he gives us opportunity to deny his authority. Do you see how his disciples fail to follow our Laws and customs?"

What is Yosef talking about?

"They have failed to follow the ritual of hand washing before eating. And yet there is sufficient water right over there," he said, pointing to the town well. "They mock us and all we stand for."

Yosef and the priests moved forward through the crowd. There was a sense of alarm amongst the people, but they cleared, allowing the delegation to stand before Yeshua.

Yosef looked around at his followers with disdain. He then addressed Yeshua directly. "Why don't your followers live in accordance with the tradition of the elders, but instead eat with ritually unclean hands?"

The crowd looked upon Yeshua and his followers. John realized this was true. He had never seen a rabbi eat without first performing the hand washing ceremony.

A murmuring went through the crowd, and Yosef had a look of satisfaction on his face.

Yeshua did not seem frightened by the obvious mistake. Instead, he turned indignant. "Yesha`yahu was right when he prophesied about you hypocrites—as it is written, 'These people honor me with their lips, but their hearts are far away from me.'"

Yosef's face quickly changed from a look of superiority to a look of alarm. "Yesha`yahu does not speak today. Our forefathers are the proper subject of that passage."

Yeshua was not persuaded by the argument. "'Their worship of me is useless, because they teach man-made rules as if they were doctrines.' You depart from God's command and hold on to human tradition."

Yosef turned red with rage. "We do not make the Laws of God. His Laws through tradition. They have been passed down to us from the time of Moshe."

Yeshua pointed at the P'rushim. "For Moshe said, 'Honor your father and your mother,' and 'Anyone who curses his father or mother must be put to death.' But you say, 'If someone says to his father or mother, "I have promised as a gift to God what I might have used to help you," then you no longer let him do anything for his father or mother.'"

Yeshua's words cut to John's heart, as he remembered the encounter with his uncle just that morning.

At this, the members of both Councils began shouting in anger at Yeshua. The crowd began yelling back, and there was pandemonium.

Yeshua held up his hand to quiet the crowd.

Yosef spoke. "You misjudge us, and that is your sin, not ours. We teach the Word of God. We teach as our fathers taught before us, and their fathers before them."

The Council nodded in approval.

Yeshua looked over the crowd. "Thus, with your tradition which you had handed down to you, you nullify the Word of God! And you do other things like this."

Yosef breathed in deeply. "How can we nullify God's Word? It is eternal. You are the ones who eat in defiance of the Laws of Adonai. You are the ones who have been made unclean in His eyes!"

Yeshua called to the crowd to come and hear. "Listen to me, all of you, and understand this! There is nothing outside a person which, by going into him, can make him unclean. Rather, it is the things that come out of a person which make a person unclean!"

Without giving the priests a chance to reply, Yeshua turned and walked into a nearby house. Yosef stood there silent as the crowd dispersed. When he finally spoke, it was with well-thought and angry words.

"Who is this man who accuses us of not following Scripture?" he said. "He acts as if he thinks himself a god."

The crowd refused to listen, instead shouting insults at the priests. John feared they would do something dangerous.

"Let's get out of here," Nakdimon said.

At Nakdimon's house, Yosef tried to place the confrontation in the best possible light. "Clearly, we were not properly prepared," he said. "It was my fault. I was so zealous in silencing him I erred in approaching him while still weary from the long journey. My desire to trap him overtook my senses. We will confront him again, tomorrow, after we are rested."

Nakdimon called for one of the servants to show Yosef and his delegation to their rooms. When they were alone, Nakdimon turned to John. "What did you think of the encounter?"

John cleared his throat, almost afraid to speak. "It is not my place, Master," he said, "to question the Council's decisions."

"No one is asking you to question decisions," Nakdimon said in a soothing voice. "You have been around this man from the very beginning. In many ways, you have the most experience with this Yeshua and how he operates. I am just interested in your opinion, nothing more."

John looked at the older man, searching for any signs of deceit, but he saw none. "Yeshua speaks the truth," he started, slowly.

John expected Nakdimon to be angry, but instead he remained calm. "Interesting. Can you explain how you came to this decision?"

John didn't want to say anything more. He felt trapped.

"Earlier today, while you were away, I went to Temple to give an offering, a korban, as required by the Law."

"That is a good and right thing to do."

John nodded in agreement. "I understand our Law and I know what is expected. But today was different." John stopped, ashamed at the memory.

Nakdimon spoke in reassuring tones. "How was today different?"

Tear began to well in his eyes. "Today, I saw my uncle, my mother's husband, begging. I felt ashamed. I was embarrassed that I even knew someone who would beg, much less that it was someone who was my family."

Tears began rolling down John's cheeks, and he quickly wiped them away, hoping they would not continue. "He wanted my offering, the korban I was to give to God, but I refused to do it. I thought it more important to give an offering to God than to help my own family."

John wiped his eyes again, and looked down, afraid of his master's reaction.

Nakdimon reached into his pocket. He withdrew his coin purse, which was bulging. "I do not agree with Yeshua on all things, but on this he speaks the truth. Here," he reached into the purse and removed a silver coin, "take this, and fulfill your obligations to both God and your family." He handed the coin to John.

The embarrassment he felt in his heart gave way to joy over his master's generosity. He was not sure of the right way to respond, but he knew what his heart was telling him to do. He reached up with both arms and hugged his teacher.

If Nakdimon was surprised or angered at the physical contact, he did not show it.

"Thank you." John released his hold quickly and ran out the door.

When he was outside and sitting to put on his sandals, he had a moment to look at the gift Nakdimon had given him. He assumed it was another korban to replace the one he should have given his uncle. But in his hand was a Roman denarius, enough money to buy his family food for a month.

John sniffed as his nose began to run, then wiped his eyes and ran to his mother.

16

The Followers

"John, I have an important assignment for you."

The setting sun streamed past the figure of his master in the doorway.

"Come, follow me," Nakdimon said as he turned and headed to the rear of the house.

John stood and followed Nakdimon into the back courtyard. Philo was there, along with Sha'ul and several other members of the P'rushim. Upon seeing his old friend, John wanted to rush up to him and find out when he had gotten into town, what he had been doing and what his plans were, but John knew now was neither the right time nor the right place.

Nakdimon turned to John. "I understand that you have several... 'friends'... in Yeshua's camp," he began.

Nakdimon glanced at Philo, and John immediately knew where Nakdimon received his information.

"We need to understand better what is happening with our adversary. I have seen with my own eyes how you have upheld the high standards of your training even in difficult circumstances. It is for this reason I want you to take on this assignment."

John didn't understand what Nakdimon was talking about. "What assignment?"

Nakdimon motioned to one of his servants, who brought forth a basket filled with bread and fish. "We need to know where Yeshua will be going tomorrow so that we may intercept him on the road. This may make it easier for us to trap him than in the towns where he is popular. But to do that, we need someone to infiltrate their camp and find out what his plans are. We think you would be the least conspicuous of all of us."

John was flattered that Nakdimon had thought of him for this assignment. "I am not sure how invisible I can be, but I will try."

Nakdimon motioned to the basket. "You will dress as a simple townsman, and carry this basket of bread and fish into the encampment. It numbers now well over five thousand men, with their wives and children. Yeshua has been teaching there all day. Now that the sun has set, the crowd should disperse for dinner, making it easy for you to walk through the encampment. Keep your eyes open and your ears sharp. Stay hidden behind the basket, and try to find out what his next moves will be."

John lifted the basket of fish and bread onto his shoulder. "I will do everything possible for you, Master."

As he was leaving, he heard Philo speaking softly under his breath, "He's still carrying fish."

John reached the outskirts of the encampment. It was a large hill adjacent to the shoreline. He saw several boats at anchor just off the beach, and several others that had been dragged onto land for the night.

The crowd was vast. As far as John could see, there were people everywhere. Many small fires were burning, filling the air with smoke and the smell of charcoal. Several fires had pots on them filled with fish and vegetables, adding to the other smells in the air. If this was how the crowd looked after they dispersed, as Nakdimon said, he could hardly imagine what they looked like before when Yeshua was preaching.

He walked carefully through the campsite, trying not to make eye contact with anyone, listening as intently as he could for any conversations that might allow him to complete his mission.

"You there, boy," a voice cried out in his direction. "Come here. What are you carrying?"

John turned the opposite direction and continued walking as if he hadn't heard anything, but the man repeated his question. John heard footsteps moving quickly as he approached.

Suddenly, a hand grabbed his shoulder and spun him so quickly that he almost lost control of the basket. He recognized the man, although the man showed no such recognition of him. It was Y'hudah, one of Yeshua's talmidim.

"I said, what are you carrying, eh?" the man said. "Let me see."

He grabbed the basket from John and looked inside.

"Bread... fish... excellent. My master has need of these items."

Y'hudah turned before John could argue and began carrying the basket back in the direction he came from. John had no choice but to follow.

When Y'hudah reached the edge of the shore, he stopped before Yeshua himself.

"I have some food here," Y'hudah said. "Let's see..." He began moving things around, "we have some bread."

"How much?" Shim'on asked.

"Five loaves. And two fish," replied Y'hudah.

"Bring them here to me," said Yeshua.

John watched Y'hudah take his basket. Yeshua called over a few other of his talmidim and spoke softly to them, so softly, John could not hear. The men quickly moved off and began calling out to the crowds.

"Sit down, all of you," yelled Shim'on, "we are going to give you a little..." he glanced back at Yeshua, "...a tiny bite to eat. Sit, please, sit."

The people, on hearing the news that a meal was to be served, began sitting and murmuring excitedly over the food. All of Yeshua's talmidim seemed nervous as they walked through the crowds.

John glanced back at Yeshua. He was kneeling in the grass, the basket before him. He lifted the small basket with both hands above his head, up to the heavens. He called out, "Father, glorify your Son, so that the Son may glorify you."

Yeshua brought the basket down on to the cool evening grass then sat beside it. He reached in with both hands and began pulling off large chunks of bread, handing them to followers nearby who took them into the crowds. Time and time again, he reached in and pulled large pieces of bread out, handing them to those who had formed a line to assist in distributing the meal.

He also began bringing out fish, but not just the two John knew to be in there, but fish too numerous to count. These, too, were distributed to the crowd. John watched, amazed, as Yeshua spent several hours reaching into his small basket and producing handful after handful of food.

John could not imagine how he was accomplishing this.

There had to be a false bottom to the basket Nakdimon had given him, and Yeshua must have buried a large supply of food for just this occasion; there was no other possible answer.

John was handed a large piece of bread and a fish. Curious, he bit into the bread. It was soft and moist and tasted of the sweetest honey. This was nothing like the bread he was used to from Nakdimon's home. Why would Nakdimon give him the finest of his breads to take on this assignment?

John looked at the fish. It was raw and uncooked, to him the least appealing way to eat fish. He felt a queasiness in his stomach as he contemplated trying it. He placed the fish to his lips and took a small bite. The taste was not at all what he expected. The fish was delicious, like it had been prepared by a great cook, and reminded him of the fish he had eaten at Ya'ir's last year, the fish that came from Shim'on's boat.

After many hours, Yeshua's talmidim began to return with baskets filled with leftover pieces of fish and bread. Each man had his own basket filled to the brim with these scraps. John looked around; everyone who had been fed seemed content, many having already drifted off to sleep.

Yeshua, finished serving, reached in and began serving his talmidim. They ate heartily, laughing and talking amongst themselves. Yeshua, too, enjoyed the meal with his followers.

When all was over, Yeshua placed the twelve large baskets filled with pieces of bread and fish over by the shoreline. Y'hudah brought over the original small basket John had brought and handed it to John.

"My master thanks you for sharing your meal with us," he said.

John looked into the basket for some type of opening. Not only could he not find one, but there were still the original five small loaves and two fish he had arrived with.

John returned, but dared not tell his master of what he had witnessed. Instead, he said, "Yeshua sent his talmidim across the sea, towards Beit-Tzadiah. Yeshua himself dismissed the crowds. He is walking alone into the hills."

"Alone!" cried Nakdimon joyfully. "Now is our chance."

Indeed, John had never heard of Yeshua traveling by himself. He always had several of his talmidim and a small crowd.

Immediately, Nakdimon called for some soldiers to join them, and the entire Council headed out the gates, with John leading them to the location of the meal. John pointed out the direction he last saw Yeshua, and soldiers ran off, searching.

John looked around for Philo, but his friend was not in the group. Although a full moon was high in the night sky and easily illuminated the hills with a silvery light, they saw no sign of the Natzerene. The search was called off just before daybreak.

John did not see Yeshua or his talmidim that morning, or for many days after that.

The main door opened and a hot wind penetrated John's robe. Two mysterious figures entered with Nakdimon. They were ushered quickly into a private room, and John heard no sounds through the door that might reveal their identity or explain their goal.

John returned to his studies, struggling to maintain focus on the words he was reading. A servant called his name, and John jumped up quickly, happy to no longer have to concentrate.

"The master has asked for you," said the servant boy.

John straightened his robe and followed the servant across the home.

"They are in there," said the boy, pointing to the door that the two men had gone through. The servant turned without raising his head and disappeared into the dark hallway.

John cracked the door open a hair. Four men were seated in the room, and all turned to see who had opened the door.

John recognized Sha'ul and Nakdimon, but the other two figures were still concealed behind their travel robes, their faces in darkness.

"Come in, my apprentice," said Nakdimon.

John opened the door wide and stepped in, then closed it tightly behind him.

"Have a seat here," said Sha'ul, motioning to a small chair next to him. "Nakdimon was about to introduce our guests."

Nakdimon stood. "I have received troubling news about Yeshua. He has been sighted on the main road. It is believed that he will be in the city within the hour."

"Where does this news come from?" asked Sha'ul.

Nakdimon motioned to the two strangers, who cast off their travel cloaks. John recognized them immediately. One was dressed splendidly in a fine purple robe; it was Yosef from the Sanhedrin in Yerushalayim. The other was dressed as a poor townsperson, a dirty brown robe caked with dust. John was surprised to see his old friend.

John wanted to jump up and greet Philo, but forced himself to remain seated and quiet.

"We were on the road from Yerushalayim when we came upon a large traveling party. As we overtook and passed them, we could clearly see Yeshua and his talmidim," said Yosef. "We quickened our pace to try and arrive before him."

"We estimate he is no more than one hour behind us," added Philo.

"What is it we are to do?" asked Nakdimon.

"You are to do nothing. We do not believe Yeshua plans to spend any time here in K'far Nachum. However, we do need to place someone in his midst, someone who will not bring suspicion on the Council or yourselves," said Yosef.

"My father is well aware of the situation, and he has formulated a plan. I have been asked to infiltrate the Natzerene's followers and find out all I can about his plans and ambitions," said Philo.

John felt a twinge of jealousy at Philo's orders. He would have enjoyed himself following Yeshua to find out something that might finally silence this man.

"And that is why you have been summoned here, young John," said Nakdimon, turning to face him. "We do not want the high priest's son on such a mission by himself. You are to accompany him and report back when you have important news."

"Two boys walking with his followers would not raise

suspicions the way we would," said Yosef. He turned to John. "Since you were already a spy in his camp last month, we are certain you will be able to infiltrate and report back with ease."

"I know we will," said John.

The older men laughed at his zeal. "This is why we chose you. You have the fire and desire we need to make this happen, not to mention the experience," said Yosef, nodding knowingly to Nakdimon.

"When will we begin?" John asked.

"You need to go, now, to your room. Clothes have been laid out for you that will help in your deception, along with a pack of clothing and some food for the journey. Do not take anything that would give you away as being my apprentice," said Nakdimon.

John thanked the men and returned to his room. All was as Nakdimon had said, with dirty clothes that matched Philo's laid on his bed, and a pack of similar clothes ready for the trip. John changed and met Philo at the door.

"Was this your idea to include me?" John asked Philo as they prepared to leave.

"No, this was actually Nakdimon's idea," said Philo. "I think it's a very good one. I have so much to tell you."

"And I, you," said John.

As they turned to leave, Sha'ul handed each of them a sack of coins. "This is for you to use in emergencies. Keep it close, as I am sure most of Yeshua's followers do not have such wealth. Try to blend in. Don't confront Yeshua directly, don't interfere with his talmidim, or his plans."

Nakdimon handed John a small satchel. "In here is paper and writing supplies. Try to document each day the Natzerene's crimes, so that we might use them against him in the future."

"Most of all," said Yosef, "be safe. If you feel threatened or you are exposed, return as fast as you can. I have sent word to my contacts in the area that you will be part of his followers, but I cannot guarantee they will be able to protect. Don't try to be heroes.

"We will," said Philo.

With a final blessing, the two exited Nakdimon's courtyard and began their journey.

It didn't take long before Yeshua and his party came through the town's east gate shortly after John and Philo had arrived. When news of Yeshua's return spread through town, hundreds came running, and he and Philo were able to join the throng undetected.

Yeshua did not spend any time in K'far Nachum, just as Yosef suspected. Yeshua exited through the west gate less than an hour later, traveling along the road. Most of the townspeople followed him to the city walls, but not through the gate. John and Philo stayed with his band of followers, keeping quiet, only speaking when absolutely necessary.

John longed to pull Philo aside and pelt him with a hundred questions, but knew that he would expose them if he did, and so kept to himself to minimize that possibility. He was grateful that he did not recognize any other of Yeshua's followers, other than the twelve. His biggest fear was that Myriam would be with this group and might reveal them to Yeshua.

John and Philo followed the long, ragged column of people walking with Yeshua. There was a set order to how the mass traveled. First was Yeshua, alone with his twelve talmidim. Then a gap of several hundred feet, enough to give them privacy but not so much that they would disappear from view. After them came the men, about two hundred or so by John's count. These men were interested in talking about themselves and the future, what being followers of the mashiach would mean to them both here and in an afterlife. Next came the women and small children. They were more pragmatic, talking about life on the road and the difficulties of traveling long distances without resting. Next came the older children, the ones who were able to walk and be by themselves. To them, this was just some great adventure. In total, John estimated that there were about a thousand people in the crowd.

Philo and John were last, keeping distance between themselves and the children so they did not have to worry about revealing their true mission.

They headed west for several hours. He moved closer enough to Philo to ask a question. "Where do you think we're going?"

Philo did not respond immediately. "I do not know. That is why we are here, to find out."

John didn't like the answer. He felt uncomfortable not knowing what was around each bend, and he was concerned that they would be discovered at some point.

The road itself was pleasant enough. Wide enough to allow travelers heading east to pass without conflict, fairly level and well maintained. There were few rocks to trip on, and few indentations to stumble upon. In fact, the most difficult part of the journey for John initially was keeping pace with the crowd. They were far more use to traveling than he was, and his legs quickly grew tired from the constant exertion.

He was most relieved when evening fell and Yeshua signaled a stop for the night. They had already passed Mount Korazim, which was now to their north and east, and they made camp in the foothills of the Naftali Mountains just ahead.

At the signal to stop for the night, Yeshua and his talmidim moved off the road to the south, and those following him set up an encampment north of the road, giving them some privacy. Campfires were lit, meals were prepared, and everyone was polite to the two spies. As people drifted off to sleep, John saw his opportunity. He motioned to Philo to follow him, and they walked off a ways until the conversations dropped to a level that could not be discerned.

"I was so surprised to see you," John said. "How have things been in Yerushalayim?"

"It has been hectic," said Philo. "My father has been struggling with reports of this Natzerene for months now. We thought we had him at Herod's, but since those plans fell through, he has been all over Y'hudah. He is spreading his heresies, and we seem to be powerless to stop him."

"Why do you think that is?"

Philo gave John a strange look. "I don't know. We should have had him any number of occasions, but he always seems to find a way to slip thorough our traps."

Philo rolled a large rock beside another, and patted it, suggesting that John take a seat. When both were comfortable, Philo said, "By the way, happy birthday."

John was dumbfounded. He did some quick math in his head and, indeed, today was his birthday. "How did you know?" he asked.

"It would be stupid of me to forget my friend's fifteenth birthday."

Fifteen. It was difficult for John to believe he had been at this for three years. When he turned thirteen, he had gone home, but his uncle was so mean and angry that John chose never to return again. Nakdimon had not celebrated his fourteenth last year, and today, he was far from friends or family, except for Philo.

"I have a small gift for you," Philo said.

"You didn't need to do that."

"No, but I wanted to. Here." Philo handed him a small satchel held closed with a drawstring.

"What is it?" John asked.

"Open it and find out."

John loosened the drawstrings and pulled on the ends of the bag until it opened. He turned the bag over and emptied the contents into his right hand. Two small, black leather boxes rested there, with leather straps coming out from each end.

"It's a *tefillin*," said Philo.

John knew what it was. All of the priests and Council members wore them on occasions. They served as a reminder of God's intervention at the time of the Exodus from Egypt. They wore them on their foreheads and on their arms, and kept the Word of God in them, in the form of small parchments with Scripture on them.

"I thought, if you want to be a rabbi, then you should have one. You will be needing to wear it in the future, anyway."

"Thank you," said John, "I will treasure this always."

"Good, now, put it away before someone sees it and sounds an alarm. What has been going on since last we saw each other?"

John relayed to Philo some of the things he had seen, including the episode with the basket.

Philo whistled. "And there was no way he could have snuck that food into your basket?"

"Philo, there was a lot of food. We're talking five thousand men, plus their wives and children. Half a year's wages wouldn't buy enough bread for them—each one would get only a bite! I don't have any logical explanation where this food came from, other than it was provided miraculously."

"Don't say that. Not even in jest. That is what he wants everyone to believe. There has to be a logical answer."

"If there is one, I can't find it."

"Well, we needn't worry about that right now," Philo said. "The important thing is to focus on our mission, see what we can discover and report back."

"What does your father believe this man is?"

Philo raised an eyebrow at the question. "What does he think he is? Why, just a man, like the others. Why do you ask?"

"I've seen him do an awful lot of things. Things that can't be explained unless he had some spiritual help to do them."

Philo scoffed at the idea. "Nothing he has done requires a spiritual explanation."

"Bringing Rivkah back from the dead?"

"We told you, she was misdiagnosed."

"Driving a demon from Hadad?"

"He probably paid him off to act that way."

"Healing that man with leprosy?"

"That hasn't been confirmed. And even if it was, our own priests and rabbis have done the same thing. It doesn't make him a mashiach."

John nodded in agreement. "No, but it does make him a holy man. Demons can't drive out demons. Demons don't heal."

Philo let out a deep sigh. "What is your point?"

"My point," said John, carefully picking his words, "is maybe this man isn't a threat, maybe he can be an ally. Have we ever thought to approach him and invite him to meet with us as equals?"

Philo stood up so quickly, it startled John. "I will not listen to this anymore," he said, so loudly his words echoed back from the hills.

John stood and tried to calm his friend, before they were revealed; before their mission even started. "Keep your voice down. I'm just asking questions. It doesn't mean anything. Do you want to give us away?"

Philo glanced over to see if his cry had been detected in the camp, but no one seemed to stir. They both sat down and resumed talking in quiet tones.

"This is heresy," said Philo. "Maybe it was a mistake bringing you on this mission. Maybe you've been too close to the situation all along."

John did not want to be dismissed in the first day. "No, I'm not doubting our job. I'm just asking questions. You have to admit it is a little confusing."

Philo shook his head. "There is no confusion. I know our course is true and just. This is what Adonai expects... no demands from us. To shut down this heretic, this vile hater of our way of life, before he destroys everything we have built."

Something in what Philo said struck John as odd. "I always thought this was about God, not our way of life?"

Philo leaned away from John, his eyebrows pursed in a puzzled expression. "It is about God."

"But you seem more angry at losing your position than about attacks on Adonai."

Philo stammered. "No... no... It's just..." He took a deep breath. "It's just that if he continues to spread his lies, he will bring wars to our people. Rome will wipe out everyone in Y'hudah."

John couldn't see how one man could be such a threat to Rome, but he backed down. "Okay, I see it your way. I don't really doubt our position, I just wanted to go over the good and bad points, to make sure we were together on this."

Philo licked his lips. "Okay." He spoke in such a tone that said, "I'm not sure I believe you."

John reached out and placed a hand on his friend's shoulder. "I am on your side. I always will be."

Eager to change the conversation, John asked, "Where do you think he is headed?"

Philo had become well traveled over the past several months, but his journeys were to the south, between K'far Nachum and Yerushalayim. "I have never ventured this far north or west. I do not know. Based on the direction we are headed, I think it is safe to guess we will be walking the Huleh Valley. Why, I don't know."

Philo stood up and offered John a hand to help him to

his feet. "We should probably get back to the camp. We don't want to raise suspicions."

They parted company, one heading north, the other south, so they would enter camp alone and from opposite directions, to minimize the possibility that they would be seen together.

John found an empty patch of land, lowered his pack and leaned against it as a pillow.

He drifted off to sleep replaying the argument with Philo against all of the things he had witnessed.

Philo's fervent shaking woke John awoke the next morning. "Get up, they are leaving already!"

John rubbed sleep from his eyes and looked to the south. Yeshua's talmidim were already packing, getting ready for the day's travel. John could still see stars in the morning sky, although there were the first rays of the rising sun off to the east.

The people in his encampment were scrambling to follow. Some rolled their bed sheets, while others put out fires or prepared a small morsel to eat. Hungry, John reached into his pack for a piece of bread.

Yeshua's talmidim were on the road, heading west again. John and Philo quickly fell in a few minutes behind them. Although the morning sun had not fully risen, John counted only twelve men in the group ahead of them.

"I don't see Yeshua. Where is he?" asked John.

"I did not see him when I arose. He must have left during the night."

"What should we do?" The whole point of their mission was to follow Yeshua. And here they had lost him after the first night.

"Let's keep following his talmidim," said Philo, "and see if he reunites with them this morning."

It was a good idea, as after an hour, Yeshua met up with his followers along the road. He had apparently been in the hills during the night.

Around nine o'clock they came to a fork, and Yeshua and his followers turned north. Those following Yeshua split, about half had turning off the road and heading south.

The road twisted and turned until they saw the city of

Tzfat in the distance. By midmorning, they had passed the city gates and continued along the northern road.

Despite repeated guesses, they could not fathom what Yeshua was doing or were he was headed. Each town along their path he bypassed. He made no effort to interact with or teach the crowd following him. With each town they passed, that slowly decreased. By the second nightfall, the followers had been cut in half to five hundred, and cut in half again by the third night.

At the northern end of the Huleh Valley, Yeshua turned west and headed towards the Via Maris, the famed north-south trade road that ran along the Mediterranean Sea.

"If the Via Maris is our destination, what cities would he be heading towards?" asked Philo.

"Caesarea and Yafo to the south, Ptolemais, Tzor and Tzidon to the north. Or he could be looking to get a ship to take him west to Rome or Greece."

Philo puzzled over the statement. "Going to Rome or Greece doesn't make sense. Why leave all of his followers now?"

John looked at the crowd they were in. "I'd say his followers are leaving him."

"All of those towns are Gentile, and hostile to our way of life. Why would he lead us there?"

"Or go there himself?" added John. "It doesn't make sense."

As the days continued, John and Philo found themselves walking together more and more, as the crowd continued to thin the further into the country of the P'lishtims they went. Several times a day, armed groups traveling in the opposite direction threatened them and their party, and it was only their size that seemed to protect them. But as more followers dropped out, they began to wonder if they would be safe.

On the fourth day, they reached the Via Maris and turned north again.

"Tzor, definitely Tzor," said Philo.

"Or Tzidon," corrected John.

The end of the fourth day found them camping just south of Tzor. The next morning had them packing and marching past the city, again heading north.

"What lies north?" asked Philo.

John searched his memory of the maps he had seen. "Tzidon. After that, I don't know. I don't think I have seen any maps of the territories further to the north."

Philo shook his head. "I don't like this one bit. Mission or no mission, if Yeshua heads north of Tzidon, I think we had better turn east and make for Caesaria Phillipi and K'far Nachum. This is dangerous territory we are in."

John couldn't agree more.

That evening, the eighth day in the month of Sivan, they finally arrived at the city of Tzidon. Up ahead, Shim'on held up a hand to stop the procession, and everyone came to a halt.

He left his group and walked over to their small band, which now numbered less than twenty. "Yeshua will be entering this city. He has asked that all of you remain here, please, outside the city, while we go in. It will only be for a few days."

There were groans and anger coming from some that they would be separated.

John was glad for this reprieve. They had walked with Yeshua for several days, and he had not once talked to them, always talking only to his talmidim. John couldn't understand why these people still followed him. He didn't seem to be much of a teacher.

The crowd followed Shim'on's request and set up an encampment at the edge of the city. Several, however, disgruntled at being left behind by Yeshua, went into the city after him.

Philo found John near a newly lit fire. "We must go into the city."

"But you heard Shim'on. He wants us to wait here for him."

Philo closed his eyes, keeping calm, then opened them and looked deeply at John. "We are not one of his followers. We have a mission to complete. Come."

John left the fire and accompanied Philo through the open city gate.

They made inquiries of the locals as to where Yeshua had gone. As word spread that Yeshua was here, in their town, a strange reaction took place. John had expected that there would be anger and resentment at the news that someone from Natzerene had invaded their city, but the opposite was true. People spoke in hushed, excited tones to the news that a great Hebrew prophet had arrived. John heard bits and pieces of conversations about some of the things Yeshua supposedly had done. They were even more fanciful and amazing than what he himself had seen.

He and Philo made some inquiries and found that Yeshua and his talmidim had located a house to stay in. If Yeshua was expecting anonymity, he failed. A crowd of Kena'an Gentiles surrounded the house, asking for favors, healings and miracles.

Yeshua and his talmidim left the house to address the crowd. John and Philo pushed through to better hear.

"... and so we only wish to rest after our long journey," they heard Shim'on say as they got within hearing distance. "Please, leave this place and allow us some peace."

"A healing," cried someone in the crowd.

"Show us a sign," shouted someone else.

Shim'on sighed and turned to Yeshua with a look of resignation on his face. Yeshua raised his hand and the crowd quieted to a low murmur.

"Sir, have pity on me. Son of David!" cried a woman, breaking the quiet. She was not a Hebrew, for her dress clearly identified her as a woman from Kena'an.

If Yeshua was going to say something, he remained silent.

Seizing the moment, she made her request. "My daughter is cruelly held under the power of demons!"

The crowd began talking excitedly at her remarks. Their words rose like the the bubbling of a fast moving stream. Concerned about all of the commotion accompanying her request, Yeshua's talmidim began talking loudly, imploring their master to dismiss her request, concerned that if Yeshua granted it, they would be forced to grant everyone's.

"Send her away because she is following us and keeps pestering us with her crying," said Y'hudah, one of the twelve.

Yeshua raised his hand and again the crowd quieted. He walked over and stood in front of the woman. "I was sent only to the lost sheep of the house of Isra'el," he told her. "Let the children be fed first, for it is not right to take the children's food and toss it to their pet dogs."

The woman dropped to her knees and bowed her head in reverence. "That is true, sir, but even the dogs under the table eat the children's leftovers." Her gaze never rose to see Yeshua's reaction.

Yeshua's expression remained unchanged for only a moment then a broad grin spread across his face. He laughed heartily. "For such an answer you may go on home. The demon has left your daughter."

The woman raised her head in disbelief, but Yeshua reached down and gently lifted her by her arm, bringing her to her feet.

Unsure what to do, she instinctively reached out and embraced Yeshua in thanks, then quickly departed through the crowd, anxious to see if his statement was true.

"Again, with expelling demons," said Philo, disgustedly. "At least this time there is no proof."

Proof or not, that was all the crowd needed, as the demands for miracles and cures erupted anew. Yeshua and his talmidim had their hands full trying to answer and control the requests.

John and Philo stayed there for several hours, taking note of everything that was said and done.

It was late in the evening when they returned to the encampment outside of town. John immediately went off a distance and began writing what he had seen and heard, as per Nakdimon's request. Philo went to sleep, with the understanding that John would wake him when he was finished recording, so that he could take a turn to keep watch.

When he was finished, he woke Philo and laid down himself, falling fast asleep. But it seemed to be for only a moment, as Philo again shook him awake far too early.

"They are leaving Tzidon!" said Philo, excitedly.

Yawning, John forced himself off the ground. "Which way are they headed?" he asked.

"South."

John was puzzled. "Back the way we just came?" he asked.

Philo nodded.

This didn't make any sense at all. Why would Yeshua travel all this way to spend a single night in a Gentile town then return?

"I don't know his destination. I just know we need to follow him," said Philo.

John quickly packed—he was getting quite good at that—and they fell in with the crowd following Yeshua and his talmidim.

The twenty or so Jews who remained from the original crowd of over a thousand was supplanted by about a hundred Gentiles from Tzidon. The newcomers spoke excitedly about the events of the previous night. Several attempted to engage Philo and John, but they politely refused to get drawn into conversations. Others from their original group were less distant, and readily conversed with the newcomers.

"Jews walking and talking with Goyim," Philo said with a hint of disgust in his voice. "If this is Yeshua's great plan, then we should have no problem getting him arrested when we return to K'far Nachum."

A lone cloud hid the summit of Mount Korazim in the distance. It had been a long, though uneventful, walk back to this familiar countryside, and John, for one, was happy to see some familiar sites.

"One more day and I'll be able to sleep in my own bed," he said to Philo. "I'm so sick and tired of sleeping on the cold, hard ground."

"Being a rabbi's apprentice is making you weak," Philo kidded.

They both shared a laugh over the thought.

Around them, the crowd of followers had swelled to almost two thousand. Gentiles had been joining their ranks steadily since the events in Tzidon, and once they had entered Y'hudah proper, Jews joined them also. There was much buzzing and excitement at following Yeshua, although he still maintained a separation between his talmidim and the crowd that followed.

"I wonder where we'll be stopping this evening," John asked, not really expecting an answer.

A young girl who was walking near them flashed a smile. "How long have you been following Yeshua?" she asked. Her hair and eyes reminded him of Myriam, and he suddenly felt a strong desire to see his friend again.

John was not sure how to answer. "Since... since Yochanan immersed people in the Yarden River."

The girl's eyes lit up at his statement. "You saw Yochanan at the Yarden? That must have been the most amazing thing to see."

John chose not to answer.

She turned to a few of her friends walking with her and mentioned that John had seen Yochanan. They immediately surrounded him, asking questions and speaking quickly between themselves.

John looked over to see Philo had moved away, separating himself from John and his new "friends." Philo had a look of humor and disgust on his face.

"What was Yochanan like?"

"Did he immerse you?"

"Have you seen Yeshua perform any miracles?"

"Have you ever spoken to Yeshua?"

John was pelted with question after question, and he tried his best to deflect each one, but it was getting difficult to do so.

"Please, I have been traveling for a long time. I am tired, and I don't feel like answering a lot of questions," he pleaded, with little success.

Up ahead, Yeshua and his talmidim where being encircled by a crowd walking in the opposite direction. They stopped, and it was only a moment before the two crowds had completely surrounded the twelve.

"Are you Yeshua, the healer?" one of the men asked.

Shim'on shook his head, and pointed out his master. "He is Yeshua. But please do not delay us. We have important work to do."

The man bowed his head in humility. "Forgive me, but I have to insist that I speak to him right away."

Shim'on, Mattityahu, and several others of Yeshua's talmidim tried to create a barrier between their master and these men. But the one who had spoken would not accept that answer. He began running quickly from one side of the wall to the other, trying to find an opening, all the time calling to Yeshua, "Please, my friend can neither hear nor speak. Please, just lay a hand on him and heal him."

The more he tried to break through, the more the talmidim seemed determined to stop him. They were at an impasse until Yeshua, without saying a word, walked past his followers and right up to the man's friend.

He led the man off the road, away from the crowds. There was an olive grove about a hundred feet from the road, offering shade from the sun, and Yeshua took the man there.

He motioned for the man to drop to his knees. Then, Yeshua placed his index fingers into the man's ears, moved them around before removing them. He then cupped his hands together, spat into them, and touched his hands to the man's tongue. He placed his fingers back into the man's ears, looked up to heaven and gave out a loud groan that startled many people. Looking back at the man, he said in a loud voice, "Hippatach—Be opened!," pulling his fingers quickly from the man's head.

The crowd suddenly fell silent, listening intently to see if anything had happened. The man kneeling in front of Yeshua made no sound, no indication that anything had happened. Then, a quail suddenly burst from under some brush at the edge of the grove. The man turned at the sound, and watched the bird fly up into the sky. A smile broke over his face. "A quail!" he said in a most excited tone. "I heard the quail."

He stood and embraced Yeshua, then dropped immediately to his knees, burying his head in the tall grass.

"Forgive me," he said.

Jesus merely reached out and helped the man to his feet.

He turned and saw his friends, still in the crowd. He began walking, then running, over to them. "Did you hear the quail?" he asked in a most excited voice.

Tears streamed down his friends' faces. "Yes we did," they both said, embracing the man when he arrived.

The three of them began speaking in hurried, quick

tones, all the time looking at each other and occasionally over at Yeshua, who still stood by the olive grove.

"Tell no one of what has happened," Yeshua commanded them.

The three men looked perplexed. "Tell no one?" they asked. "This is the most miraculous thing I have ever seen."

"Tell no one," Yeshua again said.

The three men became quiet then started walking through the crowd back towards K'far Nachum. "I can hear," the man said. "I can speak." He said this to anyone and everyone whom he passed.

The crowd became excited with the news. "The deaf hear," one woman shouted.

Yeshua repeated his command to the crowd, then began walking back to be with his talmidim.

The crowd, somewhat intimidated by him and what he had just accomplished, gave him a berth, and they began at once walking east towards K'far Nachum.

As they walked, the crowd chattered loudly. Whenever travelers heading west passed, people began telling them hurriedly what had happened.

John and Philo walked together, saying nothing. Philo had that look on his face once more, the look that said, "I don't believe his sorcerer's tricks." John knew better than to try and engage him in conversation at this time.

The girl they had spoken to earlier was back. "Did you see what happened?" she asked John.

He nodded, saying nothing.

"It's a miracle. We just witnessed a miracle by Adonai." Her face shone like a golden menorah.

Philo wanted nothing to do with her. "It's just cheap tricks. He is a conjurer and a sorcerer."

She looked at Philo in disbelief. "How can you say that? Don't you believe he is the mashiach?"

John stepped between her and Philo. "The mashiach is someone we are looking for, not Gentiles," he said. "What do you know of the mashiach?"

She stepped back, slightly alarmed at their two boys' anger. "I mean nothing by it. Aren't you always looking for your mashiach, your king?"

Philo spat on the ground. "King? Look at him. He is a

dirty beggar. He has no throne, no kingdom, no place to lay his head. How can he be king of any peoples, let alone of the great nation of Isra'el?"

"But look what He can accomplish," she continued. "Everything He does, He does well!" she said. "He even makes the deaf hear and the dumb speak!"

Philo had all he could stand. "Leave me alone, or I will not be responsible for my actions!" he said in a most terrifying tone.

Her eyes grew wide in fear, and she and her friends backed away slowly, then turned and ran over to another group. They began speaking quietly amongst themselves, occasionally glancing back at Philo.

When things calmed down, John leaned over. "You sure have a way of making friends," he said, hoping to elicit a smile.

It worked. The anger left Philo's face, and a smile appeared, if only briefly. "I cannot stand these idiots who are willing to accept everything at face value. Can't they see that he is just good at tricks?"

John didn't know how to respond, so he chose to say nothing at all.

They walked along together in silence, and also alone.

The sun had just set below the western mountain range when Shim'on signaled a stop for the night. John guessed they were about four hours from K'far Nachum and his soft bed, and he longed to continue, but Philo talked him out of it. "It's been a long day, we haven't eaten in six hours, and the road is no place to be by ourselves during the night. We will be much safer here. You can see your bed tomorrow."

John had to agree, and they stole a spot of soft grass and sat down. Campfires were lit, but food had grown scarce over the long journey. The crowd which had numbered about two thousand this morning had more than doubled since the news went out about the healing earlier. Many were hungry and grumbling about their stomachs.

John and Philo stood and walked away from the group, back towards the road. When they got to the edge of the road, they could overhear Yeshua and his talmidim speaking. Trying to not appear to be eavesdropping, both boys listened intently to the conversation.

Yeshua's voice came across the road loud and clear. "I feel sorry for these people, because they have been with me three days, and now they have nothing to eat," he said.

A voice answered, one that sounded to John like Y'hudah from K'riot, "We have not enough food to feed such a crowd."

Yeshua would not relent. "If I send them off to their homes hungry, they will collapse on the way. Some of them have come a long distance."

Another voice spoke up. John recognized his old tormentor, Ya'akov. "How can anyone find enough bread to satisfy these people in a remote place like this?"

There was silence, and John heard the talmidim talking amongst themselves about the hopelessness of the situation.

"How many loaves do you have?" Yeshua asked.

His talmidim began looking through their baskets and provisions. "Seven," said T'oma, "and a few fish."

Yeshua motioned for them to bring them to him. When all of the food was delivered, he placed it into a single basket. Just as John had seen before, he lifted the basket to heaven, and called out, "Father, glorify your Son, so that the Son may glorify you."

Shim'on began yelling to the crowd and motioning, "Sit down, everyone, just take a seat where you are. We will bring you a meal."

Yeshua lowered the basket to the ground, and sat next to it. He reached in with both hands and began pulling off large chunks of bread.

"What is he doing?" asked Philo.

"Watch," said John.

Over and over, he reached in and pulled out large pieces of bread. His talmidim took what was handed to them, gave it to some in the crowd, and returned for more. Yeshua also handed them fish.

Ya'akov's brother, Yochanan, came over with bread for Philo and John. He looked at them strangely. If he recognized them, he didn't acknowledge it. "This is for you," he said. "Adonai bless you."

Philo refused to accept the food, so John took both pieces. Yochanan returned to the line.

John took a bite of the bread. It was just as delicious as he remembered. "Here," he said, offering a piece to Philo.

"I don't want to eat that rancid bread," Philo said.

"Rancid?" John said. "This is the most delectable, sweet, soft bread I have ever eaten. You really must try a piece."

He gave Philo a tiny morsel. Philo popped it into his mouth, then turned and looked at John with surprise in his eyes.

Ya'akov was over with another handful. "Adonai bless you," he said, handing the bread to Philo.

Philo took a large bite, and handed some more to John. The two ate the bread quickly, not realizing how hungry they were.

Soon Taddai came by with two fish. Philo took one bite and said, "This is amazing. This can't be dried fish, packed for a trip. This is better than fresh fish just out of the nets."

John gave him an "I told you so" look.

Yeshua's talmidim continued bringing them bread and fish, and they ate until they were full. Philo took several pieces of bread and placed them into his bag. "I want to show this to Nakdimon when we get back," he said.

John nodded.

It was almost midnight when Yeshua stopped distributing food. John looked around and everyone in the crowd was well fed. Many had fallen asleep with the meal, while others stood around lit fires speaking in hushed tones about how great Yeshua was.

Yeshua's talmidim took several baskets through the crowd, picking up whatever was left over. John slapped Philo on the arm and pointed across the road.

There were seven baskets filled with leftover bread and fish. Each basket was twice the size of the basket Yeshua pulled the food from.

Yeshua and his talmidim walked off towards a grove of palm trees, leaving the baskets alone. Several people crossed the road to look at the baskets, and Philo pulled John with him. "Let's go see how he did that," he said.

John already knew, but followed his friend.

Philo picked up the basket Yeshua had been reaching into. There were seven dried loaves of bread, untouched, and two smoked fish. Philo dumped the contents onto the ground. He reached in with his hand and hit the bottom of the basket, as if he expected it to open. Nothing happened.

He dropped to his knees and ran his hands along the ground where the basket sat. "There's no opening," he exclaimed. "All I feel is grass."

He looked at one of the baskets of leftovers. "This bread doesn't even match what was in the basket," he said. He picked up a half-eaten fish. "This is fresh, not smoked."

He turned to John with the bread in his right hand and the fish in his left. "Can you explain this?"

John shook his head. "This is just like the other time."

Philo looked befuddled. He was clearly at a loss for words.

"Sorcery, I tell you. That is the only explanation."

A few of the men from the crowd heard him. "What do you mean, sorcery?" one asked.

Philo looked up, not realizing there was anyone there but himself. "Can you explain this?" he asked.

One of the men broke into a smile. "Isn't it obvious to you? This is a gift from Adonai. Just as He fed manna to our forefathers for forty years, His servant here has fed us."

Philo refused to accept that explanation. "We are not our forefathers. God is not feeding the nation. This is one man, providing one meal."

There was another man there, a large man who was pulling pieces out of the basket and stuffing them into his mouth. "Yes, but what a meal. Have you ever tasted better bread or eaten tastier fish?" He licked his fingers before reaching for another mouthful.

Philo was disgusted by his display. "Is this all you care about? A free meal? Doesn't it bother you not knowing where it comes from?"

One man laughed. He was as thin as a papyrus reed, and a stark contrast to his overweight friend. "We know where it came from, from Yeshua, the mashiach."

Philo's anger exploded. He threw the food in his hands to the ground. "What do you know about the mashiach?

Have you studied the scrolls? Do you know when he will arrive, how he will appear? Are you rabbis?"

His anger caught the men off guard, and they shrunk back from him.

"We are not rabbis, we are but humble men. He is a miracle worker, no? Doesn't our text say He will be a miracle worker?"

"Where does it say that in the text?" Philo yelled.

His voice carried into the crowd, and a few more came across the road.

"Tell me which scroll says the mashiach will feed crowds of fools who follow him," he screamed.

One of the newcomers reached out in a friendly gesture. "Brother, calm yourself. You're getting worked up for no reason."

Philo yanked himself away from the man and took two steps backwards. "You're all blind. You see only what you want to see. This man is leading you to your doom. He is not the true mashiach. He is a false teacher. His ways are not Moshe's ways."

More people made their way across the road to see what the commotion was all about.

"How do you know?" asked one man.

"I've been following Yeshua for six months. I've never seen you before," said another.

John suddenly had a queasy feeling in his stomach. The crowd seemed on the verge of turning against Philo. He had no doubt Philo was sure he could win any fight, but the odds were overwhelmingly against them.

"Come," he said softly, trying to get Philo's attention. "This is neither the time nor the place." He pulled Philo's arm sharply, turning him away from the crowd and towards himself.

Philo raised a fist as if to strike him, then recognized who had pulled him.

"We'd best get out of here while we can."

Philo turned and saw about a dozen men moving slowly towards them. Some had picked up rocks, and a few had thick branches in their hands.

"Your friend is right. You'd better go now," said the fat man, as he approached with a large rock in his hand where the bread had been a moment earlier. "We don't exactly like the way you're talking."

Philo turned, and the two of them walked straight towards Yeshua and his talmidim. John felt that between the crowd with sticks and rocks and Yeshua, they were safer with Yeshua.

The crowd followed for several steps, lost interest, and returned to the road.

John let out a sigh of relief. "You almost got us killed," he said.

Philo kept walking. "I'm sorry if you were scared," he said. "It's just these people who follow this man blindly like sheep to their shepherd make me so angry. I want them to use their brains to think. I want them to see the Natzerene for what he really is."

When Philo said, 'Sheep to their shepherd,' a strange feeling came over John.

"What's the matter with you?" Philo asked.

John hesitated before answering. "Do you remember when you asked the crowd if they knew how the mashiach would appear?"

Philo nodded.

> *He will stand and feed his flock*
> *in the strength of Adonai,*
> *in the majesty of the name*
> *of Adonai his God;*
> *and they will stay put, as he grows great*
> *to the very ends of the earth*

"The scroll of Mikhah," said John. "The prophet spoke of a mashiach that would feed His flock."

Philo remained silent.

"You don't think we just witnessed that here, do you?"

"Are you telling me you think this filthy peasant is your king?" he asked, in a voice dripping with disdain.

John carefully thought about his answer. "No," he said, meekly.

Philo sighed. "Tomorrow, we will tell Nakdimon all about this, and he will decide what best to do."

They walked along in silence, circling back to their belongings. They thought it best to sleep separately from the rest of the crowd.

17

A Faith Shaken

"Miracles?" asked Nakdimon.

Philo nodded. "The crowds follow him, not because they agree with his teachings, but because they want to see miracles."

"And he provides these miracles?" asked Sha'ul.

Again, Philo nodded. "While I don't think they are legitimate supernatural miracles from Adonai, his followers are completely accepting of them."

Nakdimon and Sha'ul turned to each other and spoke in soft whispers.

"Do you think they believe us?" asked John.

Philo shushed him and nodded. "Miracles are nothing new. We have seen them performed by a number of other so-called prophets."

"But his miracles are quite spectacular," John said.

"Healings are easy to fake. That thing with the bread and the fish, that was impressive, but there has to be a logical way he accomplished it. We just haven't figured it out yet."

Nakdimon turned back to the boys. "You say that he performed these 'miracles' while on the road from Tzion?" he asked.

Philo nodded. "About four hours west of here."

Nakdimon and Sha'ul conferred for another moment. "He must have had the food planted there specifically for that moment," said Nakdimon. "This could work to our advantage. If we can force him to perform one of these 'miracles' at a time of our choosing, when he is not prepared, we may be able to turn the crowd against him."

"Where is he now?" asked Sha'ul.

"I believe he is in the town square," said John.

"We shall go at once and put a stop to these infernal demonstrations," said Nakdimon.

Sha'ul did not move. "I must return to Yerushalayim tonight. I have been summoned. You go without us."

John saw Sha'ul leave the room, followed by Philo.

When the Council arrived at the square an hour later, Yosef from the Sanhedrin had joined them. There were several townspeople already waiting for Yeshua. At the sight of the Council approaching, several of the larger men pushed their way forward, creating a wall to protect the younger and weaker if there should be a fight.

Yosef raised his hand. "What is the meaning of this?" he asked. "Why do you impede our way?"

One of the men in the crowd spoke. "Rabbi, I am a common man. I do not have your learning, your authority, or your wealth. But I saw yesterday your two spies with Yeshua, the one we call the mashiach."

Yosef immediately waved him off. "He is no mashiach. He is but a simple man from Natzeret."

The crowd disagreed. "You have not seen Him as we have," another said.

"I've seen him heal the sick," said one.

"He healed my brother from leprosy," said another.

"I was there when He healed a woman by the road."

"I hear He raised a dead girl."

Nakdimon stepped forward and tried to quite the crowd. "These stories are just that, nothing but stories. No man has the power to do any of these things."

"He does," cried a woman from the back. "He is the mashiach."

The crowd's murmurings grew. Suddenly one shouted, "There he is, by the docks." The crowd ran from the square towards the shore.

Yeshua and several of his disciples were readying a boat for sail. Yosef again pushed his way through the crowds.

"We will put to rest this nonsense of him being from God," Yosef said, and turned to Yeshua. "You there, Yeshua of Natzeret. Give us a miraculous sign from heaven to prove yourself."

Yeshua sighed deeply, as if it came straight from his heart. "Why does this generation want a sign? Yes! I tell you, no sign will be given to this generation!"

John watched the crowd's reaction to Yosef's demands. The citizens of K'far-Nachum, like his uncle, may not fully trust the priests, but at least they had always been respectful.

Yosef would not back down. "Are you saying you cannot perform even the simplest of miracles? These people," he waved at the crowd that had surrounded them, "they call you the mashiach. This is blasphemy, unless you really are who they say you are. Prove yourself. Put this issue to rest. Show us even the most simple of signs, and we will believe you too."

Yeshua turned to Yosef. "You will believe? When it is evening, you say, 'Fair weather ahead,' because the sky is red, and in the morning you say, 'Storm today!' because the sky is red and overcast. You know how to read the appearance of the sky, but you can't read the signs of the times!"

This man from Natzeret showed no respect for the office of the priests, John thought. It had to be that he was a false prophet. No true prophet of Adonai would trample and discredit His servants here on earth.

"These are not the signs we are speaking of," said Nakdimon. "Prove yourself, or stopping leading these people on."

Yeshua turned to the crowd, ignoring the priests. "A wicked and adulterous generation is asking for a sign? It will certainly not be given a sign—except the sign of JoYonah!"

Without waiting for further discussion, he walked up the ramp and disappeared into the boat.

Yosef stood there, open-mouthed. He took a deep breath, than carried on his attack. "Is it then that you cannot perform miracles?"

No one paid him any attention. Yeshua's followers completed their preparations to get under way.

"You cannot leave like this," Nakdimon yelled. "As the religious authority in this town, I demand you answer me."

The crowd laughed.

"He even has power to silence priests," mocked one man.

"Our own rabbis are powerless in his presence."

"He is the mashiach."

John could not understand why his fellow townspeople followed Yeshua, agreeing with him so easily. Don't they see he had to be a liar?

Yosef addressed the Council, loud enough so the crowd could hear. "We will leave now," he said, trying to regain some dignity. "This man is not worthy of our efforts." He headed back to Nakdimon's home, ignoring the taunts coming from some of the crowd.

John watched as the ship departed from K'far-Nachum for the other side of the lake.

Yosef rested under Nakdimon's olive trees with the other priests.

"I have never been so treated. I am sorry, I should have listened. You were correct," he apologized to Nakdimon.

"It is as I have stated. Every confrontation we have with this man ends similarly. His speech is unprecedented, his answers most amazing. He is unlike any other false prophet we have dealt with."

Yosef nodded in agreement. "We must find a way to get through him. More confrontations like this only give him credibility amongst the crowds. Who is he that he can speak like that? I thought he was a peasant."

Nakdimon did not hesitate in his answer. "He is Yeshua ben-Yosef of Natzeret. Until a few years ago, he was a simple carpenter. Now, he may be the greatest threat ever to our way of life."

Yosef paused. He rubbed his eyes, breathed deeply, and slowly exhaled. "He speaks well, no?" he asked.

Everyone assembled nodded in agreement.

"Master," offered John, "what of his followers, his talmidim?"

Yosef turned and glared at John. "Boy, who are you to be listening in on my conversations?"

Nakdimon quickly came to John's defense. "This boy is one of my brightest pupils. He has gifts and I believe he will one day make a fine rabbi."

John wilted under the glare of the representative from the Sanhedrin.

"You were saying, boy?" barked Yosef. "What about his talmidim?"

John swallowed hard, trying to steady his nerves. "All I was asking, Excellency, is I have seen his followers off preaching his words alone. When Yeshua is not around."

Yosef's eyes widened and a smile began to form. "Is this

true?" he asked Nakdimon.

"I have never seen this."

"But I have," pleaded John. "His followers travel about without their teacher to protect them. Perhaps if we started by discrediting them, we can more easily get to Yeshua."

Yosef paused only a moment to consider the idea. Yosef addressed Nakdimon. "Send your fine student here to locate some of his followers alone, and come back and bring me to them. I will finish this task, and the sooner the better." Yosef headed into the coolness of the house.

John sprinted across the courtyard and out the front gates.

It took him less than an hour to find two of Yeshua's talmidim off by themselves, preaching his blasphemy. When he did, he had a young boy send word to the Council while he stayed with the men lest they should leave.

They were at a small rock wall separating two tracts of land. Both men dressed in old, worn robes of brown and tan, with dust visible along the hems. They took turns preaching the words of their teacher.

Around them sat several dozen men, women and children, all equally dirty and unkempt. They were silent, drinking in every word being spoken. Occasionally, a murmur went throughout the assembled mass as they agreed with a particular point or comment, but for the most part, it was silent except for the voices of the men speaking. John stood along the road, separated by several dozen feet from the group, watching intently.

John heard some commotion behind him and saw that Yosef and the others were approaching. Yosef leaned over to speak softly into John's ear. "Do you know those men?"

"The one on the left, his name is Bartholomew and the other is called Y'hudah. He is from K'riot. Both of them are students of the rabbi Yeshua."

Yosef snorted at the title given. "You there," he called out.

At the sudden sound of Yosef's voice, several of the women near the back jumped, startled by the priest's proximity. Many of the men, when they saw to whom the voice belonged, began to clench their fists and breathe deeply, perhaps getting ready to protect Yeshua's men.

The crowd became nervous as they realized members of the Council were standing so close.

"I am Yosef of Ramatayim, a member of the Sanhedrin in Yerushalayim."

Everyone backed off giving Yosef a clear line to the two men.

Bartholomew and Y'hudah did not seem intimidated. "What is your business here?" asked Y'hudah.

Yosef stood tall and put on his most authoritative voice. "We have received word in Yerushalayim of your teacher, Yeshua. We have come a long way to speak with him."

"He is not here," said Y'hudah.

Yosef bit his lower lip and shook his head, as if he was disappointed. "That is too bad. We had hoped to learn a little more about his teachings. Are you his talmidim?"

Y'hudah and Bartholomew exchanged nervous looks. "Yes," they replied in unison.

Yosef's smile was warm and inviting.

John looked at the other priests. They too smiled. The crowd nearby began to relax. *Whatever you're going to do, Yosef, get on with it.*

"Good, good. Then perhaps we can ask you some questions."

Y'hudah and Bartholomew nodded their agreement.

"And where does your teacher hail from?" he began.

Y'hudah stepped forward, prepared to take most of the questions. "He is from Natzeret."

Yosef snorted. "Natzeret? I have been to Natzeret. Nothing good has ever come out of such a place."

The crowd laughed a little at Yosef's statements. John knew the citizens of his city looked poorly on anyone or anything from Natzeret. It was such a very small and unimportant little village, it was hard to imagine anyone important coming from there, much less the mashiach.

"Is it true he claims to be the mashiach?" asked Yosef.

Y'hudah answered thoughtfully. "There are those who make that claim," he said.

"Does he?"

Y'hudah hesitated a moment. "I believe he is the mashiach."

Yosef scoffed and addressed the crowd. "You believe?

And who are you to believe? What is your background? What gives you the authority to make such a claim? Are you a learned scholar of our Scriptures?"

Y'hudah shook his head. "No, I am but a humble man. I have no learning on these matters other than what my rabbi has taught me."

Yosef seemed pleased. "So tell me, are you familiar with the scroll of Micah?"

John leaned over to speak softly to Nakdimon. "What is he doing?"

Nakdimon shrugged his shoulders. "I don't know. Let's see where he takes this."

Yosef repeated his question.

Y'hudah and Bartholomew both seemed puzzled. "No, I cannot recall any specific passages from that scroll."

Yosef addressed the crowd. It had almost doubled as word spread that the priests had arrived to engage Yeshua's men in debate.

"You have not read our sacred scrolls? Are you not the talmidim of the great Yeshua of Natzeret, followers of the true mashiach?"

Y'hudah and Bartholomew remained silent.

Yosef cleared his throat. "Mikhah the Morashti, was a prophet of Judah. He knew Yesha'yahu, and during his life, Jotham, Ahaz, and Hezekiah were kings of Judah."

John understood what Yosef was doing. By naming these three kings from the ancient history, he was placing the context of the Scripture in its proper place. He looked around and saw most of the crowd nodded in agreement, for they were familiar with these names.

"He wrote a scroll that prophesied the coming of the mashiach. Would you like me to quote you from it?" Yosef continued without giving Yeshua's men a chance to respond. "It says:

> *But you, Beit-Lechem near Efrat,*
> *so small among the clans of Y'hudah,*
> *out of you will come forth to me*
> *the future ruler of Isra'el,*
> *whose origins are far in the past,*
> *back in ancient times.*
> *Therefore he will give up Isra'el*

only until she who is in labor gives birth.
Then the rest of his kinsmen
will return to the people of Isra'el.
He will stand and feed his flock
in the strength of Adonai,
in the majesty of the name
of Adonai his God;
and they will stay put, as he grows great
to the very ends of the earth;
and this will be peace."

John's eyes widened as Yosef spoke. "He's using the prophecies of the mashiach against them," he whispered to Nakdimon.

His master shushed him.

"This scroll speaks of the coming mashiach. Let me ask you," said Yosef, addressing Y'hudah directly, "Where does your teacher come from again?"

Y'hudah looked alarmed. "From Natzeret."

"From Natzeret," Yosef said loudly, turning to address the crowd, "But our sacred prophets say he will come from Beit-Lechem. How can this be?"

Y'hudah did not answer.

"It's true. The priest speaks the truth," said a woman next to John. Immediately the entire crowd whispered about the point Yosef had made.

Yosef waited only a moment. "Our sacred prophet says this mashiach will have origins from the distant past. Tell me, who was Yeshua's father?"

"His father was Yosef."

"And what is his profession?"

"He is a carpenter in Natzeret."

Yosef laughed loudly, and many in the crowd joined him. "A carpenter? Does this carpenter have origins from a distant past? Is this carpenter descended from a line of kings?"

The crowd started to talk loudly amongst themselves.

Yosef raised his hand to try to quiet them. "Our sacred prophets say the mashiach will be a ruler of all Israel. Tell me, from where does your teacher rule?"

Y'hudah stood silent, unwilling to answer. Bartholomew began to breathe heavily through his nose, as if trying to calm himself.

"Our sacred prophet says he will be highly honored around the world. Tell me, what honors has your teacher received?"

Y'hudah and Bartholomew remained silent.

Yosef stepped forward until he stood right under Y'hudah and Bartholomew. "Can this nomadic mashiach from Natzeret perform miracles?"

Y'hudah answered. "I have seen it many times, with my own eyes. He has the power of God in him."

Yosef addressed the crowd. "They say your teacher can heal, cast out demons, and such. Since you are such learned students of his, surely you too can perform miracles?"

Y'hudah was playing right into Yosef's trap.

"Then I would say to you, if he truly is the mashiach, these powers are also in you, his closest talmidim."

Yosef addressed the crowd. "Who here needs healing today? Come forth and see if these men are truly what they say they are."

Before Y'hudah or Bartholomew could protest, several people came forward with various problems. One, though, stood out from the others. A large man stepped forward, tall, though thin. His long, dark hair was unkempt and streaked with gray, as was his long beard.

John gasped. It was his uncle!

"Teacher, I have here my son."

John pushed aside some of the crowd for a better view. He saw his uncle and with him, his younger brother David.

"I beg you, heal him. He is only four, yet I have never heard him speak, because he is possessed by an evil spirit that won't let him talk."

Uncle pushed David out until he stood alone in front of Yosef and the talmidim. The crowd backed away, fearful the demon might make itself known at any moment.

Yosef turned to Y'hudah. "Well, are you the talmidim of the true mashiach? Cast out this demon and I will bow my knee to him and be his talmid."

Y'hudah came down from the wall and walked up to David.

The boy stared at the ground.

Y'hudah raised his hand and spoke. "In the name of Yeshua of Natzeret, I command you evil spirit to leave this boy and never return," he said in a loud voice.

David continued to stare at the ground.

Yosef leaned over and spoke into Y'hudah's ear. "Maybe he didn't hear you."

The crowd laughed.

Y'hudah's eyes darted back and forth at the crowd's laughter, but he tried again. "Do not toy with me, foul demon, or you shall feel my teacher's wrath. Leave this boy NOW!"

David turned to face Y'hudah. His brow furled in anger and he began to breathe heavily. John feared one of David's episodes was about to start. John ran out of the crowd and knelt by David, trying to soothe the boy.

Several people in the crowd recognized John.

"You're scaring him," John pleaded with Y'hudah. "He's just a little boy."

Yosef's smile never slacked, but John could sense anger in his eyes. "Perhaps the demon is deaf," he said to the crowd's great amusement. "Perhaps you should try healing the demon before trying to remove him."

The people howled with laughter.

Yosef smug face made him look as if he had finally begun to get the upper hand.

Before Y'hudah could try again, a murmur went through the crowd. Like small animals sensing an approaching predator, all of them simultaneously looked to the west.

Bartholomew, who still stood on the wall above everyone else, turned to see what was causing the commotion, and smiled.

John saw Yeshua and several of his disciples approaching. The laughter in the crowd quickly silenced, as a child caught by a parent in an act of disobedience.

Yeshua walked right up to Y'hudah and Yosef. "What's the discussion about?" he asked

Uncle knelt before Yeshua with his head lowered. In all of his years, John never recalled seeing his uncle approach anyone humbly.

"Rabbi, I brought my son to you because he has an evil spirit in him that makes him unable to talk. Whenever it seizes him, it throws him to the ground—he foams at the mouth, grinds his teeth and becomes stiff all over. I asked your talmidim to drive the spirit out, but they couldn't do it."

John stood silent, seeing how Yeshua would answer this request. A part of him secretly hoped he was wrong and Yeshua had the power to heal.

Yeshua faced the crowd.

"People without any trust! How long will I be with you? How long must I put up with you? Bring him to me!"

John walked David towards the Natzerene. The boy took a few steps, and then fell to the ground in a violent convulsion, writhing and foaming at the mouth.

John fell away from his brother. He had seen this too many times in the past. But today, now, something was different. The convulsions seemed far more severe. "You're killing him!" John cried.

Yeshua turned and spoke to Uncle. "How long has this been happening to him?"

"Aren't you the mashiach? Wouldn't you know how long this has been happening?" Yosef asked sarcastically.

A few nervous chuckles circulated through the audience.

John's uncle refused to raise his head and address Yeshua directly. He replied, "Ever since childhood, and it often tries to kill him by throwing him into the fire or into the water." His uncle looked directly at Yeshua for the first time. "But if you can do anything, have pity on us and help us!"

Yeshua's eyes grew large at Uncle's request, and he raised his eyebrows in a look of bewilderment. "What do you mean, 'if you can'?" Yeshua asked. "Everything is possible to someone who has trust!"

Uncle immediately dropped his head to the dirt. "I do trust—help my lack of trust!"

Yeshua looked out over the crowd. It had swelled to almost a thousand, and more still were coming.

He turned to David, who was still convulsing in the sand. "You deaf and dumb spirit! I command you: come out of him, and never go back into him again!"

A hideous howl came from David. He began bucking and twitching as if being devoured from the inside. Some of the women watching could not bear it and tuned away.

Yosef looked on, dumbfounded.

Just as suddenly, all was still. David lay there motionless.

John leaned over his little brother, who lay motionless in the dirt. He reached down and tried to determine if he was breathing. David's skin felt cold and wet. John feared the worst and glared at Yeshua. "What have you done to him?"

"He's dead," said someone in the crowd. A murmur ran through the crowd, "Yeshua killed him," they all said.

John held his little brother's hand, when suddenly the boy stirred. John saw see his chest move, indicating he was still alive.

Yeshua knelt gently by the prone body. He grasped the small hand in his. Instantly David's eyes opened and Yeshua helped him to his feet.

The crowd marveled, and many fell to their knees before Yeshua.

John fell back onto the dry sand. There before him stood Yeshua and David. John's eyes were the same height as his little brother's and, for the first time, there was a look of peace and joy in them. David took John's hand and smiled at him.

"It is all right, brother," David said.

John felt tears in his eyes. David spoke! Oh, how he wished his mother was here to see this. John gave David a hug, and the little boy squeezed back hard, forcing the tears from John's eyes.

Without addressing the priests, Yeshua turned and left. Much of the crowd followed him.

Uncle ran forward to his son. He dropped to his knees. "David?" he asked, tentatively.

"Yes, Papa?" the boy replied.

His uncle cried. "Oh, my boy, my beautiful boy," he said, as he swallowed David in an enormous hug.

Yosef and the priests remained silent. Without a word, they turned back to Nakdimon's house.

Is this possible? Could this false teacher have healed my brother?

The square emptied, until only the three of them remained. Across the square stood the lone figure of a girl,

Myriam. Slowly, she made her way over to him.

"Now do you believe?" she asked.

John said nothing.

She turned and followed the crowd after Yeshua.

"Boy," cried Nakdimon. John snapped out of his stupor and saw his master and the others were quite a ways off. He jumped to his feet and ran after them.

John turned one last time to the scene. His uncle and brother were hugging and smiling. John suddenly felt shame that he was not there, that he was with his master. John felt envy for what had happened to David. John wished deeply to again be a part of his family, but knew that life was gone, and Nakdimon and the priests were his family now. Anger swelled over what had happened, anger that it hurt his current family and anger that it had not happened to him.

Then David, without leaving his father's grasp, raised one small hand and waved to his older brother.

John turned his back on them and rejoined Nikdimon.

He caught up quickly. Yosef walked several steps ahead, fuming over the latest failure.

Nakdimon quietly asked John, "That was your father, wasn't it?"

John chose not to look at the older man. "Stepfather, actually," he said.

Nakdimon shook his head. "And the boy?"

"My brother," said John.

Nakdimon sighed. "I was afraid of that. Is there any chance your uncle staged this entire show for the Natzeret? Perhaps for some silver?"

John considered it. He had no doubts his uncle would do just about anything for a little extra money. "No, I have known my brother for all of his life. His illness was real, and so, I must assume his cure is also."

"Dangerous business," said Nakdimon, "dangerous business. Yosef cannot allow such displays to continue. We've tolerated this man far too long. I fear what steps Yerushalayim will take next."

John swallowed at the thought that his uncle and brother might be the cause of an invasion of K'far-Nachum.

They arrived at the gates to Nakdimon's home. "We

will retire for the remainder of the day," announced Yosef. "Tomorrow we will depart to Yerushalayim for the Passover."

John was surprised Yosef seemed to be giving up so quickly. "At sunrise, we will be at the south gate." He spoke to Nakdimon. "I expect you and your closest advisors to accompany us. You will report to Kayafa everything you have seen and done, and then we will decide how best to deal with this man."

Nakdimon's eyes grew wide in surprise at the invitation to spend the Passover in Yerushalayim. "Yes, Excellency, I will arrange for donkeys and porters for the long trip." He turned to John. "You have been most closely monitoring this man, I expect you to join us."

Yerushalayim! John had longed to visit that fabled city.

Nakdimon and the priests from Yerushalayim entered the gates and disappeared into the house.

Sha'ul and Philo were just inside the wall. They were dressed for travel, with several servants and pack animals prepared for the trip. "We have heard what happened," Sha'ul said.

John could not answer, ashamed that his family was part of the heretic's deceptions.

"Before we leave," Sha'ul said, "we need to know for sure. Seek out your family and find out if this healing was true or false."

John said his farewells to his friend and the master, then ran off towards his home.

The afternoon sun was low on the horizon when John reached his family home. He knocked several times on the door, but there was no answer. He pushed open the door and walked inside.

The house was in disarray. It looked as if no one had lived in it for several weeks. A layer of sand coated everything. Dust and dirt were everywhere.

John turned to leave, only to see a familiar face at the door. "Hello, John," said Myriam.

John's eyes widened at the sight of his old friend. "Myriam, how are..." He paused. "Have you seen my family?" he asked.

Myriam looked down at her feet. "I thought you saw

them today, in the square. You were there."

The memory of his reaction this afternoon shamed John. "Yes. But where are they now, where have they gone?"

Myriam looked up and into John's eyes. "Your family has been with us for the last month. They had no food, no income, and we took them in because your mother was always so nice to mine when she was ill."

John's anger boiled inside him, not at Myriam or her family, but at himself for not being there for them. He could have given them more, more money and more time, but he'd been interested in his own life, not theirs.

"I talked to them about Yeshua. They understand now. Your stepfather, your mother, your brother, they all know the power, the truth of Yeshua."

John did not answer.

"Are you so blinded by your studies, that you cannot see the truth, also?"

John did not know what to say.

She grabbed his hand and said, "Come with me, I want to show you something."

John took Myriam's hand and they were silent as they walked south, out of the city.

They walked along in silence. Myriam seemed content only in having John with her.

They passed through the northern city gate. As they walked up the road to the crest of the hill, they passed several beggars, pleading for a few coins. John thought back to Yeshua's statements about their wealth, and he felt ashamed. He had a few small coins, and he gave them to some of the beggars. When he was out of coins, they continued until they reached the top of the hill.

"I recognize this place," said John. "This is the road to the Yarden, where the Immerser used to preach."

Myriam's eye saddened at the mention of Yochanan's name. "Yes," she said, "just over this hill is where he used to preach. Why don't you go up there and take a look." She stopped and sat down by the side of the road. "I'll wait for you here."

"What's up there?" asked John. "What is it you want me to see?"

Myriam made no effort to answer.

John hesitated a moment, and then walked up the hill. Just before he got to the top, he heard a low roar, like a thousand insects swarming in one place. When he reached the top, he could see the entire valley, all the way to the mountains of the north.

Over every visible piece of land, he saw people. Thousands and thousands, like some vast camp for an approaching army. There were tents and wagons, livestock and fires. He could make out groups of people, individuals, and families. They were all talking, but from this distance, he could not make out any of the conversations, only the low drone of their voices. He stood there for several minutes looking.

He looked to his right and saw that Myriam had joined him.

"Amazing, isn't it?" she asked.

"Who are they?"

Myriam laughed quietly then caught herself. "Don't you know?" she asked, "Haven't you guessed?"

John stood silent for a few moments. "There must be thousands of them," he said.

"Tens of thousands, actually," replied Myriam. "All of them touched in some way by Yeshua. All of them believers in who He is and what He stands for."

John could not believe what he saw. The P'rushim had assumed he had at best a few hundred hardened followers. Certainly, his followers grew as he approached town, but didn't he just have smaller groups that traveled between towns? Had the Council thought he had a thousand, they would have been terrified. But this...

"What are they all doing?"

"Waiting," said Myriam.

"Waiting for what?"

Myriam turned to John. "Waiting for Yeshua to fulfill the prophecy, waiting for Him to take His place at the throne of David."

John could not believe what he was hearing. "This man is not the mashiach," he said sternly. "Your wait will be in vain."

"How do you know?" demanded Myriam. "Is it just because He doesn't fit your view of what the mashiach will be?"

John was not sure how to answer. "Myriam, I have done a lot of study on the writings of our fathers. They very clearly give us signs to look for." Even as he spoke, the words of Nakdimon rang in his ears.

"Clear signs?" she asked. "I would never say I know as much about our religious writings as you, but how can you deny He isn't sent by God? You've seen His miracles. You know what His powers are, how He speaks, how He acts. This is no man seeking glory for Himself. This is the Son of God standing before us. Can't you accept that?"

John thought back to all he had seen, all he had heard. From the baptizer to Rivkah to Myriam's mother to his own family, he had to admit this man had performed many miraculous things over the last few years.

"But, he does not fit the prophecies," he tried again. "The scrolls are very clear."

Myriam would have none of it. "I don't care how clear you think the scrolls are. Maybe you aren't reading them correctly. Maybe you don't have all of the answers." She turned to look at him, gazing deep into his eyes. "John, you know who He is. You've seen what He can do. Are you so blinded by the beliefs of your teachers you cannot see what is plainly in front of you?"

John could not answer. He could not think of what to say. He looked back at the mass of people. "Are your parents down there?" he asked.

Myriam pointed off a few degrees to the west. "Over there. My mother is healed. We have chosen to follow Yeshua wherever He may lead us."

John looked over the mass. "What of Rivkah? And Ya'ir?" he asked.

Myriam shifted her arm right. "When last I spoke to them, they were over in that area. Rivkah is doing well. Ya'ir knows we are friends. He asks about you all of the time. Do you want to go see him?"

John shook his head.

"Ya'ir thanks Adonai for that night you brought him to Yeshua. Ya'ir knows, had you not done that, he would be dead to the world."

John did not want to accept responsibility for Ya'ir's decision. John had one more question, but was afraid to ask it.

As if sensing his problem, Myriam said, "Come, if you want, I can take you to your family. Yes, they are here also." She took several steps towards the crowd, but John could not move.

"Don't you want to see them?" she asked.

John didn't know what he wanted. Three years ago, it was nothing more than to leave his family. Then God had granted him every wish he had wanted. Now it seemed he wanted nothing more but to go back to them.

John stood up straight and proud. "I cannot go," he said. "My life is with the priests. I can't go down there."

Large tears flooded Myriam's eyes. "John, don't do this," she pleaded. "They have blinded you. Open your eyes. Look at the truth you have seen."

John felt like he was on the verge of crying too, although he kept a tight face so Myriam would not catch on. "I can't. Even if I wanted to, I can't abandon my studies."

"Why?" asked Myriam, fighting back tears.

"Because..." John let his voice trail off. "Because, this is not what I want," he finally said, gesturing out at the mass of people. "I want to get out of this city and be something. As a rabbi, people will respect me. I want people to know me, not see me as one more face in a mass of people."

Tears streamed down Myriam's face. "John," she pleaded, "don't do this to yourself. You're better than that. Open your eyes to the truth."

When John did not reply, she added, "Please, I need you."

John's mind raced as he tried to understand what was happening. "I can't go with you," he said. "I can't."

John turned and ran down the hill. Myriam called for him to come back.

As John ran from Myriam, his watering eyes made it difficult to see.

John ran down the road, back to the northern gate and the city, back to Nakdimon and his "family."

Before he could reach it, the gate opened and several hundred people came through. The crowd was large and noisy. John soon realized they were some more of Yeshua's followers. Some of them discussed David's healing earlier today.

All of the beggars outside the gate stood and pleaded with the crowd for money. One of them said nothing. He just sat and tried to understand what was going on. John recognized him. He was Timaeus' son. He had lost his sight many years ago, and had been begging ever since.

He remained still for some time as the crowds passed by, then suddenly he yelled as loudly as he could. "Yeshua, Son of David, have mercy on me!"

Some of the people in the crowd became nervous. "Be quiet!" they yelled at him.

But the blind beggar would not be silenced. He only shouted louder, "Son of David, have mercy on me!"

This went on for several minutes. Suddenly, to John's astonishment, Yeshua himself was there with his talmidim. When Yeshua heard the man's cries, he stopped. He turned to the crowd and said, "Tell him to come here."

The crowd around the blind man opened up and allowed him clear access to Yeshua. "Cheer up," they said. "Come on, he's calling you!"

The blind beggar threw aside his coat, jumped up, and came to Yeshua.

"What do you want me to do for you?" Yeshua asked.

The blind man did not look down, as others had. He looked forward, straight and true, although he of course could not see. "Teacher," he said, "I want to see!"

Yeshua said to him, "Go your way. Your faith has healed you."

The blind man's face changed. Instead of having the appearance of looking off into the distance, his countenance fell. He turned and looked first at Yeshua, then over at the disciples, then over at the crowd. With each turn of his head, a smile grew broader and broader. John saw tears streaming down the man's cheeks.

"My eyes are open," he cried. "I can see. Yeshua has made me see. I can see."

The crowd was very happy for him, and he walked around them, seeing many for the first time.

Yeshua said nothing, but turned and headed down the

road, to where John had left Myriam. The crowd followed him.

When it again became quiet, John emerged from behind the bush. He remembered his training. Without another thought, he turned and walked through the gate, back to his studies.

18

The Triumphal Entry

It was early in the evening when Yosef, Nakdimon, and their entire party finally crested the road and caught their first glimpse of Yerushalayim. The long journey exhausted John, so quickly had they walked the dusty road. Yet even in his exhaustion, he could not contain his excitement to finally see the holy city. He had heard so much about Yerushalayim while he was growing up. He had always dreamed to see it, and now the time had come.

As they walked along the road from Beit-Anyah, John could make out the tall wall of the city, a mass of stones some fifty feet in height. On either side of the road a small, three-foot-high stone wall stood. People were coming and going through the small gate in the wall into the city. John could not see into the city with any clarity, as it was in shadow compared to the bright sunlight at the road.

When they reached the gate, a delegation came out of the shadows to greet them. They were dressed in the deep purple robes of the P'rushim, the same as the robes worn by Yosef. John did not know any of them except for the one whom he met at Herod's, Anan.

"My brother," Anan said, "have you returned with good news?"

Yosef shook his head. "Sadly, no. It is as we were told. This man speaks as if he has been empowered by God Himself."

The men in purple were dismayed. "What are we to do?"

Yosef motioned to the party. "These men have all dealt with this man from Natzeret. I have brought them so they may celebrate the Passover here, and that they may instruct us in the ways of this man."

The welcoming party greeted the delegation from K'far-Nachum. John saw Philo. His heart jumped at seeing his friend. He made his way over to greet him.

"Philo, it's great to see you."

Philo gave John a hug that lifted him off the ground. "It's good to see you too, old friend," he said.

John leaned over and spoke in a softer tone. "This is an incredible situation we are in," he said.

Philo nodded in agreement.

"Who are all of these men?"

Philo pointed to several. "He is Mattat'i. He is Mal'ah. He is Yochanan. And, of course, you remember Anan, my uncle."

John heard loud voices as if from a distance. Philo hopped onto one of the walls along the road to get a better view, then reached down to help John up.

Several men came running quickly along the road, yelling as they ran past the priests. "He is coming," they yelled, "he is here." Within moments, men and women of all ages poured out through the gate, heading back down the road.

"What is the meaning of this?" one of the priests asked. No one stopped to answer. From John's vantage point, he was able to see further than the priests. His heart sank as he saw who was approaching.

"Yeshua comes," he said quietly, to Nakdimon.

Nakdimon relayed John's observation to Yosef, who in turn relayed it to the priests in purple.

"What," they said, "he is coming now?"

Nakdimon looked to John for an answer, and John nodded his head.

With a bit of indifference, the priests stepped back to see what was going to happen. After a few moments, the crowd spilled out onto the road, lining both sides of the narrow street. John could not hear what they were saying, but the general tone seemed to be one of happiness and joy.

"What foolish people," Philo whispered to him.

Several men in the crowd removed their dusty cloaks and laid them on the ground as a covering. When the women, who did not have cloaks, saw this, they began to break off leaves from the palms lining the road and laid them on the ground. John and Philo looked at each other with disgust at what the crowd was doing.

Then, Yeshua and his followers came. Yeshua sat high above the others. This puzzled John, until Yeshua came into clear view. He was riding on a donkey! John could not believe this. "That is their mashiach," he said in a mocking tone to Philo, "riding on a simple beast of burden?"

A smile came across Philo's lips. "This man cannot possibly think he is a king. How ridiculous."

Some of the first people of the crowd passed by them, and John began to understand what they were shouting.

"Please! Deliver us!" cried some.

"Blessed is he who comes in the name of Adonai!" said others.

"Blessed is the coming Kingdom of our father David!" cried yet another.

Still others shouted, "You in the highest heaven! Please! Deliver us!"

Anan could hold back no longer. "Who is this?" he demanded.

Several of the men in the crowd turned and answered, "This is Yeshua, the prophet from Natzeret in the Galil."

The men returned to their yells and praise. The priests waited for the proper moment.

Anan was becoming furious at the cries of the people. "It is blasphemous," he called out to the crowd, "to call this Natzeret a prophet. He comes not in the name of Adonai, our God, but as a false teacher."

As soon as Yeshua was next to them, Anan shouted out to him, "Rabbi! Reprimand your talmidim! Tell them not to blaspheme in this way."

Yeshua stopped the colt just across from the delegation of P'rushim. His followers looked as if they wished to attack the men, but all became silent.

Again Anan cried out in a loud voice, "Rabbi! Reprimand your talmidim!"

Yeshua did not take the bait. He looked directly at Anan then pointed at the stone wall where John and Philo stood. "I tell you that if they keep quiet, the stones will shout!"

The crowd, hearing this response, again cheered. New shouts of "Blessed is the King who is coming in the name of Adonai!" "Shalom in heaven!" and "Glory in the highest places!"

The P'rushim had no recourse. By now, Yeshua had

moved past them and through the gates into the city. So large was the crowd that even if they wanted to arrest him, they could not get near him.

When the crowd had passed and all again became quiet, Anan addressed his colleagues. "I see now how dangerous this man has become. Come, let us go to Kayafa and tell him of this. His arrival here should make it easier to address this situation once and for all."

As the men followed Anan into the city, John whispered to Philo, "I've heard them say that before."

Philo shushed him to be silent. "My father has expected this. We are not completely unprepared. We actually have many plans ready for this Yeshua. Be patient, my old friend, for today you have seen the beginning of the end of this man from Natzeret and his blasphemous teachings."

As the men walked through the streets, Nakdimon and Anan were deep in conversation. The other P'rushim were listening intently, totally ignoring John and Philo.

John quickly told Philo all that had happened since last they met. "And you, why have I not seen more of you?" he asked his old friend.

Philo looked about to be sure no one was listening. "My father has sent me out through all of Y'hudah," he said. "I have been gathering information on Yeshua and his talmidim for the last six months."

John was surprised to hear what Philo had been doing. "For what purpose?" he asked. "Were you following him?"

"Not like you and I did. No, I was visiting the towns he went to and learning what he did there, and documenting it."

Philo stopped and grabbed his friend's arm. "You must tell no one," he said, "but I have formed a friendship with one of Yeshua's talmidim. One of his inner twelve does not believe Yeshua is as the others say he is."

John was shocked to hear this news. "I thought all of his talmidim were loyal?" he asked.

Philo again walked quickly to catch up to the men ahead. "No, not all are loyal. We have one who is on our side. Soon, I will introduce him to you."

It was dark when the delegation finally reached Kayafa's home. It was a magnificent structure, so much grander than his old home in K'far-Nachum. John marveled at the marble columns and the second story windows.

As the delegation mingled in the courtyard, servants came and washed the dust off the feet of the men. John too had his feet washed by a servant, which was for him a new experience.

When all were refreshed, Kayafa came out himself to greet them. "I have heard the news," he said in a loud, authoritative voice. "I know Yeshua and his followers have entered the city, and I know crowds came with them."

"What shall we do?" asked one of the men.

"For the moment, he has left the city."

Some of the men seemed surprised Kayafa knew more than they did.

"I do not expect him to be gone for long," he continued. "You must be tired from your long journey. Come, enter into my house and refresh yourselves. Nothing more can be done tonight. In the morning, we will tell you of our plans to deal with this man and his followers."

Nakdimon, Yosef and the others seemed surprised Kayafa was so confident. Yet, they were tired and rest seemed to be a good idea.

As John and Philo were about to enter the home, Kayafa came up to his son.

"Tell me your news," he said, barely acknowledging John standing next to him.

Philo told his father of what had happened. "The crowds have become quite large," he said. "That man rode into the city on a beast of burden, just as the scrolls predicted."

John did not understand what he was saying. Philo explained, "One of our scrolls, the scroll of Z'kharyah.

> *Rejoice with all your heart, daughter of Tziyon! Shout out loud, daughter of Yerushalayim! Look! Your king is coming to you. He is righteous, and he is victorious. Yet he is humble — he's riding on a donkey, yes, on a lowly donkey's colt."*

John had not yet read Z'kharyah's scroll. "Does this mean he is the mashiach?" John asked. He regretted the question the moment it came from his mouth.

Kayafa turned very angry. "All this means is the man is a student of the Scriptures. He knew that verse was in there, and he manipulated the situation to make himself appear to be the mashiach." He calmed down, then continued, "This should be the final proof we need to put our plan into action."

Kayafa turned to his son. "Philologus, I need you to go once more out of the city and find this Yeshua. Do not approach him, only observe, so we may know his movements." Kayafa handed him a small sack of coins. "You know who this is for?" he asked.

Philo nodded. Kayafa turned to John. "I know you must be tired from your journey, but I need you to accompany my son. This may be the most important thing either of you do."

John nodded his head in agreement, and without a moment's hesitation, he followed Philo back out of the city.

"Where do you think he went?" John asked.

"Our sources tell us he is spending the night in Beit-Anyah. When we get there, there is someone I want you to meet."

The journey to Beit-Anyah was quick, and John soon found himself standing outside a small home. There were perhaps a hundred people lining the streets in front of it.

Philo pointed at the home. "He is staying there for the night."

As the moon rose higher, many of the people simply curled up and slept wherever they had been standing. Quietly, the door opened and a stream of light illuminated the streets. A man snuck through, checked to see if anyone had seen him and quickly closed the door. Philo stood up and walked over to him, with John following.

When the man recognized Philo, he motioned to keep quiet. He grabbed Philo by the arm and ushered him into a darkened alley between two buildings. John could make out no features of the man as he stood in the darkened space.

"Who is this?" the man demanded, pointing at John.

Philo introduced his friend. "This is my friend, Yochanan ben Elioenai. He is an apprentice of Nakdimon, from K'far-Nachum. He has traveled a long way, and is to be completely trusted."

The man looked at John with disdain. "I trust no one, least of all someone from K'far-Nachum."

John did not understand the man's apprehension towards him. Then the man stepped into the light. John was astonished.

"Do you know me, boy?" the man asked.

John was without speech momentarily. "I... I know who you are. You are Y'hudah. You are one of the talmidim of Yeshua."

The man did not seem pleased to find out John knew who he was. "Have we met before, boy?" he asked.

John nodded. "Once, outside K'far-Nachum, when you were with Bartholomew."

Y'hudah tried to remember. "Yes, you were with Yosef when he confronted us."

Philo interrupted. "We have little time for this," he said.

Immediately Y'hudah was back on task. "You are correct."

"What has happened?" asked Philo.

"After we entered the city, he went to the Temple. I do not know why, for he looked about, then we left."

"What did he want with the Temple?" asked Philo.

Y'hudah grew angry. "I just told you, I don't know," he said.

Philo kept quiet, not interrupting.

"But I do know he will be there again tomorrow morning. We will be leaving at dawn. Will you be there to see?"

"What will he do?" asked Philo.

Y'hudah shook his head. "I do not know. He must have gone there this evening for a reason. All I know is he told us to be ready to return at dawn tomorrow."

Philo handed Y'hudah a small sack of coins. "This is from the P'rushim, in thanks for all you have done."

The man took the coin sack. "I don't need your money," he said, and he offered it back to Philo.

"Keep it," said Philo. "It is but a token. But there will be more where that came from if you continue with the plans we have discussed."

Y'hudah placed the sack within his robes. "I must get back to the home before the others become suspicious. Wait here until the moon arrives overhead, so that no one suspects our meeting."

Philo nodded and Y'hudah headed off into the night.

John watched until the man disappeared from sight. "What plan?" he asked Philo.

Philo was still searching the street to be sure no one had seen them. "All will be revealed soon, old friend."

19

Chaos at the Market

John was having a wonderful dream that he, Philo and Myriam were back in K'far-Nachum when he felt his body shake violently. He opened his eyes to see Philo standing over him. "It's before dawn. Get up and get dressed. We are going to the Temple."

John wiped the sleep from his eyes, then immediately got dressed. He soon found himself approaching Mount Mariah and the most holy of places, Herod's Temple at Yerushalayim.

They approached it from the south. John's heart pounded in anticipation of his first glimpse of the building. John and Philo joined other worshippers there in the pre-morning air ascending a monumental stone staircase that was at least two hundred feet wide. They would take a step up and then have to walk a few paces before reaching the next step. As they climbed, John focused on the massive limestone wall at the top of the staircase. It must have risen eighty feet into the air. Its base was plain with no details, but about thirty feet up, it had been constructed to look like stone columns were embedded into the wall for support.

They finally reached the top of the staircase and stopped to catch their breath. There were two identical openings in the wall, fifteen feet wide and twenty feet high, separated by a thick wall that Philo and he could have comfortably stood behind and no one would have known they were there. Although the openings were plain in appearance, the gate had the most beautiful underground passageways John had ever seen.

"This is called the Beautiful Gate," said Philo. "Do you see those?" Philo pointed at the magnificent columns supporting the carved stone ceiling.

"They are made of Corinthian brass, one of our most precious metals."

The ceiling was made of stone, was arched and consisted of seven large domes, each supported by columns. John was amazed at the level of intricacy of the geometric and floral stone carvings in the ceiling. As they stepped through the gate, they walked in a tunnel straight through the rock wall. John kept looking up at the carved ceiling until his neck hurt.

As they approached the end, daylight once again streamed through and John's heart raced at the thought of finally seeing the fabled Temple up close. But first, they had to climb another long staircase until they reached the top and finally emerged into the fresh morning air.

Before John stood the Temple, his first view of it at such a close distance, although to say it was close would have been a lie. They were still an amazingly long distance away from it. They now stood in its courtyard, and all John could really make out was its brilliantly white marble walls and its gleaming golden roof.

"This is the Court of the Goyim," said Philo.

It seemed bigger than all of K'far-Nachum! Hundreds of people stood in its courtyard and it looked empty. John and Philo stepped off to the side to let worshippers through.

"Turn around," Philo said.

John slowly turned his body, not wanting to take his eyes off the Temple. He snapped his head around and was stunned by the image before his eyes.

There stood a magnificent building containing hundreds and hundreds of columns more magnificent than the ones he had just seen. They were made not of limestone, but of marble, and gold shone off their tops.

"That is the Royal Porch," Philo said, "although some call it the Royal Colonnade."

Seeing all of the columns, John could understand why. "Can we go into it?" he asked.

"Absolutely."

As they walked over towards the colonnade, John turned his head all the way to the left and then all the way to the right. It was the only way he could see the length of the building. It rose at least fifty feet into the air, which supported a red clay roof. Above that, set back about thirty feet, was the center portion of the colonnade, which had openings to let light shine in and illuminate the inside.

As they reached the edge, John was again overwhelmed by the size and scale. Each column, which had seemed slender when he first saw it from a distance, was so wide that even if Philo and he stood on either side and tried, they could not touch hands. Each column hid other columns that John didn't originally notice, so that there were a total of four rows of columns. Each column supported an arch of stone that in turn supported the carved stone ceiling. As a game, he counted the number of steps from the outer edge of columns to the inner, and it was twenty.

This massive beauty hid the Center Hall, which was twice as tall as the outer aisles. John saw it illuminated with sunlight from the massive openings along its upper clerestory wall. The tall ceilings were alive with the sounds of the merchants and worshippers doing business, which seemed to be the main purpose of the building.

The busiest of places was the tables of the moneychangers. These were located just inside the outer aisles. Being subject to the Romans, many worshipers had only Roman coins. But the Temple Law required everyone entering the grounds to pay a tribute to the service of the sanctuary of "half a shekel," a Jewish coin. So that's what these men did, exchange half shekels for Roman money. Of course, they would demand a small sum for the exchange. With a hundred thousand pilgrims expected this week for the Pesach Feast, John imagined these men would make a healthy profit in the coming days.

Near the money changers were the dove merchants. Worshippers were required to offer doves in sacrifice, yet it was difficult to travel long distances with them. This was another of the businesses John imagined would make a healthy profit in the coming days.

John noticed a faint wisp of the *calaniot* flower, and realized the table he was standing next to was for selling incense. The table next to that had pots of wine needed for sacrifice in the temple. All around him, people chattered. Coins exchanged hands and were plinked in money bags.

As John saw the men working at these tables, he thought of his uncle. His uncle would be right at home with these men, as John saw one arguing with a widow over the price of a dove. The price he was demanding was so much higher than the cost would have been outside the Temple walls. These men were taking advantage of their positions by selling what they had at an enormous increase.

John flinched as a thundering crash echoed off the ceilings, followed by intense shouts. He pivoted to see Yeshua standing before one of the money changers' tables, enraged.

Like a lion on a sheep, Yeshua turned on the adjacent table, lifting it high into the air as he overtuned it. Gold and silver coins bounced off the stone floor, sliding and rolling in all directions. Any man who tried to stop him was promptly sent flying to the ground.

John could not believe any man claiming to be a rabbi could do such a thing. His first instinct was to try and stop him, to help the merchants, but Philo held him back.

"This is incredible," Philo said. "He is doing more damage to himself here than we could ever imagine."

They watched Yeshua attack the dove merchants next, turning over their tables and releasing the doves into the air.

At table after table, the merchants stood by helplessly as Yeshua disrupted their sales. A few merchants tried to escape with their supplies, but he grabbed them, too.

After the colonnade was a total shambles, Yeshua finally stopped. He breathed heavily, laboring to get air after all of his exertion.

One merchant looked at his overturned table and asked, "Why?"

Yeshua's fury calmed down. "Isn't it written in the Tanakh, 'My house will be called a house of prayer for all the Goyim'? But you have made it into a den of robbers!"

Yeshua took another deep breath and addressed all of the merchants there. "You have all made it into a den of robbers." He wiped tears from his eyes.

The merchants stood there, dumbfounded. Then Yeshua and his followers turned and left as quietly as they had come.

Philo walked into the midst of the caranage, his brilliant white robes resplendent in the morning sun. The merchants walked about with dazed looks on their faces. Some had begun to pick up the mess, while others just stood around.

One man looked up and saw Philo's robes. "Teacher," he asked, "by what authority does he to do these things? Who gave him this authority?"

Philo bent down to help the man. "I do not know."

John stood with Philo in the foyer of Anan's house. Although paling in comparison to the Royal Porch he visited that morning, it was nonetheless a magnificent structure, if this entry room was any indication. The room itself seemed to be at least as big as Ya'ir's whole house. The plaster walls were fifteen feet high, painted a deep, rich red. Each wall had a painted pattern of gold and black, their repetitive design accentuating the depth of the room. The ceiling was a brilliant white, with a green and white mosaic pattern embedded into it. Plush, multi-colored rugs covered the polished marble floors.

In the adjoining room stood the Sanhedrin, the ruling council of Yerushalyaim and all Y'hudah. John and Philo watched though the doorway as Kayafa cleared his throat and addressed the assembled P'rushim.

"My friends, for too long we have lived in fear, afraid to take action. For too long, we have allowed this Yeshua to freely move from town to town, poisoning the minds of our citizens. We have been patient, we have been lenient."

Kayafa circled the room, talking loudly while still appearing to be speaking to each member of the P'rushim personally. "We have tried to contain him, we have tried to discredit him. We have sought to expose him and to denounce him. Yet, despite our best efforts, he remains a strong and very real threat to us and to our way of life."

"But what can we do?" cried a voice from the back.

Kayafa turned to face the questioner. "Yes, what can we do? We must decide, here, what our course shall be. We must decide, now, how we will end this once and for all."

John felt a sick pit forming in his stomach. He had heard this speech once before.

"He must be put to death," said Kayafa, in a soft voice.

"No," cried many of the men there.

The great rabbi Gamli'el, visiting from Tarsus, stepped forward. "Excellency, you cannot ask us to do this. We are

Jews. He is a Jew. Jew does not kill Jew."

The others said the same thing. Kayafa waited a moment then raised his hand for silence. "We cannot kill Jew, you are correct. However…" He turned to Nakdimon. "However, I have cultivated certain relationships over my years as president of the Sanhedrin. The Roman governor of all Y'hudah is visiting here in Yerushalayim, a man named Pontius Pilate. He is a friend. We must arrest the Natzerene and bring him before the governor."

"Not during the festival, or the people will riot," said Gamli'el. The priests agreed almost in unison that they could not control the citizens if that happened.

"That is why we must do it now, before the festival of Matzah," said Kayafa. "If we delay, we risk the wrath of the city."

John feared the direction Kayafa was taking this. True, they had to stop this man. But death? That was wrong. It went against everything he read in the Tanakh. He could keep quiet no longer. He crept over to Nakdimon. "Master, this man's teachings do not justify such a sentence. His followers will protect him."

Kayafa glared at John so intently John bowed his head to hide his eyes. "His teachings are of no consequence," Kayafa said. "His followers will not defend him. We must bring him before Pilate."

The priests agreed with John. "These crowds will save him. We will never get near enough to arrest him."

"We must try once more to discredit him."

One of the priests near the rear shouted, "Perhaps if he was by himself?"

"He is never by himself," scoffed Nakdimon. "We have no way to get him alone."

"Actually, we do."

The entire P'rushim turned to see who had spoken.

Philo walked over to his father. "I have been in contact with one of Yeshua's trusted followers. This man made me aware of Yeshua's plans. Tomorrow at sunrise, he will be at the Temple to teach to all who gather there."

The priests again argued. "Do you intend to arrest this man on the Temple grounds in front of his followers?"

Kayafa held up a hand to silence the critics and let his son finish talking.

"You heard what he did at the Temple today," said Philo. "He has no respect for the Temple or its grounds. As to his followers, there will be few there at that early morning hour."

Kayafa interjected. "My friends, we must take action. I will go tomorrow morning and confront this man myself. If he fails my tests, he will be arrested, I assure you."

Nakdimon spoke loudly for all to hear. "I for one will support Kayafa." The two men faced each other and placed a hand on each other's shoulder. "I will join you."

One by one, the rest of the P'rushim shouted support.

John watched the crowd, fascinated.

I have a bad feeling about this.

20

The First Confrontation

The morning sun had not cleared the eastern mountains when the P'rushim, led by Kayafa, arrived at the Temple before dawn. The money changers and merchants were there, though not as many as yesterday. Most hid in shadows near the porches. The P'rushim stood next to the western gate and waited.

The morning sun was high when Yeshua and his followers entered. They took up a position near the eastern gate and he began teaching from the scrolls of Shlomo.

Kayafa led the P'rushim to the eastern gate. John reluctantly followed.

Kayafa stood before Yeshua and, with great disdain in his voice, interrupted Yeshua's discourse on the holy writ. "What s'mikhah do you have that authorizes you to do these things? Who gave you this s'mikhah authorizing you to do them?"

Several of Yeshua's followers jumped in surprise at Kayafa's voice. Three men stood and placed themselves between their teacher and the priests. Others glared at Kayafa and the others.

Yeshua did not appear annoyed by the interruption. "I will ask you just one question: answer me, and I will tell you by what s'mikhah I do these things."

Kayafa's eyes burned in fury at the way Yeshua controlled the conversation.

Yeshua had a twinkle in his eye, almost as if he was enjoying what was happening. "The immersion of Yochanan—was it from Heaven or from a human source?" he asked. "Answer me."

Of all the ways John had imagined this playing out, this question was entirely unexpected. What was Yeshua up to?

Kayafa turned his back to Yeshua and whispered quietly to the priests. "I know how to answer this," he whispered, "but how will his followers respond?"

Nakdimon spoke first. "If we say, 'From Heaven,' he will say, 'Then why didn't you believe him?'"

"Are we to say it was human?"

Gamli'el and others looked around the crowd that had gathered. "Many of these people are from Galil," Nakdimon said. "They all regarded Yochanan as a genuine prophet. Do we dare say it was merely human?"

John whispered to Philo. "But if we say, 'From a human source'..." Suddenly John realized the trap Yeshua had set. "He must not answer."

Philo leaned over to his father and whispered in his ear.

Kayafa nodded. He turned back to Yeshua. With a forced smile upon his lips, Kayafa answered. "We don't know."

John held his breath, hoping that by refusing to fall into the trap, the Natzeret would implicate himself.

Yeshua only smiled. "Then, I won't tell you by what s'mikhah I do these things."

Kayafa's smile disappeared at the slight. His face twisted into a rage that appeared to be difficult to control. "How dare you." He glared at the Natzeret.

John stood wide-eyed as the two men stared at each other.

Philo whispered, "Now my father has no choice. The Natzeret has laid the foundation stones for his own demise."

John nodded in agreement.

Kayafa stood furious. "You won't tell us," he snarled at Yeshua. "Who are you to refuse to answer?"

Yeshua said nothing. As the tension mounted, Shim'on stepped forward to defend his teacher. "Who is this? I'll tell you who he is. He is the mashiach, the Son of God."

Kayafa gave Sh`imon a stern look. "Beware your words, boy. Thoughts like that are blasphemous and punishable by death."

Shim'on refused to back down. Yeshua's other talmidim stepped forward to restrain him. "Quiet down, or they'll arrest us all."

Kayafa ignored the threats and spoke directly to Yeshua. "I am the president of the Sanhedrin. What right do you have to refuse to answer?"

If Yeshua feared Kayafa, he didn't show it. He motioned to his talmidim to sit down then sat as if he were teaching a class. "A man planted a vineyard," he began. "He put a wall around it, dug a pit for the wine press and built a tower, then he rented it to tenant-farmers and left."

John was lost as to what Yeshua was doing.

"What is this story?" asked Kayafa. "Answer my question."

Yeshua ignored Kayafa. "When harvest time came, he sent a servant to the tenants to collect his share of the crop from the vineyard. But they took him, beat him and sent him away empty-handed."

Kayafa's mouth opened and closed several times, as if he had something to say but chose not to. He remained quiet, waiting to see where the Natzeret was taking this story.

Yeshua continued. "So he sent another servant. This one they punched in the head and insulted. He sent another one, and him they killed, and so with many others—some they beat up, others they killed.

"He had still one person left, a son whom he loved. In the end, he sent his son to them, saying, 'My son they will respect.' But the tenants said to each other, 'This is the heir. Come, let's kill him, and the inheritance will be ours!'

"So they seized him, killed him and threw him out of the vineyard."

Yeshua looked directly at Kayafa. "What will the owner of the vineyard do? He will come, destroy those tenants and give the vineyard to others! Haven't you read the passage in the Tanakh that says, 'The very rock which the builders rejected has become the cornerstone! This has come from Adonai, and in our eyes it is amazing'?"

Yeshua made a motion and his talmidim arose. Kayafa's face had turned bright red in anger, and he looked as if he were about to burst from the effort of keeping quiet.

Yeshua's fearlessness amazed John. He understood the story. The priests and the P'rushim were the evil farmers. Yeshua was saying that they were rejecting Adonai, not him. That truly was blasphemy.

Kayafa had enough. "Arrest that heretic," he said to the priests.

Several of the priests looked at each other nervously, and then moved forward to capture Yeshua and his talmidim. The crowd that had been listening surrounded Yeshua to protect him.

"Come, let us remember our plan," said Anan, as he grabbed Kayafa's arm. "Now is not the time or place."

Kayafa glared at Yeshua, then turned and left. Anan and several of the P'rushim followed him.

Nakdimon did not. He stepped forward. "Rabbi, we know that you tell the truth and are not concerned with what people think about you. You pay no attention to a person's status, but really teach God's way. Does the Torah say that taxes are to be paid to the Roman Emperor, or not?"

Nakdimon's flattery surprised John, and several of the crowd appeared to visibly relax. Perhaps speaking to Yeshua in this tone would cause him to trip and speak falsely.

Yeshua was not easily blinded by flattery. "Why are you trying to trap me? Bring me a denarius so I can look at it."

Nakdimon motioned to John, and he brought forth a money sack filled with Roman coins. He reached in and handed one to Nakdimon, who in turn handed it to Yeshua.

Yeshua held it up into the sunlight for all to see. "Whose name and picture are these?" he asked in a loud voice for all to hear.

"The Emperor's," they replied, almost in unison.

Yeshua handed the coin back to Nakdimon. "Give the Emperor what belongs to the Emperor. And give to God what belongs to God!"

John dropped his jaw in disbelief. He was so sure that Nakdimon had finally gained the upper hand over the Natzerene, but once again, the man had slipped away. John was beginning to think he was like a greased sow; nothing was going to cause him trouble.

Nakdimon, seeing his gambit had failed, walked off after Kayafa.

Yosef stepped forward. "Rabbi, Moshe wrote for us that

if a man's brother dies and leaves a wife but no child, his brother must take the wife and have children to preserve the man's family line," he began.

Yeshua turned to hear his question.

"There were seven brothers. The first one took a wife, and when he died, he left no children. Then the second one took her and died without leaving children, and the third likewise, and none of the seven left children. Last of all, the woman also died."

John saw where this was going. It was the same laws his uncle had used on his mother to get her to marry him, although the law was no longer in effect since she had already given birth to John.

Yosef paused, and then asked his question in a loud voice so everyone in the crowd could hear it. "In the Resurrection, whose wife will she be? For all seven had her as wife." He smiled at Yeshua.

John liked this question. Yeshua could not deny the writings of their most holy prophet.

Yeshua's smile never lowered. "Isn't this the reason that you go astray? Because you are ignorant both of the Tanakh and of the power of God?"

It was Yosef whose smile dropped. The crowd listened intently to Yeshua's answer.

Yeshua continued, the gleam in his eye getting brighter. "For when people rise from the dead, neither men nor women marry—they are like angels in heaven. And as for the dead being raised, haven't you read in the book of Moshe, in the passage about the bush, how God said to him, 'I am the God of Avraham, the God of Yitz'chak, and the God of Ya'akov'? He is God not of the dead, but of the living! You are going far astray!"

The crowd murmured in admiration for how skillfully Yeshua had answered the question. Yosef left to find the others.

John looked around. It seemed he was the only one left. Suddenly, he felt the eyes of the crowd on him, and a fear rose up in him. *No, if this is truly the life I want to lead, I must try.*

John stepped forward, his mouth parched. A sick feeling bubbled in his stomach. Even so, he felt compelled to ask his question.

He walked up to Yeshua, standing just before him. "Which is the most important mitzvah of them all?"

Yeshua smiled at him. This smile, though, differed from the smiles he had given before. This one was warm, inviting, as if Yeshua was looking at John not as an adversary, but as a pupil.

"The most important is, 'Hear, O Isra'el, the Lord our God, the Lord is one, and you are to love Adonai your God with all your heart, with all your soul, with all your understanding and with all your strength.'

"The second is this, 'You are to love your neighbor as yourself.' There is no other mitzvah greater than these."

John recognized the Scripture. He had to admit, he too felt the same way. "Well said, Rabbi." John lowered his eyes, afraid that if he continued to look at Yeshua, the man would see into his soul. "You speak the truth when you say that he is one, and that there is no other besides him, and that loving him with all one's heart, understanding and strength, and loving one's neighbor as oneself, mean more than all the burnt offerings and sacrifices."

Yeshua smiled at John. He bent down so they were at eye level. Yeshua touched him lightly on the shoulder. "You are not far from the Kingdom of God."

He motioned to John to sit and join them. John looked around, but he saw none of the P'rushim. He sat down to hear what Yeshua had to say. Yeshua asked him a question. "Tell me your view concerning the mashiach. Whose son is he?"

John considered the question. His mind raced through all of the Scripture he had memorized, but there was only one possible answer. "David's," he said.

Yeshua's eyes lit. "Then how is it," he asked, "that David, inspired by the Spirit, calls him 'Lord,' when he says, 'Adonai said to my Lord, "Sit here at my right hand until I put your enemies under your feet"'?"

John realized the difficulty of the question.

Before he could offer a response, Yeshua continued. "If David thus calls him 'Lord,' how is he His son?"

John thought hard, trying to recognize the passage Yeshua referenced. Then he remembered it was from one of King David's psalms.

> *Adonai says to my Lord, "Sit at my right hand, until I make your enemies your footstool.*

It was one of the most important, most divinely inspired psalms David had written. He said that the coming mashiach would not be simply one of his offspring, one of his sons, he will also be David's Lord.

There was no way for John to deny the conclusion Yeshua had presented. The mashiach was not only the descendent of David by birth, but also the Lord of David by His Divine nature. John realized he was trapped; there was no way to invalidate the argument. He could not deny the prophecy.

"I do not know," he admitted.

The great crowd listened eagerly to him.

Yeshua seemed to take pity on him. "Watch out for the kind of Torah-teachers who like to walk around in robes and be greeted deferentially in the marketplaces," he said to John, "who like to have the best seats in the synagogues and take the places of honor at banquets, who like to swallow up widows' houses while making a show of davvening at great length."

John realized Yeshua was talking about his teachers.

Yeshua looked him directly in the eye. "Their punishment will be all the worse!"

John thought about everyone he had learned from over the last three years, Ya'ir, Nakdimon, Sha'ul, Kayafa, and Yosef. The thought that these men would be punished rather than praised for what they did seemed unbelievable.

Yeshua appeared finished. He stood, and then helped John to his feet. Without another word, he turned and took his talmidim down the street and around the corner. The crowds followed, leaving John alone in the square.

21

The Pesach Meal

John awoke at dawn. It was the thirteenth day of the month of Nissan, the day to celebrate the Pesach meal.

While John appreciated everything the priests had done for him, while he appreciated all of the places he had gone and all of the teachings he had received, there was still one duty of his apprenticeship which he hated. And that was the task of preparing for the Pesach Feast. John knew this was going to be a long and difficult day. The only joy John found in this task was that today, here, Kayafa's talmidim would have to work also.

Because of the confrontations with Yeshua, they had not been able to complete the ceremonial cleansing of the home the night before. John knew the Law, before the P'rushim sat for the Feast, he and the others would have to clean the house of anything made with the grains wheat, rye, barley, oats, and spelt. Even with all of the boys, including Philo, helping, it still was late into the afternoon before their task was completed.

Evening approached, and they set places for each of the priests who would attend that meal. Philo, as Kayafa's son, would set the Seder plate.

After the table was set, the members of the P'rushim arrived. Each wore his finest priestly robes made from a rich blue fabric. Blue, red, and crimson pomegranates and bells of gold thickly lined each robe. Their walk was almost musical when the bells clinked against each other as the men walked. Each wore a turban of dark blue.

Behind each priest stood one of their talmidim. When all was in place, Kayafa's wife and other children entered, dressed in their finest clothing, and sat at an adjacent table in the room.

It was only after everyone sat and the room was silent did Kayafa finally enter. He appeared almost as an angel, for he was dressed in the brilliant white kitl burial robe, symbolizing the verse, "Our sins shall be made as white as snow." He walked slowly, clearly reveling in his position as the leader of the Feast.

John stood along a darkened wall with all of the other talmidim. In the dim light, Kayafa appeared more solemn and regal than John had ever seen him. It was hard for John to relate to him as Philo's father, for he had never seen him in this role before.

Kayafa reached his seat and, with great ceremony, he reached down to the table and lifted an ornate gold flask containing the ceremonial wine. In a somber tone, he recited the traditional blessing over the flask of wine and then poured cups for each of his invited guests, being certain to fill them almost to the brim. When each man had received his portion, in unison, they slowly bowed their heads and drained their cups. Each talmidim then stepped forward and refilled the chalices.

Kayafa then began a long retelling of the story of their ancestors' flight from slavery in Egypt.

When this was finished, Kayafa began the ritual washing of the hands in total silence.

Each man at the table now reached over and dipped parsley into a bowl of salt water, as a reminder of the tears shed by their enslaved ancestors.

Kayafa reached over to a silver plate containing three covered matzot, removed the cloth, and broke the middle one. He removed one half, and hid it from view, returning the smaller portion to the plate.

With these ceremonial sections complete, Kayafa unrolled a large, ornate scroll, and read.

"Now Moshe was tending the sheep of Yitro his father-in-law, the priest of Midyan. Leading the flock to the far side of the desert, he came to the mountain of God, to Horev. The angel of Adonai appeared to him in a fire blazing from the middle of a bush. He looked and saw that although the bush was flaming with fire, yet the bush was not being burned up. Moshe said, 'I'm going to go over and see this amazing sight and find out why the bush isn't being burned up.'"

With these words, Kayafa told the story of the great prophet Moshe who led his ancestors from slavery in misery of Egypt, and of their great journey to a land flowing with milk and honey.

Kayafa again uncovered the matzot. All of the

assembled priests, in unison, spoke an Aramaic invitation to all who were hungry or needy to join in the Seder. They then repeated the invitation in Hebrew, and finally repeated it one more time in Greek.

Then Kayafa's youngest son stepped forward into the light around the table. If he was nervous, he didn't show it. With a loud voice, he asked the first ceremonial question.

"Why is this night different from all other nights?"

All of those seated at the table repeated the question quietly to themselves, so that a deep, reverent murmur reverberated throughout the room.

The young boy intoned the second question. "Why is it that on all other nights we do not dip even once, but on this night we dip them twice?"

Again in a low voice, the question was repeated.

"Why is it that on all other nights during the year we eat either leavened bread or matzat, but on this night we eat only matzat? Why is it that on all other nights we eat meat either roasted, marinated, or cooked, but on this night it is entirely roasted?"

The boy returned to the table and sat by his mother. He appeared very proud of himself for having done such a good job with the questions. His mother looked down at him and gave him her approval, which made him smile more.

Kayafa produced a second scroll.

> *Then, in the presence of Adonai your God, you are to say, "My ancestor was a nomad from Aram. He went down into Egypt few in number and stayed. There he became a great, strong, populous nation. But the Egyptians treated us badly; they oppressed us and imposed harsh slavery on us. So we cried out to Adonai, the God of our ancestors. Adonai heard us and saw our misery, toil and oppression; and Adonai brought us out of Egypt with a strong hand and a stretched-out arm, with great terror, and with signs and wonders."*

This was the point John was most dreading. Kayafa, as was the tradition, began an elaborate commentary on these verses of Scripture. John felt weak from having fasted all day, and the combination of the darkness of the wall and Kayafa's slow, deliberate tones almost caused him to nod off.

As Kayafa spoke about each of the ten plagues Adonai brought against their Egyptian captors, each person removed a drop of wine from their cup with his or her fingertip.

After what seemed an unbelievably long explanation by Kayafa, he finally finished. Each person then raised a second cup of wine and drank it.

After a second round of ritual hand washing, Kayafa blessed the matzot, then a second blessing, and a third blessing. Kayafa broke the matzot in half and passed them to each man seated next to him. John and the other talmidim brought matzot to everyone in the room, and then returned to the darkness of the wall.

John was finally allowed to eat. He picked up his matzot and raised it to his mouth. Normally, he found them unappealing, but the combination of the fast, the hard work and the wine made them seem delicious.

Next, John ate the bitter root as a symbol of their former slavery. The bitter taste of the root brought a wave of nausea over him, but it soon passed. While John could only handle a small amount, Kayafa and the other priests made a grand show of how much of the root they could consume.

Finally, Kayafa's servants brought in the main meal, and John allowed himself to fill his stomach.

A third cup of wine was poured, and Kayafa recited the grace after the meal. Everyone drank the third cup of wine.

Kayafa's young son stood and walked over to the front door and opened it wide. When he returned to his seat, Kayafa spoke once more.

"Pour out your wrath on the nations that don't know you, on the kingdoms that don't call out your name; for they have devoured Ya`akov and left his home a waste."

John poured his fourth and final cup of wine.

As Kayafa poured the ceremonial fifth cup, the Cup of

Eliyahu, an alarming thought jumped into John's mind. The fifth cup was supposed to signify the coming mashiach. John glanced at the door, almost expecting to see Eliyahu walk in with Yeshua.

Kayafa began the final part of the ceremony. After reciting several Psalms, Kayafa said a final blessing over the last cup of wine, and everyone drank. "The Pesach Seder is now complete," he announced. "My prayer is that each of you will be able to join me here next year in Yerushalayim, where we will greet our mashiach."

With that, Kayafa left the room in a stately manner, followed by his wife and family. Only after they had left did the priests sitting around the table get up. Many of them needed their talmidim to help, due to their age and the amount of time seated on the floor.

John was glad when it was over. Exhausted from the fasting, the work, the meal and the wine, he made his way quickly back to his room, changed into his nightshirt, and lay down to sleep.

22

In the Garden

"John, get up," said a voice, as someone violently shook him. John opened one eye and saw Philo kneeling by his bed, a lit lamp in his hand.

"Is it morning already?" he asked, lying back down.

Philo shook him even more violently. "John, get up now. The soldiers are here. They are going to arrest the Natzerene."

Instantly John bolted out of bed. "When are they leaving?" he asked, looking around for his clothes.

"No time for that," Philo said, pushing him towards the door. "They left a few moments ago. We will have to run to catch them."

And that is how John ended up on the streets of Yerushalayim wearing nothing more than his nightshirt, trying desperately to keep up with Philo.

Because of his time here, Philo knew a few shortcuts. They turned and raced up a narrow alley that was only wide enough to fit one person. Philo's lamp danced to the left and the right, and John was thankful for the full moon on more than one occasion when the lamp disappeared completely. The coolness of the night made the sweat on his skin feel clammy, and he wished they would just arrive and be done with all of this running.

They came to an olive grove. It was quiet, seemingly abandoned. John spied Yeshua by himself in the center of the garden, kneeling amongst the gnarled trees. He was obviously deep in prayer, and John almost felt ashamed to be interrupting him. His followers were there also, lying asleep amongst the tree's roots.

The full moon was high up in the night sky, but Yeshua's face was hidden in the shade from the moonlight. John was alarmed at his appearance. Over the past several days, every time he had encountered this man, his clothing seemed clean and new. It was as if the sand and dust that clung to so many in this part of the world had no affect on him.

Although it was a cool night, sweat stained his shirt as he prayed. John looked more closely. Was that blood mixed in with the sweat?

Yeshua finished his prayer. He hesitated a moment, then raised himself to his feet. He walked over to where his talmidim were lying.

"For now, go on sleeping, take your rest.... There, that's enough! The time has come!" said Yeshua. "Look! The Son of Man is being betrayed into the hands of sinners!"

John and Philo looked over to the entrance to the grove. "There's Y'hudah, with the Roman guards," said John. "I wasn't sure if he would actually go through with it."

"My father gave him thirty pieces of silver this afternoon. He'd better go through with it."

Y'hudah walked into the grove, dressed in a dark brown cloak. Behind him marched two dozen Roman soldiers, well armed with both clubs and swords.

Philo stepped out from their concealment. "Where are you going?" whispered John, frantically.

Philo just shushed him and kept walking. Too scared to follow, John stayed where he was.

"Get up! Let's go!" Yeshua yelled at the sleeping figures. "Here comes my betrayer!"

The three men on the ground quickly got to their feet and surrounded Yeshua, as if to protect him from the soldiers. But without weapons and vastly outnumbered, there was little they could do.

Philo walked up to the captain of the guard. No words were spoken, but it was obvious to John that the captain recognized Philo, who took a place between Y'hudah and several soldiers.

Y'hudah walked straight to his friends, smiling, his arms spread wide. "Rabbi!" he exclaimed, walking up to Yeshua. He grabbed Yeshua's shoulders, still smiling broadly, and then gently kissed him on the cheek.

Yeshua did not release himself from Y'hudah's grasp, but his question spoke volumes. "Y'hudah, are you betraying the Son of Man with a kiss?"

Y'hudah dropped his hands quickly, and the guards moved forward to make the arrest.

"Yeshua of Natzeret," Philo said, "you are under arrest for blasphemy against the laws of Moshe.

"And for insurrection against the rule of Rome," added the captain.

Two soldiers stood on either side of Yeshua to escort him out of the grove.

Shim'on pushed against the soldier closest to him, knocking him into another. A struggle broke out between the soldier and the two men. Within moments, all the men grabbed and pushed each other. Several soldiers drew their swords. Shim'on pulled a sword from the sheath of a nearby soldier. Before anyone knew what was happening, he had swung at the soldier. The man deflected the blow, and the sword fell across Philo's face.

Philo screamed as he dropped to his knees, his hands trying to stop the blood flowing from the side of his head.

John gasped at the sight of his friend severely wounded. He stood, ready to go to lend aid, but his fear kept him in hiding.

"Enough," shouted the captain of the guard. Everyone froze.

Yeshua raised his hand and looked at Philo. "So you came out to take me with swords and clubs, the way you would the leader of a rebellion? Every day I was with you in the Temple court, teaching, and you didn't seize me then! But let the Tanakh be fulfilled."

He twisted to release from the guard's grip and walked over to Philo, who knelt on the ground moaning in pain. Yeshua reached down and picked something up from the grass, than touched Philo's head. Immediately Philo stood up as though nothing had happened.

The two soldiers again grabbed Yeshua's arms.

"If anyone else interferes," shouted the captain of the guard, "arrest him."

John stood on the edge of the clearing. One of the soldiers noticed him and pointed. "There's another one."

The captain motioned to two of his soldiers, and they gathered their weapons and began to head over to where John stood.

The soldiers moved near enough to John that they could lunge at him. One grabbed John with his hand.

Since the soldier had only grabbed him by his shirt, John twisted, trying to break free. The soldier grabbed him with his other hand, and John twisted back and forth, trying to extract himself from the situation.

The soldier yelled at one of his colleagues to come and help him.

John dropped to his knees. His shirt ripped along a seam. The soldier released him momentarily to get a better grip, but John used the opportunity. He bolted up straight, lunging for the pathway. The soldier gave one last mighty tug. John's nightshirt tore again, then ripped clear of him.

He ran, naked, from the olive grove straight through the early morning streets.

23

The Second Confrontation

John arrived back at Kayafa's house and stood by the gate, peering into the courtyard. In his condition, he had hoped the grounds would be empty, but soldiers and townspeople filled the space. He slipped into the courtyard undetected. Ashamed by his nakedness, he prayed no one would catch him. He looked around, hoping Philo had escaped also, but he could not make out his friend amongst everyone there.

Despite the late hour, bright light poured from the house. He heard voices inside, although he could not make out what they were saying.

He hid in a dark shadow behind a grove of fig trees, certain no one would see him without a deliberate search. The moon rose in the night sky, and the evening air grew cool. He shivered.

A commotion down the street signalled the guards' arrival with their captive.

He peered through the leaves of the tree and saw the captain of the guard walk through Kayafa's entryway. Yeshua, his hands shackled before him, was alone; none of his talmidim had been captured along with him. Philo was not in chains either, and for this, John was grateful.

Several of the guards accompanied the captain into Kayafa's house, while the rest of them warmed themselves by a small fire in the courtyard.

John longed to join them, as the early morning air was cold upon his bare skin. As he watched, he saw a dark figure peer around the gatepost, then slowly move towards the fire.

John felt a tap on his shoulder and he jumped.

"Hold on, it's just me," said the familiar voice.

"Philo!" John exclaimed, pleased to see his friend. "I was so worried. How are you? How is your head?"

Philo shook his head. "I don't want to talk about it. Here," he said, removing his outer garment, "You must be freezing." He handed the robe to John, who quickly covered up. There was dried blood on the robe.

"What happened in the garden? I saw the sword hit your head. I saw you drop in pain."

Philo glared at him. "I said I do not want to talk about it."

"But your ear?" John said.

Philo grabbed John by the shoulders. "Yes, the sword hit me. There was some bleeding. But it is better now. Will you please just drop it?"

John nodded, though his friend's behavior puzzled him. "What is going on?" John asked.

Philo raised a finger to his lips, saying, "Be quiet," and then motioned for John to follow him. They moved quietly through the courtyard undetected by the soldiers and officials, until they came to the stand of trees near the house. Philo gave John a boost to the lowest branch, then climbed up himself. They moved up several branches until they were both hidden from the visitors in the courtyard and near enough the windows they could see and hear what was going on.

Inside the home, the voices grew. John peered through the open window and recognized several of them. He heard Anan speaking, and Nakdimon, Yosef, Sha'ul, Kayafa, and Gamli'el were also there, as well as most of the P'rushim.

"What charges are brought against this man, Yeshua of Natzeret?" asked Anan.

He heard several men raise their voices in answer. Anan chose one man at random.

"I heard him say he was raising an army to overthrow Rome," the man said.

At the statement, several men shouted the man down. "He has never said any such thing," one said. Others agreed with the dissenter.

Anan grew tired of the arguments. He asked for another charge.

"He is subverting our nation, forbidding us to pay taxes to the Emperor," another said.

"No," said Nakdimon, "we have never heard it said of him he incites rebellion against Rome. And he has said we are to render to Caesar what is Caesar's."

Anan continued. "Another, then. Has anyone else seen

a crime to charge this man with?"

Another man came forward. "What of his talmidim? He has been inciting the people with his teaching wherever he travels in Y'hudah. He started in the Galil, and now he's spreading his blasphemy here."

"Rome will not execute this man simply because he is a teacher. I need something else."

Man after man came forward, but Kayafa dismissed each one. For several hours, no one seemed to remember anything for Kayafa to justify Yeshua's execution. As accusation after accusation was made and dismissed, John grew more and more weary. Once, Philo had to shake him to keep him awake and, after that, the fear of falling did the job.

As the sun rose over the eastern mountains, someone John recognized came forward.

"I am Sha'ul of Tarsus," he said. "Three years ago, I was here in Yerushalayim for the festival of Pesach, studying under my master, Gamli'el. We stood on the Temple grounds. Do you recall that day?"

Yeshua said nothing, not even acknowledging the priest. "You came in and attacked the merchants doing business. You had a whip made from cords and drove them all out of the Temple grounds, the sheep and cattle as well. You knocked over the money changers' tables, scattering their coins."

Many members of the P'rushim agreed, remembering a similar incident from a few days ago.

Sha'ul continued. "Once you were finished, I approached you. 'What miraculous sign can you show us to prove you have the right to do all this?' I asked. You said, 'I will destroy this Temple made with hands; and in three days I will build another one, not made with hands.'"

Now the P'rushim howled with rage.

Kayafa restored order and asked Yeshua, "Have you nothing to say to the accusations these men are making?"

Yeshua sighed deeply without acknowledging Kayafa.

"What of your followers, your talmidim. Are they also under your delusions? What have you been teaching them?"

Yeshua finally answered. "I have spoken quite openly

to everyone, I have always taught in a synagogue or in the Temple where all Jews meet together, and I have said nothing in secret, so why are you questioning me? Question the ones who heard what I said to them, look, they know what I said."

Yeshua motioned at Sha'ul, who had made the accusation against him.

Anan slapped Yeshua hard across the face. "This is how you talk to the cohen hagadol?"

Yeshua looked into Kayafa's eyes. "If I said something wrong, state publicly what was wrong. But if I was right, why are you hitting me?"

Kayafa paced around the prisoner, clearly enjoying the man's predicament. "I put you under oath! By the living God, tell us if you are the Mashiach, the Son of God!"

Yeshua finally raised his head and glared at Kayafa. "The words are your own. But I tell you that one day you will see the Son of Man sitting at the right hand of HaG'vurah and coming on the clouds of heaven."

"That should do it," Philo whispered. "By invoking the same name Adonai had used with Moshe, Yeshua has effectively written his own death sentence. The P'rushim cannot excuse such blasphemous talk."

John knew Philo spoke the truth. Despite the years of following this man, of trying to discredit him or have him arrested, despite the trips to Herod and the time spent on the road, John suddenly felt shame and pity that the P'rushim would treat him this way.

Kayafa grabbed at the collar of his robe and strongly pulled it apart, ripping the garment into two pieces.

"Why do we still need witnesses?" he said in an anguished voice. "You heard him blaspheme! What is your decision?"

In unison, they all declared him guilty.

With the decision made, they surrounded Yeshua, who did not utter a sound. An elderly rabbi with a long white beard walked up to Yeshua, then spit in his face. Others followed his lead.

Yosef, who had watched the proceedings without speaking, suddenly stepped forward. "Why do you do this? You've already declared him guilty. Don't lower yourselves any further by behaving like this."

The P'rushim began yelling at Yosef, telling him to be quiet and move. One elderly priest actually pushed him aside, causing Yosef to stagger and fall.

"This is getting ugly," said Philo. "We'd better get out of here while we still can." They began moving down the tree.

As they jumped to the ground, they saw Roman guards trying to force their way into the house, only to have the P'rushim refusing them entrance. There was a lot of yelling and shouting, and one soldier raised a sword, but was quickly stopped by his commander, who reminded all of them that they were at the home of the High Priest, and no blood was to be spilt here.

Philo began walking quickly towards the crowd.

"Wait," John yelled, unwilling to leave the cover of the trees.

Philo motioned for John to join him, then turned and reached the edge of the crowd.

The Roman commander spoke to Kayafa. "Release your prisoner to our care. We will insure his safety."

"If you are going to lead him away," said an old priest, "then blindfold him, as we do not want his blaspheming eyes viewing our holy city."

One of the guards reached out to Yeshua. He had a soiled cloth hanging from his belt. He removed it, and fashioned a crude blindfold about the man's eyes. Once this was secure, they yanked him in the direction of the door, so hard he almost lost his balance and fell.

Philo happened to be standing there and caught him then thought better of it and punched Yeshua.

"Let's see you prophesy!" he shouted.

The guards made their way through the crowd of Council members and out the front door into the courtyard. John shifted his position so he could see what was happening.

As the captain of the guard left Kayafa's home with the prisoner, the other guards warming themselves by the fire came over and surrounded Yeshua. Seeing the blindfold and the rough way the guards handled him, they too beat him with their fists. Despite the heavy blows, Yeshua said nothing.

Behind Yeshua, the entire P'rushim was emptying out

of Kayafa's home.

All of the noise and commotion had woken all the members of Kayafa's household. All of the talmidim of the Sanhedrin who had been staying in and around the courtyard were awake and talking about what had happened, as were Kayafa's servants.

The sun was just rising over the horizon, and the courtyard brightened. John looked towards the fire, and saw someone he did not expect.

It was Shim'on. In all of the confusion at the garden, John had assumed he had run off with the other talmidim.

One of Kayafa's serving girls stared at Shim'on. "You were with the man from Natzeret. Yeshua!"

Shim'on looked about nervously. All in the courtyard looked to see who she was accusing, and then turned their gaze upon him. He stood up nervously, as if looking for an exit.

He turned to the girl. "I haven't the faintest idea what you're talking about!"

Shim'on moved quickly away from the fire, into Kayafa's entryway which was still in shadow. Off in the distance, John heard a rooster crowing as he welcomed the morning light.

The girl did not let it end. Other talmidim gathered around them. She pointed at Shim'on. "This fellow is one of them."

From within the entryway, Shim'on pleaded his case. "I don't know the man!" he said.

The other talmidim moved towards Shim'on. The man was clearly nervous. One of the older boys, a talmidim of Yosef, looked at Shim'on. "You must be one of them, because you're from the Galil. Your accent gives you away."

Shim'on appeared crazed with fear. "I swear to you, I do not know this man you are telling me about!" As he was speaking, John again heard the rooster off in the distance.

Yeshua looked directly at Shim'on. It was the first time John had seen Yeshua acknowledge anyone since his arrest.

Shim'on saw his rabbi looking at him. John could not

believe his ears. Shim'on had followed and ate and learned at the feet of this man for three years, yet out of fear, denied even knowing him. This was no longer the same Shim'on.

Shim'on suddenly burst into tears and sobbed furiously.

One of the guards struck Yeshua sharply in the back, dropping the man onto one knee. The guard violently pulled him back up, and shoved him out through the entryway.

All of the P'rushim followed through the open entryway, along with most of the talmidim. As soon as they were on the streets, Kayafa's servants returned to the house, and the courtyard became still.

John waited, then slipped inside and ran straight to his room. He discarded Philo's blood stained robe and dressed himself in a spare robe, grabbed his sandals, and exited the house.

At the entryway, he heard sobbing sounds. Shim'on was still lying on the ground, his body heaving desperately. John stopped, not sure what to do.

Shim'on looked up and recognized him. "John?" he asked, through sobs.

John only nodded in agreement.

Another wave of guilt overwhelmed Shim'on, and he again cried violently.

"He knew, John. He knew," Shim'on said. "Everything He said would happen has happened."

John knelt next to the man, and placed a hand on his shoulder to comfort him.

Shim'on looked up into John's eyes, and placed his hand on John's shoulders. "You've seen Him. You know who He is."

"Do you know where they are taking him?" John asked.

Shim'on shuddered. "At the Pesach last night, He told us, 'The Son of Man will die, just as the Tanakh says He will, but woe to that man by whom the Son of Man is betrayed! It would have been better for him had he never been born!'"

Shim'on had a look of fear, as if he saw death. "I denied Him! Three times I denied Him! Am I His betrayer?"

Shim'on released his grip on John and fell to the

ground. For the longest time, he did not move, and John feared he had died. Then Shim'on breathed in deeply, and sobbed violently.

John did not know what, if anything he could do. He was confused. He had seen Yeshua heal, bring back the dead, argue and win over Kayafa. Now he accurately predicted these events? John had to find out for himself.

He did not know for certain where they were taking Yeshua, but he knew he had to find them.

24

The Trial

The morning sun rose over the roofs of the buildings of Yerushalayim. The citizens of the city, awakening and beginning their morning routines, heard the passing and looked out of windows. A Jewish man, surrounded by Roman guards and following the P'rushim, was too strange a sight to leave alone. Many left their homes to follow. By the time they reached the center of the city, the crowd had swelled to several thousand.

John saw Philo, standing with his father and the other priests, and walked over to him.

"Why didn't you come with us?" Philo asked.

The memory of the night's events shamed John. It hurt more than the teasing he got from the older boys, more than the pain he felt when his actions disappointed Myriam, more than the pain of how he had treated his own family. This was a shame that bore deep into his soul. "I don't want to talk about it."

He wondered if he could tell Philo of the pain last night's events caused him. Every part of him wanted to discuss his concerns with his friend, but he knew that any such attempt would be futile. Ultimately, he decided not to push it, letting Philo think what he wished. "Where are we?"

"This building houses the headquarters of the Roman government here in Yerushalayim."

The building was not that impressive, nothing like what John had imagined a Roman government building would be. While it was a two-story building, so were most of the others in this part of town. He had expected marble columns, massive stone statues, something more. It looked as if Pilate had just taken over somebody's home.

As his father stepped forward to address the Roman officers, Philo raised his hand to his mouth motioning John to keep quiet.

Kayafa stopped in front of the government headquarters, placing himself between Yeshua and the building. Joining Kayafa were all of the heads of the Sanhedrin.

A door to a balcony on the second floor opened. A Roman officer, adjusting and straightening his robes as he walked to the railing, called down to them.

"What is the meaning of this mob?" he asked in an authoritative voice. John immediately recognized him as Sergius Paulus, the Roman official he had met with Philo back in K'far-Nachum.

John watched Kayafa step forward, his long regal robes shimmering in the morning light. He walked with the gait of a man in complete control. "Long live Caesar. I am Yosef Bar Kayafa. My colleagues are members of the P'rushim here at Yerushalayim."

"Why do you bring such a crowd to us this morning?"

Kayafa positioned himself almost directly under the balcony. "We have a prisoner here, a Jew. We must speak with your Prefect, Pontius Pilate."

Sergius did not seem impressed. "My Prefect has important duties this morning. He does not have time to deal with this now. Take your prisoner and come back tomorrow." He turned as if to walk away.

"Excellency, I must insist. This matter cannot be delayed for even one day. Tell your Prefect who is here. He will come."

Sergius looked once at Kayafa, and then went into the building.

"Do you think Pilate will appear?" asked John.

Philo uttered a grunt. "He will."

Secretly, John hoped that Pilate had left. His mind began to build a fantasy of Pilate summoned to Rome, left the night before. Maybe this would save Yeshua. The return of Sergius with another man dashed John's daydreams.

"That's Pontius Pilate, the sixth Procurator of Y'hudah. He is the Roman governor over all Israel," said Philo.

At the sight of the Roman governor, John suddenly felt small and insignificant. It was the same feeling he often had in the presence of his uncle. Physically, Pilate was an intimidating sight. He towered over Sergius. Based on the grayness of his hair, John believed him to be in his early fifties. The gold band he wore on his head hid his closely shorn hair. While for some men, his nose may have seemed too large, somehow it seemed well proportioned to his chiseled face. John's eyes actually hurt at the sight of the fine white robe he wore. In this bright morning light, it made Pilate look like a brightly lit lamp.

"Kayafa, by what right do you bring this crowd to my doorstep?" he asked. His voice was deep and strong, and seemed to echo slightly off the buildings.

"Before you," said Kayafa, "I have brought a Jewish citizen. We have interrogated him and found him to be a threat to Rome."

Pilate scoffed. "A threat to Rome? One man?"

Kayafa nodded. "We found this man subverting our nation, forbidding us to pay taxes to the Emperor and claiming he himself as our mashiach—a king of Jews!"

John could not understand why Kayafa would make up such an outrageous lie. Was he so determined in his course of action that he would say anything to get the man executed? He whispered to Philo, "What is your father doing? That never happened. I thought the charge was going to be about the Temple and the moneychangers?"

"That charge would not be acceptable to the Romans," Philo said. "That charge would only get him a prison sentence, not an execution."

Pilate walked to the edge of the balcony and placed his hands on its marble balustrade. "Bring him forward that I may see."

The P'rushim parted and allowed the Roman soldiers to bring Yeshua forward.

Pilate looked down at him. "Is this true? Are you the King of the Jews?"

Yeshua looked up. If there was any fear in him at standing before the Prefect of Y'hudah, he did not show it. "The words are yours."

Kayafa spoke up. "This man has been inciting people against Rome. He is teaching he will become their king. He opposes the paying of taxes to Caesar." Kayafa turned to Yeshua. "Tell him. Admit what you have admitted to us."

Yeshua remained silent.

Pilate waited. "Aren't you going to answer? Look how

many charges they are making against you!"

Yeshua did not reply. Pilate and Sergius conferred for several minutes. Finally, Pilate addressed Kayafa.

"I find no ground for a charge against this man."

John's heart leapt for joy at Pilate's pronouncement. So much for what Shim'on said. He remembered back to the interrogation last night and how Yeshua showed more restraint than most of those questioning him. Pilate's vindication made John think that the governor had to have been in the room with them and seen how poorly the P'rushim treated Yeshua.

A murmur went through the crowd. Several members of the Council spoke softly to themselves, but Kayafa quickly quieted them.

"He is inciting the people with his teaching throughout all Y'hudah," Kayafa pleaded. "He started in the Galil, and now he's here!"

"Then he is not from Yerushalayim, but from the Galil?" asked Sergius.

"Where he is from is of no concern. He is here, now, under your authority," replied Kayafa.

Pilate scolded the priest. "Anything that happens in Y'hudah is my concern. But this man is under the authority of Herod. I find no crimes against Rome. If he is guilty of crimes against Jews, then it is Herod's authority to punish him, not mine."

Pilate turned to address the captain of the guard. "Herod is here in Yerushalayim. Take him to Herod for trial." Pilate returned to his office without another word.

"Oh no," said Philo. "Herod won't condemn Yeshua to death. Pilate is the only man to order that."

Inside, John smiled. He knew that he should be supporting his masters, but he felt a great joy that Pilate denied Kayafa's death sentence against Yeshua. He agreed that Yeshua needed to be arrested, but the idea that Yeshua deserved death made him ill.

John thought all of Kayafa's planning was about to unravel. "What will happen next?"

Philo wrinkled his brow and massaged his temples. "My father will have to do as Pilate has ordered. Perhaps Herod will arrest him."

John's mind raced back to Herod's palace, Salome's

dance, and the awful sight of Yochanan's head on the platter. Would Herod risk arresting this man? "I thought your father didn't want Herod to arrest him?"

"He doesn't," Philo said, "but he also doesn't want this man poisoning Herod as Yochanan did."

"What will your father do?"

Philo remained silent. Kayafa and the others began to lead Yeshua through the streets of Yerushalayim, presumably to Herod's quarters.

"I don't know." Philo closed his eyes for a few moments, and then opened them suddenly. "John, you must do me a favor."

"Of course."

Philo sighed and placed a hand against the side of his head, where the sword had struck. "I need to have this looked at. I cannot follow my father through the streets of the city. You must go with him. Tell me everything that happens."

"Where will you be?"

"I need to see a physician. I am returning to my father's house. Follow them for me, please."

25

The Shepherd

John followed Kayafa and the guards as they took Yeshua to Herod. Many in the crowd went, also, but many more left the streets. John walked towards the P'rushim, but something at the edge of the crowd caught his eye.

An elderly man leaned on an old shepherd's crook to support himself. His face was weathered and he had the mark of a man who had spent most of his life outdoors. Why John noticed this man out of every other person in the crowd, he did not know. For some reason, he felt an overwhelming desire to talk to the shepherd.

"Do you know the man they are taking to see Herod?" asked John.

The old man shook his head. "No, I have never seen him before. Who is he?"

"His name is Yeshua."

At the name, the shepherd excitedly grabbed John shoulders. "Yeshua!" His eyes twinkled as he spoke. "Tell me, how old is he?"

What difference could the man's age make? He thought back to the conversations he had with Philo about Yeshua. "He is, I believe, thirty-three. He is a carpenter, from Natzeret."

The old man raised his hands to the heavens, a broad smile on his weathered face. "Praise be to Adonai! He has allowed me to see Him once more before I die."

John felt as if a hand had taken hold of his heart. He did not know why, but suddenly the words of the shepherd seemed extremely important. "Him?" he asked, "Who is he?"

The old man looked John in the eyes. "He is the mashiach. The one we have been waiting for."

The forcefulness and conviction in the man's voice stunned him. How could the old man be so certain? John thought back to every encounter with Yeshua. Had he missed something? "What do you mean? Until a moment ago, you said you had never seen him?"

The old man walked away without answering. John followed him.

The words of Nakdimon and Kayafa suddenly sprang into his ears. "He cannot be the mashiach. Our Scripture is very precise. The prophet Mikhah the Morashti prophesied the mashiach comes from Beit-Lechem." Even as he spoke the words, John remembered the shepherd's conviction and felt doubt welling inside him.

The old man did not answer.

John quoted the Scripture verse.

> *But you, Beit-Lechem near Efrat, so small among the clans of Y'hudah, out of you will come forth to me the future ruler of Isra'el, whose origins are far in the past, back in ancient times.*

"He is from Natzeret, so he cannot be the mashiach. We all know that."

The old man sat at a bench in the shade. "Allow an old man to rest his weary bones. I have been on this earth a long, long time. My days are almost finished. But I thank Adonai He allowed me to see the mashiach one last time."

Again the man's convictions grasped at John's heart. How could he claim Yeshua was the mashiach, and not recognize him? He could not be one of his talmidim. John did not remember ever seeing the old shepherd at any of his encounters with Yeshua. Confused, John chose not to respond. He just stood there silently, waiting for him to continue.

The old shepherd closed his eyes, and John was afraid he was going to sleep. Then a smile slowly came across his face.

"I was a lot younger then," he began, speaking as if to a large audience rather than one boy. "It was a beautiful evening. It was warm, but not so warm that it was uncomfortable. The stars shone in the sky as if Adonai Himself had dipped His fingers in starlight and splashed them on the curtain of the night.

"I was there with several of my brothers. We were actually glad to be out that night. Because of a Roman census, people from every city were in Beit-Lechem. They had come from all over to register. Some had even come from Natzeret."

At the mention of Beit-Lechem, John suddenly realized his great error, the error the Council was about to make. How could he have been so led astray? Why didn't he search deeper?

"I remember as if it was just last night. I was looking up in the sky, and I saw a star appear. I had never seen a star appear. I pointed it out to my brothers. It grew brighter and brighter. It was not like the wandering stars, the bright ones that moved across the night. This star remained where it was. From where we stood, it seemed as if it was right over Beit-Lechem."

Years ago, when John lived with his mother and uncle, he had spent many evenings out amongst the stars. He had never seen one appear, and tried to recall anyone else who had claimed to see one appear. He could think of no one. The shepherd's story began to intrigue him.

"I heard a soft sound in my ear, a wonderful, soft sound. At first, it was like music, but it was like no music I had ever heard. It sounded like speech, but it was no language I could understand.

"The music grew along with the star. I realized it was not a star. It gave off light, but not starlight, not moonlight, but a brilliant light, as bright as the rising sun. I knew it was not the dawn, for that was hours away."

John sat, mesmerized by the old man's story. He suddenly longed to return to his old life, before the priests and the teaching, back when his mama took care of his every need. A strong desire to sit and spend an evening on the edge of the desert, looking into Adonai's beautiful creation came over him. He felt a longing in his heart, a longing to have been with the shepherd that evening so long ago.

The old man remained silent, smiling at the memory.

"It frightened me. I didn't know what it was. But it became clear to me the light and the sound were one.

"I have never heard of light making speech. I have never heard of music giving light. I fell to the ground, as did my brothers. We were terrified. I shut my eyes and clasped my hands over my ears. But the sound did not get softer. The light became so bright I could see it through my closed eyes.

"I opened them. I saw our sheep, grazing peacefully. They showed no fear. I could not believe they hadn't scattered at the sound and the light."

John's mind imagined the scene, the sheep walking in the cool night air as bright light shown illuminated their fields. He did not understand what caused this to happen, but the joy in the man's voice and the peaceful images he conveyed made John know that it was a wonderful thing.

"I looked up and saw an angel of Adonai, there, in the sky. It was angelic light that shown about us. It was the Sh'khinah of Adonai that shone around us."

Tears welled in the man's eyes. "The angel spoke to me, to us. I will never forget his words. They were like spoken music, not songs, not lyrics, but spoken music. It was as if he was singing and I understood what the notes meant.

"He said, 'Don't be afraid, because I am here announcing to you Good News that will bring great joy to all the people. This very day, in the town of David, there was born for you a Deliverer who is the mashiach, the Lord. Here is how you will know: you will find a baby wrapped in cloth and lying in a feeding trough.'"

When the shepherd mentioned the visitation by the angel, John felt a twinge of envy creep into his heart. He read so many accounts of angels speaking to his ancestors, yet he had never once tried to visualize how the conversation happened. He imagined the songs Moshe must have heard as he stood on the mountain before the bush that burned but was not consumed.

"I did not think it possible, but the music grew even louder. I was fascinated at the sound and the sight. I could not see them, but somehow I knew my brothers felt the same way."

The old man stared off into the distance.

John closed his eyes, trying to place himself into the scene the man was painting for him. As he did, he felt a peace and calm overcome him. He heard no other sounds but his own breathing and the old man's soothing voice.

"I noticed the angel was not alone. Before my eyes, I saw the army of heaven. All of Adonai's angels were there. Behind them, I could see heaven itself. The sound became almost deafening, but it did not bother me in the slightest."

John opened his eyes. He felt the tears welling, threatening to become a flood. He wiped his face, hoping the movement would hold back the deep emotions he was feeling, the deep longing that now burned inside him.

The shepherd continued. "This heavenly chorus of Adonai began to sing. And each note came with a powerful message. They said, 'In the highest heaven, glory to God! And on earth, peace among people of good will!'

"Without warning, it became quiet. The light was gone. The stars were out, as they had been before. The breezes were cool, as they had been before. The sheep grazed as they had before."

The man turned and looked directly at John. Both of them had large tears running down their cheeks.

"I looked at my brothers. They were crying, just like me, just like you."

John wiped at his eyes several times. He knew what the man said was true. He knew in his heart now that he was wrong, that Kayafa, Anan, Yosef, and all of the others were wrong. He knew that he himself had seen the mashiach.

"It took us several minutes before we could speak. When we did, we made no sense. It took awhile for us to regain enough sense to communicate. We said, 'Let's go over to Beit-Lechem and see this thing that has happened, that Adonai has told us about.' So we left our sheep and went into the town."

The man looked down at the ground. "It was quiet. Everyone was asleep, or so it seemed. This amazed us—how could they sleep through all of that light, all of that sound.

"We did not know where we were going. Behind us we saw a lamb, one from our flock. It was perfect, without blemish. It walked with us.

"We stopped, not knowing where to go. The lamb continued and turned down a street, towards the area of the town's stables. Remembering the angel's words He would be laid in a feeding trough, we followed."

John knew what the shepherd was about to say. In fact,

he had always known. With a great sickening feeling, he realized it was his desire for respect, his desire to be more than Adonai had made him that had blinded him to the truth. He felt ashamed that he had listened to the voice of men rather than to the voice of God. He was disgusted with himself for choosing to place his own desires before Adonai's.

"We found the lamb standing before a cave. A man and his wife where inside the cave, out of the night's air. When he saw us, he said, 'I am Yosef, from the town of Natzeret in the Galil. This is my wife, Myriam.' Lying there, in an old wooden feeding manger, lay a newborn baby, wrapped in a clean cloth.

"His mother smiled warmly and invited us in to see. 'This is my son. He was born this night. We have named Him Yeshua, the name given to Him by Adonai.'"

John's anger and disgust at himself suddenly gave over to a feeling of great love. It was true; Yeshua was the mashiach Adonai had promised so long ago! John felt as if his heart was about to burst from the joy. He knew that it did not matter what his old motivations were, all that mattered was that he knew the truth.

The old man, having finished his story, stood up.

"Since that day, I have been content to be a shepherd. Every day on this earth is a gift from Adonai, and every day here I ache to return and hear the angels sing once more." He walked away, and John chose not to follow.

John sat on that bench for a long time. He replayed every moment of the shepherd's story repeatedly in his mind. As he did, the feelings of peace and contentment grew in his heart. But he also began to feel a longing, a desire to tell someone, anyone about the truth.

He thought of Kayafa, Nakdimon, and the others. None of them would listen to a boy. Somehow, he had to stop Herod and Pilate. Somehow, he had to arrange for his mashiach's release. He had to find someone he could convince that would help him convince them of the truth.

Instantly, John knew what to do.

By the time John got to Kayafa's house, he was out of breath and could barely stand.

"PHILO," he screamed, as soon as he regained his

voice. "PHILO!"

John stood there in the courtyard, screaming his friend's name. Several of Kayafa's staff came out, trying to silence him, but John refused to be quiet. "PHILO!" he screamed.

Philo emerged, a bandage on his ear.

"What is it? I asked you to follow my father. What happened at Herod's?"

A great love for Philo fell over him. They had been friends for so long, John did not think he could feel any closer to Philo, but his new feelings placed his old, to his shame. He knew he had to convince Philo, not for his sake or Yeshua's, but so that Philo could know of Adonai's great love.

"Philo, they have the wrong man. Yeshua must not be put to death."

"What are you talking about? This is what my father has worked for."

John grabbed Philo's arms. *Adonai. I beg you, please open Philo's eyes to the truth.* He took a deep breath. "Yeshua is from Beit-Lechem."

"No he's not, he's from Natzeret. You know that."

"No, he was raised in Natzeret. He was born in Beit-Lechem."

John became silent, trying to determine if Philo understood the significance.

"The scrolls," John pleaded, "the scroll of Mikhah. It tells of the mashiach being born in Beit-Lechem."

Philo pushed John away hard, knocking him to the ground. "He is no mashiach," Philo screamed at him. He raised a fist, daring John to stand, threatening to knock him down again.

Despite Philo's anger, John found himself unafraid. It did not matter to John if Philo hurt him. All that he wanted was for his friend to believe. Philo needed to know the truth. "He is the mashiach. I can prove it. Come down to the square with me. There is an old man, an old man from Beit-Lechem, who was there at Yeshua's birth. He will tell you the truth."

Philo stood still, refusing to follow.

John pleaded with him. "Please, please come and listen. We must stop the Council. Listen to the shepherd's story, tell me he's lying."

"The Council will not take the word of one crazed old man."

John forgot about the danger Yeshua was in. It no longer mattered. All he could think of was freeing his friend. "What about you? Will you at least listen to him?"

It took a very long time for Philo to answer. "I will come, but only to prove this old man wrong." His fist turned into a hand to help John up.

Thank you Adonai for changing Philo's heart.

Immediately, John knew what he had to do. After he convinced Philo, the two of them could approach the Council. With the old shepherd at their side, the priests would have to release Yeshua. Delight flowed over John that Adonai had provided a solution to free the mashiach.

"Thank you, thank you," he said to Philo. "You will not regret this."

John turned and ran back to the town. Philo followed at a significantly slower pace.

The town square was crowded, as the citizens of Yerushalayim were busy with their daily lives.

"Where is this old man you spoke of?" said Philo accusingly.

There were too many people for John to see one specific person. *Adonai, bring us to this man. Let Philo see him.*

John walked, Philo following not far behind. John's eyes darted, looking at faces, trying to recognize him.

At the far end of the square, he saw a figure seated on a bench wearing the same gray cloak as the shepherd. John hurried Philo along and they ran to him.

"I've brought a friend. You must tell him your story," said John as he got to the bench.

There would be no story. The old man sat still, his eyes open and looking to heaven.

Both of them stared at the body of the old man. All of the hope, all of the joy drained from John's heart. He felt a crushing defeat. How could he convince Philo now?

John began to search the square. He found two Roman soldiers. "There is an old man over there, on that bench. I think he has died."

The Roman soldiers looked at each other, and then

reluctantly walked over. Philo stepped aside to let them examine the body.

One of soldiers slapped the man a few times, and then closed the man's eyes.

"We will have someone take the body. Do you know who he is?"

"I never asked him his name."

The guard seemed perturbed John could not offer any more information. "Okay, we'll notify the proper people. Do you want to stay with the body?"

John' mind was in a panic. He thought back to all of the events that had led him to this time and this place, wishing only that he had arrived five minutes sooner.

Philo turned and walked away. John turned to follow, but his heart told him to stay. "I will," he said to the Roman soldier.

The Roman shrugged, and walked off to make his report. John sat down on the opposite end of the bench.

"John?" said a soft, quiet voice behind him. He turned to see who would know him all the way down here.

"Myriam?" said John, hardly able to believe his fortune. He stood and she ran over to him. They gave each other a hug. The people standing around looked disapprovingly at them.

He had not expected to see her. Maybe it was Adonai's plan. Maybe Myriam could help him convince Philo. "Why are you here?" he asked.

Myriam stepped back a moment. "I know you don't believe in Him, but I am here with Yeshua. Why are you here?"

John gazed into her eyes. He ached to tell her of the shepherd and the story, but he knew where he had to start. "Do you know where Yeshua is now?" he asked softly.

Her eyes grew wide with fear. "No, what has happened?"

He took a deep breath. "I am here with the Council. We came down here to get the Romans to agree to..." He hesitated, "to deal with Yeshua." The words brought pangs of guilt upon him.

"Deal with him how?" she demanded.

John swallowed. "It was the Council's decision, not

mine," he said.

Myriam's eyes watered. "What have you done, John? Where have they taken Him?"

John pleaded with her. "It was not my fault. I didn't know the truth."

Myriam stood up and placed her hands on her hips. "Where is He, John?" she demanded.

"They've taken Him to Herod. They've taken Him to Herod to arrange an arrest."

Myriam slapped John hard across the face.

John did not move. Myriam dropped to her knees beside him and cried.

"I know the truth now," said John softly. "I know all about Him."

Myriam looked up at him hopefully. "Is there anything you can do to stop this?"

He tried to imagine any way he could convince Kayafa. He just shook his head. "Kayafa's mind is made up, his heart has grown cold. Yeshua's life is in His Father's hands now."

Myriam grew hopeful. "And Adonai would never let His Son die, would He?"

"We can only pray."

26

The Final Confrontation

The crowds had returned as John and Myriam approached the government building, not sure where to turn. He felt a strong hand on his shoulder.

Yosef of Ramatayim stood tall, but John sensed that something was different.

"Did they speak to Herod?" John asked.

Yosef nodded. "Herod chose to return him to Pilate."

John's hopes grew. Perhaps Adonai would spare the man. "The way this is playing out...this is not what I want," he said. "I have seen Yeshua, His strength and His character. Kayafa has made a mistake."

John told Yosef what the old shepherd had told him.

"Can we do anything to stop this?" John asked.

"Kayafa and the others will be back any moment. When I saw how Herod treated him, I could not watch any longer and left early."

"We can go to Pilate and tell him the truth," said John, excitedly.

Yosef shook his head. "Tell Pilate Yeshua is truly the King of the Jews? That he is the fulfillment of our prophecy? That would insure his execution."

John could not think of anything else. Pilate had to know Yeshua was Adonai's chosen mashiach. He had to agree to set Him free.

"There may be a way," said Yosef. "We need to get to Pilate." Yosef walked quickly into the government headquarters, with John and Myriam right behind him.

Yosef used his status in the Sanhedrin to get the guards to let him in to see Pilate. He was able to bring John, explaining he was his talmidim and needed to remain with his master. Myriam was not allowed to enter, and stayed outside.

They walked up a long stone staircase to Pilate's dimly lit office. John felt a chill as he moved deeper into the Roman complex.

It was a small room with several desks and chairs. Sergius Paulus sat at one of the desks, and several Roman guards stood watch.

"Who are you?" he asked. "How did you get in here?"

Yosef crossed the room to approach Paulus, keeping a wary eye on the guards.

"I am Yosef of Ramatayim. I am a member of the Sanhedrin."

Sergius scoffed. "The Sanhedrin? Pilate already spoke to you this morning."

Yosef shook his head. "No, he spoke to Kayafa. Kayafa left out some important details Pilate must know."

Sergius seemed unimpressed. "Pilate has made his decision. Herod will deal with the Galilean."

Again, Yosef shook his head. "No, I was with Kayafa and Yeshua at Herod's. Herod has refused to act. Kayafa is on his way back to have Pilate complete this man's sentence."

Sergius took a deep breath and slowly exhaled, as if to keep himself calm at the news. He hesitated, looking at Pilate's door and back at Yosef. After several moments, he rose and knocked on the door.

After Sergius had left, Yosef spoke to John softly, so the guards could not overhear. "We have only one option."

John suddenly had hope. It was dashed when he heard the loud crash of a door striking a wall and saw an angry Pontius Pilate pointing at Yosef. "You, come into my office now."

Yosef showed no fear of the Roman governor. With head held high, he strode into the room, beckoning John to follow.

Pilate sat on a wooden chair on a large, wooden dais. It gave him the appearance of a king, which was important for him when dealing with the townspeople. There were no other seats in the room. The doors to the balcony behind him were open, allowing the morning's soft breezes to cool the room.

"Herod has refused to deal with this man?" he asked.

"Yes, Excellency."

"I cannot have an uprising this close to the Festival. If I were to release my soldiers to control a raucous crowd, relations in this city will be strained for months, if not years."

Yosef paused but a moment, and then boldly moved forward with his plan. "Excellency, forgive me, but isn't it the custom that during the festival of Pesach, you offer to release one prisoner, whomever the crowd requests?"

Pilate was silent.

"Could you not ask the crowd to release this Yeshua?"

Through the open doors came the sounds of an approaching party. John turned to listen, and realized Kayafa was returning with Yeshua.

Pilate walked into Sergius' office. Yosef and John remained.

"Kayafa is returning with the Galilean. As soon as they arrive, I want the prisoner brought to me."

Yeshua stood before Pilate. Several Roman guards surrounded him and Yosef, while John remained in the dim light at the back of the office.

Pilate addressed Yosef. "You brought this man before me on a charge of subverting the people. I examined him in your presence and did not find the man guilty of the crime you are accusing him of."

Pilate paused before continuing. "And neither did Herod, because he sent him back to us. Clearly, he has not done anything that merits the death penalty. Therefore, what I will do is have him flogged and release him."

John's hopes rose. Pilate walked through the open doors onto his balcony. In the town square below, the crowd had grown by several thousand.

He addressed the crowd. "This man has done nothing wrong. What charge are you bringing against him?"

"If he hadn't done something wrong, we wouldn't have brought him to you." John recognized Kayafa's voice from below.

Pilate did not like the response. "You take him and judge him according to your own law."

Kayafa replied, "We have judged him, and found him guilty. We don't have the legal power to put anyone to death."

"And so you do not want me to judge him, you want me to serve as your executioner? That is not why Rome is here. We are not here to serve you." Pilate called out to his guards. "Bring the prisoner before me."

The soldiers pushed Yeshua onto the balcony, for the crowd to see. Hissing and booing grew loudly from the assembled masses.

"Are you the King of the Jews?" asked Pilate, getting right to the crux of the issue.

Despite the bruises on his face from the beatings, and the dried blood on his garments, Yeshua remained calm, showing no outward sign of fear of tribulation. "Are you asking this on your own, or have other people told you about me?"

Pilate glared at the prisoner in anger. "Am I a Jew?" he asked, his voice rising. "Your own nation and head cohanim have handed you over to me. What have you done?"

Yeshua remained calm despite the tenseness of the situation. "My kingship does not derive its authority from this world's order of things. If it did, my men would have fought to keep me from being arrested by the Judeans. But my kingship does not come from here."

Pilate's eyes lit. "So then," Pilate said to him, "You are a king, after all."

Yeshua answered, "You say I am a king. The reason I have been born, the reason I have come into the world, is to bear witness to the truth. Everyone who belongs to the truth listens to me."

Pilate leaned forward. "Truth? What is truth?" he spat at him.

Yeshua did not answer.

Pilate waited a few moments. As the silenced continued, he began pacing from side to side, not dropping his gaze at the prisoner.

Yeshua made no further response.

Pilate turned again to address Kayafa and the crowd.

"I don't find any case against him. However, we have a custom at your Pesach Feast to set one prisoner free. Do you want me to set free for you the 'king of the Jews'?"

John's hope rose to a point he could hardly contain it. They had done it. Adonai had found a way to save the life of the mashiach.

The crowd did not respond immediately. Suddenly,

Sha'ul cried in a loud voice, "Free Bar-Abba!"

Upon hearing the name, the rest of the crowd joined him. "No, not this man but Bar-Abba!" they cried.

Pilate appeared surprised at the response. "I have before you your king. Do you not want him released?"

"Free Bar-Abba! Put Yeshua to death on the stake! Put him to death on the stake!"

John could not believe what he was hearing. Tears ran down his cheeks. Then he looked at Yeshua, who still did not show any concern.

Pilate returned from the balcony and walked to the outer office. The crowd continued to chant behind him.

"Go to the jail and bring me Bar-Abba, immediately," he barked.

Moments later, soldiers shoved a large, unwashed man into the office. Pilate ordered both prisoners brought onto the balcony with him.

A third time Pilate asked those milling below, "But what has this man done wrong? I haven't found any reason to put him to death. So I'm going to have him flogged and set free."

The crowd went out of control. They continued to yell, "Put him to death on the stake and Free Bar-Abba!" It became a chant, repeated over and over. The volume was deafening.

Pilate walked over to a marble basin filled with water, and placed his hands in it. He addressed the crowd. "My hands are clean of this man's blood—it's your responsibility."

The crowd did not back down. "His blood is on us and on our children! Put him to death on the stake and free Bar-Abba!"

Pilate returned to his office with both prisoners. He turned to one of the guards and nodded at Bar-Abba. "Set this man free."

Bar-Abba's eyes grew wide as the soldiers led him from the office.

Then Pilate turned to the other guard. "This man is to be flogged. After that, remove him to Gulgolta. I want him on a crucifixion tree by nine." He returned to his throne. "The rest of you, get out of my office before I have you join him."

The guards took Yosef and John through the outer office and down the stairs. They opened the outer doors, which streamed bright sunlight into the hall.

As Yosef and John emerged from the Roman headquarters, Kayafa took notice of them. He appeared ready to make a comment, but became distracted when two guards removed Bar-Abba's shackles, and pushed him roughly into the streets.

The doors slammed shut.

The crowd dispersed to watch the flogging of Yeshua. Kayafa and the Sanhedrin headed in that direction also. John watched Kayafa accept congratulations from the rest of the P'rushim with a large grin.

The square soon emptied and grew quiet. Only Yosef, Myriam, and John remained.

"Myriam, will you ever forgive me? You tried to tell me. Why didn't I listen?"

"I don't know. I feel sick inside. What can we do now?" she asked.

Yosef shook his head. "There is nothing that can stop this now. Yeshua is already nailed to the execution-stake, as far as Pilate is concerned."

John felt the guilt rising in him. "It's my fault. It's all my fault," he said, over and over.

Yosef placed a hand on John's shoulder. "You are not at fault."

John shrugged the hand off and walked a few feet away. "I did kill Yeshua. I knew who He was, but I refused to accept it. Maybe if I had spoken, maybe if I had fought for Him, He might still live."

Despite the situation, Yosef managed a smile. "You, a young boy, only a few years into apprenticeship, believe you can take on Kayafa and the whole Sanhedrin? How could you have done that?"

John realized Yosef was right. "Maybe I couldn't. But I should not have assisted them. I should have left the moment I saw Yeshua. I should have listened to Myriam."

Yosef looked down and locked eyes with John's as tears began to fall. "You are not responsible for this, do you hear me?"

John wiped his tears and nodded.

Yosef sighed deeply. "If anyone could have prevented it, I should have. It was my testimony that condemned this man."

Yosef lifted John's chin. "Are you a good student? Do you know your Scriptures?"

"Yes."

"Then tell me," the older man asked, "for whom is the mashiach born?"

John thought about how to respond.

"Do you know Yesha`yahu?"

John searched his memory.

> *In fact, it was our diseases he bore, our pains from which he suffered; yet we regarded him as punished, stricken and afflicted by God. But he was wounded because of our crimes, crushed because of our sins; the disciplining that makes us whole fell on him, and by his bruises we are healed.*

Yosef was impressed. "Everything they say about you is true. For whose crimes did the prophet say the mashiach would be wounded for?"

John understood. "For our crimes?"

"Yes. All of this time we were looking of a mashiach, thinking He would be freeing us from Rome. We are small minded. We are worried about captivity, and look to Him to free us from oppression.

"But what is the one thing separating us from Adonai? Is it the Romans? Is it the Bavlims? No, they all will pass. Only one thing separates us from Adonai."

"Sin," said John and Myriam together.

Yosef nodded. "I understand now. I have been such a fool all of these years. I thought it would be a war. I thought Adonai would crush the Romans. I prayed it would happen in my lifetime." A single tear fell down his cheek. "Yeshua was born to pay for my sins."

"There was nothing I could have done?" John asked.

Yosef shook his head. "Unless you think you can stop Adonai's plan from before the fall of Adam."

John's eyebrows dropped in confusion. "What do you mean? Why would God possibly choose to let His own Son die, even before Adam had sinned? That doesn't make any sense."

Yosef smiled. "Do you not know the scroll of Yesha'yahu?"

"Yes," John said, tentatively.

"Near the end," Yosef said. "Do you know where the prophet says,

> *Seek Adonai while he is available, call on him while he is still nearby. Let the wicked person abandon his way and the evil person his thoughts. Let him return to Adonai and he will have mercy on him, let him return to our God, for he will freely forgive."*

John nodded.

"Now, what does it say next?"

John tried to picture the scroll before him. "It says,

> *'For my thoughts are not your thoughts, and your ways are not my ways,' says Adonai. 'As high as the sky is above the earth are my ways higher than your ways, and my thoughts than your thoughts.'"*

There was silence while Yosef let the thought settle.

"It doesn't lessen the pain," John said. "He doesn't deserve what is about to happen to Him."

Yosef shook his head. "No, that is laid squarely on you and me. We deserve it."

John saw how this made sense.

"What shall we do now?"

Yosef stood up. "I do not want to do what I know I must."

John and Myriam looked at him quizzically.

"If the mashiach is to die for me, the least I can do is be there for Him."

John knew what that meant. "I will go with you. I will watch Him be scourged and nailed to my tree."

Yosef smiled. "You marvel me. I had heard you were wise beyond your years. I had heard you knew Scripture as well as the cohen hagadol. But I never knew you were mature enough to see a man die in your place."

John should have felt proud, but he was ashamed.

Myriam turned to John. "I cannot go with you. I cannot watch this. I love this man." Tears flowed freely on her cheeks.

John took her hands tenderly into his. "I know. I will be back for you."

She nodded, biting her lower lip to keep it from trembling. "I must go and see my parents and let them know what has happened." She turned and ran off.

John watched her until she turned behind a building and was gone. Then he and Yosef left Pilate's headquarters and began the walk to the courtyard where the sentence would be handed down.

By the time Yosef and John arrived, spectators ringed the entire courtyard. Yosef and John tried to get a better view, but the crowds were too thick. Finally, Yosef used his authority as a member of the Sanhedrin to force a few people to let them through.

The courtyard was large, ringed by the two-story building that was the government headquarters, a large olive tree at its center. Roman soldiers stood three deep, shoulder to shoulder, preventing anyone from pushing through to the prisoner.

Cheers erupted from the far side. John saw some movement, and then Yeshua came into view.

It was a horrifying image. He was Yeshua, but the guards had badly mistreated Him. He wore an old purple robe, one that barely hung to His knees. A large soldier led Him on a long chain attached to the bands around His hands. If He slowed or stumbled, a hard pull would move Him along.

"Adonai, no!" gasped John, on seeing Yeshua's face. The most obvious thing was that there was no beard. It was just gone. Judging by the blood dripping, John could only assume the guards had ripped it out. So bruised and swollen were both eyes, it was amazing He could even see. His nose bled freely, and atop His head, the Romans soldiers had weaved thorns into a makeshift "crown." Wherever the thorns touched flesh, blood trickled.

The Roman soldiers on either side of Yeshua shouted and belittled their prisoner, bowing deeply, trying to incite the crowd to join them. "Hail to the King of the Jews," they would say, bowing deeply in mock admiration. Some would run behind Yeshua and strike Him in the head with a stick. Others would walk up and spit on His face.

When they arrived at the olive tree in the center, they removed the crown and purple robe. Yeshua was naked underneath. They removed the chain from the bands about His wrists and led Him to a large wooden post. They attached the bands to a large metal hook, stretching His arms high above His head. Yeshua had to balance on His toes just to breathe.

Sergius Paulus stood with a proclamation. The crowd quieted to hear. "Yeshua ben Yosef of Natzeret, by order of Pontius Pilate, Prefect of the Roman Province of Judaea, on this day you shall be flogged for crimes against the Empire."

Two Roman executioners lined up on either side of Yeshua. Each had in his hand a flagrum, a short-handled whip with three long thick leather thongs. They held the flagrums loosely in their hands, the lead balls at the tips bouncing slightly with their movements, the ping of the metal sounding faintly musical.

Sergius took his position in front of Yeshua. Yeshua stared at him with a blank expression. When the Roman official was satisfied everything was in place, he gave the order to begin.

With a loud crack, the first guard struck Yeshua's left side. Where the whip hit, a large bruise began to swell, and blood trickled out. Yeshua grimaced and His body stiffened.

The second came to His right. The guards took turns swinging their evil weapons repeatedly, striking Yeshua on the back, on the shoulders, on the buttocks and on the thighs of His legs. Yeshua, who stood bravely silent at first, cried out with every impact. His entire back became black and red from bruises and blood.

John looked away, tears streaming down his cheeks. *No, He is doing this willingly in my place.* He forced himself to turn back and watch.

After about two minutes, the beating was so severe Yeshua finally passed out from the torture. Sergius ordered the beating stopped, and both guards held their whips.

The Roman official walked over to a small wooden table, and poured water from a ceramic jug into a chalice. He stood before Yeshua and tossed the water into His face, reviving him. Sergius bent down and looked into Yeshua's eyes. Satisfied Yeshua could withstand more, he ordered the beating to continue.

Three times Yeshua fell unconscious from the torture, and three times Sergius revived Him and ordered it to continue. Every strike of the whip caused damage; each blow removed tissue and blood. Because of the devastation they were causing to the back, the guards stepped closer, allowing their foul whips to reach around and strike His sides, and then His front.

Finally, Yeshua's eyes closed. Sergius ordered a halt, and then raised each eyelid. No pupil was visible, only the white.

"It is over," said Yosef, relieved. "Sergius has judged that this was enough, that Yeshua cannot withstand another blow."

The guards brutally lifted Yeshua off the hook, and He immediately collapsed to the ground. They kicked Him in the side, sending sand and gravel into the open wounds they had just created, and then roughly grabbed Him by the arms and pulled Him to his feet.

The prisoner who left the courtyard was no longer recognizable as Yeshua.

Excited crowds ran from the courtyard to line the streets for the short walk to Gulgolta. John and Yosef joined them along the route.

Yeshua emerged from the headquarters. The guards lashed a thick wooden beam to each hand, held up by the back that only ten minutes earlier they had been beaten. To say He was in agony would have been an understatement of immense proportions. Every step, every tortured, staggered step, Yeshua grimaced and cried out. Behind Him, Roman guards with whips would occasionally lash at Him, just to keep Him moving.

As they walked the last part to the top of the hill, Yeshua's strength ran out, and He collapsed onto the wooden beam. His body heaved heavily as He tried to fill his lungs with air. The guards kicked at Him several times, but He could no longer support the weight of the beam.

John stood frozen. It all seemed like a dream, a nightmare. He had never seen anyone so brutally treated in his entire life.

The officers looked into the crowd at the side of the road and pointed at John. "You, untie him and carry that beam. I won't have him dying in the road on me. We have other things planned for him."

John was incredulous. He began to move forward, but the large man standing behind him pushed him aside. The man looked in wonder at the officer. "Me? Why should I carry his penalty?"

"Pick it up now, or we will perch you next to him."

The man swallowed hard, and bent down and untied Yeshua's hands. He picked up one end of the heavy beam and placed it onto his shoulders then hauled it to the top of the hill.

Two soldiers grabbed Yeshua by either arm and dragged Him behind the beam.

27

The Death of Yeshua

The execution grounds were located just outside the city walls, set along the road north out of Yerushalayim. At a crest before its descent out of the city limits, the Romans had prepared an area for executions. This location insured that a maximum number of people would witness what was about to take place.

On the left side of the road was an escarpment. It rose maybe two dozen feet. John noticed a formation of rock outcroppings that bore an eerie resemblance to a human face, with sunken eyes and no nose. This must be why they call this the place of the skull.

Four holes had been chiseled out of the solid rock at the base of the escarpment. Three were aligned at the edge of the road, and a fourth was placed at an outcropping of rock about five feet above them. Crucifixion stakes occupied two of the lower holes, and two men were set there. A large wooden column was set in the upper hole, flanked by two ladders. The two prisoners cried out in agony as they raised themselves up to try and keep breathing.

As Yeshua approached, two guards took the wooden beam the stranger carried and ordered him away. The man gladly left. They placed the bean on the ground. Three other soldiers forced Yeshua onto his knees, then swung him around so his back was against the wooden beam, his arms outstretched. Two soldiers held his right arm down.

One soldier came over with a large steel spike. He made a show of trying to decide where to place it, moving it from palm to wrist and back.

Without warning, he lifted his hammer and drilled the spike into Yeshua's hand, just above the spot where the thumb attached. A stream of red poured from the wound. John, feeling sick, had to turn away. He heard Yeshua let out a tremendous cry of agony. Looking back, he saw the soldier pound quickly until the spike had come out through his wrist and was driven deep into the wooden beam.

He moved over to the other arm. Yeshua, despite his weakened condition, struggled to pull his arm back. Two soldiers were required to keep it in the approximate place the executioner wanted it.

"Hold him still," he cursed. Finally, he brought the hammer down and attached Yeshua's other hand to the beam. Then, two more soldiers lashed each arm to the wooden beam.

Once secured, they lifted the beam with Yeshua attached, and handed it to the guards perched on the ladders. They struggled to raise the beam over their heads, and dropped it harshly atop the wooden column. They maneuvered it until the hole in its top lined up with the column, then dropped into the hole with a thud. Yeshua cried out as it was set. The time was nine o'clock in the morning.

The executioner grabbed a third spike and drove it into Yeshua's feet as two soldiers held them still, securing him to a block at the bottom of the column. He then stepped back to view his work.

And so John saw his mashiach hanging there, on the execution stake. Yeshua appeared to be dead, or unconscious. As his body starved for air, he raised himself up onto his newly pierced feet to allow himself to draw in air then slumped back down to rest.

One soldier handed the executioner a bundle. "These are the prisoner's belongings."

The executioner removed Yeshua's robe and sandals from the sack, but he was much larger than they were, and they would never fit him.

"Nah, I don't need these. Who wants them?" he asked the men accompanying him. Three men who were about the right size raised their hands. Unable to decide, he threw the sack to the ground. "You decide," he said, and he turned to walk back into the city.

John watched the soldiers look at each other, trying to decide who should get it. One said, "I know, let's gamble for them." The man produced some dice called tesserae, cut from the bones of a former prisoner, marked with crude pips died black. "Highest roll wins."

John moved in for a closer look. The first man placed the dice in a cup and rolled, but was only able to get a four. The next man rolled a seven. The last man took the dice and threw them. When they finally stopped rolling, it was only a two.

The second man let out a cry of joy at his good luck and picked up the sack. All three then went back with their comrades.

The crowd's murmurs grew silent. John saw them part as Pilate and several Roman officials made their way to the crucifixion site.

Behind Yeshua, on the face of the rock, John noticed that the Romans had carved out three large recesses, almost like shelves in the rock's side. Each one was about John's size in width, and half that in height, maybe six inches deep. Pilate approached with several lesser officials carrying large paper banners. He took the one on top and motioned for the nearest soldier to take the other two.

"Place them in the upper niches," he barked.

As the soldier climbed a ladder, Pilate placed his in the lowest niche. When everyone stepped back, John was able to view all three signs.

The first was written in Latin. It said:

IESUS NAZARENVS REX IVDAEORVM

The second was in Hebrew:

היהודים מלך מנצרת ישו

And finally, in the Greek, or common tongue:

ΙΗΣΟΥΣ Ο ΝΑΖΩΡΑΙΟΣ Ο ΒΑΣΙΛΕΥΕ ΤΩΝ ΙΟΥΔΑΙΩΝ

All three said the same thing:

YESHUA FROM NATZERET, THE KING OF THE JEWS

It was then that John noticed some of the members of the crowd included some of the lesser members of the

Sanhedrin. One approached Pilate, head held low in humility.

"Forgive me, governor," he asked, "But could you change the inscription?"

Pilate looked at him dumbfounded. "What?"

The man trembled slightly at the Roman's voice. "Don't write, 'The King of the Jews,' but write instead, 'He said, "I am King of the Jews."'"

Pilate looked up at what the man spoke about, but finally turned and said, "What I have written, I have written." And with that, he turned and left.

The other man looked at the notices, fixating on the words in Hebrew. John looked closer at what was written.

John couldn't believe his eyes! The words in Hebrew, Yeshua Ha'Netzeret V'mlech Ha'Yehudim, had a message. *Yeshua Ha'Netzeret V'mlech Ha'Yehudim.* Y H V H. YHVH.

In the sign behind Yeshua, John saw the tetragram of the name Yahweh, the name of Adonai!

He fell to his knees and began to cry.

No one else in the crowd seemed to realize. He felt like running forward and pointing it out for all to see, but said nothing out of fear.

After an hour, the main crowd began to thin. The Romans left only a small party of men to keep order. Feeling more secure, many began to move up to the edge of the crucifixion grounds. Some cried, some spat at him, and some insulted him. "Aha! So you can destroy the Temple, can you, and rebuild it in three days? Save yourself and come down from the stake!"

Kayafa, Anan, and several other other Council members walked up to the foot of Yeshua. Kayafa had a look of contentment on his face, as one who had finally had a tremendous burden removed.

Anan looked up. "He saved others, but he can't save himself!" he said to Kayafa. They shared a laugh.

"So he's the Messiah, is he?" said Kayafa, "The King of Isra'el? Let him come down now from the stake! If we see that, then we'll believe him!"

The robber on Yeshua's left, hearing who he was, mocked him also. "Aren't you the Messiah? Save yourself and us!" Despite the tremendous pain he was in, he managed a small laugh at his little joke.

The man hanging to his right became angry. "Have you no fear of God? You're getting the same punishment as He is. Ours is only fair; we're getting what we deserve for what we did. But this man did nothing wrong."

Unable to stay erect, he slipped down his pole, his strength weakening, and then forced himself back up. "Yeshua, remember me when you come as King."

Yeshua forced himself up so he could speak. "Yes! I promise that you will be with me today in Gan-`Eden."

Yeshua had hung there for almost three hours. Many had come and gone in that time. Kayafa was probably already at his home, celebrating his victory.

Yosef and John remained. None of Yeshua's talmidim where present, at least none they could see. John no longer felt any emotion, and it puzzled him. He thought he should be horrified at the sight, or terrified, but in truth, he felt nothing. It felt as if something tore all of his emotion from his body.

At noon, there was a tremendous shudder, as if an earthquake was starting. Everyone there screamed, fearful the earth would open up. The three men on the posts swayed slightly in the tremble.

The trembling did not continue. Instead, the skies became dark, so dark John saw stars. People ran screaming in horror, not sure what to make of it.

John and Yosef were bewildered. "What does it mean?" John asked Yosef, but he was at a loss. The wind rose from the south, and dust and sand blew off the ground.

Many people in the crowd had enough. They left rather hastily. At last, only a hundred or so remained.

Nothing else happened. It remained dark, and the wind was strong, but they felt no further tremors, nor did any other signs occur. Those who stayed became calm at the situation.

Ashamed at seeing the mashiach hanging there, submitting willingly to Adonai for the sins John had committed, John wanted desperately to do something, anything, to help Him through this torture. There was nothing he could do. Every time he moved close to the stake, one of the guards ordered him to keep back.

The only sounds John heard were the wind, the soft sounds of the women sobbing, and the occasional cry of each crucified man as he raised himself up to keep breathing. Every instinct told John to get off this mountain, to get himself away from this horrifying sight, but he knew he could not leave.

At about three o'clock, Yeshua gave out a loud cry. "*Elohi! Elohi! L'mah sh'vaktani?*"

One of the people standing to John's right said, "Look! He's calling for Eliyahu!"

John knew differently. John recognized what Yeshua was saying. It was in the old Hebrew, the language he had been studying. It was the first line of one of King David's psalms. John remembered one line in particular.

> *Dogs are all around me, a pack of villains closes in on me like a lion at my hands and feet. I can count every one of my bones, while they gaze at me and gloat. They divide my garments among themselves; for my clothing they cast lots.*

John leered at the Council members who were still there, gloating over their supposive victory. He stared at the broken body of Yeshua as He hung there in pain, seeing His ribs pressed against His bloodied flesh, His legs and arms straining at the weight of keeping Him alive. And he watched as the soldier who had won Yeshua's robe held it as a spoil of war. Here, before his very eyes, the words of the prophecy King David had penned almost a millennia ago came to life!

Next to him, Yosef was making the same startling discovery.

Yeshua again lost the strength to stay erect, sliding down his pole. After a few moments, he forced himself back up. "I'm thirsty," he said.

No one moved. John could no longer stand it. He walked up to one of the soldiers. "He's thirsty. Can't a dying man get one last drink?"

The soldier stared blankly at John like he didn't understand the request. He motioned to the sergeant-of-the-guard, who shrugged. "We don't have anything here for him to drink."

John surveyed the area. There were many items left littered by the crowds before they dispersed. He found a small jug of cheap wine. He removed the plug, and could tell by the odor it had soured in the heat. Nevertheless, it was the only thing drinkable around.

He returned to the guard. "How do I get up there to give him this?" he asked.

The guard said nothing, and made no effort to help. John looked around. He found a sponge lying on the ground, so he wrapped a cord around a hyssop branch and used the cord to attach the sponge. He then poured what was left of the sour wine onto the sponge, and carefully lifted it to Yeshua's mouth.

"Wait!" said someone in the crowd, "Let's see if Eliyahu will come and take him down."

As he approached Yeshua, John was able to see the extent of his injuries up close. His skin was gone in so many places. Blood had dried, although fresh ripples oozed every time He lifted himself to breathe. John smelled blood mixed with dust of the ground, and could only imagine the agony he must be in. At the base of the crucifixion stake, John saw the white bone of Yeshua's lower legs visible where His calves should have been. His mouth filled with bile, and he thought he might get sick, but he forced it down and concentrated on lifting the branch so that his mashiach would get the drink He yearned for.

Yeshua saw the sponge before him, and stretched himself to take a taste. "*Teleō*," he said and, letting his head droop, Yeshua died.

John recognized the Greek phrase tax collectors used. He stood there, holding the pole, hoping Yeshua would rise, but He did not move. The earth shuddered again. This time, it was not a minor temblor, as before; this time, the entire ground shook violently. Large cracks appeared in the earth around Yeshua's stake. John dropped the pole and ran back to Yosef.

Both of them struggled to keep their footing as the ground threw them violently back and forth. Several in the crowd had given up and dropped to the ground, only to be rolled back and forth as the ground shook. John saw trees in the distance swaying violently at the motion; some larger ones toppled.

Many men screamed in horror. "Save us, Adonai," they cried in unison.

The three men on the stakes rocked back and forth, their cross beams spinning them almost completely around the execution stakes. The criminals on either side of Yeshua screamed in pain as their limbs were torn and buffeted by the movement. Only Yeshua made no sound.

Debris rolled down the rock cliff behind the men. Sand and rocks rained down, tumbling past the stakes and into the road. Several people were hit by boulders.

Then, John grew terrified as he saw the face of the rock itself begin to separate. All along the cliff, and down past the men on the stakes, the rock tore. Bushes and dirt fell into the chasm being created. It grew vertically until it reached the base of the cliff then crossed the execution grounds right past Yeshua's stake. It stopped a few feet later, and a hissing sound rose from the split.

Just when he thought he could take it no longer, the shaking lessened. Rumbling sounds in the distance began to subside, and he found he was able to stand upright with little effort. The crucifixion stakes stopped swaying and began to settle down.

One of the Roman guards walked over to the corpse on the pole. He looked up into the bloodied face of Yeshua. "This man really was a son of God!" he said in awe. After a moment, he walked away.

Several members of the Sanhedrin who had remained walked up to the sergeant-of-the-guard. They adjusted their clothing and tried to make themselves look presentable.

"It is three o'clock," one said, "and our Shabbat is drawing near. We do not want these men hanging here after sundown, defiling our ceremonies."

"What would you have me do?" asked the Roman.

"Can you not hasten their deaths in some way?"

"Break their legs," he ordered.

John watched as two soldiers walked over to each robber and methodically broke their thighbones. Each man cried out in pain when he tried to raise himself up to continue breathing, but was unable.

When the soldiers came to Yeshua, one of the men said, "He's already gone."

The officer did not want any mistakes. He raised his spear and thrust it into the corpse's right side. A mixture of blood and water came out, flowing into the large chasm that had opened at his side.

"He's gone," said the guard. The officer grunted his approval, and then told the men to return to the barracks.

Within moments, everything was still. With the spectacle over, the crowd dispersed. Several women remained, looking at Yeshua's body. Yosef came up to John.

"I am proud for what you did," he said. "You were the only one to show Him mercy. I am sure Adonai will reward you in Gan-`Eden for your act."

John did not want to think about that. That was not why he did it. All he could think of was the pain Yeshua went through for his sake.

The darkness that had begun three hours earlier ended and the stars went back to their daytime slumber. "What shall we do now?" John asked.

Yosef saw the women leaving. "Do you know any of them?" he asked.

John looked at the faces. One appeared to be Yeshua's mother, but it was difficult to be sure because of all of the crying. The others were strangers. Then they parted and he noticed on girl near the back.

"Myriam," he called out.

When she heard his voice, she excused herself and went over to them.

"I thought you weren't going to come?" he asked.

She stared at the ground, not raising her face in shame. "I didn't want to, but I could not stay away. I had to be here when He died."

Introductions were in order. "Myriam, this is Yosef of Ramatayim. He is a member of the Sanhedrin."

Myriam gave John a peculiar look.

"No, it is all right. He knows the truth about Yeshua."

Reaching into his change purse, Yosef pulled out two large Roman gold coins and gave them to her. "Here," he said, "take this into town and buy a burial cloth. We may have mistreated Him in life, but we will not mistreat Him in death."

Myriam thanked him, took the money and headed out on her chore.

"Come with me," Yosef said. He and John were only a few steps behind her.

As Yosef walked up to the door of Pilate's office, John was not sure what to expect. Yosef entered into the outer office. Sergius sat at his post.

"Now what do you need?" he asked. "Have we not done enough for you today?"

Yosef bowed his head out of respect. "Forgive me, but the prisoner your Prefect sentenced has died. We would like to remove the body before sundown. It is our way."

Sergius gave him a strange look. "Just a moment." He went over and knocked softly on Pilate's door. When allowed, he entered.

Yosef and John just stood there for several minutes. The door opened and Pilate himself came out.

"He is dead already?"

"Yes," said Yosef.

Pilate did not look pleased. "Bring me the sergeant-of-the-guard."

"Yes, Prefect," Sergius said, and left the room. Pilate returned to his office, leaving the door opened.

In about ten minutes, Sergius returned with the sergeant. Pilate came out. "I have been told the Natzeret is already dead?"

"Yes, Prefect," the man said.

Pilate looked puzzled.

Sergius spoke up. "Prefect, remember how this all started. That deceiver told his followers while he was still alive, 'After three days I will be raised.'"

Pilate turned to Yosef. "Is this true?"

"Yes, I'm afraid it is."

Pilate smirked. "His followers may rob the grave. Then they can continue their insurrection, saying, 'He was raised from the dead.' This last deception will be worse than the first."

He turned to the sergeant-of-the-guard. "Release the prisoner's body to these men. You may have your guard.

Go and make the grave as secure as you know how."

The sergeant saluted, and Pilate returned to his office.

When John and Yosef returned to the execution spot with the four soldiers assigned to the guard detail, Myriam was already there with the linen cloth. There was another man standing there, a hood concealing his face.

As they approached, he lowered the hood. It was Nakdimon. John did not know what to make of this.

"What is your purpose here?" Yosef barked.

"Is he dead?" Nakdimon asked.

"Yes."

He pointed at several chests at the foot of the stake. "I have brought some seventy pounds of spices—a mixture of myrrh and aloes."

He looked up at the lifeless body. "I have spent the last three years pursuing this man to achieve his death. Now that I have succeeded, it sickens me. He did not deserve what we did. He did not deserve to die as a common criminal." Nakdimon looked up almost reverently. "He was a good man."

Nakdimon left. Yosef reached up to begin to remove Yeshua's body. "This will make us ritually unclean. We will be unable to attend Temple, or participate in any festivals until we are cleaned and make the appropriate offerings."

"I don't care," said John.

Yosef smiled at his willingness to help.

They wrapped him in the burial cloth Myriam had purchased, using the spices Nakdimon had delivered. With the help of several porters, they moved his body off the hill.

"Where shall we take Him?" John asked.

Yosef pointed down to the road. "I have purchased a new tomb just on the other side of that garden. I was intending it for my own use, but we shall place Him there."

John and Yosef emerged from the mouth of the tomb. There was a large, round stone to the right. It took eight guards to roll it into place, sealing the tomb with Yeshua's body inside.

"He has suffered enough," said Yosef. "I do not want His grave defiled."

The guard said, "No one will enter, I guarantee it. Pilate has ordered the tomb sealed." The soldiers took a thick iron chain and some stakes. First, they pounded one through the chain at the right side of the round stone, then they threaded it through the metal handle in the middle of the seal stone, and finally, they pounded a second large stake just to the right of the stone. "There, no one will be able to move this without removing the stake and this seal, and anyone who does is under penalty of death. The body will not be disturbed."

As the last rays of the setting sun peeked over the mountains, the night's full moon rose on the eastern horizon. As it grew higher in the sky, John saw that it was not nearly as bright as it usually was. In fact, this moon was red, almost blood red.

"Tonight, a blood moon arises," said Yosef, as they walked to Yosef's home.

John shivered at the thought. After the events of this day, Adonai chose to raise a blood moon.

28

Redemption

John and Yosef sat under the starlight sky in Yosef's courtyard. The blood moon had turned back to a normal full moon.

"How could Adonai let Him die?" John asked.

"You are very good at your studies, aren't you?" Yosef said

John nodded.

"Nakdimon tells me you have already committed the entire Tanakh to memory. It takes most of us ten years to do that, yet you did it in less than three."

John looked down to avoid Yosef's gaze. He felt ashamed that Yosef would bring this up so soon after Yeshua's death.

"But have you ever considered this? For more than two thousand five hundred years, from Adam until Moshe wrote the Torah, the world was without a written revelation from God. Do you believe Adonai left Himself without a witness, without a way to tell Avraham, Yitz'chak, and Ya'kov His plan for their redemption?"

John had never considered this before. "I don't think Adonai would have left them without an idea of His plan."

Yosef pointed off into the night sky. "There is an old tradition some rabbis hold that Adonai told Adam how He would forgive mankind for Adam's sin. But there were no books available, so Adonai wrote it in the night skies."

John looked up at the beautiful, peaceful lights of the stars. "I've never heard that, what do you mean?"

"Adonai told Adam His plan for redemption in the Mazzaroth, the constellations He had placed there. I studied this in my youth. I was fascinated by the idea, but I haven't thought about it for a long time."

"Why are you bringing this up now?"

Yosef took a deep breath of the cool night air. "I did not understand what the Mazzaroth was saying, so I dismissed it. But after these events, it is becoming clear.

"One of the constellations is called in the common

tongue Lupus. You may know it as a wolf. But this wolf has been slain, and is in the act of falling down dead. Its ancient Hebrew name is Asedah, which means to be slain."

John looked puzzled.

"I too was confused. Why would Adonai talk about His mashiach and then talk about His death? I could not understand. Until today."

John looked at the older man, and then back up at the night sky. "Are you saying Adonai told Adam that the mashiach would be killed?"

"Yes."

John swallowed at the thought. The night's sky suddenly seemed overwhelming to him.

"The really interesting thing is the constellation that proceeds the slaying of the mashiach. Its Hebrew name was Adom, which means cutting off. It is covered in Daniel's book. Do you know where?"

John thought hard, for it had been awhile since he had read Daniel. "Do you mean,

Then, after the sixty-two weeks, Mashiach will be cut off and have nothing."

"Exactly. Daniel prophesied Yeshua's death. Perhaps he was looking at the Mazzaroth as he did so. But this constellation, the one that talks of being cut off, in the common tongue is called the Cross."

John gasped at what Yosef was saying.

Yosef pointed to the horizon. "You can see the Cross rising over the mountains. It is where Adonai put it."

John strained to see what Yosef was talking about. "I see it. Is that how the Mazzaroth ends, with the stake and the slaying?"

Yosef smiled. "Hardly. The very next constellation is Atarah in the ancient Hebrew. Today we call it Corona, or the Crown. I don't believe Adonai would slay His mashiach and then crown Him."

"Then what do you think it means?"

Yosef smiled and the moonlight twinkled in his eyes in delight. "I think it means that Yeshua will come again. I don't know how, but I don't think we have seen Adonai's entire plan."

John awoke yet again in a strange room. He rubbed his eyes a few times, trying to get the cobwebs of the night's sleep from his head.

After a moment, he remembered the events of yesterday. His heart filled with sadness at his role Yeshua's death. His only desire was to pull the covers over his head and hide from the world. Perhaps he could hide here in Yosef's home. No one would look for him here. Or maybe he could try and find Myriam or his parents. Or Ya'ir.

He came to the reality of the situation and knew no amount of hiding would change what had happened. He rose and dressed before opening the door and heading out of the room.

Yosef's house was large and impressive, like Kayafa's and the other members of the Sanhedrin he had met on this visit. The room he had slept in was not in the servant's quarters, nor was it with the other talmidim under Yosef's tutelage. He had been given guest quarters within the main house.

He headed into the main room, and saw Yosef and his family at the table having a breakfast of bread and sweet honey.

"Good morning," John said, stifling a yawn as he did.

Yosef stood to greet him, as did his family. "I let you sleep. You seemed tired."

"I was."

Yosef placed his hands on his wife's shoulders. "Let me introduce you to my family. This is my wife, Shlomit. My daughters, Na'omi and Marah, and my son, 'Eli."

John greeted the family, and then all of them sat at the breakfast table.

Yosef passed him the bowl of bread. "Now that you're awake, what are your plans for the day?"

John took a loaf of bread gratefully. "I don't know. I can't go back to Nakdimon."

Yosef looked confused. "Why not?"

"I can't learn the old ways anymore. Not since I know the truth."

"What about showing him the new ways?"

John had not considered that. "I don't think he'll listen to the opinions of a fifteen year-old boy."

"Maybe not, but he deserves to know the truth."

John hesitated. *How can I hope to convince someone who was so adamant that Yeshua was not the mashiach?*

"As a member of the Sanhedrin, I must perform the cleansing ceremony and make the ritual offerings. Meet with me after services tonight. I will speak to Nakdimon. I will also speak to Kayafa, Anan, and the rest of the Sanhedrin."

"They won't listen to you."

"No, but I fear the discipline of Adonai if I don't spread His Word with them."

John understood what Yosef was saying. If they truly believed that Yeshua was the Son of God, they would be bound to spread His truth to everyone they met, even if it was to those who stood in opposition to Yeshua's teachings.

Yosef's daughters rose from the table and began clearing the scraps. John offered to help, but they would not allow it. He sat back down at his place.

"And what will you do today?" Yosef asked, as he was preparing to leave.

"I am not ready to see those from my life for the last three years," he said, "but I will see those from before. I'm going to try and find my family."

It was mid-morning when John reached the outskirts of the city. He had made several inquiries, and found that the followers of Yeshua had remained at Beit-Pagei on the outskirts of the city, not far from the Mount of Olives. As John approached, there seemed to be twice as many people as the last time he had seen Yeshua's followers. Unlike last time, though, he did not fear entering their midst.

John felt lost as he roamed the great expanse of tents and people. People moved to and fro, either unaware or unfazed by their prophet's death yesterday. Several smiled and welcomed him as they passed. This was not the mannerisms he was expecting.

"Are you lost?" asked a man's voice behind him.

John turned to see an elderly man in a brown robe. His beard was long and his clothing dust covered, but his face held a warm and inviting smile.

"I have never been here before, but I am looking for someone from K'far-Nachum."

"K'far-Nachum! We have many people here from that great city."

John still had not gotten use to the idea of his old town being considered a great city. "Do you know where some of them may be?"

The old man raised a bony finger and pointed off to the east. "Most from there have settled over by that grove of fig trees."

John thanked the man and headed into the direction shown.

It took several hours, but he finally found someone who knew his mama, and took him to her.

When John saw her, tears welled in his eyes. He thought he was prepared to see her, but knowing that she was a follower of Yeshua, he suddenly feared she would blame him for his execution.

"John!" she cried as soon as she saw him.

John ran over and threw his arms around her, squeezing her tightly and sobbing softly into the folds of her cloak.

"Hush, hush my son. What is wrong?"

John told everything he had been involved in since he had become Ya'ir's apprentice.

His mother listened as only a mother can, and then said, "What is past is past. You cannot change what you have done. All you can do is move forward with the truth."

John wiped his tears and held her hands.

"I promise you, Mama, I will."

There was a silence between them, but an understanding also.

"How has your life been? How is David?"

His mother smiled at the mention of his brother. "Life has been wonderful ever since Yeshua cleansed David. Everything has changed. Your uncle is like a new man. He gave up drinking and cursing. He has been diligent in his studies of the Tanakh."

John smiled at the thought of Uncle deep in studies at the Temple.

"And he has returned to work."

"Selling fish?"

His mother shook her head. "No, he is now catching them. He bought Shim'on's old boat—"

"Father's boat?" John interrupted.

"She nodded. "Yes your father's boat. He has become a very good fisherman, not as good as Shim'on, or your father, but good enough to provide for his family. I no longer have to work the marketplace, but can stay at home with David."

"And how is David?"

If his Mama's smile had been large talking about her husband, it grew twice the size at the mention of his brother.

"He is wonderful. He is such a joy to have around now. David has been learning the Tanakh. He does not remember anything from the time he was possessed, which is probably best. All he knows is Adonai's love and how it manifests itself in his life."

John was truly grateful to hear that everything was going so well for her.

"I am happier than I have ever been since your father. Your uncle has become attentive to my needs, and works hard to provide for his family. We are not rich, but we are far from poor. We have even been able to leave Myriam's family and move back into our own home."

"And you know the love of Adonai," John added.

His mother nodded.

After spending several hours with his family, John sought out Ya'ir. He found him leading a study on the Tanakh with about a dozen youth.

When Ya'ir saw John, he dismissed his class. "John, my boy. What are you doing here?"

John told Ya'ir all that had happened.

"I am sorry it took you so long to see the truth, but I am glad you finally have."

John nodded. "How is Rivkah?"

At the mention of her name, she emerged from the tent. John had never seen anyone so beautiful. He suddenly felt his heart tug with a desire for her.

"I am wonderful." She ran up and gave him a hug and quick kiss on the cheek. "My father has told me what you did for me, how you persuaded him to seek out Yeshua when he couldn't. I owe you my life."

John blushed at the kiss and the compliment. "You owe me nothing. I had nothing to do with it, in fact..." His voice trailed off.

"Yes?" she asked.

"I'm ashamed to tell you this. I hoped that Yeshua would fail. At that time, I hoped that your death would prove He was a false prophet." John wiped tears from his eyes. "Can you forgive me?"

Rivkah's laughter surprised John. "Of course I forgive you. Do you think you were following your own will, or Adonai's? God is so great He can even use a non-believer as you were to fulfill His will."

John was amazed at her answer. "I can't think of myself as being part of God's plan."

Rivkah agreed. "Well, I still see you as Adonai's instrument in my life."

"I may never be able to repay you for what you did," said Ya'ir.

John suddenly felt very exposed from all of the compliments.

"What are you doing now?" asked Ya'ir. "Will you still apprentice with Nakdimon?"

"I don't see how I can."

"Then come here with me. I have been teaching all of the children. Your experiences would be a valuable addition to my teachings."

John was tempted by Ya'ir's offer, but knew he would not accept it. "I'll consider it," he offered, trying to be diplomatic.

Ya'ir frowned. "It seems you never agree to my offers to teach you."

John laughed at the memory of the first offer of apprenticeship, an offer that seemed a lifetime ago.

"I promise you, I will consider it."

Many hours passed before John walked into a particular campsite in the cool evening air. He heard the one voice he longed to hear.

"John?" asked Myriam.

John smiled broadly as he turned to greet her. She ran and threw her arms around him.

"I have wanted to see you since yesterday," she said. "You left with Yosef so quickly, we didn't have time to talk."

"I know, I'm sorry about that. I'm afraid we won't have much time tonight, either."

Myriam frowned at the comment.

"It doesn't matter," she said, "as long as you have accepted the truth."

"I have."

Myriam offered him a seat on the stone wall and John sat.

"I do have one question I hope you can help me with," she asked.

"I can try."

Myriam hesitated. "Why did He have to die?"

John had considered the question several times himself. "Because Scripture said He would."

Myriam did not seem to accept the answer. "Why would Adonai send His Son if He knew that death was the final outcome?"

John thought back to his lessons. "Do you remember what Moshe wrote in the first book of the Torah?"

Myriam nodded, but did not offer an answer.

"After Adam had eaten from the tree and sinned against Adonai, what did Adonai say to the serpent?"

Myriam looked blankly at him.

"He said,

> 'I will put animosity between you and the woman, and between your descendant and her descendant; he will bruise your head, and you will bruise his heel.'"

Myriam still did not seem to understand.

"Don't you see? Adonai knew we would sin, and He knew we would need a redeemer. Yeshua came to fulfill these words."

Myriam seemed to understand.

"Yeshua died to put away sin by the sacrifice of Himself, and to destroy Satan, who has the power of death. He bruises Satan's head—destroys his power and control over mankind, turning us from the power of Satan to Adonai. And Satan bruises His heel. Adonai chose this so that our salvation could only be brought about by the death of Yeshua."

"Are you saying that Adonai planned for Yeshua to die?"

"Yes."

Myriam pondered the concept a while. "Then, is His work finished?"

John had been thinking about this ever since he helped place Yeshua in the tomb. "I don't know. But my heart tells me that His work is not done."

Myriam smiled at the thought. "I hope you're right. I ache to see Him one more time."

John thought back to Rivkah and what he had seen. With Adonai, anything was possible.

It was well into the evening when John returned to Yosef's house. Despite the lateness of the hour, the lamps were lit and he could hear voices discussing something. He removed his sandals and quietly entered the home.

Yosef and Nakdimon sat on the floor. They were in such deep discussion they did not immediately notice his entrance.

"Are you saying that Adonai sent Yeshua to die?" asked Nakdimon.

"It is the only answer."

Nakdimon shook his head. "I cannot believe such a thing. Why would Adonai choose this way to redeem men? Why not have us prove our love through the Law?"

Yosef shook his head. "That is not possible. Do you keep the Law?"

Nakdimon nodded.

Yosef pressed. "Do you believe that Adonai will allow you into Gan-`Eden if you do not follow the Law?"

"Of course not."

"What if you keep only half of the Law? Will He allow you in then?"

"No."

"How about three-quarters? Seven-eighths? Fifteen-sixteenths?"

"You are being ridiculous," Nakdimon snarled. "What is your point?"

"My point," said Yosef with a smile, "is that unless you keep the whole Law, every part of it, then you are accountable for all of it. Adonai does not discriminate sin. False witness and murder are equal in His eyes."

"I do not see how this is relevant."

Yosef softened his voice. "Kayafa is guilty of breaking the Law in his handling of Yeshua. What he did was wrong. You know it and I know it."

Nakdimon remained silent.

"It is true," said John, emerging from the shadows. "What Kayafa did was because of his love for his way of life. It was strictly for himself. What Yeshua did, dying in our place, was the purest form of love. It was the love only Adonai can shower on His children."

Nakdimon's eyes locked on John's. "I do not disagree with what you have said," he began to say, "but I cannot condone his teachings. They went against all of our traditions, everything handed down to us from our fathers."

"You're wrong," John said, surprising himself at how forcefully he spoke to his former master. "All of history has pointed to the coming of the one who would redeem us. Yeshua did not come to condemn our ways, but instead to show us the true way."

Nakdimon shook his head. "No, you're wrong."

"Am I?" interrupted John. "You know the Tanakh. What does it say about the mashiach?"

Nakdimon paused.

"I'll tell you what it says. Yesha`yahu said,

> *He was wounded because of our crimes, crushed because of our sins; the disciplining that makes us whole fell on him, and in fellowship with him we are healed.*'

"You where there when Yeshua died, were you not?"

Nakdimon nodded.

"Did you not see David's great psalm come to life before your eyes?"

Nakdimon dropped his head, unable to hold John's gaze. "I did."

"Then how can you deny what your heart knows is

true?"

Nakdimon let out a deep sigh before continuing. "When I saw how Kayafa and the others treated him, I was sickened. I knew in my heart that it was wrong. Now that it is over, though, what can I do?"

Yosef reached out and placed a comforting hand on Nakdimon's arm. "My friend, you can help us to get the word out about Yeshua. You can tell everyone what you know."

Nakdimon shook his head. "I cannot. It is too far from what I have grown up believing."

Yosef stood up and offered a hand to Nakdimon. "In time, you will. You know the truth. It will gnaw at your insides until you have to proclaim it from every rooftop."

It was well past midnight when Nakdimon left and Yosef and John retired for the evening. As John laid his head down, his mind raced through everything he had done that day, everyone he had seen and spoken with.

He realized there was one other person he needed to speak with.

Tomorrow, he would find Philo and tell him the truth.

29

A Life Saved

"PHILO!" John cried as he walked along the warm streets, the morning sun rising in the sky. He had been searching for Philo for several hours without any luck.

As he called out for Philo, he was surprised to hear his own name in the distance. By the sound of the voice, he knew it had to be Myriam.

As soon as she saw him, she ran to him. "Where are your priestly robes?"

It was true. John no longer wore the fine clothing he had received while studying under Nakdimon. He asked for and received from Yosef an old hand-me-down robe.

"I will not wear those robes again," he replied. "Those men I looked up to are evil. They falsely accused an innocent man, and sent Him to die."

Myriam grinned at him, a grin so bright and happy that he could not understand it.

"But you're wrong. He is not dead! He is alive. Just as He said."

"What?"

"It is true. This morning, as the sun was rising, Myriam of Magdala, Myriam the mother of Ya`akov, and Ya`ir's wife Shlomit bought spices in order to go and anoint Yeshua. I went with them since I knew which tomb we had sealed Him in."

John looked on, afraid to interrupt her, hoping she was telling the truth.

"As we walked up the road to the tomb, we were asking each other, 'Who will roll away the stone from the entrance to the tomb for us?' We didn't know if the guards would allow it, or if there were even enough soldiers there to do it. I knew how big it was, and how many Roman soldiers it took to secure it three days earlier."

John nodded, remembering the labor involved in sealing the tomb.

"But when we got there, we saw that the stone had been rolled back already. The tomb was open.

"The women I was with were nervous. They looked at each other, afraid as to what had happened. But I was not. I walked up to the entrance to the tomb, and peered in."

"What did you see?"

Myriam smiled again. "It was amazing. I saw a young man dressed in a white robe sitting on the right. It was confusing. I could not imagine what a young boy would be doing there.

"I realized that it was a son of God, one of Adonai's angels! He said to us, 'Don't be so surprised! You're looking for Yeshua from Natzeret, who was executed on the stake. He has risen, He's not here! Look at the place where they laid Him. But go and tell his talmidim, especially Kefa, that He is going to the Galil ahead of you. You will see Him there, just as he told you.'

"Suddenly the man vanished. All of us looked at each other, not sure of what to think. We then agreed to follow the angel's charge. We split up and headed into the city. I knew I had to find you. I've been looking for hours."

John was thrilled that he was the first person she thought of with this news. But it did not make any sense.

"I don't understand. Are you saying that Yeshua has returned from the grave?"

Myriam nodded enthusiastically.

John's knees grew weak. He placed a hand on her shoulder to steady himself. "I'm not sure what this means."

Myriam helped him to a bench were he sat to regain his composure.

"How could He come back from death?"

Myriam smiled. "Let me understand this. Two minutes ago you were convinced that He was the mashiach, the only Son of God, now you question whether He has the ability to rule over death?"

She always knew how to make him smile. "I guess that is silly. Of course if He can raise Rivkah, He has that power."

They walked back to the city, back into Yerushalayim. "What are you going to do now," he asked, "now that He is alive?"

She ran ahead of him, skipping. "I'm going to tell everyone the news, the good news. I'm going to shout it from the highest rafters. I'm going to scream it from the tallest rooftops."

Then she turned serious. "I'm going to find Philo," she said.

John thought of his friend. Even Philo's father had condemned the man. Philo seen it all too.

"Going to find me for what?" said the familiar voice from behind them.

They turned their heads so quickly it almost broke their necks. The sight of their old friend was overwhelming. They both ran to him and hugged him, talking loudly.

Philo pushed them off. "Slow down, both of you. I'm glad to see you too, but I can't listen to you both at the same time."

"How is your ear?" John asked, reaching for the bandage.

Philo forced his hand away before he could touch it. "It is okay, leave it alone."

John began to tell Philo of the discussion he had the night before with Yosef.

"You are not going to try and tell me that you two think Yeshua was a mashiach?"

John held his tongue.

Philo took a deep breath through his nose, exhaling through his mouth, his mouth ending in a grimace. He interlocked his hands, touching the tip of his nose with his index fingers. "We have finally taken care of his heresy, and now you want to start it all over again?" He looked at Myriam with disgust. "I'll bet it was you putting all of this foolishness into his head. Let me save you the trouble; Yeshua was no better than a common thief. His death should have proved that to you."

Myriam began smiling, first at Philo, and then at John. So infectious was it that John could not help but smile too.

"What? Why are you smiling like that?"

"What would you say if we told you we could prove that Yeshua was the mashiach?"

Philo scrunched his face in puzzlement. "You can't

prove that. The man is dead and buried."

"Or is he?" said Myriam. "You see, I was there when we placed Him in the tomb, and I was there this morning when I saw that it was empty. Yeshua is alive. I saw an angel from Adonai, who told me this."

Philo's puzzlement turned to anger. "Yeshua is dead. If his tomb was empty, his talmidim had to have come in the dead of night and stolen the body."

"From a sealed tomb? With Roman guards?" John asked. "Where were his talmidim when Yeshua was arrested, tried, and executed. What makes you think they would suddenly have the courage to confront Roman soldiers and steal His body at night?"

Philo considered John's argument. "If not that, then maybe Yeshua didn't really die. Maybe he just fainted."

John laughed at the thought.

Philo looked as if he was about to punch his friend.

"A man, beaten and nailed to a Roman stake, pierced by a Roman spear, carried and sealed in a tomb, can revive, move the sealed stone and walk out without the guards stopping Him? That's the craziest thing I've ever heard."

"No, the craziest thing I've ever heard is a man coming back to life. That just doesn't happen every day."

"But could a mashiach do that? Would He have the power?"

"He was no mashiach."

I have to get through to him. "I didn't see you when Yeshua died on the cross. Where were you?"

"I went to the Temple. I offered prayers to Adonai, thanking Him for silencing the Natzerene."

"Did anything unusual happen?"

Philo said nothing.

Philo's silence puzzled John. "When Yeshua died, there was a great earthquake. Did you feel that?"

Philo nodded. "I did. Several of the Sanhedrin had joined me in prayer when the earth shook. My father was in the Temple when the earthquake hit. He told me it was so violent the curtain that hung separating the Holy of Holies tore right down the middle, from top to bottom."

"Do you believe that Adonai would allow all of this to happen, show all of these signs, if Yeshua was a liar or a lunatic?"

"I have to admit that it doesn't make sense. But why would Adonai send a mashiach that did nothing, that didn't free his people from the Romans, who was mocked, ridiculed and crucified? That makes far less sense."

John smiled at his friend's question. "That is because you are looking at this from your point of view. Have you ever considered what Adonai's plan might be?"

"We know his plan, it's in the Tanakh. He gave Moshe the Laws, and we are to follow them."

John shook his head. "I used to think that way too. It doesn't make any sense. How can Adonai expect us to overcome sin? How does keeping the Laws conquer our imperfections? It can't be done."

"And how does the killing of His mashiach make more sense?"

John shrugged his shoulders. "I'm not sure I can answer that, but Adonai must have wanted it to happen, it's the only conclusion."

Philo smirked at the thought. "An all-powerful God who cannot keep His Son alive?"

"Are there other Scriptures that match what happened to Yeshua?" asked Myriam.

Philo looked as though fire might come out from his ears, but he held his tongue. "Yes, John," his contempt dripping with every word, "tell her where Scripture speaks of a dying mashiach."

John ran all of the Scripture he knew through his mind, all that related to the mashiach. Suddenly he widened his eyes. "Our Scriptures do tell us about Him. I don't know why I didn't see this before.

'Then, after the sixty-two weeks, mashiach will be cut off and have nothing.'

"Daniel himself prophesied that Yeshua would die for someone else."

Philo remained silent as he considered the implications of the verse. "Yes, I guess you could say that can be interpreted to mean that he might die," he offered feebly.

John suddenly knew he had Philo rethinking his position. "There's the prophecies of Yesha'yahu.

> *I offered my back to those who struck me, my cheeks to those who plucked out my beard; I did not hide my face from insult and spitting.*

"I watched Him be scourged. I saw them spit in His face, and His beard was torn from his face."

Myriam looked as if she was going to be sick from the description.

"You were there," he said to Philo, "the first time Yeshua stood before Pilate. He did not utter a word, just as Yesha-yahu said:

> *'Though mistreated, he was submissive—he did not open his mouth. Like a lamb led to be slaughtered, like a sheep silent before its shearers, he did not open his mouth.'"*

Philo offered no opposition.

"Oh my." John's eyes suddenly widened, and a look of horror spread across his face.

"What is it?" Myriam and Philo asked at the same time.

John swallowed hard. "I just remembered the words of one of King David's psalms.

> *In my thirst, they gave me vinegar to drink.*

"I did that! I was the one who gave Him vinegar to drink."

Myriam placed her hands on his to comfort him.

John dismissed the idea from his mind. It was too overwhelming to think that the great King David had seen him in a vision. "Do you remember how dark it became when Yeshua was on the stake?"

"Yes."

"The prophet 'Amos wrote,

> *"When that time comes," says Adonai Elohim, "I will make the sun go down at noon and darken the earth in broad daylight."*

"This cannot be coincidence. This has to be the work of Adonai," Myriam pleaded.

"I agree," said John.

The three of them just sat there for several minutes looking at each other. They tried to understand the enormity of what they now realized.

"I still cannot believe it," said Philo quietly, almost a whisper.

"Why?" John asked. "Because you were a part of it? Because you were the instrument used by Adonai to bring forth His prophecies from two thousand years ago?"

Philo nodded his head, but remained silent.

"That's awfully boastful of you to say that Adonai's prophecy can't be true because one talmid doesn't want to believe his part in it."

"I remember." Myriam smiled at him. "Once, Yeshua said that no greater love can a man do than lay his life down for his brother. Adonai sent Yeshua to die for us to show us the meaning of love."

John added, "He sent Yeshua to us for that purpose. He poured all of His wrath and anger and hatred of sin on His mashiach, because He knew we couldn't bear it, but He could."

"Let me see that ear," John said, changing the subject.

Philo pushed John away. "I said no, not now."

Myriam got into the act. "Then let me see."

The two of them began poking at Philo, laughing as they did, but Philo remained very serious.

"It's my injury, let it be"

With all of the tussling, the bandage came loose and fell to the ground.

John gasped. "There is no wound there at all!"

Myriam pushed the ear back, trying to see where the sword had struck. Philo made no effort to stop her.

"I don't even see a scar. Are you sure this is where he was struck?" she asked.

John nodded. "What happened? I saw the sword hit you. I saw the blood."

Philo looked at the ground, defeated. "I cannot explain it. Yes, you are right, the sword did hit me. It was very painful. I remember holding my hand against the side of my head to try and stop the bleeding. But when I got home, there was no wound."

"Then why the bandage?" Myriam asked.

Philo sighed. "I knew a lot of people had seen the cut. I wanted to cover it up, so that no one would think..." His words trailed off.

"So that no one would think Yeshua miraculously healed you?" John asked.

Philo nodded.

"When Yeshua bent down to the grass and picked something up, what was it?"

"My ear," said Philo, quietly.

John and Myriam looked at each other, dumbfounded.

"Yeshua miraculously healed you, and you still won't believe?" Myriam asked, flabbergasted.

Philo dropped his head into his hands. "I can't." Philo sat down to ponder everything they were saying. "I cannot believe that Adonai would do all of that and then kill off His mashiach. A dead mashiach can't show love for anyone."

"But what of a living one?" asked Myriam, her voice filled with hope.

"What are you talking about?" asked Philo.

"He is alive! His tomb is empty. I saw it this morning. Yeshua is alive!"

Philo looked dumbfounded. "Alive? I cannot believe that."

"Because you choose not to?" asked John. "Whether you choose to believe it or not, it does not negate the facts that she told you. Yeshua, God's mashiach, is alive."

Philo stood suddenly. "Then take me to him now. Show him to me, with the wounds in his hands and stripes on his back..." He glanced from Myriam to John, then back. "These stripes you say he took for me. Show this to me and I will not refuse to believe."

Myriam stood between the two boys, linking her arms into each of theirs. "Then come with me. We haven't a moment to lose."

30

Wanderings

John stopped suddenly as he passed the boulder, remembering that he used to hide behind it as a child. That seemed so long ago, almost another lifetime.

It had been three days since he left Yerushalayim, three days since he and Myriam tried to convince Philo that Yeshua was alive. When they couldn't locate Him, Philo became upset and went back to his father. Nakdimon, on the other hand, understood, and left Kayafa and the other priests to return home. John, not knowing what to do, went with Nakdimon, who walked with him now.

"What is it?" asked Nakdimon.

John waved his hand almost to dismiss the question. "It's nothing. I was just remembering that it was on this spot I saw Yochanan come out of the desert all those years ago."

He joined Nakdimon on the path into the city. He was returning home to K'far-Nachum, but he was no longer the same boy who left.

As they entered the city, Nakdimon stopped. "I must return to the Temple. I need to find out what has happened while we were in Yerushalayim."

John nodded, clasping the man's right forearm as they parted. "I want to see my family. I enjoyed our travel together. I look forward to seeing you again soon."

"As do I."

The two men parted in opposite directions, but with similar hearts and desires.

John entered his home. It was clean and neat, the total opposite of how he remembered it from his last visit.

His mother was the first to see him. "John!" she cried, running across the room.

David looked up and saw his older brother, and ran too. It took several moments before the three of them could separate.

"I have good news," John said. "Yeshua is alive!"

His mother shushed him. "Do not speak of the dead like that, unless you mean alive in your heart."

John shook his head vigorously. "No, I mean alive. The tomb I empty. He lives again."

"Where is He?" his mother demanded.

"I do not know. I did not see Him in Yerushalayim. I came back here with Nakdimon, hoping He might be here."

"I have not seen Him. But if what you say is true, this is wonderful news."

John felt a tug on his robe. "How long are you home?" David asked.

John bent down and rubbed his little brother's tussled hair. "For as long as Adonai wants me to be."

"What of your studies?" Mama asked.

John sighed. "I have done all I can with learning from the others. What I need to do now is tell everyone about what I saw and learned."

Mama fixed him a glass of wine and bread with honey, and the three sat and talked for several hours as John told them everything that had happened since they last saw each other.

It was late afternoon when the door opened and Uncle walked in.

John initially froze, the sight of the man in his house triggering all of the fear and apprehension he had as a child.

When Uncle recognized who was visiting, he bounded over. "John, my boy, it is so good to see you." He bent down and gave John a hug.

John momentarily was at a loss, but then remembered the changes he had heard about his uncle. He stood and returned the embrace.

"Tell me everything that has happened since we were last together," Uncle asked, sitting down to hear John's story.

John sighed at the thought of repeating his conversation of the last few hours, and then laughed at how absurd this situation would have been three years ago.

"What is so funny?" David asked.

"Nothing," said John, taking up a seat next to his uncle. "It's just so good to be home."

It was late in the evening before John had finally answered all of his uncle's questions and was ready to retire.

"But not me," Uncle said. "It is a full moon out tonight, and I'll be spending the evening on the lake."

John looked at his mother, puzzled.

"Your Papa has purchased a fishing boat, Shim'on's old boat, actually."

"Father's boat?" John asked.

They both nodded.

"It seems that since Shim'on left, there's been a real need for fishermen here. Say, why don't you come with me? We can talk some more while we are fishing."

John shook his head. "I'd like that, I really would," he said, a half-truth, "but I've traveled a long distance today and I'm exhausted. How about I see you in the morning?"

Uncle's lower lip pouted in disappointment. "I understand. You get your rest. You can sleep in your old room, unless you have somewhere else you plan to be tonight."

John shook his head and turned towards his old bed.

"And make sure you are there at sunrise to load those fish into baskets!" Uncle suddenly barked in a fierce tone.

John was stunned at the command and turned, expecting to see the evil uncle standing there, again trying to take over his life.

But his uncle had a devilish smile on his face, apparently pleased at his little joke.

He laughed deeply, causing everyone to join in.

John stood on the shores of the lake at dawn, just as his uncle had asked. He wasn't sure why he rose so early, or what compelled him to come back, but he believed that Adonai was trying to show him something, and he knew he'd better listen.

His uncle's boat had not yet appeared on the horizon, so he began to wander the docks, the smell of salt and drying fish stinging his nostrils, delivering powerful memories of a lost time.

"Aren't you the fish merchant's son?" he heard someone ask behind him.

John turned and saw an amazing sight. Standing on the dock was Shim'on, the talmid of Yeshua. John nodded his head, not sure what the man was doing there or what he might want.

Shim'on bounded across the deck in three steps and placed his arm around him. "John, it's so good to see you. I thought you were in Yerushalayim?"

"I was. I'm here now. Hav you seen Him?"

"Yeshua?" Shim'on asked.

John nodded.

Shim'on shook his head. "Alas, no. I have seen His tomb. I know He lives, but I have not seen Him."

"Then why are you here?"

"I wanted to see K'far-Nachum one last time, see my old boat, these docks, before I leave." Shim'on was smiling broadly. "You were there, though. You know what happened."

John nodded.

"Good. I could use a friend now. Come, walk with me."

The two left the docks and sat by the road.

"Tell me about yourself," Shim'on said.

John launched into an abbreviated description of the events of the last three weeks.

"So, now you believe the truth? Now you know Yeshua is God?"

John nodded. "I do."

"And what do you plan to do with this knowledge?"

John tried to beat back a pride he felt swelling in him. "I plan to tell everyone I meet the truth. I wanted to teach the old Laws, but now I want to teach the new truth. I want everyone to know what I know."

"And if they still want to follow the old Laws?" Kefa asked.

John smiled. "They won't. I'll get through to them even if I have to beat them over the head with a hammer."

They sat in silence for a few minutes, listening to the caw of gulls.

"After His resurrection," Shim'on began, "I decided to spread His good news throughout the land. I'll be heading back to Yerushalayim. I could use some help. Would you join me?"

John had to think about it. Philo and Myriam were gone. With everything that had happened, he could never return to his studies. His mother was finally happy, and she didn't need him. "Shim'on, I think I'd like that," he replied.

A broad smile broke over the older man. "My son, that is great news."

They stood and began walking back into town.

"But I am no longer Shim'on. That name means nothing to me. When Yeshua asked me to be His talmid, my life was reborn. The man that I was, the drinking, cursing, vile dirty fisherman died, and I was reborn. When Yeshua did this for me, He also gave me a new name. I was no longer Shim'on, the fisherman, but now I am Kefa"

"Why did He call you Kefa?"

"In Aramaic, *kefa* means rock. Yeshua said that He would build His church on the rock of my belief. I am the talmid of the risen Mashiach."

John's eyes twinkled brightly, and he grinned widely. "I love the way that sounds. 'A talmid of the risen Mashiach.' That's what I want to be."

"If you are going to be with me, to be my talmid, then I will rename you also, to show your rebirth. From this moment on, I think I will call you..." He paused as he considered a name. "You will be Marcus, or Mark, if you prefer."

"Why Mark?"

"Do you know what Mark means?"

John shook his head no.

"It means 'smashing hammer.'"

They both laughed at the joke.

The gesture touched John deeply. "I am John-Marcus," he replied wiping tears from his eyes to look strong. "And you may call me Mark."

That evening, they set up an encampment off the main road. As a fire crackled, Kefa asked him when he first met Yeshua.

"I was there at the Yarden River when Yochanan the

Immerser was preaching," John-Mark said, and he told Kefa about his experience.

The two men sat again in silence. The older man stretched out, as if to sleep.

"Master," John-Mark said, "May I ask you a question?"

Kefa did not open his eyes. "Yes, anything."

John-Mark took a moment to work up the courage for his question. "I was there when Yeshua spoke to the crowd about a farmer scattering seed. Do you remember that?"

The older man smiled without opening his eyes. "Yes, I remember that."

"Well," John-Mark continued, "I was confused by that. I thought He would be talking to us about Scripture. Instead He talked about farming. I was very confused. What did it mean?"

Kefa sighed, not out of disgust at the question, but out of sheer exhaustion. "You and I will be like that farmer," he said. "The seed we will be sowing is the good news of all of the things we saw. Some will not listen. They will call us fanatics or lunatics and walk away. That is like the seed falling on the footpath. They won't listen to us, and the Adversary will snatch them away."

Kefa shifted to a more comfortable position. "Some people we will meet will be happy, and leave us quite content. But when they tell their families and friends, they will be laughed at, and they won't continue. They're like the seed falling on shallow soil."

"I see," John-Mark cried out. "It's all making sense. The seed that fell among the thorns would be like people who hear our news, but that news gets choked out, like weeds choking out growing plants."

"Yes," said Kefa, smiling. "And some people will hear, will believe, and will tell others. They are like the seed that fell on fertile ground."

At last, Mark understood. "Master, I have another question," he began.

Kefa raised his hand. "Slow down, little one. We will have plenty of time together in the years ahead. Can you write?"

"Of course, it is what I did for my masters," replied John-Mark.

He reached into his travel sack and pulled out a bundle tied with string. "I have here some writing materials. I'm not very good at writing. Would you start writing down some of your questions? Or some of the things you witnessed?" He handed the items to John-Mark.

"Of course I could. When would you like me to start?"

"Whenever Adonai leads you," Kefa said.

John-Mark accepted the gift and sat back for a few moments to think. He soon heard light snoring coming from the still form next to him.

John-Mark sat by the glow of the firelight, and thought about all of the things he had witnessed, from Yochanan the Immerser to Herod's palace to the Pharisees plotting to Yeshua nailed to the cross, and then he suddenly knew how he would start. He began writing.

The beginning of the Good News of Yeshua the mashiach, the Son of God: It is written in the prophet Yesha'yahu,
"See, I am sending my messenger ahead of you;
he will prepare the way before you."
"The voice of someone crying out:
'In the desert prepare the way for Adonai!
Make straight paths for him!'"

About the Author

W. R. (Will) Sander was born in Liberia and grew up on the east coast. He currently resides in the Kansas City, Missouri area with his wife Kim and his sons Bradley and Benjamin. He has been a Christian since September 26, 1997, when God spoke to him at 30,000 feet on a flight from Kansas City.

He is active in the leadership of his church, and performs with the Praise Band.

This is his first novel.

Author's Notes

This novel is intended to help in witnessing the Good News (Gospel) of Yeshua (Jesus). I hope you have enjoyed reading it, but I ask that when you are done, you pass it along to someone else who may need to read it.

People often wonder how authors or artists are inspired to create their works. To help with the witnessing, I'm going to explain how this book came to be. But before I begin, this will state some "spoilers," so if you haven't read the book yet, please finish it before turning this page.

Author's Notes

Since you're here, I'll assume you've either finished the book or don't care if there are any surprises.

I was inspired to write this book while I was preparing a Bible study on the Gospel of Mark. As I was doing some background research on the author, I read an unusual statement in my study Bible. In Mark 14, verses 51-52, the writer of the Gospel states:

> "*51 There was one young man who did try to follow him; but he was wearing only a nightshirt; and when they tried to seize him, 52 he slipped out of the nightshirt and ran away naked.*"

The Bible commentary I was consulting stated that there was speculation that this young man was actually the writer of the Gospel himself. The thought intrigued me; what if the writer of the Gospel of Mark was actually a young boy present not only in Gethsemane, but throughout Jesus' ministry?

As soon as I had that thought, I knew two things about my book; it would contain this very scene in the garden of Gethsemane (chapter 22, In the Garden), and it would end with the opening strains of the Gospel of Mark. Now all I needed to do was fill in the beginning and the middle parts.

As I wrote, I used the Gospel of Mark as my guide, taking the scenes that unfolded there and expounding upon them to create the novel you just read, using actual Scripture for the dialogue. I decided my novel would open where Mark's Gospel did, with the ministry of John the Baptist, so my first scene became the appearance of Yochanan the Immerser outside of John's hometown.

My next decision was how would I go about making the main character available at all of the important scenes in Christ's life. In studying the Scriptures, I realized that one group was present throughout Jesus' ministry, and I'm not talking about His disciples. I'm talking about the priests, the ones who tried repeatedly to stop or discredit Jesus. That idea made for an interesting thought, how about telling the Gospel story from the point of view of someone not interested in it? In other words, if I wanted to use this narrative as a witnessing tool, why not make the main character initially against Jesus, and have him slowly become a believer over the course of the

Author's Notes

book, as I hoped the reader might do? It was certainly a novel idea, and one I don't think many have explored, so I began writing by finding ways to make this happen.

As I was writing, the Harry Potter books were all the rage. If our youth accepted a boy learning to become a wizard, why not have my character have some similar super-human ability, and that's when I decided to give John his eidetic memory. Not only did it allow the character to be discovered and used by the priests, it allowed me to bring Scripture into the story verbatim in a natural way.

Now that I had my main character, I needed to flesh out the other characters. Early on, I knew I wanted John to be torn between two other characters on opposite sides. This became Philo, who would champion the non-believer position, and Myriam, who would be a follower. I hope that their dialogues back and forth asked and answered typical questions non-believers might have about the Gospel. I chose Philo's name, since he is an obscure character in the New Testament, mentioned once by Paul in Romans 18:15. I thought the nickname of Philo (FI-low) would make sense and be easily remembered.

Myriam was chosen because it is such a common name, and easy to identify with.

John, of course, had to be John-Mark.

But in the earliest drafts of the book, I used Anglicized names; John, Mary, Jair, Nicodemous, Caiaphas, but it soon got confusing when I tried to write John into the scenes with John the Baptist. Also, it didn't really sound right to use modern names in the first century context.

I discovered and purchased a copy of the Complete Jewish Bible by David H. Stern, and I immediately latched onto the idea of using Scripture quotes from this source rather than the King James or some modern translation. This translation takes the original Greek manuscript of the New Testament and connects it to the Jewishness of the Messiah. Names and locations are transliterated to the original Hebrew. This not only gave an authentic feel to the names, places and dialogue, it masked the true nature of the novel (a retelling of the Gospel) so that, I hoped, non-beleivers would become invested in the characters and story by the time they realized it was a Christian novel, and might continue to read to the end. Thus, Jairus became Ya'ir, Nicodemus became Nakdimon, Caiaphas

Author's Notes

became Kayafa, Capernaum became K'far-Nachum and John the Baptist became the wonderful Yochanon the Immerser.

But John stayed John. My target audience was today's youth, and I feared that The Book of Yochanan would not be very appealing, nor would the reader identify with that character name. So I made John a nickname for Yochanan, just as I made Philo a nickname for Philologus.

I researched and tried to paint an authentic image of the life and times in the first century, but I also tried to keep the dialogue accessible to today's modern reader. The scenes and dialogue are right from the Gospels, but the descriptions and some of the mannerisms are more modern than I had hoped. I did take some poetic license with the characters; for example, there is no evidence that Caiaphas was ever a priest in Capernaum, but then again, it is at least possible. Please don't use this novel as your only source of information on the Gospels. Yes, I tried to follow it accurately, but if you want a full understanding of Jesus' life and ministry, I would recommend you begin reading the entire Gospel of Mark, and then do as I did; search out the other Gospels to either expand your understanding of the scenes Mark wrote about, or discover events in Jesus' life that Mark did not write about.

Scripture Verses

To assist you, I have compiled a list of all of the Scripture verses referenced in this novel, either by themselves or as dialogue:

1 Samuel 2:9, Mark 1:7, Deuteronomy 18:15, Isaiah 6:1-3, Matthew 3:2, Mark 1:7-8, Luke 3:7-9, Matthew 3:11-12, John 1:19-23, Isaiah 40:3, John 1:25-26, Luke 3:10-14, Matthew 3:14-15, John 1:29-34, Matthew 3:15, Exodus 20:7, Isaiah 52:13, Mark 1:15, Luke 5:4-5, Luke 5:8, Luke 5:10, Isaiah 9:1, Mark 1:15, Mark 1:24-25, Mark 1:27, John 3:2-7, John 3:9-21, Daniel 7:13-14, Mark 1:15, Deuteronomy 13:2-6, John 1:34, Mark 3:22, Mark 2:5, Mark 2:7, Mark 2:10-12, Mark 2:14, Mark 2:16-22, Mark 3:3-5, Mark 4:3, Mark 4:5-9, Mark 3:8, Mark 3:18-19, Mark 3:21, Matthew 12:23, Mark 3:22-27, Mark 3:30, Mark 3:28-29, Mark 3:32-35, Mark 4:21-32, Deuteronomy 5:6-10, Mark 5:23, Mark 5:30-31, Mark 5:34-36, Mark 5:39, Mark 5:41, Mark 6:18, Mark 6:22-25, Mark 7:5-8, Mark 7:10-15, Mark 6:38, Matthew 14-18, John 6:7, Matthew 15:22-24, Mark 7:27-29, Mark 7:34, Mark 7:37, Mark 8:2-4, Matthew 15:34, Micah 5:3, Mark 8:12, Matthew 16:2-4, Micah 5:1-4, Mark 9:16-19, Mark 9:21-25, Mark 11:9-10, Matthew 21:10-11, Luke 19:39-40, Luke 19:38, Zechariah 9:9, Mark 11:17, Mark 14:2, Mark 11:28-33, Mark 12:1-11, Mark 12:14-17, Mark 12:19-34, Matthew 22:42-45, Psalm 110:1, Mark 12:38-40, Mark 14:41-42, Mark 14:45, Luke 22:48, Mark 14:48-49, John 2:18, Mark 14:58, Mark 14:60, John 18:20-23, Matthew 26:63-66, Mark 14:65, Mark 14:67-71, Mark 14:21, Luke 23:2, Mark 15:2, Mark 15:4, Luke 23:5, Micah 5:1, Luke 2:10-12, Luke 2:14-15, John 18:29-31, John 18:33, John 18:35-40, Luke 23:21-22, Matthew 27:24-25, Isaiah 53:4-5, John 19:21-22, Mark 15:29, Mark 15:31-32, Luke 23:39-43, Mark 15:34-35, Psalm 22:17-19, John 19:28, Matthew 27:49, Mark 15:39, Matthew 27:65, Daniel 9:26, Isaiah 50:6, Isaiah 53:7, Psalm 69:21, Amos 8:9, and Mark 1:1-3.

Glossary

Hebrew Name	Pronunciation	Modern Name
Adom	ah-DAHM	Adam
Adonai	AH-doh-neigh	A name of God
Anan	ah-NON	Annas
Avraham	OV-ra-ham	Abraham
Bar-Abba	bar-AB-ba	Barrabas
Bar-Talmai	bar-TELL-my	Bartholomew
Beit-Anyah	bait-AN-yah	Bethany
Beit-Lechem	bait-LE*CH*-em	Bethlehem
Beit-Pagei	bait-PUG-eh	Bethphage
Cohen Hagadol	co-HEN-hag-DOLE	High Priest
Daniel	donny-EL	
David	dah-VEED	
Eliyahu	ELLIE-eye-who	Elijah
Elohim	el-oh-HEEM	A name of God
Galil	GULL-leel	Galilee
Gamli'el	gam-LEE-el	Gamaliel
Gulgolta	GULL-gol-ta	Golgotha
Isra'el	is-RYE-elle	Israel
Kayafa	kie-A-FA	Caiaphas
Kefa	kay-FA	Cephas (Peter)
K'far-Nachum	k-FAR-KNO*CK*-oom	Capernaum
Kinneret	kin-AIR-et	Sea of Galilee
Korazim	COOR-a-zeem	Chorazin
K'riot	kree-OAT	Iscariot
Levi	LUH-vee	
Mashiach	ma-SHE-a*ck*	Messiah
Mattityahu	MAT-tee-yeh-you	Matthew
Moshe	moe-SHAY	Moses
Myriam	MER-REE-ahm	Mary
Nakdimon	nak-DEE-mon	Nicodemus
Natzerene	knot-ZAR-teen	Nazarene
Natzeret	knot-ZAR-et	Nazareth

Note: To pronounce the *italicized* portions, produce a rolling sound in the throat.

Glossary

Hebrew Name	Pronunciation	Modern Name
Philo	FI-low	Philologus
Philologus	FILL-uh-LOW-gus	
P'rushim	prooh-SHEEM	Pharisees
Ramatayim	rama-TIME	Arimathea
Rivkah	riv-KAH	Rebecca
Ruach HaKodesh	ru-A*CK*-ha-CODE-esh	Holy Spirit
Sanhedrin	san-HEAD-ren	
Satan	su-TAN	
Sergius Paulus	SURGE-ee-es POW-loose	
Shabbat	sha-BOT	Sabbath
Sha'ul	SHA-ool	Saul
Shim'on	SHEEM-oan	Simon
Sh'mu'el	sha-MOO-el	Samuel
s'mikhah	smee-*K*AH	Authority
talmid	tal-MEAD	Disciple
talmidim	tal-ME-deem	Disciples
Tanakh	tu-KNO*CK*	Old Testament
Tarsus	TAR-sis	
T'oma	TOE-ma	Thomas
Torah	tore-RAH	Pentateuch
Ya'akov	ya-ahh-COVE	Jacob
Yahweh	YAH-way	A name of God
Ya'ir	yah-EAR	Jairus
Yarden	YAR-den	Jordan
Yerushalayim	ya-ROOSH-a-LIE-em	Jerusalem
Yeshua	ya-SHOE-ah	Jesus
Y'hudah	YOU-dah	Judea
Yitz'chak	yit-ZOCK	Issac
Yochanan	YOKE-a-non	John (Jonathan)
Yosef	YO-sef	Joseph
Z'kharyah	z*ek*-HAR-ree-ah	Zacharias
Zavdai	zov-DIE	Zebedee

Coming Soon

The continuation of the trilogy that began with
Talmid – The Book of John

Emissary – The Book of Kefa
Slave – The Book of Sha'ul

Made in the USA
San Bernardino, CA
12 February 2014